D0501971

The Burning Chambers

BOOK ONE

ALSO BY KATE MOSSE

The Languedoc Trilogy

Labyrinth

Sepulchre

Citadel

Other Fiction & Stories

The Winter Ghosts

The Mistletoe Bride & Other Haunting Tales

The Taxidermist's Daughter

KATE MOSSE

The Burning Chambers

MINOTAUR BOOKS
NEW YORK

This is a work of fiction. All of the characters, organizations, and events portrayed in this novel are either products of the author's imagination or are used fictitiously.

www.minotaurbooks.com

Part-title pages photography © Benjamin Graham: p. 8 Rue du Trésau, La Cité, Carcassonne; p. 152 Notre-Dame La Dalbade Church, Toulouse; p. 442 The Keep, Château de Puivert

Map artwork by Neil Gower

Library of Congress Cataloging-in-Publication Data

Names: Mosse, Kate, 1961– author.
Title: The burning chambers / Kate Mosse.
Description: First U.S. edition. | New York : Minotaur Books, 2019.
Identifiers: LCCN 2019002773 | ISBN 9781250202161 (hardcover) | ISBN 9781250202178 (ebook)
Classification: LCC PR6113.O884 B87 2019 | DDC 823/.92—dc23
LC record available at https://lccn.loc.gov/2019002773

Our books may be purchased in bulk for promotional, educational, or business use. Please contact your local bookseller or the Macmillan Corporate and Premium Sales Department at 1-800-221-7945, extension 5442, or by email at MacmillanSpecialMarkets@macmillan.com.

First published in Great Britain by Mantle, an imprint of Pan Macmillan

First U.S. Edition: June 2019

10 9 8 7 6 5 4 3 2 1

As always, for my beloved

Greg & Martha & Felix

and also for my wonderful mother-in-law,

Granny Rosie

To every thing there is a season, and a time to
every purpose under the heaven:
a time to be born, and a time to die;
a time to plant, and a time to pluck up that
which is planted;
a time to kill, and a time to heal;
a time to break down, and a time to build up;
a time to weep, and a time to laugh;
a time to mourn, and a time to dance;
a time to cast away stones, and a time to
gather stones together;
a time to embrace, and a time to refrain from
embracing;
a time to get, and a time to lose;
a time to keep, and a time to cast away;
a time to rend, and a time to sew;
a time to keep silence, and a time to speak;
a time to love, and a time to hate;
a time of war, and a time of peace.

[Ecclesiastes 3:1–8, King James Version]

CONTENTS

⚜

Note on the Wars of Religion

⚜

The Wars of Religion were a sequence of eight civil wars, which began after years of conflict on 1st March, 1562 with the massacre of unarmed Huguenots in Vassy by the Catholic forces of Francis, Duke of Guise. They ended, after several million had died or been displaced, with the signing of the Edict of Nantes on 13th April, 1598 by the previously Protestant King, Henri IV, Henri of Navarre. The most notorious engagement of the Wars is the St Bartholomew's Day Massacre in Paris, commencing just before dawn on 24th August, 1572. But there were many similar events in towns and cities the length and breadth of France before and after that, including in Toulouse between 13th and 16th May, 1562, when more than four thousand people were slaughtered.

The Edict of Nantes, when it came, was less a genuine reflection of a desire for religious tolerance than an expression of exhaustion and military stalemate. It brought a grudging peace to a country that had torn itself apart over matters of doctrine, religion and sovereignty, and all but bankrupted itself in the process. Henri IV's great-grandson, Louis IX, revoked the Edict at Fontainebleau on 22nd October, 1685, precipitating the exodus of those Huguenots still remaining in France.

Huguenots never numbered more than a tenth of the French population, yet their influence was significant. The story of French Protestantism is part of the larger European story of the Reformation, from Martin Luther's hammering his 77 Edicts to the church door in Wittenberg on All Saints Day, 1517, Henry VIII of England's dissolution of the monasteries, which began in

1536, to the missionary Evangelist Calvin setting up his safe haven in Geneva for French refugees in 1541 and the safe haven offered to Protestant refugees in Amsterdam and Rotterdam from the late 1560s onwards. In France, key points at issue were the right to worship in one's own language; a rejection of the cult of relics and intercession; a more rigorous focus on the words of the Bible itself and a desire to worship simply, based on the rules for living laid down in scripture; a rejection of the excesses and abuses of the Catholic Church that were repugnant to many; the nature of the host, transubstantiation as opposed to consubstantiation. For most people, though, these matters of doctrine were remote.

There are many excellent histories of the Huguenots and the influence of this small community is extraordinary, a diaspora that took them – as skilled refugees – to Holland, to Germany, to England, to Canada and to South Africa.

'The Burning Chambers' is a series of novels set against the backdrop of three hundred years of history, from sixteenth-century France to nineteenth-century Southern Africa. The characters and their families, unless otherwise specified, are imagined, though inspired by the sort of people who might have lived. Ordinary women and men, struggling to live, love and survive against a backdrop of religious war and displacement.

Some things do not change.

Garonne
Toulouse
N.G
Paris
Vassy
FRANCE
La Rochelle
St Antonin-Noble-Val
Toulouse
Carcassonne
SPAIN
0
10
15
Miles
Carcassonne
Chalabre
Aude
Puivert
PYRENEES
Mediterranean Sea

Principal Characters

⚜

In Carcassonne – La Cité

Marguerite (Minou) Joubert
Bernard Joubert, her father
Aimeric, her brother
Alis, her sister
Rixende, their servant
Bérenger, a sergeant-at-arms of the Royal Garrison
Marie Galy, a local girl

In Carcassonne – The Bastide

Cécile Noubel (formerly Cordier), owner of a boarding house
Monsieur Sanchez, a *Converso* and neighbour
Charles Sanchez, his eldest son
Oliver Crompton, a Huguenot commander
Philippe Devereux, his cousin
Alphonse Bonnet, a labourer
Michel Cazès, a Huguenot soldier

In Toulouse

Piet Reydon, a Huguenot
Vidal (Monsignor Valentin), a nobleman and priest
Madame Boussay, Minou's aunt
Monsieur Boussay, Minou's uncle

Madame Montfort, his widowed sister and housekeeper
Martineau, steward to the Boussay household
Jacques Bonal, assassin and manservant to Vidal
Jasper McCone, an English craftsman and Protestant
Félix Prouvaire, a Huguenot student

In Puivert

Blanche de Bruyère, the Chatelaine of Puivert
Achille Lizier, a village gossip
Guilhem Lizier, his great-nephew and soldier at the château de Puivert
Paul Cordier, the village apothecary and cousin to Cécile Noubel
Anne Gabignaud, the village midwife
Marguerite de Bruyère, the late Chatelaine of Puivert

Historical Characters

Pierre Delpech, a Catholic arms dealer in Toulouse
Pierre Hunault, nobleman and Huguenot commander in Toulouse
Captain Saux, a Huguenot commander in Toulouse
Jean Barrelles, Pastor of the Huguenot Temple of Toulouse
Jean de Mansencal, President of the Parliament in Toulouse
François, Duke of Guise and Lorraine, leader of the Catholic Faction
Henri, his eldest son and heir
Charles, his brother and Cardinal of Lorraine

PROLOGUE

⚜

Franschhoek
28th February, 1862

The woman stands alone beneath a sharp blue sky. Evergreen cypress and rough grasses bound the graveyard. The grey headstones are bleached the colour of bone by the fierce Cape sun.

Hier Rust. Here lies.

She is tall, with the distinctive eyes of the women of her family going back generations, though she does not know it. She bends forward to read the names and dates on the tombstone, obscured by lichen or moss. Between her high white collar and the dust-caked brim of her leather hat, the white skin on the back of her neck is already burning red. The sun is too strong for her European complexion and she has been riding across the veldt for days.

She removes her gloves, folding one inside the other. She has mislaid too many to be careless and, besides, how would she acquire another pair? There are two general stores in this hospitable frontier town but she has little left with which to barter and her inheritance is gone, spent on the long journey from Toulouse to Amsterdam, then from Amsterdam to the Cape of Good Hope. Every last franc has been spent on provisions and letters of introduction, hiring horses and a trustworthy guide to lead her through this unfamiliar land.

She drops the gloves to the ground at her feet. A powder of

copper-red Cape dust puffs into a cloud, then settles. A black beetle, hard-backed and resolute, scuttles for cover.

The woman draws breath. At last, she is here.

She has followed this trail from the banks of the river Aude and the Garonne and the Amstel, over the wildest seas to where the Atlantic Sea meets the Indian Ocean, to the Cap de Bonne Espérance.

Sometimes the trail has blazed bright. The story of two families and a secret passed down from generation to generation. Her mother and grandmother, then further back to her great-grandmother and her mother before that. Their names have been lost, taken up in those of their husbands and brothers and lovers, but their spirits live in her. She knows it. Finally, her quest ends here. In Franschhoek.

Ci gît. Here lies.

The woman removes her leather riding hat and fans herself, the wide brim shifting the blistering air. There is no respite. It is as hot as an oven and her flaxen hair is dark with sweat. She cares little for her appearance. She has survived the storms, the assaults on her reputation and her person, the theft of her possessions and the loss of friendships that she had thought were built to last. All to bring her here.

To this unkempt cemetery in this frontier town.

She undoes the buckle on her saddlebag and reaches inside. Her fingers skim the small antique bible – a talisman she carries with her for luck – but it is the journal she pulls out: a soft tan leather cover, held shut by a thin cord wrapped twice around it. Tucked inside are letters and hand-drawn maps, a Will. Some pages are loose, their corners spiking out like the points of a diamond. This is the record of her family's quest, the anatomy of a feud. If she is right, this sixteenth-century notebook is the means to claim what is rightfully hers. After more than three hundred years the fortunes and the good name of the Joubert family will, finally, be restored. Justice will be done.

If she is right.

Still, she cannot bring herself to look at the name on the gravestone. Wishing to savour this last moment of hope a little longer, she opens the journal instead. The spidery browned ink, the antique language reaching forward to her across hundreds of years, she knows every syllable like a catechism learnt in Sunday School. The first entry.

This is the day of my death.

She hears the whistling of a red-wing starling in flight and the shriek of a hadida in the scrubland at the boundary of the cemetery. It seems impossible that a month ago such sounds were exotic to her ears, and now they are commonplace. Her knuckles are white, clasped tight. What, after all, if she is wrong? What if this is an end, not a beginning?

As the Lord God is my witness, here, by my own hand, do I set this down. My last Will and Testament.

The woman does not pray. She cannot. The history of the injustices done in the name of religion – to her ancestors – surely proves that there is no God. For what God would allow so many to die in agony and fear and terror in His name?

All the same, she glances up as if she might glimpse heaven. The sky here in the Cape in February is the same vivid blue as it is in Languedoc. The same fierce winds catch the dust in the hinterlands of the Cap de Bonne Espérance as they do in the Garrigue of the Midi. A kind of heat, a breath that sets the red earth swirling and scatters a veil across the eyes. It whistles through the grey and green mountain passes of the interior, tracks worn by the movement of men and of animals. Here, in this outback land they once called the Elephant's Corner, before the French came.

Now the air is still. The air is hot. Little stirs in the heat of the noonday sun. The dogs and the farm workers have taken shelter in the shade. Black railings mark out each plot – the de Villiers family, the le Roux family, the Jourdan family – all those of the Reformed Religion who fled France in search of sanctuary. The year of Grace of the Lord sixteen hundred and eighty-eight.

Her ancestors too?

In the distance, behind the stone angels and the headstones, the Franschhoek mountains frame the picture and the woman is suddenly pierced by a memory of the Pyrenees: a sharp and desperate longing for home, like an iron band around her ribs. The mountains are white in winter, green in the spring and early summer. In autumn, the grey rocks turn to copper before the cycle begins once more. What she would give to set eyes on them again.

Then she sighs, for she is here. She is a long way from home.

From between the well-worn covers of the leather journal, she takes the map. She knows every mark, every crease and drip of ink, yet she examines it all the same. Reads again the names of the farms, of the first Huguenot settlers who found themselves here, after years of exile and wandering.

Finally, the woman crouches down and reaches out to trace the letters carved on the headstone. She is so absorbed, that she – who has learnt to be vigilant – does not hear the footsteps behind her in the dirt. She does not register the shadow blocking out the sun. She does not acknowledge the smell of sweat, of clinker and leather, of a long journey across the veldt, until the push of the muzzle of a gun is at her neck.

'Get up.'

She tries to turn, to see his face, but the cold metal is jabbed against her skin. Slowly, she stands.

'Give me the journal,' he says. 'If you do, I will not harm you.'

She knows he is lying, for this man has hunted her for too long and there is too much at stake. For three hundred years his family has tried to destroy hers. How could he let her go free?

'Give it to me. Slowly, now.'

The coldness in her enemy's voice is more frightening than anger and, instinctively, her grasp tightens on the journal and the precious papers it holds. After all that she has endured, she will not make it easy. But now his sharp fingers are pinching at her shoulder, driving into the muscle hard and fierce, through the white cotton of her shirt. Her grip cannot hold. The diary falls to the dirt and bursts open, scattering the Will and the deeds into the dust of the graveyard.

'Did you follow me from Cape Town?'

There is no answer.

She has no gun, but she has a knife. When he leans down to pick up the papers, she pulls the dagger from her boot and stabs at his arm. If she can disable him, if only for a moment, she might steal the papers back and outrun him. But he has anticipated such an attack and shifts his weight sideways. Her blade only grazes his hand.

She is aware, just before it connects with the side of her head, of the downward strike of his arm. A glimpse of black hair, divided by a seam of white. Then an explosion of pain as the pistol splits open her skin. She feels the split of blood on her temple, the heat of it, and she falls.

In her last seconds of consciousness, she grieves to think this is how the story will end. In a forgotten corner of a graveyard on the other side of the world. The story of a stolen journal and an inheritance. A tale that began three hundred years ago, on the eve of the civil wars that brought France to her knees.

This is the day of my death.

PART ONE

⚜

Carcassonne
Winter 1562

CHAPTER ONE

⚜

INQUISITIONAL PRISON, TOULOUSE
Saturday, 24th January

'You are a traitor?'

'No, my lord.' The prisoner was not sure if he spoke out loud or answered only within his own ruined mind.

Broken teeth and shifting bone, the taste of dried blood pooled in his mouth. How long had he been here? Hours, days?

Always?

The inquisitor gave a flick of his hand. The prisoner heard the rasp of a blade being sharpened, saw the irons and pincers lying on a wooden table beside a fireplace. A squeeze of the bellows to fan the coals. He experienced an odd moment of respite, as terror of the next torture momentarily banished the agony of the raw skin on his flayed back. Fear of what was to come drowned, if only for an instant, his shame at being too weak to endure what was being done to him. He was a soldier. He had fought well and bravely on the battlefield. How was it that now he was too fragile to withstand this?

'You are a traitor.' The inquisitor's voice sounded dull and flat. 'You are disloyal to the King, and to France. We have evidence from many attesting to it. They denounce you!' He tapped a sheaf of papers on his desk. 'Protestants – men like you – give succour to our enemies. It is treason.'

'No!' the prisoner whispered, as he felt the breath of the

gaoler warm upon his neck. His right eye was swollen shut from a previous beating, but he could sense his persecutor coming close. 'No, I –'

He stopped, for what could he say in his defence? Here, in the inquisitional prison in Toulouse, he was the enemy.

Huguenots were the enemy.

'I am loyal to the Crown. My Protestant faith does not mean –'

'Your faith brands you a heretic. You have turned away from the one true God.'

'It is not so. Please. This is all a mistake.'

He could hear the pleading in his own voice, and he felt ashamed. And he knew, when the pain came again, he would say whatever they wanted to hear. Truth or not, he had no strength left to resist.

There was a moment of tenderness, or so it seemed to him in his desperate state. A gentle lifting of his hand, like a lord romancing his lady. For a fleeting instant, the man remembered the wonderful things that existed in the world. Love and music, the sweetness of springtime flowers. Women, children, men walking arm-in-arm through the elegant streets of Toulouse. A place where people might argue and disagree, might put their case with passion and knowledge, but also with respect and honour. There, wine glasses were filled to overflowing and there was plenty to eat: figs and cured mountain ham and honey. There, in the world where once he had lived, the sun shone and the endless blue of the Midi sky stretched over the city like a canopy.

'Honey,' he murmured.

Here, in this hell below earth, time no longer existed. The *oubliettes*, they called them, where a man might disappear and never be seen again.

The shock of the assault, when it came, was the worse for being unheralded. A squeezing, then a pressure, then the metal teeth of the pliers splintering his skin and his muscle and his bones.

As pain embraced him in her arms, he thought he heard the voice of a fellow prisoner from a neighbouring chamber. An educated man, a man of letters, for several days they had been held in the same cell. He knew him to be a man of honour, a bookseller, who loved his three children and spoke with gentle grief of his wife who had died.

He could hear the murmuring of another inquisitor behind the dripping cell wall: his friend was being interrogated too. Then he identified the sound of the *chatte de griffe* slicing through the air, the thud as the talons connected with skin, and it shocked him to hear his fellow prisoner screaming. He was a man of fortitude who, until now, had borne his suffering in silence.

The prisoner heard the opening and closing of a door, and knew another man had come into the cell. His cell or the one next door? Then murmuring, the shifting of paper on paper. For a beautiful moment, he thought his ordeal might end. Then the inquisitor cleared his throat and the questioning began again.

'What you know about the Shroud of Antioch?'

'I know nothing of any relic.' This was true, though the prisoner knew his words counted for nothing.

'The Holy Relic was stolen from the Eglise Saint-Taur some five years past. There are those who claim you were one of those responsible.'

'How could I be?' the prisoner cried, suddenly defiant. 'I have never set foot in Toulouse until . . . until now.'

The inquisitor pressed on. 'If you tell us where the Shroud

is being hidden, this conversation between us will stop. The Holy Mother Church will, in Her mercy, open Her arms and welcome you back into Her grace.'

'My lord, I give you my word I –'

He smelt the searing of his flesh before he felt it. How quickly is a man reduced to an animal, to meat.

'Consider your answer carefully. I shall ask you again.'

Now this pain, the worst yet, was granting him a temporary reprieve. It was pulling him down into darkness, a place where he was strong enough to withstand their questioning, and where speaking the truth would save him.

CHAPTER TWO

⚜

La Cité

Saturday, 28th February

'In nomine Patris, et Filii, et Spiritus Sancti.'

The earth hit the lid of the coffin with a soft thud. Brown earth slipping through white fingers. Then another hand, stretching out across the open grave, then another, soil and stone pattering on the wood, like rain. A soft sobbing from a small child, shrouded in the father's black cloak.

'Almighty Father, into Your care we commend the spirit of Florence Joubert, beloved wife and mother and servant of Christ. May she rest in peace in the light of Your eternal grace. Amen.'

The light began to change. No longer the damp, grey air of the graveyard, but now an inky black. Instead of mud, red blood. Warm and fresh to the touch, slick on her palms. Trapped between the creases of her fingers. Minou looked down at her own bloodied hands.

'No!' she shouted, throwing herself awake.

For a moment Minou saw nothing. Then the chamber began to come back into focus and she realised that she had fallen asleep in her chair again. Little wonder her dreams had been troubled. Minou turned her hands over. They were clean. No soil beneath her nails, no blood on her skin.

A nightmare, nothing more. A memory of the terrible day, five years ago, when they had laid their beloved mother to rest.

Memory giving way to something else. Dark imaginings created out of air.

Minou looked at the book lying open on her lap – a meditation by the English martyr, Anne Askew – and wondered if that had contributed to her unquiet dreams.

She stretched the night from her bones and smoothed her crumpled shift. The candle had burnt out and the wax had pooled on the dark wood. What hour was it? She turned to the window. Fingers of light were slipping between the cracks in the shutters, sending a criss-cross pattern across the worn floorboards. Outside, she heard the usual early-morning sounds of La Cité waking to meet the dawn. The clinker and tramp of the watch on the ramparts, trudging down and up the steep steps to the Tour de la Marquière.

She knew she should rest longer. Saturday was the busiest day in her father's bookshop, even during Lent. Now the responsibility for the business lay upon her shoulders, she would have little time to call her own in the hours ahead. But her thoughts were spiralling like the starlings who swooped and dived over the towers of the Château Comtal in autumn.

Minou put her hand to her chest and felt the strong rhythm of her heart beating. Her dream, so vivid, had left her out of sorts. There was no reason to think their bookshop would have been targeted again – her father had done nothing wrong, he was a good Catholic – and yet she could not shake the thought that something might have happened overnight.

On the other side of the chamber, her seven-year-old sister lay lost to the world, her curls a black cloud upon the pillow. Minou touched Alis's forehead and was relieved to find her skin cool. She was relieved, too, that the truckle where their thirteen-year-old brother sometimes passed the night, when he could not sleep, was empty. Too often recently Aimeric had come creeping into their chamber, saying he was afraid of the dark. The sign of a guilty conscience, the priest had said. Would he say the same of her night terrors?

Minou splashed a little cold water on her face, wiped beneath her arms. She put on her skirt and fastened her kirtle, then, taking care not to disturb Alis, took up the borrowed book and tiptoed out of their attic room. Down the stairs, past the door to her father's chamber and the tiny box room where Aimeric slept, then down again to the level of the street.

The door that separated the passageway from their large living chamber was closed, but the frame was ill fitting, so Minou could hear the rattling of pans and the jerk of the chain above the fire as their maid hung the pail of water on the hook to boil.

She sneaked the door open and reached in, hoping to be able to lift the keys from the shelf without attracting Rixende's notice. The maid was warm-natured, but she chattered and Minou did not want to be held up this morning.

'How now, Mademoiselle,' Rixende said brightly. 'I did not think to see you up so early. No one else is yet stirring. Can I fetch you something to break your fast?'

Minou held up the keys. 'I must make haste. When my father wakes, will you say I have gone early to the Bastide to prepare the shop? To take advantage of it being market day. There is no need for him to hurry, should he intend—'

'Why, that is wonderful news that the master intends to go . . .'

Rixende stopped, halted by Minou's look.

Though it was common knowledge that her father had not left the house for weeks, it was never spoken of. Bernard Joubert had returned to Carcassonne from his winter travels a changed man. From one who smiled and had a kind word for everyone, a good neighbour and loyal friend, he was now a shadow in his own life. Grey and withdrawn, his spirit diminished, a person who no longer spoke of ideas or dreams. Minou grieved to see him brought so low and often attempted to coax him out of his black melancholy. But whenever she asked what ailed him, her father's eyes turned to glass. He murmured about the bitterness of the season and the wind, the aches and pains of age, before falling again into silence.

Rixende coloured. '*Pardon*, Mademoiselle. I will pass on your message to the master. But, are you sure you do not need something to drink? It is cold out. To eat? There is a piece of *pan de blat*, or a little of yesterday's pudding left over –'

'Good day,' Minou said firmly. 'I will see you again on Monday.'

The flagstones were cold under her stockinged feet and she could see her breath, white, in the chill air. She slipped into her leather boots, took her hood and thick green woollen cloak from the stand, put the keys and the book into the purse tied around her waist. Then, holding her gloves in her hand, she slid back the heavy metal bolt and stepped out into the silent street.

A spirit girl abroad on a chill February dawn.

CHAPTER THREE

The first rays of the sun were beginning to warm the air, setting spirals of mist dancing above the cobbled stones. The Place du Grand Puits looked tranquil in the pink light. Minou breathed in, feeling the shock of the cold in her lungs, then set off towards the main gates which led in and out of La Cité.

At first, she saw no one. The doxies who walked the streets at night had been driven inside by the light. The card sharks and dice players who haunted the Taverne Saint-Jean were long gone to their beds. Minou held up her skirts to avoid the worst of the previous evening's excesses: broken ale pots, a beggar slumped asleep with his arm balanced on the back of a flea-bitten dog. The bishop had petitioned for all inns and taverns within La Cité to be closed during Lent. The Seneschal, mindful of the King's empty coffers, had refused. It was common knowledge – according to Rixende, who knew every bit of tittle-tattle – that there was no love lost between the current occupant of the Episcopal Palace and the Château Comtal.

The gabled houses in the narrow street that led down to the Porte Narbonnaise seemed to lean towards one another as if drunk, their tiled roofs so close as to be almost touching. Minou was moving against the mass of carts and people coming through the gates, so it was slow going.

The scene could have been one from a hundred years before, Minou thought, two hundred, all the way back to the time of the troubadours. In La Cité, life went on the same, day after day after day.

Nothing changed.

Two men-at-arms were controlling the flow of traffic at the Porte Narbonnaise, waving some through without a second glance, yet stopping others and searching their belongings until coins changed hands. The weak sun glinted on their helmets and the blades of their halberds. The royal crest on their blue surcoats stood out brightly amongst the drab Lenten colours.

As she drew closer, Minou recognised Bérenger, one of many who had reason to be grateful to her father. Most of the local soldiers – as against those billeted to the garrison from Lyon or Paris – could not read the King's French. Many also favoured speaking the old language of the region, Occitan, when they thought themselves unobserved. Nonetheless, they were still served with papers and issued with written orders, and then punished if they failed to fulfil their duties to the letter. Everyone suspected it was another way of raising funds and that the Seneschal condoned it. Minou's father helped those he could from falling foul of the law by explaining what the official language meant.

At least, once he had.

Minou pulled herself up short. It did no good to brood endlessly on the change that had come over her beloved father. Or to keep picturing, in her mind's eye, his haunted and hollow face.

'Good morrow, Bérenger,' she said. 'You have quite a number here already.'

His honest, old face unfolded into a smile. 'How now, Madomaisèla Joubert! Quite a crowd, though I cannot account for it on so bitter a day. There was a host of them waiting long before first light.'

'Perhaps this Lent,' she said, 'the Seneschal has remembered his charitable duties and is giving alms to the poor. What think you of that? Is it possible?'

'That will be the day,' Bérenger guffawed. 'Our noble lord and master is not much lauded for his good works!'

Minou dropped her voice. 'Ah, what fortune would be ours if we were ruled over by a godly and pious seigneur!'

He gave another bellow of laughter, until he noticed his colleague frowning with disapproval.

'Anyhow, that's all as maybe,' he said in a more formal tone. 'What brings you out at this hour, and unaccompanied?'

'It is at my father's behest,' Minou lied. 'He has bid me open the shop for him. As it is market day, he hopes there will be plenty of customers passing through the Bastide. All of them, God willing, with full pockets and an appetite for learning.'

'Reading? Don't hold with it,' Bérenger said, pulling a face. 'But each to their own. Though would it not be right for your brother to undertake such work? It seems strange Monsieur Joubert would ask so much of a maid, when he is blessed with a son.'

Minou held her tongue, though she did not in truth resent his comment. Bérenger was a man of the Midi, raised on the old ideas and traditions. She was also aware that, at thirteen, Aimeric should have been taking over some of her father's responsibilities. The problem was her brother had neither the inclination nor the aptitude. He was more interested in shooting sparrows with his catapult or climbing trees with the gypsy boys when they came to town than in passing his days in the confines of a bookshop.

'Aimeric is needed at home this morning,' she said, smiling, 'so it falls to me. It is an honour to do what I can to assist my father.'

'Well, of course, of course it is.' He cleared his throat. 'And how goes it with Sénher Joubert? I have not seen him for some while. Not even at Mass. He is unwell, perhaps?'

Since the last outbreak of plague, any question about a person's health carried a darker strain of enquiry beneath it. Almost no family had been spared. Bérenger had lost his wife and both his children in the same epidemic that had carried away Minou's mother. She had been gone five years, but Minou still missed her company every day and, like last evening, often dreamed of her at night.

All the same, from the tone of Bérenger's question, and the way he did not meet her eye, Minou realised with a burdened heart that the rumours about her father's confinement within their house had spread more widely than she had hoped.

'He returned much fatigued from his travels in January,' she said, with a spark of defiance, 'but otherwise he is in excellent health. There is a great deal to do with the business that occupies him.'

Bérenger nodded. 'Well, I am glad to hear it, I feared that . . .' He stopped, reddening with embarrassment. 'No matter. If you would give Sénher Joubert my regards.'

Minou smiled. 'He will be glad of your good wishes.'

Bérenger thrust out his arm to block a large ham-faced woman with a squalling baby from passing in front of her. 'There you go. But you take good care, Madomaisèla, going across to the Bastide on your own, *è*? There's all manner of villains out there who'd stick a knife in your ribs as soon as spit.'

Minou smiled. 'Thank you, kind Bérenger. I will.'

The grass in the moat below the drawbridge was glistening with early morning dew, shimmering white on the green shoots. Usually, Minou's first glimpse of the world beyond La Cité lifted her spirits: the white endless sky becoming blue as the day crept in; the grey and green crags of the Montagne Noire on the horizon, the first blossoms of the apple trees in the orchards on the slopes below the citadel. But this morning the combination of her troubled night, and Bérenger's warnings, left her feeling anxious.

Minou pulled herself up. She was not some green girl, afraid of her own shadow. Besides, she was within hailing distance of the sentries. If someone did menace her, her shouts would carry back to La Cité and Bérenger would be at her side in an instant.

An ordinary day. Nothing to fear.

All the same, she was relieved to reach the outskirts of Trivalle. It was a poor but respectable suburb, inhabited mostly by those who worked in the textile mills. Wool and cloth exported to the Levant were bringing prosperity to Carcassonne and respectable families were beginning, once more, to set up their homes on the left bank.

'Here's a maid come walking by . . .'

Minou jumped as a hand closed around her ankle. 'Monsieur!'

She looked down and saw there was little to fear. Drunken fingers, too weak to hold. She shook herself free, and stepped quickly on. A young man, of perhaps one-and-twenty, was propped against the wall of one of the houses that led to the bridge. His short cloak fingered him for a gentleman, though his mustard-yellow doublet was askew and his hose stained dark with ale. Or worse.

He peered up at her through the snapped blue feather of his cap.

'Mademoiselle, how about a kiss? A kiss for Philippe. It'll cost you nothing. Not a sou, not a denier . . . which is as well, for I have nothing.'

The boy went through an elaborate pantomime of turning his purse inside out. Despite herself, Minou found herself smiling.

'Say, do I know you, lady? I think I cannot, for I would remember if I had seen so beautiful a face. Your blue eyes . . . Or brown, 'tis both.'

'You do not know me, Monsieur.'

''Tis a pity,' he murmured. 'A grievous pity. Would that I did know you . . .'

Minou knew she should not encourage him – and she could hear her mother's clear voice in her head exhorting her to walk on – but he was young and his tone was wistful.

'You should to your bed,' she said.

'Philippe,' he mumbled.

'It is morning. You will catch a chill sitting out here in the street.'

'A maid who is as wise as she is fair. Ah, that I was a wordsmith. I would write a verse. Wise words. Beautiful and wise . . .'

'Good day,' Minou said.

'Sweet lady,' he cried after her, 'may you be showered with blessings. May your—'

A casement was flung open and a woman leant out. 'That's enough!' she shrieked. 'Since nigh on four o'clock I've had to listen to your maundering and reciting, with not a moment's peace. Well, this should stop your mouth!'

Minou watched her heave a pail over the sill. Dirty grey water cascaded down the walls and over the boy's head. He leapt up, yelping, shaking his arms and legs like one afflicted by St Vitus's dance. He looked both so disconsolate yet also comical that Minou forgot herself and laughed out loud.

'I'll catch my death!' he cried, flinging his sodden cap to the ground. 'If I take a chill and die, my death – my *death* – will be on your conscience. Then you'll be sorry. If you but knew who I was. I am a guest of the bishop, I am—'

'I will rejoice at your departing!' the woman yelled. 'Students! You're idle wastrels, the lot of you! If any of you did but an honest day's work, you'd not have time to freeze to death.'

As she slammed the window shut, the women on the street applauded, the men grumbled.

'You shouldn't let her speak to you like that,' said a man with pockmarked skin. 'Got no right to speak to a gentleman of your standing. Not her place.'

'You should report her to the Seneschal,' said another. 'Setting about your person like that, it's common assault.'

The oldest of the women laughed. 'Ha! For emptying a pail of water on his head. He's lucky it wasn't a piss pot!'

Amused, Minou walked on, their squabbling growing fainter behind her. She drew level with the stables, where her father kept their old mare, Canigou, then approached the foot of the stone bridge over the river. The Aude was high, but there was no wind and the sails of the Moulin du Roi and the salt mills were quiet. On the far side, the Bastide looked serene in the early light. On the banks, the laundry women were already laying out the day's first swathes of bleached fabric to dry in the sun. Minou paused to take a sou from her purse then walked the hundred paces across the bridge.

She handed the coin to the gatekeeper for the toll. He tried it between his teeth and found it to be true. Then the girl known as Minou Joubert crossed the boundary dividing the old Carcassonne from the new.

I will not allow my inheritance to be taken from me.

The years of lying beneath his vile and sweating body. The bruises and the indignities, the blows when my flowers came each month. Submitting to his grasping fingers on my breasts, between my legs. His hands twisting my hair at the roots until the blood pinked upon my head. His sour breath. Such degradation at the hands of a pig, for nothing? For the sake of a Will attested some nineteen years past, so he says. His near-death-bed confession, the wanderings of his decaying mind? Or is there some truth in what he says?

If there is a Will, where might it be? The voices are silent.

The Book of Ecclesiastes says that to everything there is a season, and a time to every purpose under heaven.

Upon this day, with my left hand upon the Holy Catholic Bible and my right freely holding the quill, I set this down. This is my solemn vow that cannot now be broken. I swear by Almighty God that I shall not let the offspring of a Huguenot whore take from me what is rightfully mine.

I will see them dead first.

CHAPTER FOUR

⚜

La Cité

'Forgive me, Father, for I have sinned. It has been –' Piet plucked a figure from the air – 'twelve months since my last confession.'

From the other side of the confessional in the Cathedral of Saint-Nazaire, he heard a cough. Moving his face closer to the grille that separated priest from penitent, Piet suddenly smelled the distinctive hair oil of his old friend and caught his breath. Strange how a scent, after all this time, could still cause the heart strings to crack.

He had met Vidal ten years ago, whilst they had been fellow students at the Collège de Foix in Toulouse. The son of a French merchant and Dutch prostitute, who'd had no choice in her profession if she and her son were to eat, Piet was a deserving, if disadvantaged, scholar. Possessed of a quick wit and a few letters of recommendation, he had taken the opportunity of an education in canon law, civil law and theology.

Vidal came from a branch of a noble, but recently disgraced, Toulousain family. His father had been executed for treason and his lands confiscated. It was only thanks to his uncle, a prominent and wealthy ally of the Guise family, that he had been admitted to the college at all.

Outsiders both, their intellectual curiosity and application marked them out from the others in their class, most of whom had little interest in scholarship. They quickly formed a bond of friendship, spending much of their time in one another's company. Drinking, laughing, debating late into the night, they came to know one another's characters better than they knew their own, faults as well as virtues. They could finish one another's sentences and knew what the other was thinking before the thought was put into words.

They were as close as brothers.

When their studies were concluded, it was no surprise to Piet that Vidal took Holy Orders. How better to restore his family's fortunes than to be part of the establishment that had stripped them of their ancient rights? Vidal rose up quickly through the ranks: from curate in the parish church of Saint-Antonin-Noble-Val, to a position as priest-confessor to a noble household in the Haute Vallée, before returning as canon at the Cathedral of Saint-Étienne. Already, he was being spoken of as a future Bishop of Toulouse.

Piet had chosen another path.

'And what has happened to keep you so far from God's grace, my son?' Vidal asked.

Putting his kerchief across his mouth, Piet leant towards the grille separating them.

'Father, I have read forbidden books and found much to recommend within them. I have written pamphlets questioning the authority of Holy Scripture and the Church Fathers, I have sworn false oaths, I have taken the Lord's name in vain. I am guilty of the sin of pride. I have lain with women. I . . . have born false witness.'

This last confession was, at least, true.

Piet caught a sharp intake of breath. Was Vidal shocked at the litany of sins or had he recognised his voice?

'Are you heartily sorry for having offended the Lord?'

Vidal said carefully. 'Do you dread the loss of heaven and the pains of hell?'

Despite himself, Piet felt connected to the familiarity of the ritual, soothed by the knowledge of how very many people had knelt in the same place as he did now, their heads bowed, seeking forgiveness for their sins. For a moment, he felt himself connected to all those who, by this act of confession, had stepped out restored into the world once more.

All lies, of course. All untrue. Yet it was what gave the old religion such power, such a hold over people's hearts and minds. Piet was surprised to realise that even now, after all he had seen and suffered in the name of God, he was not immune to the sweet promise of superstition.

'My son?' Vidal said again. 'Why have you exiled yourself from our Lord's grace?'

This was the moment. There were no castles in the sky, there was no need for other men to speak for him in an ancient language long dead. His fate was in his own hands. Piet had to declare himself now. They had been as close as brothers once, born within a day of each other, in the third month of the same year. But the violent disagreement between them five years ago had never been resolved and, since then, the world had changed for the worse.

If Piet revealed himself and Vidal summoned the authorities, then he could expect no mercy. He had known men stretched on the rack for less. Then again, if his friend remained the principled man he had been in his youth, there was a chance that all might still be put right between them.

Piet steeled himself then, and for the first time since walking into the cathedral, he spoke in his own voice, an accent shaped by his childhood in the backstreets of Amsterdam and overlaid with the colours of the Midi.

'I have failed to honour my obligations. To my teachers and my benefactors. To my friends . . .'

'What did you say?'

'To my friends.' He swallowed. 'To those I held dear.'

'Piet, is it you? Can it be?'

'It is good to hear your voice, Vidal,' he replied, emotion catching in his throat.

He heard another intake of breath: 'That is no longer my name.'

'Once it was.'

'A long time ago.'

'Five years. Not so very long.'

Silence fell dead between them. Then, a slight shifting on the other side of the lattice. Piet hardly dared to breathe.

'My friend, I—' he began.

'You have no right to call me friend after what you did, what you said. I cannot . . .'

Vidal's voice tailed away, the chasm between them absolute. Then Piet heard a familiar sound, the drumming of fingers against the wooden walls of the confessional. In their youth, whenever Vidal was considering a particularly complex matter of law or doctrine, he had done the same. Beating out a rhythm on his desk, on a bench, on the ground beneath the elm tree in the middle of the courtyard in the Collège de Foix. Vidal claimed it helped him to think clearly. It had driven their tutors and fellow students to distraction.

Piet waited, but Vidal did not speak. Finally, he had no choice but to return to reciting the old catechism knowing that, as priest-confessor, Vidal would have no choice but to answer.

'For all these and all the sins of my past life,' Piet said, 'I ask for God's pardon. Will you give me absolution, Father?'

'How dare you! It is a serious offence to mock the holy sacrament of confession.'

'That was not my intention.'

'Yet here you are, speaking words which, by your own admission, you believe have no worth. Unless you have come to your senses and returned to the true Church.'

'Forgive me.' Piet let his head rest briefly against the wooden grille. 'I do not mean to offend you.' He paused. 'You are a difficult man to find, Vidal. I have several times written. Back in Toulouse, I had hoped to lay eyes upon you this past winter.' He paused again. 'Did you receive my letters?'

Vidal did not answer. 'The question is why you should be looking for me at all. What do you want, Piet?'

'Nothing.' Piet sighed. 'At least . . . I would give you an explanation.'

'An apology?'

'An explanation,' Piet repeated. 'The misunderstanding between us—'

'A misunderstanding! Is that what you call it? Is that how you have salved your conscience these past years?'

Piet put his hand on the partition. 'You are still angry.'

'Does that surprise you? I loved you as a brother, put my trust in you, and you repaid that love by stealing—'

'No! Not that!' Piet exclaimed. 'I know you believe I betrayed our friendship, Vidal, and yes, the evidence points to it. But, on my honour, I am not a thief. I have many times attempted to find you, in the hope of healing the rift between us.'

Piet heard Vidal sigh. He hoped, suddenly, that his words had pierced his friend's armour.

'How did you know I was in Carcassonne?' Vidal asked eventually.

'A manservant at Saint-Étienne. I paid handsomely for the information. Then again, I paid him well to pass on my letters to you, and it seems he did not.'

Piet's hand went to the leather satchel slung across his shoulder. He was in Carcassonne on a different mission. It was a strange coincidence that, having finally given up hope of ever seeing Vidal again, he should catch sight of him this morning. A coincidence, for what else could it be? Those who knew Piet was in Carcassonne could be counted upon the fingers of one hand. He had kept the details of his journey to himself. Not a soul knew where he was lodging.

'All I am asking, Vidal,' he said steadily, 'is for an hour of your time – half an hour, if that is all you will grant me. The breach between us lies heavy on my heart.'

Piet stopped. He knew if he pushed his friend, it would result in an opposite outcome. He could hear the steady beat of his own heart as he waited. All the words, said and unsaid since the fierce argument that had ended their friendship, seemed to hang in the air.

'Did you steal the Shroud?' Vidal asked.

There was no warmth in his voice and, yet, Piet felt a flicker of hope. For Vidal to be asking the question at all, surely meant he had doubts that Piet was guilty of the charge levelled against him.

'I did not,' he said in a level voice.

'But you knew the theft was to be attempted?'

'Vidal, meet with me away from here, and I will try to answer all of your questions, I give you my word.'

'Your word! This from a man who has already confessed to swearing false oaths. Your word means nothing! I ask you again. Even if it was not your hand that took it, did you know that such a crime was to be attempted? Yes, or no?'

'It's not that simple,' Piet said.

'It *is* that simple. Either you are a thief – in thought, if not in deed – or your conscience is clear.'

'Nothing is simple in this world, Vidal. As a priest, you above all men must know this. Please, my friend.' He paused, then said it again. '*Alsjeblieft, mijn vriend.*'

Behind the lattice, Piet sensed Vidal recoil and he knew his words had hit their mark. When they were students, he had taught Vidal a few words of his mother's tongue.

'That was unfair.'

'Let me put my case,' Piet replied. 'If I have still not persuaded you to think better of me, then on my honour I will—'

'What? Hand yourself over to the authorities?'

Piet sighed. 'Trouble you no further.'

He ran through the hours ahead in his mind. His rendezvous was at noon but, after that, his time was his own. He had intended to return immediately to Toulouse but, if Vidal was prepared to meet him, there was good reason to delay his departure until the following morning.

'If you do not feel it is politic to talk here in La Cité, Vidal, come to the Bastide. I'm lodging in a boarding house in rue du Marché. The owner, Madame Noubel, is a widow and discreet. We would not be disturbed. Save for an hour at midday, I shall be there all the afternoon and evening.'

Vidal laughed. 'I do not think so. The Bastide is more sympathetic to men of your persuasion, shall I say, than of mine. My robes mark me out. I would not risk those streets.'

'In which case,' Piet pressed, 'I will come to your lodgings. Or anywhere that pleases you. Choose a place and a time, and I will be there.'

Vidal's fingers began to drum again on the worn wooden partition. Piet prayed his old friend had not lost his habit of curiosity. A dangerous quality in a priest, their teachers at the Collège de Foix had cautioned, where submission and obedience counted for so much.

'I will be as mist within fog,' Piet reassured him. 'No one will see me.'

CHAPTER FIVE

⚜

The drumming got louder, more insistent. Then, just as abruptly, Vidal stopped.

'Very well,' he said.

'*Dank je wel*,' Piet breathed his thanks. 'Where will I find you?'

'My rooms are in rue de Notre Dame, in the oldest part of La Cité,' he answered, brisk now that he had reached a decision. 'A fine stone building, some three storeys high, you cannot mistake it. There is a garden at the back of the house. I will see to it that the gate is left unlocked. Come after Compline, there will be few abroad at that hour, but take every care not to be seen. Every care. No one must have any cause to associate us.'

'Thank you,' Piet said again.

'Do not thank me,' Vidal answered sharply. 'I promise no more than that I will listen.'

Suddenly, a sound reverberated through the stone alleyways of the nave. A creak, then the gravelled scrape of the heavy north doors against the flagstones.

Another penitent come at dawn to Confession?

Piet cursed himself for having acted on impulse, but the sight of Vidal walking alone into the cathedral had been too good a piece of fortune to let go. The older part of his soul, raised on miracles and relics, might have said it was a sign. His modern mind dismissed such medieval thoughts. It was Man, not God, who made the world turn.

Piet heard footsteps and his hand stole to his poniard. How many doors were there in and out of the cathedral? Several, no doubt, but he had failed to mark them. He strained to listen. Two pairs of feet rather than one? Soft, as if intending not to be heard.

'Piet?'

'We have company,' he whispered.

With the tip of his blade, Piet lifted the curtain and peered out into the nave. At first, he could see nothing. Then, in weak morning light filtering through the windows behind the altar, Piet spied two men advancing with their weapons drawn.

'Is it usual for members of the garrison to enter a holy place armed?' he asked. 'Or without the permission of the bishop?'

In Toulouse, altercations between Huguenots and Catholics were commonplace, resulting in more soldiers – both private militias and recruits in the town guard – on the streets. He had not thought such levels of unrest had spread yet to Carcassonne.

'Are they of the garrison?' Vidal asked urgently. 'Can you see the royal crest?'

Piet peered into the gloom. 'I can see little to distinguish them.'

'The Seneschal's livery is blue.'

'These men are wearing green.' He dropped his voice further. 'Vidal, if they should approach you, deny all knowledge of me. You saw no one. No one came to confession this morning. Not even a soldier would risk damning his soul by harming a priest in a state of grace.'

The assurance stuck in his throat. These were times of blood and disorder. Piet had seen enough on his journey south to Languedoc to know that a church was no longer a place of sanctuary, if, indeed, it had ever been. He looked out again.

The soldiers were moving across the transept now and searching the side chapel behind the chancel. It would not be long before they moved their attention to this side of the cathedral. He could not be discovered here.

'I entered through the north doors,' he whispered urgently. 'Save those, what other exits are there?'

'There is a door into the bishop's palace set in the west wall, and another beneath the rose window, though I fear they will be locked at this hour.' He paused for a moment. 'In the southeast corner of the cathedral there are another two doors. One leads to the tomb of Bishop Radulphe, a dead end. The other, to the sacristy. Forbidden to all but the bishop and his acolytes. It leads directly out into the cloisters.'

'Will not the sacristy door also be locked?'

'It is kept open to allow the canons access day and night. Once there, keep the refectory and infirmary buildings to your right, and you will find a gate that takes you out into Place Saint-Nazaire.'

The bells began to chime the hour, their rough clamour filling the empty aisles and giving Piet the cover he needed.

'Until tonight,' he said.

'I will pray for you,' Vidal replied. '*Dominus vobiscum.*'

Piet ducked under the heavy red curtain and ran to the closest of the huge stone pillars. He paused for a moment, then ran on to the next. As the soldiers moved along the opposite aisle, he stole widdershins up towards the door into the sacristy. He tried the handle. Despite Vidal's assurance, it was locked.

Silently, Piet cursed. He looked around until he saw that the key was hanging on a chain from a hook screwed into the stone wall. Pulling it free, Piet forced it into the lock. It was ill fitting and, at first, he could not find the catch but, just as the last chime echoed into silence, the latch gave with a heavy clunk.

Too loud. The soldiers swung around towards the noise. The taller of the two, with a vivid scar on his left cheek, dropped the visor of his helmet.

'Halt! You, stop!'

But Piet was already through the door. He slammed it behind him, then wedged a bench beneath the handle. The barricade would not hold for long, but it would slow his pursuivants' progress.

He zigzagged through the gardens, leaping over the low hedges of box and into the physic garden. Running past the chapter buildings, he spied the gate at the far end of the cloister and headed towards it. A novice priest stepped into his path, too late for him to avoid the collision. He barrelled into the boy at full pelt, sending him sprawling to the ground. Piet raised an arm in apology, but could not stop. His muscles were burning and his throat was dry, but he powered on until he reached the gate. Moments later, he flung it open and flew out into the labyrinth of La Cité.

CHAPTER SIX

⚜

The Bastide

The bells were ringing for eight o'clock as Minou walked under the Porte des Cordeliers and into the Bastide. Some of her earliest memories were of sitting at her mother's knee, listening to stories of how the two Carcassonnes had come into being: the Roman settlement of Carcasso upon the hill, the swoop of the Visigoths in the fifth century and, seven hundred and fifty years later, the Saracen conquest and the legend of Dame Carcas. Later came the rise and tragic fall of the Trencavel dynasty and the slaughter of the Cathars the young viscount had sought in vain to protect.

'Without knowing of the mistakes of the past,' Florence would say, 'how can we learn not to repeat them? History is our teacher.'

Minou knew every corner, every keystone and doorstop of La Cité, as well as she knew the rhythms of her own heart. How the carillon of the Cathedral of Saint-Nazaire stumbled between the eleventh and twelfth note of the scale. How the vines on the plains below the Porte d'Aude changed colour with the coming of the harvest: from silver to green to crimson. How the winter sun fell upon the graveyard at noon to warm those, like her mother, sleeping in the cold earth.

Minou knew it was her great fortune to have been born in such a place and have the right to call it home. But though she loved their little house in La Cité, she liked the hustle and bustle of the Bastide Saint-Louis more. The citadel was rooted in the past, in thrall to its own history. The lower town, the new Carcassonne, had its sights set on the future.

A wooden hoop wobbled into Minou's path. She caught it up and handed it back to its owner, a girl with a soot-smutted face and a blue kerchief tied around her neck.

'*Merci*,' the child said, giggling and darting back behind her mother's skirts.

Minou smiled. She had played such games in these streets, the smooth surface of the lanes of the Bastide so much better for a hoop and stick than the cobbled pathways of La Cité.

Minou carried on up rue Carrière Mage, dodging the mass of carts and ox-drays, dog traps and geese, still thinking about her mother. A memory of herself at eight years old, doing her lessons at the kitchen table in the afternoon. The sun streaming in through the open back door, lighting her slate and chalks. Her mother's clear voice, patient, turning learning into a wonderful story.

'The Bastide was founded in the mid thirteenth century, fifty years after the bloody crusade that saw Viscount Trencavel murdered in his own castle and La Cité stripped of its independence. To punish the inhabitants for rebellion against the Crown, Saint-Louis expelled every citizen of the medieval city and ordered a new town to be built on the reclaimed swamp and marshland on the left bank of the river Aude instead. Two major roads running north to south, and east to west – like this and this.' Florence drew the outline of the town on a sheet of paper. 'See? Then, here, smaller streets in between. The two cathedral churches, Saint-Michel and Saint-Vincent, that took their names from the medieval suburbs of La Cité destroyed by Simon de Montfort's Crusaders.'

'It looks like the shape of a cross.'

Florence nodded. 'A Cathar cross, so it does. The first people went to live in the Bastide in the year twelve hundred and sixty-two. A city of refugees, of honest people put forcibly from their homes. At first the Bastide lived in the grand shadow of the fortified citadel. But, little by little, the new Carcassonne began to thrive. Time marched on. Centuries passed. While the royal coffers in Paris were depleted year after year after year through wars with England, with Italy, and with the Spanish Netherlands, the Bastide survived the years of famine and plague, and grew in wealth and influence. Wool and linen and silks. Carcassonne on the hill was eclipsed by Carcassonne on the plain.'

'What does eclipsed mean?' Minou had asked, and she'd been rewarded with her mother's smile.

'It means "overshadowed",' Florence replied. 'In the Bastide, different trades set up their shops in different streets. The apothecaries and notaries in one place, the rope makers and wool merchants in another. The printers and booksellers favoured rue du Marché.'

'Like Papa?'

'Like Papa.'

The memory started to fade, as it always did, and Minou found herself alone again in the bright February morning with the familiar sense of loss. She had her mother's drawing still, though the chalk lines had grown faint on the paper, and used it now to teach Aimeric and Alis as their mother once had taught her.

Minou set her sights on the day ahead, then walked into the Grande Place. The most coveted pitches were under the covered market in the centre, or beneath the wooden colonnades that bordered the square. Even during Lent, the place was a riot of colour and commerce on market day. She tried to take pleasure in the spectacle. Hawkers, with cages of wild fowl and embroidered hoods for hunting birds, called out to the finely dressed women and men walking past.

But, in truth, despite the bustling and convivial atmosphere, her spirits were troubled. A chill wind was blowing through the Languedoc. For all that Carcassonne was some two weeks' ride from the powerful cities of the north, and the customs of the south were different, Minou feared their shop's reputation for selling books to suit all religious tastes was out of step with the increasingly intolerant times.

Bernard Joubert was a faithful Catholic, adhering to the old ways from habit as much as piety. It had been his wife who had both a skill for business and an enquiring mind to match it. Tolerance ran in her veins as steady and true as her Languedocien blood. It was she who had suggested that they should stock the words men wanted to read: Thomas Aquinas and St Paul, Zwingli and Calvin, devotional works in English and romances in Dutch.

'We shall all be reunited in God's heavenly Kingdom,' she would say to her husband when he wavered, 'whichever path we follow to get there. God is greater than anything man can comprehend. He sees all. Forgives all our sins. He expects no more than for us each to do our best to serve Him.'

Florence's instincts had been right and the business had thrived. Joubert's reputation grew. He was known to be able to acquire religious works from Geneva, from Amsterdam, Paris, Antwerp and London, and both collectors and ordinary citizens made a path to his door. Manuscripts from the English monasteries and convents looted in old King Henry's time, now circulating freely throughout the Midi, fetched a particularly good price. Most successful were Marot's translations of the Psalms into French and editions of the Gospels, which

Bernard printed on his own press. It was the bookshop that kept him putting one foot in front of the other when his grief at Florence's death threatened to overwhelm him.

At least it had.

Some weeks ago, the shutters of their bookshop had been daubed with crude accusations of blasphemy. Bernard had tried to dismiss it as the work of idle fools, stirring up mischief for mischief's sake. Minou hoped he was right. All the same, since the attack there had been a decline in the number of customers visiting the shop. Even the most loyal of patrons were anxious not to be associated with a bookseller whose name might now be on some list of heretics held in Paris or Rome. Her mother would have faced the challenge with fortitude. Bernard could not. The business was struggling and receipts were down.

Minou stopped at her usual stall to buy a fennel pie and some rose-water biscuits to take home for Alis and Aimeric later. She walked past the premises occupied by the limner and portrait painter, waved to Madame Noubel, who was sweeping the steps of her boarding house, then passed the shop selling inks, quills, brushes and easels. The owner, Monsieur Sanchez, was a Spaniard, a *Converso* who had fled the fires of the Inquisition in Barcelona and had been forced to abjure his Jewish faith. He was kind-hearted and his Dutch wife, a gaggle of beautiful, dark-featured children at her skirts, always had ready a biscuit or a piece of candied peel to give to the urchins sent into the Bastide from the villages to beg.

Their immediate neighbour was a rival bookseller, a quarrelsome man from the Montagne Noire who specialised in disreputable chap books, bawdy verses and provocative pamphlets. His shutters, cracked and in need of oil, were rusted shut. She had not seen him for days.

Minou stood in front of their blue-painted door and took a

deep breath. She told herself that of course the familiar façade would look as it always did. Why should it not? The door would be locked and untampered with. The shutters would be unmolested. The sign – B JOUBERT – LIVRES ACHAT ET VENTE – would be hanging from the metal hooks on the stone wall. There would be no repeat of the attack some weeks previously.

Minou looked.

All was well. The knot in her chest vanished. Nothing was amiss. There was no sign of malice or disorder, no evidence of interference. Everything looked just as it had when she had taken her leave the previous afternoon.

'How now!' cried Charles. 'Another cold one, I warrant.'

Minou spun round. Monsieur Sanchez's eldest son was standing on the corner of rue du Grand Séminaire, waving at her. He was lusty and strong, but simple minded. A child in a man's body.

'Good morning, Charles,' she called back.

He carried on with a smile on his broad face and a sparkle in his flattened eyes.

'A cruel wind blows in February,' he said. 'Cold, cold and cold again . . .'

'So it is.'

'Set to be fair all day, or so say the clouds.' Charles gestured to the sky with both hands, a strange flapping motion, as if he was shooing geese. Minou looked up. Thin strands of flat white cloud, like ribbon, overlaid the rising pink sun. He put his finger to his lips. 'Clouds have secrets, sshh, if we but have the wit to listen.'

Minou nodded.

Charles stared, as if only just seeing her, then began the conversation over as if for the first time.

'How now. Another cold one. Set to be fair all day!'

Not wishing to be limed in the same tangle of words, Minou held up the keys and made a pantomime of unlocking the door.

'To work,' she said, and stepped inside.

It was dark in the shop but, as Minou breathed in the familiar scent of tallow and leather and paper, she could tell everything was as she had left it: the pool of yellow wax cold on the counter, her father's inkhorn and quill, a pile of new acquisitions waiting to be catalogued and placed on the shelves, the ledger and accounts book on the desk.

She went through to the small room at the rear of the shop to fetch the tinder box. The printing press stood silent, the trays of iron letters beside it, unused now for several weeks. A square of daylight fell through the tiny window, revealing a sheen of dust on the wooden shelf where the rolls of paper were stored. Minou wiped it clean with her finger.

Would she ever hear the rattle of the press again? Her father had lost interest even in reading, let alone in printing. Though he still sat by the fire with a book open upon his lap, often he did not turn a single page.

She fetched the tinder box and struck at the stone until she had a spark, then went back into the main room. With the taper, she lit a fresh candle upon the counter, then the lamps. It was only now, as light flooded the chamber, that Minou noticed a corner of white paper sticking out from beneath the door mat.

She picked it up. Heavy paper of good quality; black ink, but in a rough hand and crude block letters. It was addressed to her, rather than to her father – and by her given name: MADEMOISELLE MARGUERITE JOUBERT. She frowned. She never received personal letters. Everyone she knew, with the exception of her estranged uncle and aunt in Toulouse, lived in

Carcassonne. In any case, she was always known by her nickname, 'Minou', never Marguerite.

Minou turned the letter over. Her interest sharpened. The letter was sealed with a family insignia, though the seal was cracked. Had she damaged it when she picked it up? Moreover, it looked like it had been applied in haste, for the parchment around it was marked with loose teardrops of red wax. Two initials, a B and a P, were set either side of some kind of mythical creature – a lion perhaps – with talons and a tied forked tail. Below that was an inscription too small to read without the aid of a magnifying glass.

In the liminal space between one breath and the next, Minou felt something shimmer inside her. A memory of such an image above a door, of a voice singing a lullaby in the old language.

'Bona nuèit, bona nuèit . . .
Braves amics, pica mièja-nuèit
Cal finir velhada.'

She frowned. Her conscious mind did not understand the words, though she had the sense that beneath the surface the meaning was clear.

Minou fetched the paper knife from the counter, slipped the tip beneath the fold and broke the seal. Inside was a single sheet of paper which looked to have been used before. At the top, the writing was obscured with what looked like soot. But, at the bottom, were five clear words written on it in black ink, in the same clumsy hand as on the outside.

SHE KNOWS THAT YOU LIVE.

Minou turned cold. What did it mean? Were the words a threat or a warning? Then the brass bell above the door rang, clattering into the silence of the shop.

Not wanting anyone to see the letter, Minou quickly thrust it into the lining of her cloak, then turned around with her working smile upon her face. The day's work had begun.

The scratch of the quill upon paper. The viscous ink staining the white pages black. The more I write, the more there is to tell. Each story gives birth to another story, and another.

There are no secrets in a village. Though time wears memory away, someone always talks in the end. Seduced by a coin in the hand, a rod upon the back, the curve of a breast beneath a summer shift. In the passing of the years, those stories intended to remain hidden and those in common sight become blurred.

Anyone and anything can be bought. Information, a soul, a promise of advancement or a bribe to be left in peace. A letter, delivered for a sou. A reputation ruined for the price of a loaf of bread. And when gold and silver fail, there is always the point of a knife.

Courage is a fair-weather friend.

Scribble, scribble. Men are frail creatures, easily turned. This I learnt at my father's knee. My education in the arts of seduction came from him, though I did not know then it was a sin. I did not know it was unnatural. He told me it was his right to make a woman of me though I was no more than ten years of age and knew no better. I was obedient. I feared a beating more than I feared what he did to me in his chamber at night. I learnt too that, when

I cried, he was angry and so punished me more harshly. Showing weakness encourages not pity but contempt.

He was my first. I killed him when his guard was down, his sword lying on the floor in his chamber and his foul appetites satisfied. I obtained the poison from a travelling apothecary, in the usual way girls are obliged to acquire things from men.

How easy it is to stop the beating of a heart.

The midwife was the second. She took longer to die, flattered by my visit. The low, white cottage at the edge of the village. Ale and a roaring fire loosened her tongue. Overjoyed to have an audience for her rambling reminiscences of those feeble-minded sons and daughters she had helped bring into the world.

Her milky eyes grew misty with the past. Many winters past, yes there had been a birth, but she was bound never to speak of it. How many years? A dozen, a score? She could not remember now. On her honour. A boy or girl? She could not say one way or the other. All these years, she had kept her word. She was not a tattle-tale.

The crack-toothed fool. She was too boastful, she was proud. And pride, as the Proverbs instruct us, is a sin hated by the Lord and one that will not go unpunished. Her clouded eyes flickered when she realised I was not a friend. But, by then, it was too late.

She bruised easily, her loose skin turning purple with each twist of my hands. White eyes turning red. A pillow, the slip stained yellow with the smoke and sweat of her many years. I had not thought she would have so much fight in her. Her bone-cracked limbs kicking and fighting as I pressed the cloth over her mouth and nose. She should be grateful that I cleansed her soul of so grievous a sin before dispatching her to her Maker.

I went from there to the chapel and confessed only my venial sins, keeping the dispatch of the midwife a secret between myself and God. The priest had no need to hear it. It is the Lord's voice I hear in my head, no other. I made a prayer of contrition. He gave me penance and absolution, secure that I repented.

Later, I gave my confessor the comfort men desire, even those who stand closest to God's heart.

CHAPTER SEVEN

⚜

La Cité

From the cover of the apothecary's doorway, Piet looked out into the street. Steam was rising from the cobblestones. Everything glistened bright with promise. Of his pursuivants, there was no sign.

Piet stepped out of the doorway, still asking himself the same question. Had he misread the situation? Was it likely that the soldiers knew who he was? No. More probable they had seen a man – a stranger to Carcassonne – making his way by stealth into the cathedral and had gone to investigate. There were rumours aplenty of priests being attacked at prayer. His reaction spoke of guilt and so, of course, they had pursued him.

On the other hand, what if there *was* more to it? Piet was certain that he had not been followed from Toulouse to Carcassonne. He'd taken a circuitous route through the Lauragais and would have noticed someone on his tail. Since arriving he had taken every care. His horse was stabled in Trivalle and he had told no one where he was lodging in the Bastide, until Vidal this past hour.

Heads or tails, a roll of the dice. Should he stay or quit Carcassonne now, while he was still at liberty? Had his description been circulated? Even now were more soldiers looking for him? Had he become a risk to his comrades? Despite every precaution, was there a spy within the group? Either in Toulouse or amongst those with whom he was due to parley at noon? Each Carcassonnais came foresworn, their loyalties vouched for, yet Piet had spent long enough in the melting pot of London to know that any one of them could be a traitor. But he was loath to abandon the rendezvous without due cause.

The sole question was should he stay until tonight, and meet with Vidal, or leave? He did not want to bring trouble to his friend's door, yet the estrangement between them lay heavy. Vidal was the first person – the only person – who had touched his heart since his beloved mother, dead for many years now. If he left Carcassonne without seeing him again, the chance to put things right between them would be lost. Perhaps forever.

Piet continued to where Vidal had said his lodgings were to be found, in the oldest part of La Cité. Red Roman tiles were layered between the grey stones of the towers and he found the house without difficulty. He examined the latch on the garden gate, noted there was a tavern opposite where he could wait out the hours between the lighting of the lamps and their meeting, then moved on.

A crowd of women and children were gathering around a large well, pails in hand, each waiting their turn to draw water. They looked healthy and well, a sharp contrast to many of the children who came into Piet's passing care in Toulouse. A little girl with a mass of black curls stood scowling up at a fine-looking boy of perhaps thirteen. Ignoring his sister, he was teasing two older girls. One had the complexion of a milkmaid and was spirited. Her cheeks were flushed a pretty pink in the pinch of the morning air and her brown eyes sparkled. Her friend was less fortunate. Her skin was pockmarked and her shoulders hunched, as if she passed her days hoping not to be noticed.

The boy swung his full pail back over the stone ledge, then set a kiss on the lips of the prettier girl.

'Aimeric, how you dare!' she cried. 'You are too bold!'

'Ha! If you don't want to be kissed, Marie, you shouldn't be so sweet on the eye.'

'I'll tell my mother!'

He feigned a swoon. 'That's no way to treat an admirer who is sick with love for you!'

He blew her another heartfelt kiss. This time, she threw out her hand to catch the imagined love-token in the air. Piet found himself smiling. What he would give to be young again and without a care.

'Adieu, Aimeric,' Marie called.

The boy took his sister's hand. 'Come, Alis,' he said, then they disappeared into a nearby house with a rambling wild rose over the lintel. Piet watched the plain friend stare at the closed door for a moment, a mixture of jealousy and longing writ clear upon her face, and his heart ached for her.

Piet made his way down rue Saint-Jean, then through the inner walls into the lists. Ahead, a narrow gate appeared to lead straight out into the countryside.

'*En garde.*'

In the tilting yard, two richly dressed boys – no doubt sons of the Seneschal's household – were practising their strokes under the gimlet eye of their fencing master.

'*Appel*, parry. *Appel*, parry. No!'

The sound of their capped foils clashed as they lunged at one another, then lunged again. Neither boy was fleet of foot, nor gave the impression of being interested in their lesson, but the instructor was unrelenting. Piet had taught himself to fight: with bare knuckles, sticks, poniard or sword, whatever got the job done. His methods were effective, if not elegant.

'Again. Try again.'

There was no one on duty at the gate. A wisp of steam

floating up into the cold air pinpointed where the guard had gone to relieve himself. Piet followed the line of the stone barbican down to the river, then retraced his steps to the stables where he had left his horse the previous evening.

'I might have need of my horse tonight, or else early on the morrow,' he said to the groom, pressing a generous tip into his hand. 'Can you keep her bridled and ready?'

'As you wish, Monsieur.'

'And there will be another sou for you if you keep your peace. No need for others to know my business.'

The boy, gap toothed, grinned. 'I never even saw you.'

CHAPTER EIGHT

⚜

LA BASTIDE

The morning trade was brisk. Minou barely had a moment to herself.

It was not until well past eleven o'clock that she dragged her father's high stool into the doorway and sat down to rest her feet. She ate the fennel pie, washing the buttery pastry down with ale, then played a wild game of pat-a-cake with the younger Sanchez children until her palms were sore. Musing on the provenance of the letter, she enquired casually of her neighbours if anyone had noticed an early visitor to the shop. No one had.

The bells were striking the quarter-hour shy of midday when Minou heard shouting. Recognising Madame Noubel's voice, she stepped out to greet her.

Cécile Noubel was a popular figure in rue du Marché. She had buried two husbands, the second of whom had settled upon her the deeds to the boarding house. In her autumn years, she finally had the freedom to live as she pleased.

'It is by order of the Seneschal,' the younger soldier was saying. A bare-faced boy, only a few wisps on his chin, he looked scarcely old enough to carry arms.

'The Seneschal? The Seneschal has no jurisdiction in the Bastide, and he most certainly has no jurisdiction over my boarding house. I pay my taxes. I know my rights.' She folded her arms. 'In any case, how do you know the villain is lodging here?'

'We have it on unimpeachable authority,' the boy was saying.

'That will do,' the captain cut in. Broad and heavily built, he had a thick brown beard and a vertical scar that ran the length of his left cheek. 'You are suspected of harbouring a known felon. Our information is that he has taken lodgings in the Bastide. We have authority to search all premises where he might be hiding. Yours included.'

Other neighbours had come into the street to see what the commotion was, or were watching from their upper windows. Madame Noubel drew herself up. Her colour was high, but she looked solid and immoveable.

'Hiding? Am I to understand that you are accusing me of knowingly harbouring a criminal?'

'Of course not, Madame Noubel,' the younger man said unhappily, 'but we are authorised, charged – that is to say, under clear orders – to search your premises. Acting on information received. The charge is serious.'

She shook her head. 'If you have a warrant from the Présidial – which, so far as I am aware, is still responsible for the governance of the Bastide, not the Seneschal in La Cité – then show it to me, and I shall give you leave to enter. If you do not have such a warrant, you can go whistle!'

'*Cinc minuta,* Madama,' the boy pleaded, dropping into the local language in an attempt to get on her good side. 'It will take but five minutes.'

'Do you have a warrant, or no?'

The captain pushed him out of the way. 'Are you refusing to comply with our orders, woman?'

'Sire,' the boy murmured, 'Madame Noubel is much

respected in Carcassonne. There are many who would speak in her defence.'

Although the crowd was enjoying the pantomime, Minou noticed the boy kept glancing at the older man and a shiver of alarm went down her spine. Were they even soldiers? They wore military surcoats, but with no insignia.

The captain prodded the boy in the chest. 'If you challenge my authority again, *paysan*,' he said in a low voice, 'I'll have you stripped until you can't walk for a week.'

The boy dropped his eyes. '*Oui, mon Capitaine*.'

'*Oui, mon Capitaine*,' the captain mimicked. 'You are a maggot, a kennel rat. You Southerners are all the same. Get on with it. Search the rooms. Every last corner of this boarding house. If the felon is here, use any force necessary to subdue him, but do not kill him. Now!' he shouted, spraying beads of spittle onto the boy's cheek. 'Unless your sympathy for these peasants means you would rather keep their company in gaol?'

In that instant, a cloud crossed the face of the noonday sun, plunging the street into grey shadow, and everything seemed to happen at once. Minou stepped closer. The boy moved awkwardly to the door, as the captain barged Madame Noubel aside to get past. He did not push hard, but she was taken off balance and fell heavily against the frame of the door, cracking her head.

Blood oozed from the wound, staining her white bonnet a vivid red and a shrill scream rang out. Monsieur Sanchez stepped forward just as Minou began to run.

'Stay back,' the captain shouted, 'all of you, else you will find yourselves arrested and charged with obstructing the Seneschal's orders. Do you understand? We seek a murderer. The law is the law, in Carcassonne as much as in the more civilised regions of France.'

Minou heard the warning but pushed through to the front of the crowd. The soldier turned on her.

'You. Tend to this harridan, this shrew. Perhaps a spell in the pillory will teach her to curb her tongue.'

Boiling with fury, Minou crouched beside her friend. Madame Noubel's eyes were closed and a thin trail of blood was dripping down her cheek.

'Madame,' she whispered, 'it is me, Minou. Do not speak, but nod if you can hear me.'

The slightest movement told Minou that her message was heard. She took a kerchief from her sleeve and dabbed away the blood.

'Any person still here by the time our search is concluded,' the captain yelled, 'will run the risk of finding themselves detained at the Seneschal's pleasure.' He grabbed Minou by the arm and dragged her to her feet. 'This woman must be able to sit unaided and answer to her own name. I will hold you responsible if she cannot. Do you understand?'

Minou nodded. He shook her again.

'Cat got your tongue? Do. You. Understand?'

Minou raised her eyes and answered. 'I do.'

He held her arm for a moment longer, then shrugged her away from him and stormed into the boarding house.

The instant he'd gone, Madame Noubel's eyes opened.

'He knocked me down. Without provocation, he knocked me down.'

'I think it was an accident,' Minou said cautiously.

'Accident or no, the result is the same! Did he apologise? Do I not own my house? I shall report him—'

'Hold still, Madame Noubel, you are still bleeding.'

'"By order of the Seneschal"! The Seneschal has no authority in the Bastide. I have run these lodgings for a dozen years without a single complaint.'

Minou glanced up at the boarding house, where the sounds of rooms being ransacked filtered out through the open windows. She was certain Madame Noubel should not antagonise such a man. Accident or no, there was something lawless about him. The local man, the boy soldier, clearly thought the same.

'Madame, come away and I will dress your wound.'

'How dare he treat me like some – some miscreant. I am a respectable widow . . . such things do not happen in Carcassonne.'

'We should leave.'

'Leave?' Madame Noubel, despite the shock, was outraged.

'I do not think you should be here when they come back out. Though they claim to come from the Seneschal, I do not believe it. Would a captain of the royal garrison behave to you as he did? Besides, the Seneschal's men wear blue. These ruffians are in green and with no markings.'

'But I asked to see their warrant—'

'Which they did not show you,' Minou said, glancing again at the boarding house. 'I am sure they are private soldiers. Or worse, mercenaries.'

'I have done nothing wrong. I will not be driven from my own home.'

'Please, Madame. Only until the so-called captain's temper has cooled. If they do not find the man they seek—'

'They will not, for he went out at first light and has not returned.'

'Then the captain's displeasure will certainly increase. He will look for someone to blame.'

Madame Noubel frowned. 'My lodger seemed a pleasant

enough fellow. Not from around here, but courteous. Hair the colour of a fox's tail.'

'The captain threatened to put you in the pillory,' Minou said, her voice urgent now.

'He would not dare. On what charge?'

'I fear it will not matter.'

All at once, the fight went out of Madame Noubel and she looked every one of her three-score years. 'But what of my house?' she said. 'It is all I have. If they damage . . .'

Charles had been hovering in the doorway of his father's shop. Loud noises frightened him, but Minou thought he would help so long as the soldiers remained out of sight.

'I will ask Monsieur Sanchez to keep watch for you,' she said, helping Madame Noubel to her feet. 'Come.'

'Another cold day,' Charles muttered, scuttling towards them with his strange, lolloping gait. 'Cold, cold, cold, cold. Set to be fine, fine all day, all day. So say the clouds.'

'Charles, listen to me. Take Madame Noubel into my father's shop. Into the bookshop, yes? Go all the way through to the room at the back where the paper and ink are stored.'

His simple face lit up. 'Look but not touch. Monsieur Joubert say not to touch.'

'That's right.' She put her finger to her lips. 'And it is a secret. No one must know, do you understand?'

Piet had witnessed the whole incident from the corner of rue du Grand Séminaire.

He watched his landlady arguing with the soldiers and then saw the attack. He saw a tall young woman, with milk-white skin and long straight brown hair, smuggle her away from under the captain's nose. He saw a strange boy, a simpleton, help them. It went against his nature not to intervene, but on this occasion, he could not.

He pressed the leather satchel to his side to reassure himself the contents were safe. The situation here proved that his reactions in the cathedral earlier had been correct. Two private soldiers in green surcoats in La Cité, two others searching his lodgings in the Bastide. Were they the same men?

Piet had spent much of his life expecting to have it taken from him. Feeling the touch of steel at his throat, the phantom ache of powder shot in his guts.

He was not Languedoc born, but it was his adoptive land and it had made him welcome. A refugee with no home, he felt a blood loyalty for this corner of France as strong as any native-born man. Tolerance and dignity and freedom: Piet was ready to lay down his life to defend these principles.

He was engaged in a battle for the very soul of France, a battle that would define how men could live and be free. Catholic or Protestant, Jew or Saracen, even those of no religion. He had learnt to trust his instincts and his instincts were telling him to get out while he had the chance. But he had made a vow, unbreakable in the eyes of God, and he would fulfil it.

Minou waited until Charles had taken Madame Noubel safely into the bookshop, then sat on the step holding the bloodied kerchief in her lap. She was only just in time. A thud of boots on the stairs, then the sergeant-at-arms reappeared, carrying a small wooden travelling chest and a leather-bound ledger, the captain fulminating at his heels.

'Where's the old woman?' he demanded. 'I told you to tend her.'

'Upon my word, I do not know.' She held out the bloody

handkerchief. 'The stink of it sent me into a faint. When I came to, she had gone.'

His eyes sharpened in anger but, this time, he controlled his temper.

'Captain Bonal—'

The captain turned on his subordinate. 'What did you say?'

'*Mon Capitaine*, forgive me,' the young soldier corrected himself, 'but I do not believe Madame Noubel is implicated in any wrong-doing or that this maid knows anything. The villain signed the register in a false name. We have this.' He held up the chest with trembling hands. 'We can set a guard. He is bound to return.'

The captain hesitated, then nodded. 'Count yourself lucky,' he growled, jabbing a grimy finger at Minou, 'that I do not put you in the pillory in the shrew's place. Get out of my sight.'

Minou got to her feet and, forcing herself not to break into a run, moved quickly away, feeling the captain's hostile eyes on her back. She refused to give him the satisfaction of letting her fear show. Only when she had rounded the corner, did her courage forsake her. She held out her arms. Her hands were shaking, but she felt exhilarated and foolhardy, brave and honourable and proud. Minou leant back against the wall, barely able to countenance how reckless she had been.

Then she began to laugh.

CHAPTER NINE

⚜

At midday Piet knocked at the appointed house in rue de l'Aigle d'Or and waited to be admitted. He heard footsteps on the stairs, then the door was opened a crack.

He blinked at the unexpected sight of a familiar face.

'Michel Cazès, by all that's holy! I had not thought to see you here.'

The door opened wider, Piet stepped inside and the two men shook hands. Five years ago, both new converts to the Huguenot cause, he and Michel had fought shoulder to shoulder in the Prince of Condé's army: Michel, a professional soldier; Piet, a civilian forced to take up arms to defend what he believed in. Since that time, Piet had not heard word of him.

Time had been cruel. Now bone thin and dressed all in black save for a white ruff and cuffs, Michel's face was scored with lines. His skin was sallow and his hair turned white. As they embraced, Piet could feel his friend's ribs beneath his clothes.

'How goes it with you?' he said, dismayed by the change in his friend.

Michel raised his arms. 'As you see, I am still here.'

At the top of the stairs, a dishevelled young man called down to them.

'Has he given the password?'

'It is not necessary,' Michel said. 'I can vouch for him.'

'All the same,' the boy said in his lazy, high-born accent.

Piet exchanged a look with Michel, but obliged. 'For the Midi.'

As they climbed the steep stairs, he noticed Michel's breathing was laboured. Twice he had to stop and hold a kerchief scented with balsam to his mouth. Piet also noticed, as Michel clutched at the banister, that two fingers were missing on his right hand.

'My friend, shall we pause –'

'I am fine,' Michel said.

They continued to the top of the building, where Piet opened his cloak to the young man to show he was armed.

'*Per lo Miègjorn*,' Piet said, repeating the password.

The boy stared at the dagger but did not ask him to remove it. His eyes were bloodshot and the stench of yesterday's ale lay strong on his skin.

'Come in, Monsieur.'

Piet stepped into a fugged room, the air thick with wood smoke and the scent of stale food. A chicken carcass picked clean sat on a wooden platter on the table, tankards sour with the smell of ale and mead.

'Let me make the introductions,' Michel said. 'Comrades, may I present to you one of the most steadfast soldiers with whom I ever had the honour to serve. Piet Reydon, originally of Amsterdam—'

'But owing allegiance to the Midi,' Piet interrupted. 'I am pleased to make your acquaintance, Messieurs.'

He looked around the room. It was a smaller group than he expected, though that was probably a good thing.

'Our Cerberus, Philippe Devereux, you have already met.'

He gave a half-bow. Closer up, the young man seemed green around the gills. His yellow doublet and hose were stained.

Michel gestured to the window sill. 'This is our commander, Oliver Crompton,' he said, stumbling over the English surname, then to a man sitting at the square wooden table. 'And Alphonse Bonnet, who is in his service.'

Piet nodded at the dark and stocky labourer, his dirty hands cupped around a rough wooden tankard, before turning to his master. Well built, with eyes close set, he wore his black beard trimmed in the English style.

'Monsieur Piet Reydon.'

Crompton held out his hand. Piet shook it and, as their eyes met, he felt a cool appraisal. His left hand tightened around the strap of his satchel.

'We have heard much of the charitable work you do for our community in Toulouse. Your reputation precedes you.'

'Much exaggerated, I am sure.' He smiled. 'Crompton?'

'English father, French mother, and a distant cousin to this young gentleman, who found the lure of the taverns of Trivalle more attractive than his own bed last evening. He is not yet recovered.'

Devereux flushed. 'On my honour, I drank no more than a gage of ale, perhaps two. I cannot account for why I was so ill affected.'

Crompton shook his head. 'You find us in the middle of a discussion, Monsieur.'

'Piet does not have time to waste,' Michel said. 'We should proceed to our business.'

'I am certain he will find much to interest him in our debate.'

Piet waved his hand. 'Please.'

'Before you arrived, Michel was saying he believes the rights of worship granted to Huguenots in the Edict of

Toleration were made in good faith, whereas my noble cousin here does not.'

'The Edict is not worth the paper it's written on,' Devereux interrupted.

'It has saved lives,' Michel said quietly.

Crompton laughed. 'Michel here believes the Queen Regent wishes for the discord between Catholics and Protestants to end. I do not.'

'I do not deny there are others who see things differently. All I say is that we should not be the ones to precipitate further conflict. We will be judged the harsher if it appears as if we refused to accept the olive branch offered.'

'This Edict,' Crompton countered, 'like all those that have been issued before, is a thing of smoke and mirrors. It is intended to give the illusion of compromise between the demands of the Catholics – by which I mean the Duke of Guise and his allies – and the moderate Catholics within the court. The Guise faction has no intention of honouring it, none whatsoever.'

'You cannot know that,' Michel said, beads of sweat glistening on his forehead. 'Guise is sequestered in his estates in Joinville. His influence is waning.'

'If you believe that, you're a fool!' Devereux said.

'Philippe, remember your manners,' Crompton warned.

'Papist dogs!' growled Bonnet, slopping ale onto the table.

'Guise and his brother have not been at court for some eighteen months,' Michel continued, struggling to breathe evenly. 'It is dangerous to portray every Catholic in the same light. It is what Guise says of us, cannot you see? He claims all Protestants are traitors to France, rebels intent on bringing down the state. He knows it to be untrue, but repeats it endlessly nevertheless.'

Piet had been party to many such conversations and the question was always the same: after years of persecution under Henri II, why should they believe his wife, Catherine, the Queen Regent, now intended to treat them fairly?

'Come,' Devereux drawled. 'You well know that if a lie is repeated often enough, in the face of the clearest evidence to the contrary, even the most level-headed of men start to believe in it. Falsehood easily becomes accepted truth.'

Michel shook his head. 'Things are not black and white. There are, on their side, as many moderate Catholics, who wish to reach a compromise, as there are those on our side who work for peace and justice.'

Crompton leant forward. 'Are these the same "moderate Catholics" who stood by and watched the violent suppression of our brethren after the Conspiracy of Amboise?'

'That was an amateurish and ill-advised plot, which turned many against us,' Michel replied.

Piet put his hand on his friend's shoulder. 'Michel is right. The Conspiracy hardened attitudes against us. Don't forget that the Duke of Guise is, to many, the saviour of France. It was he who sent the English packing and returned Calais to French hands.' He turned to Crompton. 'Forgive me if I offend you by speaking plainly.'

Crompton shook his head. 'I take no offence. My sword is for France. My mother had no choice in the matter of my conception and so, though I thank my father for the gift of life and his English name, I curse him in every other respect.' He held Piet's eye. 'The same for you? Mixed blood. You are Dutch perhaps?'

Piet smiled, but had no intention of speaking of his private circumstances in a chamber of strangers. 'For many of us, our loyalties are complicated. We each must choose our allegiance according to our own conscience.'

'Whether she o'er steps her responsibilities or not,' Michel said softly, 'the Queen Regent has decided that compromise is the way forward. For the greater good of France. I do not advocate doing nothing. I merely say we should not act rashly.'

'If we allow them to strike first, we lose the advantage,' Crompton pressed. 'As a soldier, you of all people should understand that.'

'But we have no advantage!' Michel cried. 'They have the full might of the state on their side. We do not want war.'

'*We* do not, but I fear that is exactly what Guise wants. Civil war. He will not be content until he has driven every Huguenot from France. It is said our Prince of Condé has issued a letter requesting arms and a levy to secure Toulouse. If that is so, should Carcassonne not follow where Toulouse leads?' He paused. 'Is that correct, Reydon?'

Piet had no more intention of revealing any information about the situation in Toulouse than gossiping about himself. He was here to do business, nothing more.

'A rumour, that is all.'

Alphonse Bonnet slapped his hand on the table. 'Papist vermin! Kennel rats.'

Crompton ignored him. 'Speak, Reydon,' he said, and Piet felt the atmosphere in the chamber sharpen. 'You are amongst comrades.'

He cursed the position he found himself in. The bonds of friendship made him wish to ally himself with Michel, whom he knew to be a man of honour and courage. Had any of the others in this chamber ever seen action on the battlefield? Yet at the same time, he knew how often good men – and Michel was a good man – imputed noble motives to others while failing to see the treachery around them.

He smiled. 'It is not modesty that prevents me from expressing my views, Crompton, so much as the fact that I have witnessed how harm can be done by those who proffer an opinion when they are only in partial possession of the facts. A man might do better to hold his tongue than scatter words without a care as to where they might land.'

Devereux laughed.

'But you must be aware of the murder of Jean Roset,' Crompton said, 'an innocent man shot at worship by a member of the Toulouse town guard supposedly set to protect Huguenots? And the attack on Protestants in Place Saint-Georges a week ago?'

Piet held his gaze. 'I am well aware of the situation in Toulouse. I was there and I can tell you Roset's death, though a tragedy, was an accident. Regardless, the soldier in question was arrested.'

'But it is not only Toulouse,' Devereux pressed. 'A devout Huguenot, a midwife as I heard it, was found murdered in her bed in the village of Puivert. Punished only for the crime of her faith.'

'In Puivert . . .' Michel muttered. He tried to stand, but his legs shook fiercely. Piet tried to help, but was waved away. 'It will pass, it will pass.'

'What do you say to that, Reydon?' Crompton asked.

'I know nothing of Puivert,' he said, wondering why Michel was suddenly so distressed. 'What I do know is that the situation of our Protestant sisters and brothers varies from region to region, hence my reluctance to offer advice. What holds true for Toulouse might not be so for Carcassonne.'

'Then you agree,' Devereux said, 'that we should sit on our hands and do nothing?'

Piet wondered at his confidence, which belied both his age and his dissolute appearance.

'If you are asking whether I agree that there is danger in us being perceived as the aggressor,' he replied carefully, 'then yes, I do. It will only justify prejudice against us and give licence for greater persecution. And there are Catholics at Court, who supported the amnesty for Huguenot prisoners in January which resulted in many of our comrades being released from gaol.'

'I –' Michel gasped. Piet waited until his friend caught his breath. 'We do not have the benefit of numbers,' he finally managed to say. 'We should not o'er press our cause beyond our ability to deliver it.'

'And then what?' Crompton demanded. 'Fall to our knees like nuns and pray all will be well? That is your counsel? Reydon, what say you to this?'

'My counsel is that we should all wait, and hope that the Edict will be fully implemented and that the situation will calm.'

Crompton's eyes sharpened. 'But if it does not?'

Piet glanced again at Michel, but answered honestly. 'If it does not, then we *will* be forced to act. If the truce does not hold, if our limited freedoms and liberties are denied us, we will fight for them.'

Devereux smiled, the tip of his tongue just visible.

'So in fact, Monsieur Reydon, we are in accord.'

'It is the ghost of a dream,' Michel whispered, 'to think we can take up arms against the Catholic Church and hope to win. Against Guise. Our only chance of survival lies in accepting what we have been offered. If it comes to war, we will be defeated. We will lose everything.'

'It will not come to war,' Piet said, placing his hand upon Michel's arm. 'War is in neither side's interest.'

'I need some air,' Michel said abruptly. 'Crompton, Devereux, if you will excuse me. Piet, it has been a pleasure to see you again.'

He picked up his hat and unsteadily walked from the room.

Piet followed after him. 'My friend, wait!'

Michel stopped, his hand on the wooden banister.

'You have business to conduct. Go back inside.'

'The transaction will take but minutes, then you and I can talk. Tell me where might I find you.'

Michel hesitated, then shook his head. 'It's too late,' he said softly, then continued his heavy descent down the staircase.

Piet wanted to go after him, find out what ailed him, but he stopped himself. He was in Carcassonne for a reason, one reason only. Afterwards, he would seek Michel out. There would be time enough later.

CHAPTER TEN

⚜

Michel walked away from rue de l'Aigle d'Or as fast as his failing body would allow. A whisper of despair slipped from between his dry lips. He could not remember when he last had drunk or eaten anything. He had no appetite these days.

All the tell-tale arguments – about Place Saint-Georges, Amboise, Condé, Jean Roset – were swirling around in his head, stinking of treachery. But only a traitor would know the significance of so minor an event, so far away. The final slip, when it had come, had been so small, that none but Michel would have heard it for what it was or recognised the perfidy beneath. In truth, it was only confirmation of what he had long suspected. The inconsistencies, the contradictions. Today, there could be no more doubt. Today, the villain had condemned himself out of his own mouth. It had been all Michel could do not to draw his knife and finish him then, but he knew he hadn't the strength to do it cleanly.

What of the others? Traitors too?

And Piet? Had he also sold his sword twice over? Claiming to fight for one cause, whilst promoting another? Michel pressed his hand to his chest to steady his stuttering heart. No, not that. He would swear on his dead mother's life that Piet was an honourable man.

Or despite his convictions, could he be wrong about him too? Once Michel would have been sure in his judgements. What had happened in the *oubliettes* had stripped every shred of confidence from him.

Michel looked around at the people in the Grande Place, now shrouded in the beginnings of an afternoon mist. He wondered if their lives were as simple and honest as they appeared? A solitary troubadour was singing, despite the chill. The mournful melody touched him. It was a relief to know that there were at least still things of beauty in this broken world.

The damp mist caught in his throat. Michel raised his kerchief to his mouth and it came away spotted in blood. Each time, a little more than before. The apothecary said he was unlikely to see another summer.

He wrapped his arms around his emaciated frame until the palsy had passed. Michel was afraid. He had learnt the true meaning of fear, not on the battlefields of France, but in the dungeons of the Inquisition in Toulouse. Such terrible cruelty carried out in the name of God.

Michel still did not know who had denounced him, or why, only that, shortly after the feast of Epiphany, he had been arrested and charged with treason. In those dark January days, Michel learnt how any man would throw truth to the dogs when confronted with rope or pincer. He learnt how pain would make any man swear black was white and white was black. It had taken the severing of but two of his fingers before he admitted to his part in a conspiracy that existed only in the minds of the inquisitors.

A bookseller, Bernard Joubert, had been imprisoned with him. Accused of selling seditious and heretical materials, when interrogated by the inquisitors, he had argued how it was possible to be both a good Catholic and stock works of literature and theology that reflected alternative points of view. His defence: that without understanding what the Reformers preached it was impossible to reason with them and, so, defeat their position. In knowledge lay power.

Joubert had not been stretched, but he had felt the vicious claws of the *chatte de griffe* on his skin. A whip as vicious as any on the slave ships, sharp nails set into the leather thongs, an instrument that stripped a man's skin from his back.

Unlike Michel, Joubert had withstood.

As they sat chained side by side in their stinking cell, the two men had spoken their innermost secrets to one another to keep the terror at bay. Surrounded by the stench of blood and death, by the pitiful cries of those whose bones were broken beyond repair, Bernard had spoken of his beloved wife Florence, five years dead, and of his three children; of his bookshop in rue du Marché and their house in La Cité, with wild roses trailing across the lintel. Of a secret Bernard had kept these many years.

And in return? Michel buried his head in his hands in shame.

When he and Joubert were released, without expectation and without charge, they had parted at the prison gates. At the time, it had seemed a miracle. Now Michel understood it was because of the amnesty of prisoners set down in the Edict.

Not all had been so fortunate. The scaffold had earnt its keep.

But though Michel had his liberty, the true horror had begun after he had left the gaol. The strange kindness he had received at the hands of the unknown noblewoman, being nursed at her expense in a house in the shadow of the cathedral in Toulouse. The wine, a warm bed and ointments for his wounds. This was the source of Michel's shame, that he had traded Joubert's secret for his own comfort.

Michel had not sought out Joubert since the afternoon of their release. Neither wished to be reminded of what they had endured. Now, he could think of nothing more than that he must find him. He had betrayed Joubert and he would never forgive himself for it. This was the corrosive guilt that had driven him at dawn to rue du Marché, but he had found the shop closed and shuttered. Now, after what he had just heard in the airless room above the tavern, he had to try harder. The sands were running through the hour glass. There was little time left to make amends.

CHAPTER ELEVEN

⚜

'Did you catch him?' asked Devereux, exchanging a look with Crompton. 'Did he say anything?'

'No,' Piet said. 'Should he have done?'

'Michel always lets his heart rule his head,' Crompton said dismissively. 'He will come around.'

Piet was suddenly sick of the pack of them. Schoolboys, playing at conspiracy, he had no patience for it. Dreaming of war and glory when he suspected none of them had seen action on the battlefield. They did not yet understand there was no glory in death.

'When the time comes – if the time comes – Michel will be the most steadfast of us all.' Piet knew his words sounded like a rebuke, but he did not care.

But now the moment was upon him, Piet was oddly reluctant to conclude the deal. The matter left an ugly taste in his mouth. But, they needed funds in Toulouse and Carcassonne was prepared to buy what they had to sell. Soldiers, weapons, building materials and bribes, the cost of caring for the hundreds of refugees who came in need of food and shelter. All of it came at a cost. It was too late for him to have a crisis of conscience now.

'Shall we to business? Time is short.'

'Of course,' Crompton said, and turned to Alphonse Bonnet, who stumbled to the corner of the chamber and worried at a loose floorboard. He pulled out a brown hessian bag from the cavity and handed it to his master.

'Here,' Crompton said. 'It is all there. The price as agreed.'

Piet met his gaze. 'You will forgive me if I confirm the sum. We would not wish for there to be any later misunderstanding.'

Crompton's expression hardened, but he did not object. Piet emptied the gold deniers onto the table, counting the coins back into the bag one by one.

'All there, my thanks.'

Crompton gave a curt nod. 'And now your side of the bargain.'

Piet took the satchel from his shoulder and laid it carefully flat on the table. He watched his own hand reach out, saw himself slowly unfastening the buckle and reaching inside. The air cracked with expectation.

Piet's fingers took hold of the delicate fabric within and he drew it out into the light. The pale cloth seemed to shimmer, transforming the grey gloom of the modest room into a place of light. The silk warp and the linen weft felt so delicate in his hands. He saw, as if for the first time, the delicate ornamental stitches embroidered along the length of the Shroud. The exquisite Kufic calligraphy spoke to Piet of nothing, and yet everything. For an instant, he felt he could almost smell the chill of the tomb and the exotic scents of the Holy Land, the olive groves and the bitter herbs of the sepulchre.

Except, it could not be . . . Time seemed to speed up again.

'The Shroud of Antioch,' Devereux muttered, his eyes greedy. 'I have waited long to see it.'

The relic had been carried to the Eglise Saint-Taur in Toulouse in 1392, by Crusaders returning from Antioch. A small fragment of the cloth, within which the body of Christ had been laid to rest in the sepulchre before his Resurrection, the Shroud was said to have worked countless miracles. It was the holiest of relics, one that would confer power on any who had possession of it.

'Here, Piet said roughly. 'Take it. Use it for the good of our cause.'

CHAPTER TWELVE

⚜

'There,' Minou said, dropping the last strip of muslin into the bowl of water and vinegar. The blood, rinsed from the cloth, turning the water pink. 'I do not think there will be any infection, the cut is not deep.'

Madame Noubel was sitting in a low chair in the bookshop with a horsehair blanket folded across her knees. Minou had locked the door and fastened the shutters. So far, they had not been disturbed.

'That such a thing should happen, Minou, in broad daylight in the Bastide. I scarce believe it.'

'I think it was an accident,' Minou replied carefully, 'though the captain's behaviour was reprehensible.'

'The world has gone mad,' Madame Noubel sighed, shrugging her heavy shoulders. 'But how proud your mother would have been of you. You showed great courage. Florence always stood firm. She always did what was right.'

'Anyone would have done the same.'

'Except they did not. People think only of their own skins these days. Not that I blame them.' She shook her head. 'Monsieur Sanchez is keeping an eye on my premises, you say?'

'He is. Charles is with him.'

Madame Noubel raised her eyebrows. 'More of a hindrance than a help, I'd have thought.'

'Try not to worry,' Minou said, folding the soiled muslin strips ready to take home for Rixende to bleach and wash.

'How goes it with your father?' Madame Noubel asked. 'I have not seen him these past weeks.'

Minou was on the point of deflecting the question, as she usually did, then stopped. She did not want to be disloyal, but she was in need of a friend to talk to.

'In truth, and though I have spoken to no one of it, I am much concerned. My father returned from his travels in January much distracted and burdened by melancholy. I have never seen him so low in his spirits, at least not since my mother passed away.'

Madame Noubel nodded. 'He always did rely on Florence to give him strength. When you ask what ails him, what answer does he give?'

'Sometimes, he denies there is anything amiss. Other times that it is no more than the rigours of the season. Certainly, he is plagued by soreness on his skin, but until this winter he was never so much afflicted by the dark and cold. He has not once set foot outside the house since his return.'

'In four weeks! Not even to go to Mass?'

'No, and he will not permit the priest to call upon him either.'

'Might Bernard be concerned about the bookshop, especially after that trouble you had? Rents are always rising, times are hard. We are all struggling to make ends meet.'

Minou frowned. 'It is true our finances are much on his mind and he fears for Aimeric's prospects. We cannot afford proper schooling, or the purchase of an army commission.' She paused. 'He is even talking of sending him to lodge with our aunt and her husband in Toulouse.'

'Indeed!' Madame Noubel's eyebrows arched. 'I was not aware the breach in the family had ever been healed.'

'I am not sure it has,' she said carefully, 'and yet my father is quite resolved Aimeric should go.' Minou picked at a loose thread on her skirts. 'But I think there is something more.'

The candle guttered in the brass holder on the table, casting a flickering shadow across Madame Noubel's careworn face.

'There are things in a man's life that he cannot speak of to his children, even one so close to his heart as are you.'

'I am nineteen! I'm not a child.'

'Ah, Minou,' Madame Noubel smiled, 'whatever age you are, you will always be his daughter, his little girl. He cannot help but want to protect you. It is the way of things.'

'I cannot bear to see him so burdened.'

Madame Noubel sighed. 'The suffering of those we love is harder to bear than anything we feel on our own behalf.'

'I fear that I have, by some carelessness, lost his affection,' Minou said softly.

'Never. Not you. He loves you dearly. But if it will help to put your mind at rest, I could talk to him. He might confide in me.'

Minou felt a glimmer of hope. 'Would you? I think I could bear any misfortune, and find strength to face it, if only I knew what was wrong. It is not knowing that weighs so heavily on my mind.'

The old woman patted her arm. 'That is settled, then. Do they not say that one good turn deserves another? Tell Bernard to expect me. I shall call upon him tomorrow after Mass.' She placed her broad hands upon her knees, then stood up. 'I should return home, if the soldiers are no longer there. See what those dogs have done to my house. Will you look?'

Minou unbolted and opened the door, then leapt back.

'Monsieur, you startled me!'

A man was standing on the threshold. Dressed in black,

with white ruff and cuffs, Minou's first impression was that he might be a scholar. She saw it in the stooped cast of his neck, his pale complexion and the way he blinked at the light, screwing his eyes tight into his sockets, as if the world was too bright.

'I regret the shop is closed,' she said, recovering herself. 'But if you might come back in an hour, I would be happy to help.'

'I am not a customer. I seek Bernard Joubert.' He looked up at the sign. 'These are still his premises?'

Minou pulled the door shut behind her, to shield Madame Noubel from his view.

'Why should they not be, Monsieur?'

He raised his hands in apology. 'None, no reason at all. That is to say, in these times, things change so quickly . . . I am glad to hear it.' He cleared his throat. 'Is Bernard here? I would speak with him urgently.'

'My father is not here. I manage the bookshop in his absence.'

His cheeks suddenly reddened and he started to shake, so violently that Minou feared he would collapse on the step.

'Monsieur, are you unwell?'

'Your father, so you must be Marguerite. Or, rather, Minou. Bernard talked often of you.'

She found a smile. 'Then you have the advantage over me, Monsieur. You seem to know my name, but you have not given me the honour of telling me yours.'

'My name does not matter, but I must speak with Bernard. I had thought to find him here. What hour will he return?'

'The hours he keeps vary in winter,' Minou said, disquieted by the visitor's intensity. 'I do not expect him today. If you might return on Monday, if you tell me the nature of your business, I might be able to help.'

The man seemed to fold in upon himself. 'I must see him.'

'I am sorry. My father said nothing of expecting a visitor.'

His dark eyes sparked with anger and, for the first time, Minou realised he must once have been a formidable man.

'And does he tell you everything? I warrant not, for what father would confide every private matter to his daughter?'

Minou flushed. 'I did not intend to offend you, Monsieur.'

But having given vent to his temper, he shrank back into his bones. She had thought him some two score years and ten, but Minou could see now it was only his white hair and lines upon his brow that made him seem so.

'It is I who should beg your pardon, Mademoiselle Minou. It is I who have given offence, and that was not my intention.'

'You gave no offence, so I have taken none. My father has not come to the Bastide today, but if it pleases you to write a letter, I will deliver it.'

He held up his right hand to show the raw, ruined skin where two of his fingers were missing.

'Alas, I no longer find such communication easy.'

Minou blushed at her clumsiness. 'I could write it for you.'

'Thank you, but safest not.'

'Safest?' She waited, seeing the conflict rage in his eyes, but he did not answer. 'Will you at least give me your name, Monsieur, so I might tell my father?'

He smiled. 'My name is of no value.'

'Very well. Might you tell me the name by which my father might know you for a friend?'

'A friend.' He paused, then another fleeting smile graced his face. Thought, regret, grief, all reflected there. 'Bernard told me you had the wit of ten men. Tell him Michel would speak with him. From Toulouse.'

Then suddenly he tipped his hat and was gone, as quickly as he had appeared.

Mystified, Minou went back inside.

'Who was that?' Madame Noubel asked.

'He gave his name as Michel, but only with reluctance, so who's to say if even that little is true.'

'What was it he wanted?'

'I don't rightly know,' Minou said. 'He claimed pressing business with my father, but his manner was peculiar.'

Madame Noubel waved her hand. 'Put it from your mind, Minou. There have been troubles enough for one day. If it's important, this mysterious Michel will return. If not . . .'

'I suppose so.'

'Now, did you mark if the soldiers had gone from outside my premises? We have talked the afternoon away, and I would be home.'

Still thinking about the visitor, Minou peered out again. 'They have gone, yes, though Charles is still there keeping watch.'

'Ah, he is a good, if simple, soul,' Madame Noubel said. 'Again, thank you. And, don't forget. Tell Bernard I will call after Mass tomorrow.'

Minou listened to her footsteps echoing along rue du Marché, then bent to straighten the mat. It was unlikely there would be any more customers at this hour, so she decided to close the shop. It had been a long day. A mist had come in from the mountains and a chill white light had taken hold of the Bastide. The rumble of cartwheels and the clatter of horses' hooves, all sounds muffled and distorted. Minou put the day's

takings into the strongbox beneath the floorboards, then snuffed out the candles and set off for home.

The letter with the red lion seal remained, forgotten for now, within the lining of her cloak.

Scratch, scratch, scratch go my words, the nib of the quill scoring the paper.

My carriage was waiting at the prison gates. A physician was ready to cauterise and dress his wounds. His severed fingers and poisoned skin. Ointments to soothe – and to confound.

For a day, the delirium held him like a summer sweat. His words were wild and they spoke of guilt, and of shame. Fear and pain loosen a man's tongue, but so too can kindness. A kiss, the brush of a hand upon a broken cheek, the promise of care.

How easily men tumble.

With my own hand, I gave him wine and I gave him laudanum. I let him glimpse me in my nightshift and with my hair uncovered. I gave him my own kerchief with my initials embroidered on it, to keep the thought of me close. It moved him not. There are those within the boy King's entourage who prefer the company of their own sex. Perhaps he is one of them.

No matter. There is beauty in the spilling of blood. A purification.

Gentleness succeeded where desire could not. Finally, on the third day of my ministrations, he gave me the name of the family I sought.

By God's grace, I let him live. It was not a matter of mercy. The voices whispered how, in Toulouse, it would be

harder to disguise a death and a body. In the mountains, eyes are blind.

Joubert. That is all I know, but it is a start.

Blood calls out to blood. As our Lord taught us, it is through suffering that we are redeemed.

CHAPTER THIRTEEN

⚜

La Cité

Minou walked up the hill towards the Porte Narbonnaise. The lamps of La Cité were smudged in the mist behind the walls. An owl, already out to hunt, called from the trees. The brush of a fox's tail flicked and then vanished in the undergrowth. Minou emptied her mind of the events of the day and thought only of the evening to come. She stepped up onto the drawbridge, nodded a greeting to the watch, then walked under the narrow stone arch and through the gates.

She was almost home.

A burst of blue and Minou found herself flying forward off her feet, her breath quite knocked out of her. She threw out her arms to break her fall, then felt the pressure of a hand at her elbow, helping her to her feet.

'Mademoiselle, forgive me. I did not . . .'

The man's voice broke off so abruptly that Minou raised her head in surprise. Russet-coloured hair and beard, green eyes the colour of spring. And he was staring at her too, with a look of such unwarranted surprise upon his face that she felt herself blush.

'*Jij weer*,' he muttered. 'You . . . Forgive me, are you hurt? Did I hurt you?'

'No.'

'But it is you,' he said, looking at her as if he had seen a ghost.

Minou steadied herself and took a step back.

'I think you mistake me for someone else, Monsieur.'

To her astonishment, he reached out and traced his fingers down her cheek.

Minou knew she should reprimand him for his boldness, but yet she could not speak. For a moment longer, he held his glove there, soft against her skin. Then, suddenly, as if coming to his senses, he stepped back.

'I am sorry to have alarmed you, my Lady of the Mists,' he said. 'Your servant.'

He bowed, and was gone.

One beat of her heart, two. In a daze, Minou watched him stride away towards the Château Comtal until his blue cloak vanished into the white gauze of the mist. Three beats of her heart, four and five. She raised her own hand to where his had rested and caught the lingering scent of the leather. Why had he looked at her as if to commit each of her features to memory? Why did he think she was known to him? Six beats, seven beats, eight. The bells were ringing for Vespers and she was late, but Minou could not go home. Not yet. Not with her thoughts unravelled and her senses so wild.

On through the silver mist, step by step, she went. Buildings came in and out of view. The cathedral suddenly loomed up before her, like a ghost ship breaking the surface of the sea. A huddle of clerics, black like crows with red-tipped noses in the cold, hurried across Place Saint-Nazaire and into the cathedral to pray. Minou walked on until the turrets and fortifications of the Château Comtal became visible, and wondered how the Seneschal and his household passed these eventide hours during Lent. Were they merry, the chambers filled with laughter and good cheer, or were the corridors silent with pious meditation?

Minou stopped. All around, the watch was calling the seventh hour and securing the gates of La Cité for the night. From every window and tavern, candlelight and firelight crept between the slats of shutters. Everything was the same as it always was.

Except for the scent of sandalwood and almonds. Except for the touch of a stranger's hand upon her cheek.

Piet stood outside the barbican of the Château Comtal. His heart was beating as fast as any love-sick boy.

That same girl from rue du Marché, with her extraordinary, mismatched eyes, the one blue and the other the colour of autumn leaves. Such spirit. Plain, honest clothes hanging well on her tall frame. What was it he had said? He had stammered and babbled like a simpleton. The sight of her had stolen every word from his lips.

Piet gathered his wits and headed to the tavern he had chosen earlier. He pushed open the door and was hit by a wall of noise. He ordered a gage of ale and sat at a table in a dark corner near the fire with a clear view of the door. His hand kept going to his leather satchel, now empty of its precious cargo. The bag of gold coins hung heavy at his waist.

He sipped his ale and took the measure of his drinking companions. All honest-enough-looking men, with the dark skin and black hair of the Midi. A boy came in to fetch home his father, clearly in his cups. A comely landlady stood at the casks, her plump lips set in a permanent smile. The air was blurred with easy conversation and chatter.

Piet held up his tankard. 'Madame, *s'il vous plaît*. Another!'

After a second draught, he felt the chill melt from his bones. Did the girl live within La Cité or the Bastide? La Cité surely, for her to be coming in through the gates at such an hour? Why had he not asked her name?

Piet had known many women, some with affection, others as a passing pleasure, though always – or so he hoped – with a measure of satisfaction for both him and the lady. But no one had ever touched his heart before.

He shook his head at how quickly he had been undone. He was a man who had locked away his most private feelings when a boy. Kneeling by the bed of his beloved mother as she was dying, too poor to afford the medicine that might have saved her, Piet had vowed never to allow himself to suffer such loss again.

And yet.

Now here he was, struck by the kind of *coup de foudre* about which the troubadours sang in the old songs. That moment of the world tilting on its axis. Piet raised his cup in a toast.

'To you, fair Mademoiselle, whoever you are. I salute you.'

CHAPTER FOURTEEN

The mist had soaked through her clothes and, though she did not feel cold, Minou could not delay returning home any longer. She tiptoed in, hoping to be unobserved, but got no further than hanging her cloak on its hook before her little sister came hurtling along the passageway. Memories of this strangest of days were put to flight.

'Steady, *petite*,' Minou laughed, scooping Alis up in her arms, 'else you will have me over.'

'You're so late!'

Aimeric put his head around the kitchen door. 'Oh, it's you.'

Minou tousled his hair and laughed as he crossly ducked out of reach. 'And whoever else might it be, pray?'

Their father was dozing beside the fire. Minou's heart turned over to see how pallid his skin had become. It stretched thin and taut across the bones of his cheek.

'Did Papa go out today?' she said softly. 'The sun was warm at midday.'

'Don't know.' Aimeric shrugged. 'I am so hungry, I could eat an ox.'

'Alis? Did Papa go out?'

'No, he remained at home.'

'And you, *petite*?'

The little girl beamed. 'I did. And I hardly coughed all day.'

'That is good news.'

Minou placed a light kiss upon the top of her father's sleeping head, then turned her attention to preparing supper. Rixende had left a pot bubbling over the fire, beans and turnips flavoured with thyme, bread and a goat's cheese on the table.

'Here,' she said, handing Alis the knives and spoons and giving the plates to Aimeric.

'How did you pass the day?'

'Aimeric got into trouble for talking to Marie. We were at the well, and he was saucy. Her mother came to complain.'

Alis darted behind Minou's back, out of the reach of her brother's hand, then stuck her tongue out. Minou sighed. Despite their six-year gap in age, they were too alike and argued constantly. Tonight, she had no patience for it. She emptied the sweet biscuits into a bowl and pushed Aimeric's greedy hand away.

'After supper. Don't spoil your appetite.'

'I won't! I told you, I could eat an ox!'

Minou said the Grace their mother always spoke and their eager 'Amen's woke their father, who joined them at the table. She intended to tell him about Michel and Madame Noubel's misfortune, but there would be time enough later when Alis and Aimeric were in bed.

'We were busy today,' she said. 'Charles was babbling about the clouds again. I played pat-a-cake with the younger Sanchez children until my hands were sore. I even sold that volume of verse by Anna Bijns.'

She was delighted to see the news brought a smile to his careworn face.

'Well, I confess I am surprised. I had never thought to find a home for it, but I could not resist the purchase. Such fine paper, such an elegant binding for so slim a volume. I acquired it from a Dutch printer, a man from a noble family whose passion is for books rather than ships. His workshop is on the Kalverstraat.'

'Did you go back to Amsterdam on your travels in January?' she asked. It was only a casual enquiry, intended to keep the conversation light, but a shadow fell instantly over her father's face.

'No, I did not.'

Minou wondered what she might say to recapture his light-hearted mood, but he had withdrawn back into himself. Cursing her unintended mistake, she was even grateful when Aimeric challenged Alis to a game of draughts, though it was bound to end in an argument.

To the percussive accompaniment of the counters on the wooden board, she cleared the table then settled herself by the fire and let her thoughts roam unchecked. From time to time, she glanced at her father. What was burdening him so? What had stolen the joy of his life from him? Then she thought of the touch of the stranger's hand upon her cheek, and she could not help but smile.

'What are you thinking about?' Alis asked, snuggling up to her with sleepy eyes.

'Nothing.'

'It must be a nice nothing, for you look happy.'

Minou laughed. 'We have much to be thankful for. But now, it is long past your bedtime. You too, Aimeric.'

'Why should I go to my bed at the same time as Alis? I am thirteen. She is a baby, I should—'

'*Au lit*,' Minou said sternly. 'Bid Papa goodnight, both of you.'

'*Bonne nuit*, Papa,' Alis said obediently, coughing a little. Bernard rested his hand on her head, then patted his son on the shoulder.

'Soon things will be better,' he said to Minou. 'Come the spring, I will be myself again.'

On an impulse, she put an affectionate hand on his shoulder, but he flinched and pulled away.

'When Aimeric and Alis are settled,' she said, 'I would speak with you, Father. On a serious matter.'

He sighed. 'I am weary, Minou. Can't it wait until morning?'

'If you will forgive me, I would rather tonight. It is important.'

He sighed again. 'Very well, I shall be here. Warming my bones by the fire. Indeed, there are matters I need to discuss with you, too. Your aunt requires an answer.'

'Crompton?' Michel said. 'I had not thought to see you here.' Then, peering through the wreath of fog, he realised he was in error. 'Forgive me, Monsieur. In the mist, I mistook you for another.'

'No matter,' the man said, passing by. 'Goodnight to you.'

Michel trudged slowly up towards the Porte d'Aude, every sinew of his body aching. He knew he had little time left. It was a struggle to breathe, as the hard fist of disease pushed the air from his lungs. How many weeks? When the hour came, would he find peace? Would he be forgiven for his sins and welcomed into God's presence?

In truth, he did not know.

He was late coming to La Cité, though he supposed he was more likely to find Joubert at home at this hour – if he could find the house in the dark. His exertions of the afternoon had left him exhausted and he had slept longer than he had intended.

Had he done the right thing by not speaking directly to Minou? He thought he had, for he did not know how much or how little her father had told her of her situation, and he did not wish to alarm her.

The towers loomed above him and the Château Comtal stood, half hidden and insubstantial in the mist. Michel paused, waiting for the shaking in his legs to pass. He had not gone more than a few paces further, when he felt the hair on the back of his neck stand on end. He heard the sound of breathing in the night air, somewhere behind him, and he looked over his shoulder.

Two labourers in leather jerkins and coarse, long breeches, stepped out from the sharp corner at rue Saint-Nazaire. Their faces were covered by kerchiefs tied across their mouths and their plain woollen caps pulled low on their brow. One was holding a club.

Michel heard the men's footsteps following as he tried to hurry, stumbling on the slippery cobblestones. They were getting closer. Ahead, he could see lights. If he could but make it further into La Cité.

The first blow caught him on his left temple, sending him sprawling to the ground. His nose struck a stone step and he felt the bone shatter. A second strike fell, this time to the back of his head. Michel threw up his hands to protect himself, but he was powerless against the onslaught of kicks to his ribs, his back, his hands. Then, an explosion of pain as the heel of a boot crushed down on his ankle and Michel howled. He was aware of being hauled upright, then being dragged between his assailants back down the cobbled alleyway towards the Porte d'Aude.

'Halt! Who goes there?'

The sound of the watchman gave Michel hope. He tried to call out, but he gagged on the blood filling his mouth.

'Forgive the disturbance,' Michel heard an educated voice

call back. The gentleman who had passed him earlier? Was he with them? 'Our friend is in his cups. We are taking him home to bed.'

'The Lord have pity on his wife,' the sergeant-at-arms said, and both men laughed.

Michel felt the tips of his toes dragging uselessly over the stones. Then, the sensation of passing away from the lit streets of La Cité into the velvet black of the countryside beyond the walls.

'Let me know when 'tis done,' the same voice said. 'No witnesses.'

'What in the name of God are you doing?'

'It's none of your business,' the man slurred, swaying on his feet. His breath was sour with ale and his eyes rimmed with smoke and argument. The doxy took her chance to pull her torn bodice over her breast, and slink back out of his reach.

'You've had enough, sirrah,' Piet said, standing between them. 'Go back inside. She's not for you.'

The tavern door tipped open, then shut again, spilling a ladder of passing light onto the woman. Long enough to reveal the mark of a hand on her cheek and scratches on her pale shoulders.

'Leave, Monsieur. This is over.'

'I said, what business is this of yours?' The drunk tilted forwards and back, raising his fists like a bare-knuckle fighter ready to brawl. 'Do you want to fight me for her? For that, for that doxy, that *putane*? Not even worth the price of a loaf of mouldy bread, not even . . .'

Piet glanced at the man's waist and saw no weapon. 'Go back inside. I will not warn you again.'

'Warn me,' he spluttered, 'warn me? Who do you think you

are, to tell me what to do? The "lady" and I agreed terms, then she tried to cheat me. I thought to teach her a lesson. A pox-ridden whore, she tried to cheat me.'

The man sprang forward, clamping one hand around the girl's neck and hitting her on the side of the head with the other. She flailed at him, but he was emboldened by drink and squeezed tighter.

Piet grabbed him by his jerkin and jerked him backwards, landing a punch in his soft belly, then one on his jaw. The man spun around, then collapsed on his knees on the cobblestones. Moments later, he began to snore.

'Go home, Mademoiselle,' Piet said again. 'I make no judgement on the arrangement between you, only that men when intoxicated do not always keep to their side of the bargain.'

The whore stepped back out of the shadows. 'You are a gentleman, Monsieur. My lodgings are in Place Saint-Nazaire. Business is excellent in that quartier, if you ever need a little company. No charge.'

'Go home, Mademoiselle,' Piet repeated, and turned away. The sound of her laughter followed him all the way to Vidal's lodgings in rue de Notre Dame. He crept into the dark garden, where he found a battered pail, full of water. He broke the thin layer of ice, washed the fight from his hands and then, drying them on the lining of his cloak, approached the door.

By the time Minou came back to the kitchen, having settled Alis and stood over Aimeric while he rattled through his prayers, her father's chair was empty.

She was vexed, but also relieved. She did want to tell him about the strange visitor to the bookshop, Michel. On the other hand, she had no appetite for discussing what was to become of Aimeric and whether or not they should accept the invitation for him to go to Toulouse to lodge with their aunt and uncle.

Minou took an iron and poked at the fire, causing the last of the wood to collapse in a cloud of ash. She damped down the embers and put the guard in place. Idly she picked up her mother's map from the mantelpiece and looked at the landmarks of her life sketched out in the chalk: the outline in red for La Cité, in green for the Bastide, blue for the river in between, their bookshop and their house coloured in a deep yellow.

She took a final glance around the kitchen: at the table laid ready for the morning, at Rixende's apron hanging on the back of the door, at the books on the dresser. All the things that gave their little home its character. Everything was the same as it had been at the start of this day, only she was different. Minou knew it, in her heart and her bones.

My husband is as helpless now as an infant new born. I can do with him as I wish. Run my finger down his cheek or twist my bodkin on his skin until the blood comes. Score my initials with a knife on his chest as he once marked me with bruises.

His arms are dead weights. I lift his hands, then let them drop. A marionette with no strings, he cannot prevent me. His body lies useless beneath the blanket, stewing in his own vile juices. He, who ruled by fear and his fist, is now dependent on others for everything.

It is in such things that I see the grace of God. This is God's judgement. His will. This is retribution. A fierce and terrible reckoning.

He cannot speak now, I have made sure of that too. The same potion has sapped, little by little, the strength of every muscle: fingers, toes, manhood, and now his tongue. It has thinned his blood. Sweet wines from the Orient and spices from the Indies, masking the bitter taste. Yet his eyes are sharp and clear. He has not lost his wits and, in this too, I see the grace of God. It is a delicious purgatory. He is trapped, knowing and silenced, within a husk of a body that no longer obeys him. He knows I am the architect of his illness. He knows that it is a time of reckoning. That after the years of my ill-use, the tables now are turned.

My husband wants me to show mercy, but I will not.

He prays that I might show him pity, though he would despise me if I did. When I go down to the chapel to pray for the easing of his suffering, I leave the doors ajar so that he can hear how God mocks him. How I mock him.

And I shall let him live a while longer to learn what it means to dread the sound of footsteps in the night. Just as I lay, night after night, praying he would not come to my bed. Praying to the Virgin to protect me.

If the household is surprised by the solicitude I am showing, they know better than to voice it out loud. For when he dies, I shall be mistress here and they will have me to answer to. Those who have heard the rumours of an heir to Puivert know better than to speak it in my hearing.

God forgive me, I shall have my sport a while longer. Vengeance is mine, sayeth the Lord. What are we but God's creatures to command?

CHAPTER FIFTEEN

⚜

La Cité

Piet and Vidal sat on opposite sides of the hearth. It was an elegant and well-appointed room, with generous sills and mullioned windows giving over the street. A large stone chimney and fireplace, with gleaming fire irons, a set of hand bellows and a basket of chopped logs set beside it, occupied one wall. Elsewhere, the chamber was graced with signs of devotion: a wooden crucifix above the high door, an exquisite wall hanging showing St Michel leading the archangels into battle and, between the windows, a painting in oils of St Anne. The furniture was simple, but well crafted: two polished wooden chairs, with curved arms and embroidered cushions, a table between. A box library, offering deep shelves on all four sides, was filled with religious texts in Latin, French and German. Did they belong to Vidal, or to the house itself? To Piet's eyes, everything seemed pristine, as if barely used.

The candles had burnt low and the air was hot with their words. It reminded Piet of their student days in Toulouse and of how much he missed them. Then, what united them was greater than what divided them. Faith and the years had driven them further apart, yet Piet remained hopeful. And if two men of such opposed views were prepared to try to find a spirit of agreement, then surely others might do the same?

'What I am saying is that the Edict offers us—'

'Us? You admit to being a Huguenot?'

'Admit?' Piet chided mildly. 'I did not think a private conversation between old friends constituted any kind of confession.'

Vidal waved his hand. 'You claim the Edict is not enough, and I say it is too much. Certainly, we agree it pleases neither side. Since January, there has been more religious strife, not less.'

'That fault is not of Huguenot making.'

'Monasteries sacked in the south, priests attacked at prayer, these outrages committed by Huguenots are well documented. None of this is a question of faith, it is barbarism. You must surely accept the Prince of Condé and his confederate, Coligny, have their sights on more earthly aspirations? They wish to put a Huguenot king on the throne.'

'I don't believe that. In any case, I was not talking of our leaders, but the common man. We do not want trouble.'

'No? Explain that to those monks in Rouen who arrived to worship and found the altar of their chapel defiled in the most pernicious manner. You deny any atrocities committed by Huguenots –'

'As do you those committed by Catholics. You overlook the drunken priests, the fornication, the spectacle of children being handed the keys to a bishopric as a familial inheritance. Jean de Lorraine was assistant bishop of Metz when he was but three years old and responsible for no less than thirteen sees! And you wonder why men turn away from your Church?'

Vidal laughed. 'Come, Piet, is that the best you can do? Whenever Reformers wish to attack the degeneracy of the Church, you offer that same worn example. If he is your only example of abuse, some thirty years past, then your case falls.'

'He is but one of many whose abuse of their position is driving the devout into our arms.'

Vidal made a steeple of his fingers. 'There are reports that the Reformers – the men with whom you claim kinship – are arming themselves.'

'We have the right to defend ourselves,' Piet replied. 'You cannot expect us to go like sheep to slaughter.'

'Defence, I accept. Funding private armies, smuggling weapons, all paid for by Dutch and English sympathisers, that is another matter. It is treason.'

'It is common rumour that Guise and his Catholic allies are funded by Hapsburg Spain.'

Vidal waved his hand. 'That is a ridiculous allegation.'

For a moment, they both fell silent.

'Tell me, Vidal,' said Piet eventually, 'do you never ask yourself why your Church is so threatened by the thought of us worshipping differently from you?'

'It is a matter of security. A unified state is a strong state. Those who set themselves apart weaken the whole.'

'Maybe,' Piet replied, choosing his words with care. 'Yet there are some who claim the true reason the Catholic Church tries to prevent us from being heard is because you fear we are right. You are terrified that when people hear the truth of the Gospels, God's true message as it was intended – not how it has been interpreted by generations of priests – they will join us.'

'Faith by faith alone? No need of priests, the right to worship in everyday language, no more convents, no more charity, no more good works?'

'No more buying a way to heaven regardless of the veniality of their sins.'

Vidal shook his head. 'The people want their miracles, Piet. They want their relics and the sense of the magnificence of a God beyond comprehension.'

'A blackened fingernail, a shard of bone from the body of a martyr?'

'Or a piece of cloth?'

Piet flushed at the reference. 'Is God truly to be found in such tawdry objects?'

Vidal sighed. 'If you take away the mystery of God and reduce everything to the commonplace, you take away much of the beauty in their lives.'

'How is it beauty to keep people downtrodden and unquestioning, terrified into submission? How is it beauty to stretch a man's body to save his soul? I return to my previous point. There is no reason Catholics and Protestants cannot live together, respecting one another's differences. We are all French. There is a kinship. It is dishonest to paint all Reformers as traitors.'

Vidal pressed his hands together. 'You know full well there are many of your faith who challenge the authority of the King and question his divine right to rule. As I say, my friend, that is treason.'

'I own there are some who question his *mother*'s right to rule, but that is not the same thing. Everyone knows Charles cares more for his lapdogs and for hunting than he does for affairs of state. He's a child. Every decision that is made in the name of the King is, in truth, made by Catherine, the Queen Regent.'

'You have no more idea of the realities of life at Court than do I.'

'It is common knowledge,' Piet pressed. 'The Huguenots are being offered nothing more than the chance to be second-class citizens. You know this to be true. And yet even these scraps of tolerance are challenged. Guise and his supporters do not believe we should even be citizens at all. To them, any concession is too much, even the granting of the right to worship in our own language.'

'You say that as if the right to worship in French is a small matter.'

'It was the old King himself – a true and devout Catholic – who set Marot the task of translating the Psalms from Latin into French. How can something that made a man a pious Catholic thirty years ago, now see him branded a heretic?'

'Things are different now. The world is a harsher place.'

'I tell you, if we do not take care,' Piet said fiercely, 'we will find ourselves emulating the pyres of England or the vile excesses of the Inquisition in Spain.'

'Such inhumanity will never happen in France.'

'It could, Vidal. It could. The world we know is unravelling quicker than we think. There are those in Toulouse who preach it is a pious Catholic's duty to kill Huguenots. A duty to kill in the name of God. A duty to wage a Holy War. They use the language of the Crusades even though they speak of fellow Christians.'

'Who are, to their eyes, heretics,' Vidal replied quietly. 'It seems you believe that no one who protests against any Reformist teachings – the eating of meat during Lent, say, or the ridiculing of our most sacred relics – can do so for reasons of true and devout faith.'

'That's not true,' Piet said. 'I accept there are some who are genuinely offended by our practices, but the Duke of Guise and his brother are a barrier to a lasting peace. They encourage their followers not to accept the Edict. They will lead France into civil war.'

Vidal frowned. 'You speak with the same words used in this very citadel to justify the Cathar heresy.'

'What if I do? The Inquisition, founded in the first instance to extirpate the Cathars, still has a seat here in La Cité, does it not?'

'Three hundred and fifty years have passed since St Dominic preached in the cathedral and—'

'Persuaded no one,' Piet interrupted. 'And because of his failure, so the burning chambers were born. Faith enforced in the agony of the flames.'

'Men are not so backward as in those times. France is not England, France is not Spain. Our Holy Mother Church these days seeks to lead by example.'

Piet shook his head. 'By breaking a man's spirit, his bones, to save his soul? I do not care for your theology, Vidal, if it stinks of blood and sulphur and despair.'

CHAPTER SIXTEEN

⚜

'Villain! Get your hands off me!'

There was an explosion of shouting, the sound of wood shattering, in the street outside. Piet stood up and walked directly to the window.

'Take no notice. It will be nothing,' Vidal said. 'It is a hazard of lodging opposite La Cité's most quarrelsome tavern.'

Piet looked out into the darkness. There was a knot of men staggering arm over shoulder towards the well. One fell to his knees and puked the contents of his stomach onto the cobbles. Piet recognised the drunkard who'd assaulted the doxy earlier, and he stepped away from the window.

'Revolting.'

'You are fastidious for a soldier,' Vidal said wryly. 'Are your comrades all as delicately minded as you?'

'It is a matter of decorum,' Piet countered, allowing Vidal's misapprehension about his occupation to stand. 'A man who cannot hold his drink cannot hold his tongue.'

Vidal took a sip of his wine. 'There is truth in that.'

Piet picked up his own cup and sat down. 'You cannot be unaware of the methods used by the inquisitors.'

Vidal's eyes flickered with zeal. 'If a man is found guilty of blasphemy or heresy he is handed over to the Civil Court for sentencing. You know that well enough.'

Piet laughed. 'The idea that your Church keeps her hands clean by asking the Civil Courts to dispense justice, after the horror of torture, deceives no one.'

'We concern ourselves solely with matters of doctrine. The Inquisition has no role in civil society.'

Piet paused. 'Did you say "we"?'

'We, they, what does it matter?' Vidal said, waving the word away as if swatting a fly. 'We are all servants of the same Holy and Apostolic Church.'

Ill at ease, Piet stood up again. 'You talk as if mankind has learnt the lessons of the past. That we have improved ourselves. I fear the opposite. That human beings have learnt rather to repeat the mistakes of the past, and more vilely. I fear we are sleep-walking towards a new conflict. It is why so many Frenchmen, who share my beliefs, have fled to Amsterdam.'

Vidal's mouth tightened in displeasure. 'Why do you not follow, if life in France is so disagreeable to you?'

'You are asking me that, Vidal?' Piet said, disappointed. 'When you know the debt I owe to the Midi? And why should I be exiled from my own country, simply because I think differently from those who currently hold power at Court? I am French.'

'Part French.'

'With the exception of a brief sojourn in England, and my earliest years in Amsterdam, I have lived my whole life in France, as well you know. I am French through and through.'

Piet was not speaking the entire truth. His love for his Dutch mother, who had suffered so greatly in her short life, was inextricably linked with his love for his childhood in Amsterdam. Living in boarding houses and charity missions between the waters of Rokin and the great Singel canal. Going down to the port and watching the *fluyts* getting ready to sail for the Indies. The seductive whispering in the rigging as they waited for the wind to change.

'My father's blood runs in my veins,' Piet said. 'Why should I be deprived of my birthright?'

Vidal raised his eyebrows. 'I appear to have touched a nerve.'

Piet looked at his old friend, the distinctive white flash in his hair. The line of Vidal's jaw seemed stronger, his eyes harder. They had both reached their twenty-seventh year, yet Vidal looked older.

'You are still guided by your heart not your head,' Vidal said. 'You have not changed.'

Piet took a deep breath, trying to calm himself. He blamed the Church for turning its back on his dear mother in her hour of need, but Vidal was not responsible for that. He was fighting an older battle.

He put up his hands in surrender. 'I did not seek you out to quarrel with you, Vidal.'

'Though my life is given in service to God, Piet, do you think I don't understand the way of the world? We are all frail creatures, priests and men alike. Only the Lord can judge the sins of man. Vengeance is His. Justice is His to administer.'

'I was not suggesting otherwise,' Piet said quietly. 'I know well you are a man of honour. I accept this is not a matter of abstract doctrine for you.'

'Even now, you seek to flatter me while you continue to attack the very institution to which I dedicate my life.'

A sudden knock on the door halted the conversation.

'Come,' said Vidal.

A manservant came into the chamber carrying a brass tray with a flagon of wine and two goblets, a platter of cheeses, bread, figs and sweet sugar biscuits. To Piet it struck an odd note, as if the action was somehow for show. He felt the servant's eyes on him. Dark and heavily built, the man had a ragged scar running the length of his right cheek. He looked familiar but the recollection wouldn't come.

'Set the tray down there, Bonal,' Vidal said, gesturing to the sideboard. 'We will wait upon ourselves presently.'

'Very good, Monsignor,' Bonal said, then passed his master a note. Piet watched Vidal read it, before screwing up the paper and throwing it in the fire.

'There is no answer,' Vidal said.

'Monsignor? You are a monsignor now?' Piet said lightly, once the servant had withdrawn. 'I should congratulate you.'

'A courtesy, nothing more.'

'Is he your own man from Toulouse?'

'The Chapter has many servants they deploy within the cathedral precincts and beyond. I know few of them by name.' He waved his hand. 'Shall we?'

Piet served himself to a little cheese and bread to give himself time to gather his thoughts. He knew the time had come, but he was reluctant, even now, to broach the subject that had brought him here.

Piet was suddenly weary to his bones. He shut his eyes. He registered the sound of the stopper and wine splashing into pewter goblets, then Vidal's footsteps crossing the wooden floorboards.

'Here,' he said.

'I have drunk more than my fill already.'

'This is different,' Vidal said, pressing the cup on him. 'A local wine, Guignolet. It will soothe you.'

The thick, red liquid was both sour and sweet. Piet wiped his mouth with the back of his hand. Occasional sounds from the street outside permeated the seclusion of the chamber.

'So here we sit,' Vidal said eventually, 'as we were wont to do.'

'Debating, talking late into the night.' Piet nodded. 'They were good days.'

'They were.' Vidal put his goblet down on the table. 'But we are no longer students. We no longer have the luxury of such unguarded talk.'

Piet felt his heart speed up. 'Perhaps not.'

'This morning, you said you wished to tell me of what happened that night in Toulouse when the Shroud was taken. That happier time when we were boon companions, the closest of friends.'

'Boon companions, yes.'

'It will go ill should we be discovered in conversation together. Neither my bishop – nor, I wager, your comrades-in-arms – would be minded to think this meeting of ours innocent.'

'*Dat is waar.* True.'

'If you have something you wish to say, you must speak now. The hour grows late.'

'Yes.' Piet steeled himself. 'You will forgive me my reluctance. In the cathedral this morning, you asked me if I stole the Shroud of Antioch. I give you my word, I did not.'

'But you knew the theft was to be attempted?'

'I knew nothing until after the event.'

'I see.' Vidal leant back in his chair. 'You know I was accused of being involved? That the crime of your Huguenot comrades put me under suspicion?'

'I had no idea,' Piet said. 'I am sorry for it.'

'I was put under investigation. Questioned about my faith, about my loyalty to the Church. Forced to defend myself, my friendship with you.'

'I am sorry, Vidal. Truly.'

Vidal stared at him. 'Who was responsible?'

Piet raised his hands and let them drop. 'I cannot tell you.'

'Then why are you here?' Vidal said fiercely. 'What fealty or loyalty do you owe to the thief that you continue to protect his name? Is it greater than that you owe to our friendship?'

'No!' The denial burst out of him. 'But I gave my word.'

Anger flickered in Vidal's eyes. 'In which case, I again ask why you sought me out if you can tell me – will tell me – nothing?'

Piet ran his hands through his hair. 'Because . . . because I wanted you to know that, for all my sins, I am not a thief.'

'And you think this gives me comfort?'

Piet refused to hear the bitterness in Vidal's voice. 'No one has had sight of it since that night, at least only one other. I have taken good care to make sure the Shroud remains safe.'

Piet was suddenly overwhelmed by memories of the day, each hard on the heel of the one before until he felt dizzy: the room above the tavern in rue de l'Aigle d'Or, the look of greed on Devereux's face and the awe in Crompton's eyes as fervent as any Catholic zealot; then the tailor in Toulouse who had laboured for long hours in candlelight to create a flawless copy of the Shroud, all the time spent choosing a delicate material that sang of antiquity, the faithful mirroring of the stitching, the processes required to infuse the forgery with a texture of age. His thoughts slipped further still, to the first moment when he had held the true Shroud in his hands and imagined the fabric anointed with the scents of Jerusalem and Golgotha. Then, as now, Piet felt a shiver, the clash between his reason and the ineffable and mysterious.

He took another sip of Guignolet and felt the strong heat seep into his blood. He hesitated. He could not break his vow of secrecy, but he could try to give his old friend – once his dearest friend – some fragment of hope.

'All I can promise, Vidal, is that the true Shroud is safe. I could not let something so beautiful be destroyed.'

'Even though, by your own words, you despise the "cult of relics",' Vidal said, throwing his own words back at him. 'This is cold comfort.'

'The Shroud of Antioch, even though it is but a part of the whole, is magnificent in its own right,' Piet replied. 'That, in and of itself, is sufficient to want to preserve it.'

Vidal suddenly stood up, taking Piet by surprise.

'But since I do not have it, what use is that?'

The floorboards cracked, like wood on a fire, and his red robes swirled around him like flames. The white stripe in his black hair seemed to glow silver, like a flash of lightning in a dark sky.

'Where is the Shroud now?' he snapped. 'Still in Toulouse?'

Piet opened his mouth but found he could not speak. The chamber was suddenly too hot, airless. He loosened his ruff and the hooks of his doublet, wiped his forehead with his kerchief. He took another gulp of Guignolet to slake the sudden dryness in his throat.

'Is it in your possession?' Vidal said. His voice seemed to come from a long way away. 'Do you have it?'

'No.'

Piet's eyes could not focus. His tongue felt heavy in his mouth. No more words would come. His jaw was locked shut. He closed his eyes, willing the spinning to stop.

'I am . . . the wine –'

He looked down into the deep red liquid, then up to his friend's face. Vidal looked himself, yet utterly transformed. Was he experiencing the same light-headedness, the same nausea?

Piet watched the goblet slip from his paralysed fingers,

clattering down onto the rug, sending the remains of the thick red wine spilling on the wooden floor. He tried to stand, but his legs would not obey. His vision blurred and he saw two figures, then three, crossing the room and pulling open the door. Heard them calling for help and the sound of running feet upon the stairs.

Then, nothing.

The Protestant contagion spreads unchecked. They swarm like rats through our towns and villages and cities, breathing Catholic air, infecting God's own lands. The Huguenot pastors, traitors to France, encourage civil disobedience and should be hanged for it: in Pamiers, Bélesta, Chalabre, the cancer is spreading throughout the Haute Vallée. There have been uprisings in Tarascon and Ornolac. Even here, in the village.

I have no doubt this pestilence will be defeated. And I confess such disorder serves my purpose. For what is one death, when the gibbets are full? What is a murder, when the streets are running with the blood of many? Our petty, insignificant hates and passions do not disappear when war comes. Feuds and petitions and forfeits continue unchecked beneath the surface. The vast and the insignificantly small exist side by side.

I would leave the castle, but I cannot yet take that risk. Though my husband's health is broken, too far ruined beyond the skill of any apothecary to recover, yet without my presence to keep his tongue silent in his mouth, he might yet speak. If he denounces me, then I am lost. At night, as his body becomes accustomed to the poison, he cries out.

For now, I must stay and prepare my widow's weeds. Once he is dead, then I will go to my lover. We complete one another, he and I, though he pretends not to know it. What is noble and pious in our souls is a perfect match.

There was a time when the shadows of the castle gave us the solitude we needed, but there can be other places. When I bind his wrists with cords of red velvet, it is a marriage of equals. Pleasure and pain. As our Lord taught us, we must each suffer to be reborn.

I will tell him of the creature that grows inside me. A gift from God. It will please him.

CHAPTER SEVENTEEN

⚜

La Cité
Sunday, 1st March

Minou rose still heavy with sleep and opened the shutters wide. She could not remember when she had slept for so long, so dreamlessly.

A pale mist hung over La Cité, obscuring the face of the sun, but the sky behind it was bright and the air fresh. She felt brim full of hope. It was the first day of March. Her time was her own. After Mass, she would go with Alis down to the stables in Trivalle and take their father's faithful dun mare, Canigou, out for an airing.

Minou was surprised to find Alis and Aimeric alone in the kitchen, drinking warmed milk from wide earthenware bowls. A loaf of fresh bread, a pat of newly churned butter on a wooden platter and a glistening square of honeycomb stood on the table.

'How now, my little chicks, you are out of bed early.'

Alis shook her head. ''Tis you who is late. It is past eleven. You have missed Mass.'

Minou looked around the kitchen, suddenly realising what else had snagged her attention. The chair by the fire was empty.

'Where is Papa?' she said.

Aimeric shrugged. 'He went out.'

'That's wonderful news. Where did he go?'

He shrugged again and pulled on his boots. 'I don't know.'

'He went with an old lady,' Alis said, upending her bowl to drain the last of her milk. 'It was she who brought us the honey.'

'Did the lady give her name?'

'I can't remember.' The little girl frowned. 'She had a lump on the side of her head, the size of an egg. She said you were expecting her to call.'

'Ah, Madame Noubel. Yes, I was expecting a visit, though not so early.'

'I told you, silly. It is nearly noon. You have slept the morning away and that is why Madame Cordier –' Alis's expression lightened. 'Cordier, that was the name she gave, not Noubel.'

Minou looked from one to the other. 'Which is it, Noubel or Cordier?'

Aimeric stopped in the doorway. 'Cordier was the name Father used. "Madame Cordier," he said, and he sounded surprised. Then she said, "I go by the name of Noubel now, Bernard, remember," which didn't surprise me, for she was exceedingly old. She has probably had several husbands.'

'Aimeric!' Minou chided, as he slipped into the passageway. 'Aimeric! Come back. I need you –'

His answer was the sound of the front door slamming shut.

'The lady seemed very kind,' Alis said. 'Did I do wrong to invite her to come in?'

'Not at all, *petite*. She is a kind person and a good neighbour of ours in the Bastide.' Minou smiled. 'But are you certain Papa did not say where they were going?'

'I am. Only that we were not to leave the house until you rose. And that Aimeric should not let the fire go out.'

They both looked to the hearth where the fading embers spoke of Aimeric's failure to fulfil that responsibility.

'He is wilful,' Alis said solemnly.

'Wilful! Wherever did you hear such a word?'

'Marie's mother said it to Papa yesterday.'

Minou shook her head. 'Remind me who Marie is?'

'The girl Aimeric loves. He says he will marry her as soon as he is old enough and can support a wife.'

'Ah, I remember, though he is rather too young to be thinking of marriage yet awhile. In any case, did you not tell me Marie's mother does not approve of the match?'

'She does not,' Alis said, taking the conversation seriously. 'Marie is very pretty. She has many suitors and says she intends to wed a rich man. I cannot see why she would favour Aimeric.'

Minou laughed. 'That is because he is your brother. You cannot see the virtues in him that others might. I wonder if you might like to go for a ride. Canigou has not been out of the stables for some time. Do you feel you could manage that?'

Alis clapped her hands. 'Yes! Can we go now? Marie says there is a family of otters with kits beneath the bridge. I would see them for myself.'

'Very well, but you must wrap up warmly. Have you had your medicine today?'

Alis nodded. 'And the lady brought me some liquorice to help my cough.'

'That was kind of her. Shall we take something with us, a little bread and cheese, then we can stay out for as long as we wish.'

'Until the cold gets us!'

Minou ruffled her hair. 'Until the cold gets us.'

Minou and Alis made their way down the slopes below the Porte d'Aude, hand in hand, following the line of the barbican.

It was heavy going and the brambles scratched at their

skirts. By the time they reached the Moulin du Roi the bottom of Minou's cloak was soaking wet.

'Are you warm enough, *petite*?' she asked, while her sister paused to get her breath.

'Too much warm,' Alis giggled, then squealed at a sudden splash in the water.

Minou laughed. 'It's only a river eel,' she said, pointing to the thick black tail disappearing into the muddy shallows. 'See? They will not harm us if we do not trouble them.'

At this point of the river the Aude was wide and shallow, running fast, as the melt water came down from the mountains. The wooden paddles of the mills rattled like a round of applause.

'Don't tire yourself,' she cried, as Alis ran ahead along the marshy path, setting a fast pace.

Minou breathed in the rich, earthy smell of leaf and moss on the marshland, rejoicing in the fact that the world was coming back to life after its winter hibernation. Soon it would be spring.

'On the other bank, below the hospital buildings, that's where Marie said she saw the otters.'

'Very well. When we have fetched Canigou, we can ride across the bridge to the Bastide, then down to the water. Yes?'

'Yes.'

The water cast bright reflections on the underside of the old stone bridge across the river. As they drew closer to Trivalle, Minou caught the smell of the stables, the distinctive miasma of dung and straw, tempered by the heat of the forge and the dusty scent of the horses' winter coats.

'You never go down to the river alone, do you?' she asked suddenly. Rixende did her best, but she was a careless guardian and Minou worried about what went on when she was in the bookshop and not there to supervise.

Alis shook her head. 'Aimeric said I should not. He says there are villains who would steal girls like me and sell me for a slave.'

Minou frowned. 'He has no business scaring you like that.'

Alis raised her chin defiantly. 'I am never scared.'

'I am sure you are the bravest girl ever, but you could find yourself face to face with a wild dog or a snake or even –' she tickled her – 'mean-spirited boys who might throw stones at you.'

Giggling, Alis slipped out of her grasp and climbed up onto the trunk of a fallen tree.

'Careful you don't slip into the water,' Minou said.

'Can you see it?' Alis asked, pointing to a spot on the opposite bank. 'The holt is there.'

Minou peered. 'I am not sure . . .'

'You have to let your eyes become accustomed. Then, if you are still, the kits show themselves.'

Minou looked across. In the dappled spring light, flickering like candles upon the water, her eyes were caught by something at the foot of the bridge. She edged closer, realising she was looking at a piece of fabric. Black cloth.

Minou shielded her eyes. Not a log or a stump, or flotsam. There was no doubt. The body of a man was lying on the stone ledge beneath the closest arch, half in and half out of the water. Suddenly, the cloak fell away from his face and Minou saw a shock of white hair and a ruff stained red at the neck. The river shifted again and his hands broke the surface of the water. Two fingers were missing on the right hand.

Minou lifted Alis down from the tree. 'We must go.'

'But I am not tired at all,' Alis wailed. 'We have only just arrived. We have not yet seen the otters and—'

'*Petite*, don't argue. Just come.'

At that moment, the alarum bell began to toll out across the countryside. Loud and discordant, setting the tranquillity of the day to flight. Minou felt her sister clutch her fingers tighter.

'What's happening?' Alis said in a small voice. 'Why are the bells ringing?'

Minou was almost running now, pulling her sister along behind her towards the safety of the quartier Trivalle.

'They are calling us back to La Cité before they close the gates. Hurry, now. As quick as you can.'

CHAPTER EIGHTEEN

⚜

VASSY
North-East France

It was the worst time of year for a journey. The cold had given way to endless rain, and the ground beneath his horse's hooves was slippery, clagged in mud. François, Duke of Guise, put his damp leather glove to the raw scar on his cheek and pressed, to try to take away the ache.

The weather had been against them all the way. A bitter wind, storms, few places to shelter. The further west they rode, the greater his fury at how ill-used he was. His household and his brother, the Cardinal of Lorraine, rode in sombre silence behind him. The bellies of the horses were crusted dark by the splash of the mud beneath their hooves and their heads were low. The rain fell like a steady drumbeat, bouncing off the helmets and breastplates of the duke's armed guards. The pennants, bearing the antique coat of arms of Guise, hung drab and limp on their poles.

The duke himself was soaked to the bone. His cloak lay heavy on his shoulders, his white ruff flattened by the storm. His crucifix hung like a piece of white bone on its black velvet ribbon. He glanced at his brother. The cardinal's expression reflected what he was feeling: that it was a mistake to leave the comforts and security of their estates in Joinville and head west to a reception that was far from certain.

The birthday celebrations on his estates in the Duchy of

Lorraine, his forty-third by the grace of God, had been accompanied by all the ceremony and expense due to his status. But none of it – the banquet, the masque, the players celebrating his life and times – had quelled his concerns at his loss of influence. He – the hero of Metz, of Renty, of Calais, the former Grand Chamberlain of France, standing at the right hand of the old King – was no longer welcome at court. The Queen Regent did not trust him and instead turned to those who promoted the Huguenot cause, permitting their pernicious influence to spread throughout the land.

Guise had quit the court two years previously, after the accession to the throne of Charles IX, then a boy of nine who had wept most of the way through his coronation and who still slept in his mother's bed. The duke's intention in taking his leave – that his absence would prove such a loss to the Queen that she would summon him immediately back – had backfired and he had quickly come to regret his decision. Guise sensed the same grievance in his entourage. They were loyal citizens, good Catholics all, who felt their exile to the north-eastern corner of the kingdom keenly.

It had been a gamble. He and Catherine had long been at loggerheads. She blamed him for stirring up trouble between the Reformers and her Catholic allies. He believed the 'Medici sow' was a pernicious influence, and furthermore had not taken pains enough to hide his opinion. That the boy King himself was unsatisfactory – fanatical about hunting, yet delicate and sickly and prone to temper tantrums when he did not get his own way – no one, bar the Queen herself, would deny. He was not worthy to be seen as God's representative.

As they came out from the woods into the open fields surrounding Vassy, Guise dug his spurs sharply into his horse's flank and broke into a gallop. He heard the hooves of the horses echoing down the line to the soldiers at the very back and felt a surge of determination. No doubt, he had been away from court too long. The traitor Condé, architect of the attempt to kidnap him and his brother at Amboise, was still at large and Coligny was back in favour, consolidating Huguenot influence at Court. They were the enemy within. The Queen's weakness would split the kingdom in two.

They had to be stopped.

'Boy!' he shouted.

His equerry was immediately at his side.

'What town is this?' Guise demanded, gesturing to the spires and grey slate roofs of a modest town some way in the distance. It could have been anywhere. They had been riding through the dull Champagne landscape for hours.

'It is Vassy, my lord,' the boy replied quickly.

Guise was surprised. 'Vassy, you say.' He had some limited claims of suzerainty over the town.

An idea came to him. Though the duke never failed to attend Mass on Sunday, even in the glorious days when he rode out onto the battlefield at the head of a grand army, he did not deceive himself that each of his followers shared the same sense of piety. Most soldiers were more interested in their stomachs than their souls. Moreover, in this season of Lent, they felt the lack of meat and proper victuals. Perhaps he should stop and give his troops a few hours' respite from the rain and the wind?

After they had given thanks to God, he would make sure his men were fed and warmed with a draught of ale before they rode on. François had no intention of arriving in Paris wet and saddle sore, with an entourage as exhausted and tawdry as any band of mercenaries. He was the former Grand Chancellor. He would ensure that the entire Court witnessed his glorious return.

'Boy. Ride ahead to Vassy and tell them that François, Duke of Guise, approaches with his brother, the Cardinal of Lorraine, and will honour the town with his presence. We will attend Mass. Tell them we have some forty men with us who will require food and shelter before we continue on our journey.'

'Yes, my lord,' the equerry said.

Guise sighed. His head ached and his legs pained him. Had he become too old for this young man's game? He grunted. No, he would not submit to age. Though his star might have waned, there was time yet to restore his fortunes. He looked to the heavens.

If only the rain would stop.

After another half-hour's riding, Guise could no longer feel his hands. He pulled roughly at his reins and his stallion reared again. Its hooves churned over in the mud, but the animal held its ground.

He raised an arm and his entourage started to pull up behind him with a rattling of harness, the rumble of cartwheels and grunting pack animals as the column of men and beasts came to a halt.

'What is it?' the cardinal asked.

'Quite.' Guise stared at the wooden structure looming ahead of them in the large flat countryside. 'That is the question.'

His brother followed his gaze. A broad wooden-framed barn, as tall as it was wide, stood impressive and dominant in the flat countryside outside the walls of the town. A tiled sloped roof, in the Norman style, solid walls and a run of windows upon the upper level. The spire of the church of Vassy, in the heart of the town, was dwarfed behind it.

'Do you mean that barn, Brother?' the cardinal said.

'Yes,' he snapped. 'That very large, very new, very ostentatious barn. More than a barn, a building. Outside the walls of my vassal town.'

The cardinal suddenly understood. 'A Protestant temple, think you?'

'Do you have a better explanation?'

'A barn for storing . . .' He stopped. 'No, you may well be right.'

Guise's face was set hard. 'This is what comes of allowing them to pursue their desires. A clearer symbol we could not find of how the Reformers set themselves apart from their fellow citizens and undermine our way of life.'

'By the terms of the Edict, it is now permitted for the Reformers to build a place of worship outside the walls, my lord,' the cardinal offered mildly.

'I am well aware of that. It is a grave mistake. Can you not see how their temple –' Guise all but spat the word from his mouth – 'almost obliterates the spire of our church? Today is Sunday. It is Lent. A time when all Christians show obedience and penitence, practise humility and remember the privations of our Lord. Yet they—. Such ostentation, such vulgar display, such . . . defiance.'

The cardinal glanced at his brother, saw how his eyes shone bright with zeal and, though he would not have spoken this to another living soul, with hatred. To the duke, Huguenots represented all that had gone wrong with France.

'On,' Guise commanded, spurring his horse forward.

He came to a halt within hailing distance of the town, where the young equerry was waiting with the news that the priest of Vassy would be honoured to receive them into his congregation for Mass.

'And what say they of this abomination?' He waved his hand in the direction of the temple.

The boy flushed. 'I did not ask, my lord.'

Guise's eyes narrowed. He turned to the cardinal. 'So, Brother, we do not even know how many of them there are. They breed like rats in the sewer; every day, another heretic born. Another would-be traitor.' He turned back to the equerry. 'What of their pastor? What manner of man is he, did they say?'

The boy dropped his head. 'I did not imagine you would grace the Reformed congregation with your noble presence, my lord, so I did not enquire.'

At that moment, carried by the bitter March wind, the sound of voices raised in song floated across the plains to where their horses stood waiting.

'*Que Dieu Se lève, et que Ses ennemis soient dispersés; et que fuient devant Sa face ceux qui le haïssent.*'

Guise's face flushed with anger. 'You see! They hold nothing sacred. They sing, and in the common language, during Lent. What text is it, Brother?'

The cardinal strained to hear. 'I cannot make it out.'

'*Let God arise, let His enemies be scattered; may His foes flee before him.*'

'It is Psalm sixty-eight, my lord,' the equerry said. 'It a verse the Reformers revere greatly.'

Guise stared at him. 'Do they indeed?'

'It is an affront to God,' the cardinal muttered.

'It is an affront both to God and to France,' the duke replied harshly, raising his voice. 'This is a Christian country, a Catholic country, yet we find here a nest of Calvinist vipers.'

Something of his belligerence reached the men, for their

horses scraped at the ground, restless, alert to the anger in their master's voice.

'Sire, what is your command?' the equerry asked. 'Shall I return to the town and ask how many Huguenots are numbered within Vassy?'

'Tell them these lands lie on the border of my own. It is a vassal town. I will not tolerate those who would stir up dissent. Who set themselves apart. I will not allow heresy to flourish.'

CHAPTER NINETEEN

⚜

La Cité

Piet was lying on his back. He paddled his palms gingerly around in the dirt and grass to get his bearings. His hands were bare, he realised. What had become of his gloves? The face of a girl drifted into his mind. Haunting mismatched eyes – one of blue and the other brown – full of wit and intelligence. In the white mist at the Porte Narbonnaise, he had all but knocked her to the ground. When was that? He tried to remember, but the attempt only sent her slipping further away from him.

He tried to prop himself on his elbow, but the movement made him dizzy. There was a dreadful clamouring, as if all the bells of La Cité were being rung inside his head.

Then he heard the sweet song of a blackbird, and it gave him hope. Carefully, he placed his hands on the ground on either side of his outstretched legs and raised himself into a sitting position. A rush of nausea blindsided him, setting his head and stomach spinning. He steadied himself, waited for the lurching to stop and carefully opened his eyes.

Light flooded his brain. Piet blinked, and blinked again, to clear the gauzy film between him and the world. Little by little, things came back into focus. Grey stone walls, green grass, tipped white with frost in the shadows, the distinctive outlines of the old Roman towers in the walls of medieval Carcassonne. Now he was aware of an ache at the base of his neck, and when he raised his hand, he found a lump the size of an egg. Had he been set upon by some cutpurse when taking his leave of Vidal?

Was that what had happened?

His clothes were damp from where he'd lain upon the ground, the dew seeping through his doublet. There was no sign of his cloak or hat, though his leather satchel lay a few steps away on the ridge of a low stone wall. Dread rushed through him. After all the planning, had the counterfeit relic been stolen? Then, he remembered. The airless room above the tavern, the exchange being made.

Piet snatched up the satchel, fearing the coins would be gone, before remembering he had transferred them to his purse before setting out last evening. His hand went to his waist. His purse was still there, as was his dagger. Odd. What thief would leave so fine a poniard and a full purse?

Gradually, other shards of memory came back: supping ale in the tavern to pass the hours, making his way to the fine house with its glazed casement windows. Stealing through a wrought-iron gate, leading into a small garden. His hand upon the clasp, removing his gloves to work the delicate latch. Vidal waiting with a lantern. Giving his cloak and hat to the servant in the gloom of the passageway, then . . .

He frowned. He couldn't remember. How had he come to be lying here but a few steps away? And what of Vidal? Had he also been attacked?

Piet rolled his shoulders. His arms and legs felt as if they were made of lead. Every tiny motion required a strength he did not feel he possessed. Yet, apart from the bruise on his head, he did not seem to be injured. He ground his jaw from side to side. No bones broken.

Finally, it came back to him. The memory of a thick, sweet wine on his tongue, of creeping paralysis, of falling. The rough-faced servant with the scar on his cheek, the sound of feet running as he pitched unconscious to the floor.

Piet stood, shook the fragments of grass and twigs from his clothing, then made his way back along rue de Notre Dame and tapped upon the rear door.

'Is anybody here?' The house remained silent, its shuttered windows blind and dumb. 'Hello?' he said, knocking harder. 'I would see the priest who goes by the name of . . .' Of course, Vidal would have taken a new name at his ordination but, in his joy at seeing his beloved friend again, Piet – stupidly – had failed to ask what it was. 'I wish to see the priest from Toulouse who is lodging here.'

Silence.

He looked up at the casement windows on the first floor.

'No one lives there any more, Monsieur.'

Piet turned to see a boy of about thirteen years of age standing nearby. Black curled hair, plain doublet and hose, he wore no cap. A memory slipped into his mind of a handsome boy flirting with a pretty girl beside the well.

'Aimeric, is it?' he said.

The boy fell instantly on his guard. 'How do you know my name?'

Piet smiled. 'Lucky guess,' he said. 'What do you mean, the house is untenanted?'

'As I say, Monsieur. No one has lived there since Michaelmas.'

'What would you say if I told you I had dined in this very house last evening?'

Aimeric put his head on one side. 'I would say you had mistaken the house, or had taken too much ale.'

The boy's certainty gave Piet pause for thought. 'Is this not the chapter house of the cathedral used for lodging visiting priests and clergy?'

Aimeric laughed. 'No! It belongs to Monsieur Fournier and his wife. They left after the feast of St Martin and have not returned. It's been empty these past three months. Someone's been jading you.'

'You are certain of it?'

Aimeric turned and pointed to a sweet house set opposite, framed by the bare branches of a rambling wild rose.

'I live there. I give you my word, no one has lived in the Fournier house all winter.'

Piet frowned. He did not doubt Aimeric was telling the truth – what possible reason could he have for lying? All the same, he would wager every *écu* in his possession this was where he had spent the previous evening.

Piet recreated the chamber in his mind's eye: the tapestry on the wall and a heavy sideboard where the servant had placed the tray. A library of books and Vidal's opulent red robes stirring the air as he paced up and down. A well-appointed and furnished room. He hesitated. Another memory. He'd felt the air of a chamber where no one lived, had he not thought as much? What reason would Vidal have had for claiming these were his lodgings?

'I warrant you know a way into the house, Aimeric.'

The boy's black eyes shone with mischief. 'I have no key, Monsieur.'

'I cannot think the lack of a key would be an insurmountable obstacle to a fellow of your intelligence. Look.' Piet smiled at the boy, then without warning, he drew his dagger and launched it. It sailed through the air and sliced, clean in two, a large bulb of fennel on the far side of the vegetable patch. Aimeric's eyes popped wide.

'There.' Piet walked over, retrieved his poniard and slipped it back into his belt. 'If you show me a way into the house, I will teach you how to do that. Is it a deal?'

Aimeric grinned. 'Deal.'

Piet registered the tocsin had begun to toll again as he watched Aimeric work a metal pin back and forth to release the catch.

'Would you say this lock was recently oiled?' he asked.

Aimeric nodded. 'It's clean.'

The mechanism gave, with a dull snick, and the sound stirred other memories. His breath in the cold night air. The door swinging open and Vidal himself, standing ready for him inside with a lantern.

They went in. With his hand upon his dagger, Piet climbed the stairs to the first floor, the boy following. A square of weak daylight filtered through a glazed window upon the half-landing. All the doors were closed and each creak of the floorboards seemed unnaturally loud.

'In here,' he said. 'This was the chamber where I passed the evening.'

Piet turned the handle and stepped inside. There was not a stick of furniture, no signs of comfort or habitation. No sideboard, no chairs, no table, no library of books. The tapestry that had graced the wall had gone. He walked to the hearth and crouched down. The stone was cold and the grate had been thoroughly swept.

'You are sure this is the chamber, Monsieur?'

Piet hesitated. He had been sure, but now? The room looked and felt as if no one had stepped foot in it for some time.

'Monsieur and Madame Fournier took their leave before Michaelmas, you say?'

'Yes, Monsieur.'

'Do you know where they went?'

'I heard my sister say they had gone to Nérac.'

Nérac, some leagues north of Pau, was where the Queen of Navarre had established her Huguenot court. In defiance of her husband's wishes, she had expelled all Catholic priests and the court was now a safe haven for Protestants and those escaping the political pressures of Paris. It was even more curious to think that Vidal should have been lodging in a house owned by a notable Huguenot family.

'The Fourniers are followers of the Reformed Faith?'

Aimeric dropped his gaze. 'I couldn't say.'

'I am not trying to trap you,' Piet said. 'I consider a man's religion his own business.'

Piet imagined the chamber as he had seen it last evening. This was where his chair had stood. He crouched down to examine the red stain upon the floorboards. An image came to his mind of the goblet falling from his hand, the deep crimson Guignolet spilling on the floor.

'Is it blood?' Aimeric said.

'No. Merely wine.'

Had he been drugged? The heaviness in his limbs, the lost hours, all spoke to it, but why drug him, then leave him at liberty? And what of Vidal? Had he suffered the same fate?

'What about this?' Aimeric pointed to a vivid smear on the rectangle of wall between the two windows. 'Is this also wine?'

Piet studied it. A mark, the colour of rust, ran down the white-wash as if someone had fallen back, struck their head, then slid down to the ground. Piet touched it with his fingers.

'No,' he said grimly. 'This is blood.'

CHAPTER TWENTY

⚜

Vassy
North-East France

'My lord!' the cardinal pointed to the main gates into the town. 'They have sent a welcoming party to greet you.'

The nobles of Vassy, attired in velvet and feathered caps, cloaks trimmed with ermine and golden chains of office, were standing nervously in a row.

If the Duke of Guise was pleased, he did not show it.

'Brother?' the cardinal said. 'Shall we approach the town? They wait to honour you.'

A trumpet sounded from the walls, the pennants hanging bright in the grey morning air. Guise hesitated. Then closer at hand, from within the temple, came the murmurings of a prayer.

'*J'espère en l'Eternel, mon âme espère, et j'attends Sa promesse.*'

The duke's expression darkened. He turned away from the town and drove his horse back towards the door to the temple.

'Brother,' the cardinal hissed urgently. 'See, they bring you garlands. They bring you gifts.'

But Guise's full attention was now settled upon the barn and the voices inside. He studied the wooden walls, the tiled roof, the windows cut into the higher storeys; a structure too permanent to speak of humility and gratitude. It was an affront.

The duke pulled his horse to a standstill. He raised his hand to summon the lieutenant of his guard.

'Command them to open the doors,' he said.

'My lord.' The soldier bowed in his saddle, then hammered upon the door with his fist.

'In the name of François of Lorraine, Prince of Joinville, the Duke of Aumale and of Guise,' he called, 'I bid you open these doors.'

At the duke's side, the equerry sensed the palpable shock from within. Heard, in the silence, the echo of the congregation falling quiet within the wooden walls. How many people were within? he wondered. He prayed not many.

'Open this door, by order of the Duke of Guise,' the lieutenant repeated.

The young equerry glanced back over his shoulder and saw that the concern he felt was etched upon the faces of the noblemen at the town gates. Were they also fearful of what might happen or, rather, was their concern for themselves alone? That their tolerance of Protestant worship would be held against them?

'For the third and final time of asking,' the lieutenant called for the third time, raising his voice. 'In the name of the Prince of Joinville, open this door and allow your lord admittance.'

Finally, there was the sound of a wooden latch being lifted and a creak as the heavy door was opened and the pastor stepped out.

Dressed all in black, in the sober garb of the Reformed Religion, he stood with his bare hands outstretched.

'My lord,' he said, bowing low. 'This is an honour.'

For an instant, everything hung in the balance. Then Henri, the duke's twelve-year-old son, spurred his horse past his father and attempted to force his way into the temple. The pastor was thrown violently against the door jamb. Those inside began to panic.

'*Attention! Mes amis, attention!*'

'We wish for no trouble,' the pastor cried, trying to calm both his congregation and young Guise. 'We are unarmed, a congregation gathered to worship, we are . . .'

'See how they defy the duke's command,' the lieutenant shouted and he drew his sword. 'They refuse to allow our lord to enter.'

'That is not true,' the pastor objected, 'but to bring weapons into a place of worship—'

'He challenges our noble lord.'

'We are here to observe the Sabbath,' the pastor shouted.

His words were drowned out as Guise's foot soldiers forced their way inside. A woman screamed. In the confusion, a stone was thrown and struck the duke. A trickle of blood sparked red on Guise's white cheek. For an instant, time stood still, then the cry went up.

'The duke is wounded! Our Lord Guise is assaulted!'

With a roar, the lieutenant drove his horse forward into the barn, trampling the pastor beneath his hooves. Inside, women and children tried desperately to hide, but there was nowhere to go.

CHAPTER TWENTY-ONE

⚜

La Cité

Carrying her sister on her back, Minou ran across the drawbridge to La Cité, relieved to see Bérenger was still on duty at the Porte Narbonnaise.

'Make haste!' he shouted. 'Hurry, Madomaisèla! The gates are closing.'

Minou's muscles in her arms and legs were burning, but she forced herself to keep going. She set Alis down and then tried to catch her breath.

'What's happened?' she gasped, as Bérenger pulled them inside. 'Why is the alarum ringing?'

'There's been a murder,' he said, pushing the gates shut behind them. 'They all but laid hands on the villain yesterday, but he got away. Now they think he's taken refuge in La Cité.' He dropped the heavy bar in place. 'A fellow by the name of Michel Cazès. They found his body down below the bridge at first light. Throat cut from ear to ear, or so they say.'

'At first light, but that cannot be . . .'

She stopped. Could it be the same man? She did not know his family name, but could there be two murdered men? But it made no sense. Had she not seen Michel's body undisturbed beneath the bridge shortly after noon, at the same time the tocsin began to ring? What time was that? One of the clock? Later? She wasn't sure.

'Are you certain that is the man's name? Michel.'

'Certain as I stand here.'

Minou frowned. 'And you say they began searching for the murderer yesterday?'

She remembered talking to Michel on the threshold of the bookshop as the late afternoon mist came in.

Bérenger dropped another heavy bar into place. 'So they say. Mind you, a priest is also missing, which I warrant accounts for all this fuss. From an influential Toulousain family, a guest of the Bishop of Carcassonne. The same villain was seen entering the cathedral yesterday morning, before meeting with this Cazès in the Bastide.'

Minou shook her head. 'And what is the name of the man accused of these crime? Do you know that?'

'He has red hair, that's all we've been told. A stranger, not from around here.'

Minou swallowed hard, remembering Madame Noubel's description of her lodger. Remembering the touch of a stranger's hand upon her cheek in the February mist.

'A Huguenot,' Bérenger said, rubbing a hand over his grey beard. 'That said, people see treason in everything these days. More likely a quarrel over a debt. Or a woman. Priest found him out, no doubt.' Bérenger dragged the last of the heavy bolts into place. 'There. You get off home with Alis, Madomaisèla. They say the villain is dangerous.'

'No, Cécile! I will not tell her,' Bernard repeated. 'I cannot.'

Madame Noubel was sitting at the long table in the kitchen, tracing her fingers on a chalk picture.

'Then you are a fool. If Florence was here—'

His voice faltered. 'But she is not here, Cécile. And there's the pity of it.'

'If Florence *was* here,' she said doggedly, 'she would say it was time to tell Minou the truth. Better that it comes from your lips than those of another.'

'All those who were there are either dead now, or knew nothing of what actually happened.'

'No one? What about Madame Gabignaud? You cannot be sure, Bernard. Servants talk, villagers stand and whisper around the well. Folk guard their tongues at first, then forget what was meant to be secret.'

'It was such a long time ago.'

'What about the Will?'

'I don't know what happened to it. Florence . . . she took care of everything. We did not talk of it.'

'Well, then,' Madame Noubel said impatiently. 'What if the Will does still exist? What if it comes to light? What then?'

'Why should it be found now, after all these years?'

'Bernard, these are uncertain times. War is coming, and we cannot know what secrets will start tumbling out.'

He waved his hand. 'They always say war is coming, yet it never does. Nothing changes. One month the Duke of Guise is in the ascendant, the next month fortune smiles on Coligny and Condé. What have our lives to do with any of them?'

'Don't be naïve,' Madame Noubel snapped. Then her voice softened. 'You are a ghost in your own life, Bernard. Can you not see the effect it is having on the whole family? Minou knows there is something amiss. She cares deeply for you and she worries for you. Tell her the truth.'

'I cannot.'

She sighed. 'At the very least tell her what befell you in January. She dates your decline from then. Minou is an intelligent young woman with great fortitude.' Cécile hesitated. 'She thinks you have withdrawn your affection from her, Bernard, and that saddens her greatly.'

'Withdrawn my affection . . .' he cried. 'No! But she is so young, Cécile. I want to spare her this.'

'She is nineteen. She is old enough to run the bookshop in your stead. Old enough to care for Aimeric and Alis. By rights, she should be courting or even married with a family of her own. You insult her by deciding she does not have the strength of character to bear what you have to tell her. Minou has to follow her own path, Bernard. You cannot protect her from the world forever.'

'Please, Cécile, not yet. I cannot bear it.'

'As it is,' Madame Noubel persisted, 'you risk putting distance between you and Minou because of your obdurate silence. That is the way to lose her affection. You have made yourself a prisoner in your own home, Bernard, and the whole family suffers. I implore you, tell her the truth.'

Hearing raised voices, Minou stopped in the passageway. Her fingers rested on the cold metal latch of the kitchen door, but she could not bring herself to enter. She knew she should declare her presence, not stand eavesdropping, but the apparent licence between her father and Madame Noubel gave her pause for thought. She had not considered them more than good neighbours, but they called one another by their given names. And, from time to time, slipped into the old language.

'Why do we not go in?' Alis whispered. 'Don't we have to tell Papa what we saw by the bridge?'

Minou stepped back from the door and bent down. '*Petite*, you have done so well and you have been brave. Will you do one thing more? Stay on the threshold, but see if you can spot Aimeric and bid him to come inside? You heard what Bérenger said. It is not safe to be out of doors.' She put her hands upon her sister's shoulders, turned her around and pointed her in the direction of the door. 'I will wait here, then we will go in and speak to Papa together, yes?'

Alis nodded, then ran back down the passageway to the entrance and started calling Aimeric's name. As soon as she was out of sight, Minou pressed her ear to the door.

'I have taken precautions, Cécile. I have arranged for Minou to accompany Aimeric to Toulouse. Florence's sister has offered to take him and make a gentleman of him. I have accepted the invitation. Minou will be out of harm's way there.'

'Living with Monsieur Boussay and his feather-brained wife! You think that is what Florence would want?'

'What else can I do, Cécile?' he said wearily. 'I have no other choice. Our money is almost gone. Aimeric will have a chance of advancement if I send him. There is nothing for him here.'

'What if Minou does not want to go to Toulouse?' Madame Noubel's voice was sharp with anger. 'And what's to become of Alis, deprived of her sister's care?'

'Do you not think that I have considered all of this, Cécile? It is not a decision I take lightly, but it is all I can do. The best I can do.'

'Well, then there is nothing more to be said.'

Madame Noubel opened the kitchen door. Caught out, Minou sprang back. Everyone started speaking at once.

'Minou!'

'Madame Noubel, I was—'

'Your father and I . . . Bernard and I were talking.'

'How long have you been there? Were you eavesdropping?'

'Bernard, really!'

Minou looked from one to the other, caught like conspirators in a painted tableau: her father sitting by the cold hearth, his worn face grey with worry, Madame Noubel, two pink spots on her cheeks, her hand frozen on the latch of the door.

'I have been here long enough to hear you are resolved to send Aimeric to Toulouse and me with him. As for eavesdropping, your voices were so far raised I could hardly fail to hear.'

Bernard flushed. 'Forgive me, I spoke hastily.'

'But you *do* intend for us both to go to Toulouse?'

Her father gave a long sigh. 'It is for the best.'

'Bernard believes, wrongly in my opinion, that—'

'Cécile! Allow me to decide what is right for my family.'

Madame Noubel raised her hands. 'Have it your own way.'

Minou sat down on the bench, suddenly exhausted.

'What is it, Daughter?' her father said, his voice full of concern. 'Has something happened to you?'

'No.' Minou traced a pattern on the surface of the table with her fingers, hearing and seeing nothing, until she felt the gentle pressure of Madame Noubel's hand on her shoulder.

'Minou,' she said quietly, 'are you unwell?'

She gathered herself. There was no sense wallowing in self-pity and she had to speak with her father before Aimeric and Alis came back.

'Madame, I wonder if you have told my father what happened yesterday in the Bastide?'

'I did, not least your courage in coming to my defence.'

'And of our late-afternoon visitor to the bookshop?'

'I mentioned that a man – Michel – came to call, no more than that.'

'Now I know who he is. His full name is Michel Cazès.'

Bernard took a deep breath. 'I remember him.'

Minou looked at her father. 'So, he was known to you, Father. I had hoped he was not.'

'Why? What more has happened?' Madame Noubel asked.

'Michel is dead, murdered,' she said. 'I myself saw his body in the river beneath the bridge, but a half-hour past.'

'Michel Cazès,' Bernard whispered. 'It is too cruel.'

'Are you sure it was the same man?' Madame Noubel said. 'You only saw him for a matter of minutes yesterday, you could be mistaken?'

'I remembered his clothes and, besides, he had the misfortune to be missing two fingers –'

'On his right hand,' Bernard added.

'Yes. I am sorry to be the bearer of bad news. But there is more,' Minou continued. 'His death, at least the timing of it, cannot be as they claim. The tocsin started to ring while Alis and I were down by the bridge where his body lay, from what we observed, undiscovered in the water. Yet when we fled back to La Cité, Bérenger told me the hunt for Michel's murderer had begun yesterday in the Bastide.' She turned to Madame Noubel. 'The description of the murderer they are giving out is of a man with red hair.'

'My lodger, you think?'

'Your lodger?' Bernard said, looking from face to face. 'I don't understand.'

His words were drowned by the sound of Alis shouting in the passageway.

'Minou! Papa! The soldiers have arrested Aimeric at the Fournier house,' she cried, running into the kitchen. 'They say he is a witness to murder!'

CHAPTER TWENTY-TWO

⚜

Piet pressed himself back into the shadows, waiting for the thunder of boots and leather on the battlements above to pass. All around, like pistol shots, he could hear the clatter of gates large and small being bolted, trapping him inside.

He exhaled. If Aimeric hadn't been so sharp – looking out of the window at the precise moment when four soldiers rounded the corner and headed for the exact spot where he had been left drugged – he would have been arrested. He had dispatched the boy to the stables in Trivalle to fetch his horse. Piet hoped he was reliable: he had no choice but to trust him. And still the bells kept ringing.

All this because of him?

Crouching beneath the line of the wall, Piet made his way towards the closest of the postern gates, over the straw and mud covering the wide steps. He stumbled over a vagrant slumped asleep, his breath a cloud of stale ale. A chained dog lunged at him and the geese hissed as he invaded their pen, climbing up and over the rotten struts.

He tried the handle of the postern gate, rattling the small wooden door in its frame, but it did not shift. Might he force the lock? He bent lower and ran his hand along the jamb, looking for a weakness in the hinge, but there was nothing.

Piet was about to move on to the next tower, when he felt a prickling on the back of his neck. Someone was watching him. He could feel their scrutiny, as sharp as the point of a knife on his skin.

The harsh notes of the bells ricocheted off every stone and tower, the echo chasing down every alleyway. Minou stared back along rue du Trésau and then across to rue Saint-Jean. There was no sign of Aimeric.

If he had been arrested, where would they take him?

The streets were deserted. Even the communal area around the main well, the heart of the quartier most afternoons, was abandoned. A pail swayed slightly above the drop, as if some spirit hand had touched it then vanished.

Minou ran across to the Fournier house, praying he had done nothing wrong. That he had not been caught. She had seen boys younger than him flogged so viciously, for some trivial offence or another, that they could barely walk for weeks. She hammered on the front door and called Aimeric's name, but heard only the bolts rattling top and bottom in their cradles. She doubled back to the garden behind the house. A bucket lay on its side and a bulb of fennel lay sliced clean in two beside the step, but that back door was also locked.

Minou ran out into rue Notre-Dame, at a loss where to look next. Then out of the corner of her eye, she saw something moving in the shadows beneath the battlements.

'Aimeric?' she whispered.

Then she saw a man, trying to open a door within the inner walls, and caught her breath.

It was him.

Minou stepped forward, and his hand instantly went to his dagger.

'If you try the next postern to your left, Monsieur,' she

said, calling across the space between them, 'the latch is broken and the soldiers often forget.'

Slowly, he turned. 'What?'

'I mean you no harm. I am looking for my brother.'

He sheathed his sword. 'I feared it was the soldiers coming back.'

'They will be back. There is a gate in the walls below here. If you can cross the lists without being seen, there's a path.'

He took a step towards her. 'Why would you help me? I am accused of murder. I can hear the soldiers shouting so.'

'The track winds down through orchards beside the barbican and into Trivalle.'

Piet took another pace closer. 'Did you not hear me, Mademoiselle? I am accused of murder.'

'I heard you, but you are innocent.'

'Then come with me,' he said, suddenly smiling. 'Show me the way, my Lady of the Mists.'

Minou shook her head. 'Go. You will see us both hanged if you tarry longer. If the soldiers find us together, they will arrest us both.'

'Will you at least tell me your name, Mademoiselle? I would keep it close. A keepsake, if you will.'

She hesitated, then held out her hand. 'Very well, for it costs me nothing to give you my name, I am Minou, the eldest daughter of Bernard Joubert, bookseller, of rue du Marché.'

He raised her hand to his lips. 'Mademoiselle Joubert. I saw you in the Bastide yesterday. Just before noon. You helped my landlady out of harm's way while the villains were inside ransacking my rooms.'

'Ah. Which is why you behaved as if you knew me.'

'I do know you,' he said. 'The sort of person you are, at least. It took courage to stand against the soldiers.'

'Madame Noubel is a dear neighbour,' she said, slowly withdrawing her hand. 'Monsieur, will you tell me your name in return? A fair exchange.'

'Indeed it is.' Piet touched her cheek. 'My name is Piet Reydon. If God is with me and I make it safely back to Toulouse – *la ville rose* – my door will be forever open to you for this kindness. I have lodgings there in the university quarter, close to the Eglise Saint-Taur.'

Bewildered by the turn of the conversation, Minou held his gaze.

'God speed, Monsieur Reydon.'

He nodded, as if a bargain had been struck. Then, as quickly as he had appeared, he was gone. Minou listened for the sound of the latch of the gate to know he was safely through, then breathed out.

'*La ville rose*,' she whispered.

The sound of the guards shouting behind her immediately banished all thoughts of Piet and Toulouse, and in their place came guilt. She had forgotten all about Aimeric! How could she have been so neglectful?

Minou hurried back up rue Notre-Dame only to come face to face with Bérenger and another soldier coming from the opposite direction.

'You should not be out of doors, Madomaisèla!' Bérenger said, lowering his sword. 'There's a curfew. Can you not hear the tocsin?'

Minou blushed. 'I know it, but I am searching for my brother. Alis said he had been arrested and, though I cannot believe it to be true, Aimeric has such gift for getting into trouble, I thought to fetch him home. Have you seen him, my friend?'

Bérenger's expression lightened. 'I saw him some half an

hour past, skulking about near the Fournier house. He was telling some tall tale, claiming to have spied the murderer and broken in.' He gestured behind him. 'It is boarded up, as it has been all winter. I sent him home with a flea in his ear.'

'Thank you, dear Bérenger,' Minou said, though the knot in her stomach was still there. It was a relief to know the soldiers hadn't punished him, but he had not yet arrived back at the house. Where was he?

'Never mind that,' the other soldier said, pushing Bérenger aside. 'Has anyone passed this way?'

'No one,' she said calmly.

'A man with red hair? Are you sure?'

'Oh. A man matching that description did come this way, but that was some time past.'

'Which way did he go?'

'That way,' she lied. 'Towards the Château Comtal.'

They turned and ran, Bérenger calling back over his shoulder.

'Go back indoors, Madomaisèla Minou. The villain has killed at least one man, maybe more. Take yourself out of harm's way.'

Minou watched them go. Only when they had vanished did she realise she had been holding her breath.

What had she done?

Not only helped an accused murderer escape, but also given false information to the Seneschal's men. What was the penalty for that? It hardly mattered. She knew she would do the same again.

'My Lady of the Mists.'

Standing in the pale winter's afternoon, Minou momentarily felt everything fade away: the never-ending threat of wars that never came, the daily struggle to make ends meet, the secrets her father was keeping and her worries for her brother and sister. For a moment, the world was suddenly and dazzlingly vivid, full of promise.

As she started for home, an idea started to take shape in her mind. Minou shivered at the possibility of it. How she would, without delay, tell her father she had changed her mind and that she was prepared, after all, to accompany Aimeric to Toulouse as soon as the arrangements could be put in place. She had no idea where her brother was, but since he had not been arrested, she had no doubt he would reappear as soon as the soldiers had gone.

Minou had been born and bred in Carcassonne. She had grown tall here, among the grey and sandstone colours of the Midi, amongst the vines and orchards of La Cité. A girl who had learnt her letters at the kitchen table in rue du Trésau. The footprints of her nineteen years upon the earth were here.

That girl stood now, like a shadow beside her.

Minou felt her old self take a pace back and another self take a pace forward. Carcassonne and Toulouse. Her past and her future.

PART TWO

Toulouse

Spring 1562

D·O·M

CHAPTER TWENTY-THREE

⚜

Toulouse Plains
Sunday, 8th March

'Sirrah, if you please!' Minou shouted at the driver as the carriage bounced over the brow of another hill. Its wheels were clattering over the rough ground, setting her teeth rattling in her head. She rapped sharply on the roof.

'Sirrah, stop!'

The driver pulled up the horses with such force that Minou was thrown back in her seat. Enraged, for she knew the driver had done it on purpose, she dragged the curtain back and stuck her head out.

'My brother is unwell.'

Aimeric stumbled out of the cab and, moments later, the sound of retching betrayed the weakness of his stomach.

'The motion of the carriage does not agree with him,' Minou said, though she knew full well the sweetbreads and ale he had acquired at the tavern last evening, when they had stopped to rest the horses and break the journey, were the cause of his sickness.

The pleasure at being in a closed carriage, a novelty when they left Carcassonne at first light yesterday morning, had quickly worn off. The heavy window cloth trapped the stale air inside. The short night, in a roadside tavern stinking of men and mouldy straw, had left her covered in a mass of flea bites. Minou decided she needed some air.

'How much longer? Were we not due to reach Toulouse by the ninth hour?'

'And would have done so,' the driver replied sourly, 'but for the constitution of the young gentleman.'

'I am sure the horses are grateful for a rest.'

Minou walked away from the carriage. The air was clear, a haze of mist hanging over the wet grass. Ahead was a small copse, the silver bark of the trees glistening in the early morning light. She glanced back over her shoulder. The driver was sitting on his bench, resting his whip across his knees. Of Aimeric, there was no sign.

Minou took another few steps away from the road, then slipped into the green shadow of the wood. Larch and ash trees, the last berries of the winter holly, the world coming back to life. She breathed in the sweet smell of damp soil and new leaf and, all around her, there was a carpet of tiny purple woodland violets as far as her eye could see. She kept walking, feeling the rise and fall of the uneven ground beneath her feet, heading towards the horizon beyond the tree line.

Suddenly, Minou was out of the woods and found herself standing on the top of a hill, bounded in the far distance by the white-capped peaks of the Pyrenees.

On the plains below lay Toulouse. Glorious, magnificent, glinting like a jewel in the dawn haze. She saw a wide, wide river, in front of the southern section of the city walls, like a gown of spun silver. Behind it, a myriad steeples and domes and spires, each touched by the rising sun so it seemed as if the whole city was aflame. *La ville rose*, Piet had called it.

Minou had read of how Toulouse was both a marvel of the modern age and a pearl of the Roman Empire, with its viaducts and the amphitheatre, marble columns and huge carved, sculpted heads of the pagan gods of the past. But neither her imagination, nor the most exquisite words on a page, had prepared Minou for the majesty of the city now spread out at her feet.

Then, through the trees, she heard the sound of Aimeric shouting her name.

'I'm coming,' she called back, though she did not move. Her joy at the scene before her was tempered suddenly by the thought of Alis and her father left behind. What if Alis could not manage without her or sickened? What if their departure hastened their father further into decline? What if even the best ministrations of Madame Noubel could not help him regain some measure of contentment?

What if . . .

'Minou, where are you?'

Hearing the concern in Aimeric's voice, she turned and walked back through the woods. She would not allow memories of Carcassonne to overwhelm her. Instead, she would think of the new life waiting for them in Toulouse.

The sun was rising over the plains outside the Porte Villeneuve. Piet heaved another plank onto his shoulder, bracing his legs for balance, then passed it to another, who hauled the plank up out of the sawpit and marked it with a Roman numeral to identify where it went in the frame. Others were lashing the woven wattle hurdles to the wooden scaffolding poles, ready to pulley the completed frame into place.

Piet rolled his shoulders, satisfied by the hard, physical work. He was proud to be part of an impromptu band of brothers, linked by their Protestant faith and a common purpose, who were expanding the Temple of the Reformed Church to accommodate Toulouse's growing Huguenot congregation. Whenever Piet could be spared from the almshouse in rue du

Périgord, he came here to join students, sons of wealthy merchants, clerks and yeoman farmers, standing side by side with the guildsmen and sawyers, joiners, carpenters, masons and turners. Little by little, Piet was learning the language of wood: dovetail joints and sill beams and purlins, mortise and tenon, the secret patois of skilled craftsmen.

The gold from the sale of the counterfeit shroud in Carcassonne had financed much of the work, though his role in the matter he kept secret. In idle moments, Piet worried that Oliver Crompton would discover that the Shroud was a forgery. But why would the Carcassonnais men question its authenticity? And besides, surely there was no one there who would be able to tell it from the original.

Still, doubt gnawed away at him. He could hardly explain why he had paid for a copy to be made. Except that, for all his Huguenot soul should despise the cult of relics, Piet had not been able to bring himself to hand over a piece of such antiquity and beauty. He felt guilty for deceiving his allies and for his inability to admit the truth to Vidal. Piet was still haunted by the look of disappointment on his former friend's face when he confessed he had known of the theft, albeit after the event.

'Here,' a carpenter said, heaving a beam of rough-hewn wood into his arms. 'Steady?'

Piet braced his legs and took the weight. 'I have it.'

The air was filled with wood smoke and clouds of sawdust. Flat gables were pulled up into position by mules and rope as, little by little, the building was taking shape. Simple and plain, in the style of the covered markets of the towns of the upper Languedoc – the temple was to be a wide, single space inside large enough to accommodate hundreds of worshippers. The hope was that the work would be completed by Palm Sunday some two weeks hence.

Piet had cut his hair unfashionably short and dampened down its distinctive red hues with charcoal, leaving it a strange dull grey. He'd done the same to his beard and left it untended, disguising the shape of his jaw. His pale skin had been darkened in the few weeks he'd spent outdoors in the spring sun, though he was still paler than most of the men around him. His clothes, too, were different. He had put away his ruff and doublet and wore instead the open shirt, jerkin and plain hose of a yeoman's son. From a distance, he would defy even his closest friends to recognise him.

Even Vidal.

Since returning to Toulouse, Piet's concern for his old friend had driven him to seek him out. At the *maison de charité* during the day and in the taverns of the cathedral quarter at night, he'd listened to tittle-tattle and bought gage after gage of ale, but learnt little. He'd pressed the palms of servants and sweet-talked the giggling maids in the bourgeois houses. Last week, a student from their old college admitted he'd heard gossip of the young canon with the white stripe in his black hair – already a monsignor, so they said – but had no idea where he was to be found. Since Piet did not know what name Vidal had taken at his ordination, it was all but hopeless.

Piet told himself Vidal was alive and safe, though he knew these were just words, like a catechism repeated. He would not allow himself to think Vidal might have been involved in any deception. In daylight hours, Piet dwelt on his culpability. If he had not come looking for him in Carcassonne, would his friend now be sleeping safe in his bed? He was sure, too, that the Fournier house had not been where Vidal was lodging, but Piet could only assume that it was impossible for them to have met anywhere else. He had sought out Vidal, after all, not the other way around.

In the unforgiving hours between midnight and dawn, wakeful in the dark, Piet tormented himself with the fear that Vidal had been murdered in Carcassonne – and that he himself had been accused of the killing.

Then, as news of the massacre at Vassy spread, there was much more to worry about. The facts came third hand, fifth hand, diluted and distorted in each retelling. A hundred Huguenots dead, slaughtered as they gathered in worship. Some said more. Unarmed men, women and children slaughtered by the Duke of Guise's men. What would it mean for France? For Toulouse? No one knew, only that these were lawless times. The almshouse where he worked was overwhelmed with Protestant women and children put from their homes, in desperate need of food and shelter.

'Stand clear now!'

The shouts of workers brought Piet back to the present. He clamped his fingers around the beam and strode forward, his footsteps leaving imprints in the dewed ground.

Suddenly, he felt a prickling on the back of his neck, as if someone was watching him. It was not the first time he had felt himself under observation. He looked round: a boy was idling by the midden with an insolent stare; a dark-skinned man with a Spanish beard whose eyes slid away from Piet whenever their paths crossed. Piet shook his head, surprised to be so anxious. But he was tired. The concerns that kept him awake at night were now making him see troubles where none existed.

He went back to work.

'*Merci*,' his boss said in his clumsy accent, as Piet lowered the beam to the ground ready to be hoisted up. The man in charge of constructing the section at the back of the temple was an Englishman, said to have studied in Geneva under Calvin himself. He kept his own company, but he was fair and the work ran to time.

'My pleasure,' Piet replied in English.

The man looked up in surprise. 'You speak my language.'

'A little.'

'Jasper McCone,' he said, offering his hand.

'Piet . . . Joubert.' He gave the first name that came to mind, just in case his Carcassonne troubles had followed him here.

'Most of your countrymen are not so minded to learn other tongues.'

Piet smiled. 'I spent some time in London, in the first days of your new Queen's reign. Also, Amsterdam, where many sailors know a little English.'

'But you live here now?'

'I live here.'

McCone wiped the top of a small ale flagon with his kerchief, and offered it to Piet.

'Thank you.' Piet drank, then handed it back with a nod towards the building. 'She's going up quickly.'

'We're using some of the foundations of the old building, but it's in the quality of the wood. French oak is better than English oak. Straighter and longer. Less likely to split or buckle under the load.'

'Will the work be completed on time?'

'If this weather holds,' McCone said.

For a moment, Piet was content: the taste of the hops on his tongue and the rising sun on his back, with the ache of honest labour in his arms and legs. He forgot to feel anxious. But as the ale wore off the clouds descended again; he thought of Michel, wondering if he was still in Carcassonne, and of Vidal. Then he remembered the soldiers shouting how they were hunting a murderer matching his description, and the metal band tightened around his chest again.

'I needed that,' he said, returning the flagon to McCone. 'Back to work. No time to waste if we are to be ready for Holy Week.'

Piet returned to the sawpit.

Minou stood with her arm around her brother's shoulder.

'I am sorry,' Aimeric said again.

'Do you feel better?'

He nodded. 'I truly am sorry, Minou.'

'No matter,' she said, straightening his doublet. 'There, that's not so bad. Are you well enough to continue the journey?'

'I think so.'

'Good. It's no more than five leagues now.'

'It looks closer.'

'We are high up. A few hours and we'll be there.' She smiled, and linked her arm through his. 'To pass the time, you can tell me about the day you came face to face with a murderer.'

'Not again,' Aimeric groaned as Minou helped him back into the carriage. 'I have told you everything that happened a dozen times, everything he said. In any case, you say he is wrongly accused and so not a murderer at all.'

'Then one more telling will not hurt,' she insisted, 'and it will keep your mind off the state of your stomach.' She rapped on the roof. 'Driver!'

The carriage lurched forward and soon they were hurtling down the hill towards the covered bridge that would take them over the river Garonne and into the city.

As Aimeric talked, Minou let his words wash over her. In

the days since helping him to escape La Cité, Piet was often on her mind. She never doubted he had returned safely to Toulouse, though she did not know it for a fact. From Bérenger, she had learnt that the stranger they had been seeking for Michel's murder had never been apprehended.

She imagined a myriad of invented duets between her and Piet. Sometimes they were sweet in nature, affectionate and flattering. At other times, she reprimanded him for having put Aimeric so carelessly in danger.

Now, she was in touching distance. Somewhere, within the dazzling metropolis spread out below her, she would find him.

CHAPTER TWENTY-FOUR

⚜

THE BASTIDE
Sunday, 15th March

'Let go of my arm, Alis,' Bernard cried, trying to prise his daughter's fingers from his sleeve. 'You have to stay with Madame Noubel.'

'Take me with you, Papa,' Alis cried. 'I don't want you to go.'

Cécile stepped in. 'Come, *petite*, you will wear yourself out with weeping. Here's a piece of liquorice. It will soothe your throat.'

Alis ignored her. 'Why can't I go with you? I'll be as quiet as a mouse. I'll be good.'

'It is too far. It's no place for a child.'

'Then let me go to Toulouse instead. I can stay with Minou and Aimeric. It is not fair that I should be left in Carcassonne on my own.'

'Fie, Alis, you'll not be alone, you will be with me.' Madame Noubel pressed the liquorice root into her hand. 'Your father has no choice. He has business to attend to.'

'But it's not fair –'

'*Ca suffit!*' Bernard snapped, guilt making him sharp. 'I won't be away for long.'

Madame Noubel hugged the little girl. 'We will rub along together well enough, you and I,' she said. 'Bernard, you should make ready. Alis will be fine as soon as you have gone.'

Distraught to be the cause of such unhappiness, Bernard was desperate to reassure her.

'I will not be away for long.'

'Where are you going?'

'To the mountains.'

'Where in the mountains?'

'Does it matter?' he said, feeling Cécile Noubel's eyes on him.

'If you go to the mountains, will you stop being sad?'

Her words pulled him up short. She was a sweet child, yet he felt he barely knew her. She had been only two years old when his beloved wife died. In his grief, he had left Alis to Minou's care. Now her innocent question was proof of what Cécile had warned – that his melancholy was affecting the whole family.

Blinking his failure from his eyes, Bernard studied her solemn little face. She looked so like her mother, with her black eyes and tumbling curls.

'Will you come back happy?'

'Yes,' he said, with more confidence than he felt. 'In the mountains, the air is clear and it will make me well again.'

'I see,' Alis said, and her sympathy touched him more deeply than her sorrow had done.

'Be a good girl while I'm gone,' he said. 'Work hard at your letters.'

'Yes, Papa.'

Madame Noubel stroked her hair. 'Alis, I warrant the kitten is awake now. You may give her a saucer of milk.'

The little girl's face lit up. She went up on her toes, placed a kiss on her father's cheek, then skipped up the steps into the boarding house.

'Thank you, Cécile,' he said.

'You are going to Puivert, aren't you.' It was more a statement than a question.

Bernard hesitated, then nodded. Why bother to deny it?

'Are you sure that it is wise?'

He let his hands drop. 'I have to be certain there is nothing there that could harm Minou.'

'When we talked of this two weeks ago, you were adamant that there was no danger. What has changed your mind?'

He could hardly explain it to himself, yet since Michel's murder his fears had grown and grown, like ivy on a wall.

'I told you about the inquisitional prison in Toulouse.'

'You did.'

'You cannot understand the horror of such a place, Cécile, unless you have been there. It is . . . hell. The screaming and the inhumanity, men whose bodies are broken left to die in agony in the company of those waiting for their interrogation to begin.' He exhaled deeply, as if he could rid himself of the memories. 'What I didn't tell you, was that I was held like that in the same cell as the man who was murdered, Michel Cazès.'

'Of what was he accused?'

'Treason.'

'And was the charge justified?'

'Possibly,' Bernard admitted. 'He was a Huguenot and mixed in those circles. Though that is no justification for what they did to him. Severing a man's fingers one by one to make him talk . . .'

He stopped and rubbed his eyes, sore and rimmed red from hunching over the accounts ledger in the light of a single candle each night. This month, the receipts from the bookshop would barely cover the monthly lease. He was so tired.

Bernard went to secure his meagre luggage, aware of Cécile

waiting patiently. He was grateful to her for not pressing him further. He clung to the conviction that he was doing the best thing by not confiding in Minou. He had sent her to Toulouse for her own safety, for the sake of them all. What else could he do? But it was his fault. If only he had kept his tongue still in his head. He had brought this misfortune upon himself, upon his family, and his conscience would not leave him be. He had never meant to speak his most secret thoughts, but chained to the damp, vile walls of the inquisitional prison, waiting for the torture he knew would come, he had talked to keep the darkness and pain at bay. He had revealed secrets held tight for nearly twenty years.

'I feared I would die there and no one would know,' he said. 'It was that, more than the thought of death itself, that most terrified me. Michel was certain he would hang and, of course, he suffered more. We talked and talked. But then we both believed we had no future. I told him things I should not have said.' Bernard hesitated. 'About Minou.'

'Oh, Bernard,' Madame Noubel murmured. The pity and the understanding in her voice brought another prick of tears to his eyes. 'And because Michel came looking for you, and was killed, you have convinced yourself it is all because of what you revealed to him.'

'How can it not be?' he cried. 'Michel and I had not spoken since the day of our release, but out of the blue he comes to Carcassonne. Every soldier in La Cité and the Bastide is mobilised, the tocsin is rung – even though, as Minou told us, the timing of it all made no sense. And then?' He snapped his fingers. 'Nothing. As quickly as it blew up, the matter is never mentioned again. Bérenger tells me the garrison was ordered never to speak of the murder even amongst themselves.'

'I agree it is strange, but stranger things happen every day,' Madame Noubel said. 'Can you not see your anguish spurs you to read more into this coincidence of events than might be true? Your shame for confiding in Michel drives you to assume this is all connected, but there is no proof. He probably was involved in some Huguenot conspiracy, you admitted as much. That is just as likely – more so – to be the reason for his death.'

'All I know,' Bernard said softly, 'is that I have no peace. I think about it night and day, the consequences of what I said. I am mired in regret and guilt. I have to be sure nothing in Puivert can harm Minou. To do that, I have to go back there.'

'No, the opposite is true,' she argued. 'By returning to Puivert you risk drawing attention to the old story.' She put her hand on his arm. 'I implore you, stay in Carcassonne.'

Bernard knew if things went ill and he did not return, his children would be left orphaned. Minou would grieve for him. For Aimeric and Alis, he worried less. Minou would continue to be a mother to them, as she had been every day of their lives for the past five years.

'I have to go, Cécile. After all these years, something is dragging me back to Puivert. The business with Michel. I have to go.'

Madame Noubel held his gaze, then, perhaps seeing the resolve in his eyes, she nodded.

'Very well, then. Alis will be fine with me. Minou and Aimeric are safe in Toulouse. I still have family in Puivert. I could write and let them know you are coming.'

'Thank you, but no. It's better if no one knows.'

She raised her hands. 'But take care, Bernard. Do not stay away long. These are dangerous times.'

Paris

The Duke of Guise rode through the streets of Catholic Paris towards the mighty cathedral church of Notre-Dame. His star was rising. He was once more back where he belonged. He was a force to be reckoned with again.

His eldest son, Henri, was riding on one side of him and his brother, the Cardinal of Lorraine, on the other. The black manes of the horses shone, their saddles bright and cleaned of mud. Behind them, the duke's entourage in bright livery and gleaming armour spoke of the conquering army that France needed to see.

All the bells of the churches and cathedrals were calling the faithful to Mass. François kept his expression sombre and pious, as befitted the occasion, but he felt the bells were ringing for him – the hero of Vassy, the scourge of heresy, the man who would make France strong once more.

'This homecoming is well done,' he said to his brother. 'I applaud your attention and loyalty.'

'It is no more than is rightly due to your rank and status, Brother.'

François turned and raised his arm to the crowd, then dismounted at the west door of the imposing Gothic cathedral. A messenger ran to the cardinal, bowed low, then pressed a missive into his hand.

'My lord. Brother,' he said. 'Excellent news. The Queen Regent presents her best wishes and welcomes you back to Paris. She would be grateful for your counsel. On behalf of his Majesty the King, she would be delighted to receive you at Court. She says there is much to discuss to your mutual interest.'

A slow, satisfied smile spread across Guise's narrow face. 'That is indeed good news,' the duke said.

La Cité

Vidal carefully smoothed the material flat on the ornate wooden table. He was in the private chambers of the Episcopal Palace in Carcassonne, where he had been staying for the past two weeks as a guest of the bishop. They had talked and agreed terms. Vidal was confident, when the time came for him to launch his suit to be appointed next Bishop of Toulouse, that he would have the support of the cathedral and chapter of Carcassonne.

With a magnifying glass, Vidal examined every stitch of the pale cloth, the silk warp and the linen weft, the ornamental embroidered edging and the exquisite Kufic calligraphy. There were several French churches and monasteries that also claimed to be in possession of some fragment of the Shroud in which the body of Jesus was laid in the sepulchre. Of course, most were of questionable origin. Vidal had many times studied the Shroud of Antioch when it was held in the Eglise Saint-Taur in Toulouse. He now lifted the corner of the cloth, searching for the tiniest tear in the material which he knew should be there, and found nothing. It was a very good copy, of accurate size and fashioned by an expert forger, but it was a copy of the Shroud of Antioch all the same.

Vidal glanced across the chamber to his manservant. 'A forgery, Bonal. One of the best I have seen, but counterfeit all the same.'

'I am sorry to hear it, my lord.'

'So am I.'

Vidal rolled up the delicate cloth and returned it to its leather container.

'Two things interest me, Bonal. First, why, having been missing for some five years, should the Shroud – the alleged Shroud – suddenly come to light now? I am also interested to know whether the gentleman from whom we acquired it was aware it is a forgery. That's to say, if he is party to the deception, or whether he has also been duped.'

'Shall I ask him to wait upon you, my lord?'

Vidal shook his head. 'He left for Toulouse a week ago, Bonal, in the company of his cousin. I will find occasion to talk to him there.'

'Are we to return to Toulouse, my lord?'

'As soon as I have taken my leave of my host, we will.'

'If I might make so bold, Monsignor . . .'

'Yes?'

'It occurs to me that the city fathers would be impressed by a man of action. When they consider the nominations for the next Bishop of Toulouse, surely to have retrieved the Shroud would strengthen your position.'

'I'm aware of that, Bonal. Why do you think I'm going to so much trouble?'

'Of course, Monsignor, forgive me for expressing myself poorly. My suggestion was more that it might be worth making it known that you are, and at your own expense, engaged in the search for the Shroud. It would demonstrate how you not only have money to fund such an endeavour, but also that you are a man of action. Unlike the current Bishop of Toulouse, who speaks much yet does so little.'

'There is wisdom in what you say, Bonal. I will think on it.'

'You might even let it be known that your quest has been successful.'

Vidal considered his words. 'Are you suggesting that I should – though I know it to be false – present this as the true relic recovered?'

Bonal bowed and Vidal realised his servant had lodged an idea in his mind, like a splinter, that would be hard to ignore.

He considered going into Saint-Nazaire to pray for guidance. It was Lent, and the sight of him kneeling before the altar would give comfort to the many novices and young priests of the cathedral. It was the sort of gesture that would not go unnoticed.

Vidal decided against it. His thoughts would not be still and he was now impatient to be gone. Too much time had been wasted on acquiring this false relic. Now, the hints Piet had dropped – about not letting any harm come to the Shroud – made sense. He suspected Piet was responsible for the forgery, too.

He was also frustrated with himself. Two weeks ago, buoyed by the belief that the true relic was about to come into his possession, Vidal had allowed nostalgia for their shared past to influence his decision. Rather than handing Piet over to the Carcassonne garrison, to be held on the charge of murdering Michel Cazès, he had ordered Bonal to let him go free. He had, too, a genuine concern for any testimony Piet might give under duress.

'You say Reydon gives his services at the Huguenot almshouse in Toulouse.'

'Yes, Monsignor. A breeding ground for heresy, though they claim to be engaged only in charitable works.'

'When I am bishop, I will close it down . . .' He waved his

hand. 'But, meanwhile, we will have no trouble laying our hands on him.'

The Bastide

'But that is half what the books are worth,' Bernard protested. 'Less than half. The English Book of Hours alone would raise more than you offer for my entire stock.'

The rival bookseller scratched at a pustule on his face until it started to bleed. Minou had warned him their neighbour was rarely there and had let his shop fall into disrepair. The thought of his treasures, his beautiful books, in the hands of such an uncouth individual filled him with despair.

The man shrugged. 'You're the one who came seeking me out, Joubert, not the other way around. I said I might be able to take a few volumes off your hands. Not all the foreign stuff. But stories, you know.' His eyes sparked. 'With a bit of spice to them, that kind of thing.'

'I had thought to receive a fair price,' Bernard countered weakly.

'Monsieur Joubert, we are businessmen, you and I. You need to raise a little capital, I'm prepared to help you out. A favour, if you will. It's up to you. If you don't want to sell, it's all the same to me.'

The man turned to go back inside. Bernard felt his heart crack. To give away so much of what he and Florence had worked for – that Minou had struggled to keep going during this long winter – was a betrayal. But he had no choice. He needed to leave Cécile with enough money to look after Alis while he was gone, to fund the return journey to Puivert and provide lodging while he was in the mountains.

'No, wait,' he said. 'I accept your price.'

At that moment, Charles Sanchez came shambling down rue du Marché babbling under his breath.

'Bloody idiot,' the man shouted. 'Get away with you. Go on or I'll set the dogs on you!'

'He means no harm,' Bernard muttered.

'The clouds have secrets, secrets, the clouds have secrets,' Charles chanted, his words getting faster and faster as he ran. 'Sshh. Don't tell, a secret. Don't tell!'

He ran to the end of the street and only just avoided falling under the wheels of a carriage being driven at speed up rue Carrière Mage. Bernard recognised, with a start, the black doors and golden crest of the insignia of the Bishop of Toulouse. He had grim cause to remember it. He had last seen the coach standing outside the courthouse when he and Michel were released from prison. Why should it now be in Carcassonne?

'Well?'

'Come inside, Monsieur,' Bernard said, despising himself for even speaking to such a man. 'We can conclude our business in private.'

He is dead, and I rejoice at it.

My husband, the blackest villain that ever drew breath, is dead. May his body rot in the cold ground. May his soul be in torment forever.

The funeral will take place one week from today. I will stand at his graveside, veiled and robed in black, and weep. I will play my part. The wronged wife who yet remained dutiful and constant and virtuous to the end. Once I have sole possession of these lands, who will doubt my version of the story? Who will dare raise their voice to tell a different tale?

Despite my attempts to stop his mouth, in his dying days he cried out. Rumours of a Will attested that altered the succession and disposition of his lands. Truth, or delirium? If true, who told him and when? The servants whisper and gossip of it, despite the promise of punishment. Like smoke through the cracks in the walls, the story of an heir to Puivert is slipping out beyond the castle to the village.

I have looked in every place. In my husband's private chambers, in his estate offices, in every corner of the keep and musicians' gallery, and discovered nothing. I should take comfort in this, for if I cannot find the Will, then what chance of another finding it?

I must secure my position.

When my husband's coffin is in the ground, I will let it be known that there is a quickening in my belly. How my last gift, as an obedient wife, was to give to my dying husband the comfort he craved and how, from that act of duty, came this longed-for blessing. My belly is swollen and, the Lord knows, I am too ripe to pass for being in the first months of pregnancy. But I am carrying low and my winter clothes are heavy.

In fact, this too will help my cause. My condition will explain my husband's last, delirious confession of a child. Not one of years past, but rather a child as yet unborn. There are few who will doubt it for, as the maids of the village know, my honourable husband was ruled by what hung between his legs. That he was no longer capable is knowledge that only he and I shared. That the creature growing in my belly is not his, is known only to me and to God.

Next, I shall declare it is my intention to undertake a pilgrimage to seek the Lord's blessing for the safe deliverance of the child. My absence from the castle estate so soon after my husband's death must be accounted for. There was a time when I thought my lover might be persuaded to act on my behalf. But God has shown me that this duty is mine. It is as it is written.

There is a time to be born. There is also a time to die.

CHAPTER TWENTY-FIVE

⚜

TOULOUSE
Thursday, 2nd April

Minou opened her casement window and looked out over rue du Taur.

Winter had given way to spring. On the plains beyond Toulouse, she could see the first shoots of barley and wheat. White hawthorn and glimpses of yellow broom in the hedgerows. Within the city walls, and along the banks of the river Garonne, trees were coming back into leaf. Toulouse was a city of shimmering greens, the skies above *la ville rose* a forget-me-not blue, white clouds and purple violets flourishing in window boxes. When the sun rose at dawn and fell back to earth at dusk, it lit the rust-brick buildings, sparking like a tinder box, until the whole city glistened a fiery copper and gold.

Here, now, was home.

It was barely three weeks since Minou had stood with her arm on Aimeric's shoulder, looking down on Toulouse from a distance. Not even one month, yet she felt as if she had lived here all her life. Of course, she missed her father and her little sister's sweet company, and worried about them. From time to time, she thought fondly of their neighbours in rue du Marché, but with each passing day Carcassonne drifted further away. A place she thought of with affection and nostalgia but, like a favourite toy from childhood gathering dust on a shelf, it belonged to a life now gone.

Minou spent much of her time within the confines of her aunt's house – in Toulouse it was not considered appropriate for a young woman of a good family to go about unchaperoned – so she took every opportunity to accompany her aunt when she went out. Minou was beguiled by the monumental churches and the Basilica, the sweeping arches and soaring bell towers piercing the skyline. She visited the modest medieval convents standing cheek by jowl with the imposing monasteries of the teaching friars, the twisted gargoyles of the Augustinians and the octagonal spire of the Jacobins, like an ornate dovecote fashioned in the same red brick that gave Toulouse its affectionate name. She revelled in the wide modern streets so generous that two carriages could pass one another side by side. She saw, from a distance in the fields beyond the Porte Villeneuve, the magnificent new Huguenot temple, with its soaring wooden steeple and roof.

Even the river in Toulouse was grander, the broadest stretch of water Minou had ever seen. Four times as wide as the Aude, the Garonne was filled with boats and cargo ships catching the wind to sail down to Bordeaux and away to sea. Pleasure barges that carried the noble families of Toulouse to masques and entertainments in grand houses further downstream. On the far side of the river was the garden suburb of Saint-Cyprien, linked to Toulouse by a covered bridge, crammed with shops offering the finest cloth from the Orient, spices from the Indies, jewels and stalls selling the wonderful blue dye, *pastel*, on which Toulouse's modern prosperity was founded.

And somewhere in this teeming city was Piet.

Minou looked for him wherever she went: in the morning in Place Saint-Georges; in the late afternoon from her window, when students swarmed out of the nearby colleges to hand out leaflets and to argue and debate; at dusk, in the university quarter itself, where Piet's lodgings were to be found, only a stone's throw from the Boussay residence on rue du Taur.

Her aunt's house, ornate and well-appointed, was three-storeys high and built in the traditional red Toulousain brick. The design was Italian, her aunt told her, much like the houses of Venetian or Florentine merchants. Her uncle had employed an architect from Lombardy, at great expense, to create carved pillars in a classical form boasting grapes and ears of corn, sunflowers and vines, acanthus and ivy. Constructed around a small inner courtyard, there were external balconies on the west side of the house, with polished wooden floorboards and shallow stairs. There was even a small private chapel with a painted ceiling. To Minou's eye, everything was still a little too new, a little garish, as if the house had not yet had time to settle into its own skin.

'*Paysanne!* You stupid, clumsy girl!'

Minou pitied the poor servant who was on the receiving end of Madame Montfort's anger. It did not bode well for the day ahead if she was already in an ill temper. Moments later, the door to her chamber flew open and Madame Montfort stormed in, the house keys pendulous at her waist, followed by a maid struggling beneath the weight of a heavy gown. Her uncle's widowed sister, Madame Montfort was the one who ran the household rather than her aunt, and always, it seemed, took pleasure in finding fault.

'You have not finished your toilette, Marguerite? You will make us late.'

Minou felt the familiar twist in her stomach. She had done everything to make herself agreeable, but nothing made any difference. Madame Montfort passed sly comments about Minou's height – 'unnatural and mannish' – commented that to have one blue eye and one brown suggested some 'moral deficiency', and judged that to be known by a diminutive at her age was 'childish'. Minou was careful always to be on her guard. Were her Aunt Boussay not so easily upset, Minou would have tried to talk to her about the influence Madame Montfort wielded.

'I will be ready. The last thing I would wish is to offend my aunt by making her wait upon my arrival.'

'It is God you should fear to offend.'

Minou held her tongue. Her father had counselled her to keep her opinions to herself. 'Do not argue or contradict,' he had warned, 'for it is a devout and observant household. And guard your brother well. Aimeric is restless and easily bored. He is likely to give offence.'

Minou had promised she would watch him like a hawk. She assumed, though it was never spoken out loud, that it was her father's hope that her childless aunt might remember her poor Carcassonnais relations in her Will, perhaps even name Aimeric as her sole heir. Standing at the Porte Narbonnaise in La Cité, with the fierce March wind stealing the breath from her lungs, Minou remembered teasing her father that he was worrying too much. Now, if anything, she feared it was the opposite.

Madame Montfort finished counting the linens in the chest at the foot of the bed and stood erect, the heavy ring of household keys at her waist, her embroidered sleeves slashed with red silk. Minou felt a sudden, swooping giddiness.

'What is the matter? Are you ill?'

'No. I am tired, nothing more,' she replied quickly.

Last evening, the household had sat vigil in preparation for the feast day of a local saint, St Salvador, in the hot and airless private chapel. Minou had hardly dared breathe. The heavy scent of the beeswax candles, the sharp tang of the smelling salts, the click-click of her aunt's prayer beads, the sourness of the spiced wine taken as the vigil came to its end.

'Indeed? I wonder at it. Your aunt and I find ourselves invigorated by our devotions not fatigued by them.'

Minou smiled. 'I do not doubt it, Madame. For my part, after the vigil, I spent time in private prayer. It is that, I fear, that took the remains of the night from me.'

Madame Montfort's eyes narrowed. 'In Toulouse, it is not private prayer that matters, whatever the custom in the countryside.'

'I am unaware of the practices of the country, but in Carcassonne we do not believe public devotion precludes the duty of private protestations of faith. Both are important, are they not?'

She met the older woman's gaze. Minou could see how dearly Madame Montfort wished to strike her a blow across the cheek for her impudence. Her hands tightened until the knuckles were white.

'Your aunt wishes you to accompany her in the procession.'

'I am delighted to do so and honoured by the invitation.' Then, before she had a moment to think about the wisdom of the question, she added: 'Is Aimeric also to come?'

Malice flashed in Madame Montfort's eyes. 'Indeed, he is not. It appears that your brother persuaded one of the kitchen boys to bring him something to eat after the vigil concluded. The servant has been beaten. Your brother is confined to his quarters.'

Minou's heart sank. Since the purpose of the vigil was to prepare themselves for today's procession, nothing but water should have passed her brother's lips. She had explained this to Aimeric several times.

'I will apologise to my aunt and uncle on my brother's

behalf,' Minou interrupted, unable to listen further. 'I do not excuse Aimeric's behaviour, but he is young.'

'He is thirteen! Quite old enough to know better! I'm sure I would not expect any son of mine to so abuse a host's hospitality.'

Minou bit her lip. There was no sense in antagonising Madame Montfort further and, on this occasion, Aimeric was at fault.

'The hour grows late,' Madame Montfort snapped, as if it was Minou who had kept her waiting. 'Your aunt bade me to invite you to wear this.'

Minou's spirits dipped lower. Though she had once been a pretty woman, her aunt was shorter than Minou and stout, so there was little hope that the garments would be a good fit. Madame Boussay loved clothes but had no natural eye for what suited her. Like a magpie, she gathered every crumb of information about what was worn in Paris: the colours that were in favour, those that were not; the width of skirts, of ruffs and partlets, of farthingales, of hoods. Lonely and bored in this big house, her aunt fretted endlessly about every tiny detail of cut or adornment.

'It is most kind of my aunt,' she said.

'It is not a matter of kindness,' Madame Montfort snapped, 'so much as a concern that what passes muster in Carcassonne will not be suitable in a city such as Toulouse.'

'Once more, I fear Carcassonne has been misrepresented to you, Madame. News of the latest fashions of the court reaches us too.'

'Which court?' Madame Montfort asked sharply. 'Nérac? I have heard that Huguenots are in the ascendant in certain parts of the Midi. They say the women there, even those of good society, go about in public without corsets and with their hair uncovered. And was there not some trouble with your father's premises, some accusation of—'

'I was referring to the royal court in Paris. I have no knowledge of the Protestant court of Navarre.'

'How dare you interrupt me?' Madame Montfort hissed, before remembering that this was her brother's niece, not a servant. She turned on the chambermaid instead. 'You! Why are you standing doing nothing? Hurry!'

The maid rushed to take Minou's kirtle from the wardrobe, releasing the scent of muslin and powder into the room. Minou stepped into her petticoat and stays, sucking in her breath as the girl pulled the cords, then lifted her arms for the bodice and sleeves.

Madame Montfort was prowling around the chamber, examining Minou's personal possessions; fingering her tortoiseshell comb, a lace ruff she was stitching herself, then her mother's rosary. Plain round beads of box wood and a modest crucifix, it was a far cry from Madame Montfort's elaborate double-decade of carved ivory beads and a silver cross tied to her belt.

'If you might pin the partlet tighter at the top . . .' Minou measured the distance. 'A *pouce*, or two.'

'There is no time for such vanity,' Madame Montfort snapped, 'it will do as it is. Your whole attention should be on God, Marguerite, not your appearance. Do not be late.'

The older woman rubbed Minou's mother's beads between her fingers, then dropped them back to the nightstand with such a look of scorn that, in that moment, Minou hated her.

Minou kicked the door shut after her, as she left. 'Do not be late,' she mimicked. 'In Toulouse, it is public prayer that matters.'

She dragged the comb through her hair, then twisted it

roughly into two plaits, before standing back and looking at herself in the pane of the window. Her ill humour vanished. Whatever Madame Montfort's intention had been, the borrowed gown suited her well. Though the bodice was too large, and the hem of the skirt creased where it had been let down, the texture and sheen of the velvet was beautiful. Minou was not a vain woman but, as she spun round, she took pleasure in how fine she looked.

Her aunt had given her an embroidered red cloak as a welcoming gift and she had worn it most days. But it would not match the brown dress, so she decided to wear her own green travelling cloak instead. Taking it from the hook on the back of the door, Minou was vexed to see it was still splattered with mud from her journey from Carcassonne.

Minou laid the cloak on the table and, using the stiff boot brush, rubbed vigorously, hard strokes back and forth, until the bristles snagged and the heavy wool rucked. She thrust impatient fingers into the lining to get rid of the obstruction, and drew out the letter with the red seal: the two initials, a B and a P, the hideous creature with talons and a forked tail. And her full name drawn in rough block capitals – MADEMOISELLE MARGUERITE JOUBERT.

In an instant, Minou was back in her father's bookshop picking up the letter from beneath the mat. She remembered with a thud of her heart how she had intended to speak to her father. Then the maelstrom of events, of the rest of that day and the next, that had pushed it from her mind. How extraordinary that it had been nestling inside her cloak all this time.

SHE KNOWS THAT YOU LIVE.

Minou held the note a moment longer, wondering again who had sent it and why, before hiding it beneath her mattress.

Since arriving in Toulouse, Minou had twice written to her father and paid a travelling pedlar to take her letters. He was a Carcassonnais man, so she was hopeful they had been delivered even though she had not yet received any reply. All the same, she resolved to write again this evening to ask what her father thought of the strange, haunting message.

For the first time since her arrival in Toulouse, Minou felt truly homesick.

CHAPTER TWENTY-SIX

⚜

Piet looked out of his casement window onto rue des Pénitents Gris, and saw only shadows. A stooped woman was walking slowly up and down with a panier brim-full of purple violets cradled in her arms. A pair of students looked around to see if they were being observed before rattling on the handle of the Protestant bookshop. There was nothing unusual to see, nothing out of place.

Even so . . .

For the past few weeks, Piet had felt sure he was being followed. Going to and from his lodgings to the almshouse in rue du Périgord, walking to the temple and back, he had felt a pricking on the back of his neck, an uneasiness beneath his ribs.

'Is something wrong?' McCone asked. 'Are you expecting someone?'

'No. At least, I had hoped for a message. It's not important.' Piet had delivered the letter some days past and had expected a reply before now. He turned. 'My apologies, McCone. I am a poor host.' He picked up the jug of wine from the table and held it up. 'Can I refill your cup? What you English call a splash of Dutch courage.'

'Thank you, no.' McCone pulled at a loose thread on his black cloak. 'I would that today was over.'

'At what time is the funeral?'

'At noon.'

The woman who had died was the wife of the most generous

of the supporters of the temple, a Protestant merchant with whom McCone had built a friendship.

'The cortège will make its way through faubourg Saint-Michel to our burial ground near the Porte Villeneuve.'

'Is Jean Barrelles attending?'

'Yes. Though he does not approve of such Catholic rituals, her husband wishes there to be some marking of the moment. He has asked Pastor Barrelles to say a prayer in the temple once she is laid in the ground.'

'I am glad to hear it,' Piet said. He had come to like McCone, enough to invite him to his lodgings today. He hadn't yet taken him to the almshouse, though he would. All the same, he was still careful. He could look a Dutchman in the eye, a Frenchman in the eye, and read the truth of their character. But an Englishman? So much of what they meant lay unsaid beneath the surface of their words.

'You don't sympathise with Barrelles' stance?'

Piet shrugged. 'I am aware Calvin preaches against such old ways, but I believe these rituals are as much for us left behind as for the person who has passed to a better place. Can they do any harm?'

McCone shook his head. 'How could they?'

For a moment, they were silent, their sombre moods reflected in the furrow of their foreheads and darkened eyes.

'You were a student here in Toulouse?' McCone asked.

'I was.' Piet leant back on the window ledge. 'Why do you ask?'

The Englishman shrugged. 'No reason. Curiosity. You know more of doctrine, of the law also, than most common soldiers. Or labourers,' he said, gesturing to Piet's clothing. 'You know the city well and speak of past events here as if you were witness to them.' McCone paused. 'Men listen to you. They would follow if you chose to lead them, Joubert.'

The borrowed name still caught Piet by surprise. Several times it had been on the tip of his tongue to tell McCone the truth, but somehow the right moment never came.

'Toulouse has the leaders she needs in Saux and Hunault,' he said. 'I am content to follow and to give my service in other ways.'

'How goes it at the almshouse?'

'We are full to overflowing,' Piet said. 'So many women and children left without any means of support. Refugees mostly, fleeing the conflict in the north, but we also house other desperate souls from within the city.' He shrugged. 'We do what we can.'

'It is good work.'

Piet took a sip of his drink. 'To satisfy your curiosity, I was a student in Toulouse, but at the Collège de Foix rather than the university.' He laughed at the surprise on the Englishman's face. 'Yes, I spent my formative years in the company of monks, priests and the most pious – not to say indulged – of Toulouse's favoured Catholic sons. Many of them went straight into Holy Orders without ever experiencing life, others to run their family business or manage their fathers' estates.' He raised his hands. 'But it was a good education. I have no complaints. I had hoped to be a lawyer or a notary, but it was not to be.'

'What prevented you?'

'Everything the monks taught me conspired to make me less of a Catholic, not more. Made me doubt their words and their methods. The whole machinery of the Church seemed designed to benefit the few, the bishops and the clergy, at the expense of the many. By the time my studies were complete, I was looking for different answers. I heard a Huguenot pastor preaching in Place Saint-Georges one day and what he said impressed me.'

'Why didn't you return to Amsterdam?'

'There's nothing left for me there,' he said, not inclined to share his memories of his mother. 'After finishing my studies, I spent time in England, before finding myself fighting in the Prince of Condé's army in the Loire. The soldier's life was not for me either, so I returned to Toulouse to do what I could here.'

McCone nodded. 'Things were different in England. I was an apprentice to a master carpenter, but these were the years of Queen Mary and the pyres were burning day and night. I fled to Geneva, thinking to study under Calvin. But the moment I set foot in the city I realised I hadn't the wit or the fire in my belly to become a preacher.' McCone smiled ruefully. 'And, to speak plainly, I realised that in truth all I wanted was to have enough to eat, companionship, a roof over my head and to be allowed to pass the Lord's day in peace. I had no desire to convert men or force them to my way of thinking.'

'That's it,' Piet said. 'To be treated fairly, for all men to be allowed to live as they choose within the law. Not to have every waking minute of every day determined by one's faith.' He nodded. 'I believe we understand one another, English.'

McCone smiled. 'I think we do.'

Vidal looked from the window of his priest's cell into the physic garden. The herb beds were rich and full of leaf, the first purple sprigs of lavender coming into flower. On the far side of the cloisters, the soft yellow glow from the candles in the cathedral sent diamonds of coloured light flickering like fireflies. He could hear the murmur of his brother clergy preparing for the noonday prayers and wondered if his absence would be noticed.

At a knock at the door, Vidal crossed himself and touched his fingers to his lips, then stood up. He had been there so long that his knees left an imprint in the embroidered hassock of the prie-dieu. Vidal had prayed for guidance, but there had been only silence.

'Come,' he said.

Bonal entered the chamber.

'Well? Has he talked?'

'He has not.'

Vidal turned around, hearing the hesitation in the servant's voice. 'He has said nothing? Nothing at all?'

'No, Monsignor.'

'They stretched him?'

'They did.'

Vidal frowned. 'And, even then, you are telling me he did not reveal the name of the man who commissioned him to make a copy of the Shroud?'

Bonal shifted uneasily. 'The inquisitor sends his humble apologies, but has bid me inform you that the gaoler, such was his desire to provide you with the information you require, did not exercise appropriate caution. The forger had, so it seems, a weak heart. His constitution was unable to withstand even the most moderate persuasion.'

Vidal took a step forward. 'Are you saying they've killed him?'

Bonal nodded.

'How could they be so careless?' He banged his fist on the wooden frame of the prie-dieu. 'Where's the body now?'

'They await your orders.' Bonal paused. 'If I might be so bold as to make a suggestion, Monsignor?'

Vidal waved his hand. 'Speak.'

'Since it was fear that stopped his heart, we could return the corpse to the man's workshop in the quartier Daurade and let it be discovered there. No one will know the Inquisition had any role in the matter.'

Vidal considered, then nodded. 'A sound idea, Bonal. And set a watch on the premises to see who comes calling. There is a daughter who lives with him, I believe.'

'There is.'

'Don't let her see you.'

Vidal fished a denier from inside his robes. Bonal was a rough man and occasionally over-stepped the mark, as he had with the landlady at the boarding house in Carcassonne. But he was cunning, entirely without conscience and knew how to hold his tongue.

'This also came for you, Monsignor.'

Vidal took the letter, slid his finger beneath the crease and cracked the wax.

'When was this delivered?'

'An urchin brought it to the chapter house earlier today.'

Vidal read the note, then his fist curled around the paper, crushing the words into a ball. His fingers began to drum on the wooden back of the chair, faster and faster.

'Find the boy,' he said. 'I would know how he came by this.'

Piet leant back against the sill. 'If you wish to be in faubourg Saint-Michel when the cortège moves off, you should leave. Time is passing.'

McCone stood up. 'I pray there will be no trouble.'

'You think there might?'

'There have been threats. The dead woman's family –

staunch Catholics – have issued several ultimatums. First, when they knew she was dying, they sent a priest to the house to administer extreme unction. He was refused entry. When she died, they attempted to persuade the husband to hand her body over so she could have, as they put it, a Christian burial!'

'I heard something of this. Did they not petition Parliament on the matter?'

'Yes. Their petition was rejected. The judges – Catholic to a man, of course – expressed their sympathy, but admitted they had no power to prevent a husband burying his wife in the manner he saw fit, provided it complied with the laws of the city.'

'And he has made certain of that?'

'He has,' McCone said. 'He has magistrates and attorneys of his acquaintance to call upon for advice.'

'Well, then, I cannot see what more they can do. Besides, the widower is a man of influence and wealth. I do not think that the family would risk offending him further, especially since the Court already ruled against them.'

'I hope you're right. The worst of it is that she would dislike all the fuss. She was devout and humble in her ways, a true gentlewoman.' McCone took up his hat. 'Are you coming?'

Since he had not known the lady in question or her husband, Piet felt under no personal obligation. He had to check the weekly accounts books at the almshouse, then he intended to seek out the tailor he had paid to copy the Shroud in his workshop.

'I will join you at the temple later, after the funeral,' he said.

'Very well. I will look out for you there.' McCone walked to the door. 'But Piet, if you do venture out, you might want to do something about . . .' He tapped his head. 'With hair that colour, you could be a cousin of our Queen Bess.'

Piet looked down at his hands, and saw his fingers were dusty with charcoal. His natural red was showing through, in his beard also. He laughed.

'Do we not live in strange times, McCone, when a man cannot walk in the world looking as God made him?'

CHAPTER TWENTY-SEVEN

La Cité

'When will Minou come home?' Alis said, for the tenth time that day, before being overtaken by another bout of coughing.

'Hush, child.' Madame Noubel was holding a dish of hot water with thyme beneath the little girl's chin. She was worried. Alis's skin had taken on the pallor of chalk and dark shadows smudged beneath her eyes.

'I miss her. And Papa.'

'As do I.'

'Will she be back by Ascension Day?'

'Minou will come home as soon as she can.'

'But she promised I could sit vigil with her in the cathedral. That I could stay up all night long, now I am old enough.'

'If she is not back by then, I will take you.'

'I want Minou to take me,' Alis whispered, folding back into herself.

'April will soon be over, then it will be May. The time will go faster than you think. Imagine all the things you'll have to tell Minou when she does come home. And your father, too. Won't they find you quite grown up, taller by this far at least?' She marked the air with her hand and was rewarded with a smile. 'I warrant we should expect another letter soon. Telling us all about her elegant life in Toulouse.'

'Will she take me back with her?'

'We'll see.' Madame Noubel smiled. 'Does she not love you most of her sisters?'

'I am her only sister.' Alis gave her usual answer, but Madame Noubel could hear her heart wasn't in it.

The little girl's eyes started to close. The tabby kitten, brought from the Bastide as a companion for Alis, jumped up onto the chair. For once, Madame Noubel did not shoo it away.

Alis had barely slept last evening, the repeated bouts of coughing serious enough for Madame Noubel to consider sending word to Minou. She did not want to worry her without due cause and knew Aimeric had need of Minou's presence in Toulouse as much as Alis felt the lack of it in Carcassonne. All the same, she would not forgive herself if the child—

She pushed the thought aside. Alis wasn't going to die. It was her melancholy, the absence of her family, that ailed her. Every day the weather grew milder. With the spring, Alis would improve.

Madame Noubel looked around the kitchen: at Bernard's empty chair; at Aimeric's catapult and Minou's book, all tidied away; and wondered if it might be better to take Alis to her own house after all. Here, she felt the absence of her family keenly. Perhaps in the Bastide she would be less downcast.

Rixende came into the kitchen, untying her apron. 'Is there anything more you would like me to do before I go, Madame? Anything for the little one?'

Madame Noubel shook her head. 'She will be better now the coughing has stopped,' she said. 'She misses her sister.'

'Mademoiselle Minou is like a mother to her,' Rixende said, hanging her apron on the back of the door. 'Is there any word of when the master might return?'

'It is no bus—' Madame Noubel snapped, then pulled herself up. 'If Monsieur Joubert has not returned by the tenth of the month, Rixende, I will settle what you are owed. Do not worry on that account.'

Rixende sighed. 'Thank you, Madame. I would not ask, but my family relies on me and—'

'What you are owed, you will have.'

Madame Noubel sat as the sunlight filled the yard at the back of the house and decided she would hold off writing to Minou, at least until she had received word from Bernard. He had been gone a fortnight. Had he even yet arrived in Puivert? His poor health and perhaps inclement weather in the mountains would make it slow going. She wondered if there was anyone left in the village who would remember them.

Alis had fallen asleep. Madame Noubel stroked her hair, relieved the colour was coming back to her cheeks, and softly sang the old lullaby to the troubled child.

'Bona nuèit, bona nuèit . . .
Braves amics, pica mièja-nuèit
Cal finir velhada.'

Puivert

'Hie, hie.'

Bernard Joubert clicked his tongue and his old dun mare, Canigou, lumbered over the ditch and on. Bernard's clothes and saddlebags were filthy and the white socks above his horse's hooves were hidden beneath layers of mud. The painful sores on his legs – a consequence of his imprisonment in January – were being rubbed raw again by the motion of the saddle as the ground rose and fell.

They had left Chalabre at first light, on the last leg of his pilgrimage. For once, the weather was with them. At the many crossroads, informal shrines had sprung up. Posies of pink harebells and blue forget-me-nots lay wrapped in bright ribbon; everywhere he could see crosses of twisted straw for Palm Sunday, scribbled prayers in the old language. The ancient woodlands were a meld of green and silver and, all around, the sound of birdsong.

Since leaving Carcassonne, man and beast had journeyed some fifteen leagues, keeping the snow-topped peaks of the Pyrenees ahead of them in the distance as they rode south. They had battled rain and sleet, flooded fords on the Aude and the Blau, and endured the fierce Tramontana wind. Often they found the roads near impassable in places and, elsewhere, cracked and furrowed by the winter wheels of carts and ox drays. Near Limoux, Canigou had gone lame and Bernard had lost a week waiting for her fetlock to heal.

There was also a watchful atmosphere wherever he stopped for the night. Narrowed eyes, suspicious glances. Strangers were not welcome. It had been a hard and long winter, one of the worst in living memory. Food was scarce and tempers short. Bernard had several times seen envious eyes watching as he drew a coin from his purse.

But, there was something more. The smell of fear. Rumours of the massacre of the Huguenots in Vassy had reached even these isolated villages of the Haute Vallée. The threat of being denounced terrified everyone; a man could be strung up for uttering the wrong prayer, kneeling at the wrong altar. Best to keep one's opinions to oneself and hope the trouble would pass them by.

The last time Bernard had travelled this way, nearly twenty years ago, the land had been frozen under a blanket of December snow. He had ridden his young mare hard then, terror keeping him and their precious cargo travelling through the dark, wintry night.

Joubert pulled Canigou to a halt, surprised to find his eyes pooling with tears for his beloved, lost wife. If only she had not been taken from him. Florence had always known what to do for the best.

'*Pas a pas*,' he murmured in Occitan to the old mare, pressing his aching legs into Canigou's soft belly. 'Not much longer now, girl.'

CHAPTER TWENTY-EIGHT

Toulouse

Minou looked down from the balcony onto a sea of hats and white starched ruffs.

She recognised the old gentleman who owned the bookshop in rue des Pénitents Gris – his long, trimmed grey beard hung low below his corpulent chin and jabbed at his doublet as he spoke – but mostly it was a female crowd. All lavishly overdressed in pinks and red, yellow and cerise, stiff-backed collars, embroidered bodices and velvet-trimmed hoods, like gaudy flowers in a garden bed. Some wore ornate books of hours tied to their belts, or showy rosaries of agate, coral or silver. Minou's hand went to her own waist, where she had fastened her mother's simple chaplet, and felt the better for being more plainly attired.

She scanned the faces in case Madame Montfort had had a change of heart, but there was no sign of Aimeric. Part of her was relieved. He disliked Toulouse and the petty, often arbitrary, restrictions placed upon him. He was frequently chastised for some transgression or another, last evening's misdemeanour being just one in a long line of troubles.

'There is so much at stake, Aimeric,' she had counselled as they sat in the courtyard a few days earlier. 'Our situation is precarious. I beg you, try to make yourself agreeable.'

'I do try,' he said, poking the ground with a stick. 'It would have been better if you were the boy. Everyone likes you well, except for Madame Montfort, and she hates everyone, save for Uncle's steward. She likes him. They are always in a huddle together.'

Minou was momentarily diverted. 'Are they?'

'Always. I saw them leaving the house together after dark, but two nights ago. Martineau was carrying a big, heavy bag. When he came back, it was empty.'

'Aimeric, really. You're letting your imagination run away with you. Where would they be going together, and at that time of night?'

'I'm only saying what I saw.' He shrugged. 'I hate it here. I miss Father. I miss teasing Marie. I even miss Alis, though she is annoying.' He sighed. 'I want to go home.'

Minou's heart ached for him – he was a boy who belonged out of doors, in the fields or the open spaces on the river bank, not cooped up in a town, but there was nothing to be done. For the sake of all of their futures, he had to make the best of things in Toulouse.

All the same, she vowed to confront Madame Montfort when they returned from the procession and insist that she treat Aimeric with a lighter hand.

Finally, Minou caught sight of her aunt, standing close to the wide gates that gave onto rue du Taur. She held a large open fan of feathers, though the temperature hardly merited it, and had chosen a high-backed collar, a little too tall for her neck, and crimson balloon sleeves slashed with blue to match her skirts. Her book of hours and rosary, too heavy for her belt, dragged her silhouette out of shape.

Minou felt a rush of affection. Plucked from friends and family in the modest Saint-Michel quarter, thrust into the higher echelons of Toulouse society, her aunt's open manner and informal nature set her at odds with most of the bourgeois wives. They looked down on her, and Minou could see how keenly she felt it.

Minou hurried down the stairs and slipped through the sea of people to join her. 'Good morrow, Aunt. You have quite a crowd.'

'Niece,' she said warmly. 'Oh, they are not all attending our little procession. My husband and his colleagues have an important meeting, but he was eager to walk a little of the way with me. He knows how dear I hold this feast day of St Salvador. And what a beautiful day, we are so blessed.'

'You look quite the equal of the morning, Aunt. What a fine dress, I have never seen so beautiful a colour. And thank you, too, for the generous loan of this gown. It was kind of you.'

'Well, I must own, it was my sister-in-law's idea, but it does look well on you. I would that I had your figure, but alas I have always been of less than average height.'

As the bells of Saint-Taur chimed the quarter hour, her aunt glanced anxiously to the door. 'No doubt Monsieur Boussay will be here presently. Two gentlemen from the Parliament came at first light. Inconsiderate, I call it, but they are colleagues of my husband and if he chooses to admit them at so ungodly an hour, then I would not go against his wishes. He works so very hard. So much rests upon his shoulders.'

'I know he is much relied upon.'

'Indeed so, Minou, you are so right. One of his visitors is Monsieur Delpech, a leading man of business – the wealthiest in Toulouse, some say. He is expected to be elected capitoul any day now and, though I should not say, my husband hopes some advancement might come from it. And the young priest from the cathedral. What is his name? Would that my memory was better. Such a promising man, he benefits greatly from my husband's patronage. No more than seven-and-twenty, but

Monsieur Boussay has high hopes of him. Perhaps even a future Bishop of Toulouse, though his father was much disgraced during that conspiracy when—' She broke off. 'Valentin, that was it. An odd name for a priest, though I suppose they must all be named for one saint or another . . . don't you think? What was I saying?'

'That his father had been disgraced,' Minou said.

'Indeed, more than disgraced. Executed, though I can't remember why. Ah well, it is all in the past now . . .'

Her eyes slipped away to the door once more as her voice faded.

'I am sure my uncle will be here at any moment.' Minou smiled. 'The stitching on your cloak is so fine. Quite unlike anything I have seen before. Was it made in Toulouse?'

'Oh, yes.' Madame Boussay immediately launched into a long and complicated tale of how the pattern had been copied from a garment said to be much in favour with Princess Marguerite herself, the King's sister. 'So, then I said how much I would like . . .'

Though Minou appeared to be listening, her thoughts were free. On the highest balcony, a pair of collared doves called to one another, then took flight. As she watched them spinning up into the patch of blue sky, Minou felt a moment of acute sympathy with Aimeric, remembering the liberty of her daily walks to and from the Bastide, remembering what it was to live unobserved.

'It is very fortunate to have someone so close at hand. Her father's workshop is in the quartier Daurade and, though they are Huguenots, she is more skilled with a needle than any Catholic seamstress I've found.'

'Quite,' Minou murmured.

As her aunt's words continued to ebb and flow, Minou

hoped Aimeric would find something to occupy him in his chamber. Madame Montfort was sure to have locked him in and, since the household keys were kept always at her waist, Minou feared her brother was in for a long afternoon. Her thoughts slipped to her sister in Carcassonne. She hoped her father was giving Alis the liquorice root to soothe her throat and had remembered to cut back the dead wood from the rambling wild rose above the door to let the new growth flourish.

Her aunt's voice drew Minou back.

'Though there are many skilled seamstresses and tailors in this part of the city, too. Indeed, that is one of the reasons my husband chose to build our house here. He always puts me first.' Her aunt lowered her voice. 'Mind you, he might have thought twice had we known a Protestant *maison de charité* would be set up on our doorstep in rue du Périgord. It's a scandal. Such people milling about the streets, filthy, begging. They should all be sent back to where they came from.'

'Maybe they have nowhere else to go,' Minou murmured, wondering if her aunt actually thought this or if she was simply repeating things her husband had said.

'And as for the humanist college next door, that attracts the most unsavoury types, I cannot begin to tell you. Atheists, Moors with skin as black as coal.' She dropped her voice to a whisper. 'I wouldn't be surprised if there were Jews in there as well, though of course it is the Huguenots who are the worst. Quite taking over the whole street, and the quartier Daurade, too. I am certain it was Protestants responsible for the loss of our priceless relic from the Eglise Saint-Taur.'

Minou was becoming a little dazed with the leaps and jumps of conversation. 'A relic, Aunt?'

'Don't you remember? It was quite the scandal. The Shroud of Antioch was stolen from the reliquary in plain view, five years ago it must have been. It is not the entire winding cloth, of course, just a part of it, but even so. I wonder that you can't remember, it was quite a scandal.'

Minou smiled warmly. 'I have only been in Toulouse for a little over three weeks, dear Aunt.'

'Well, so you have! You are so much one of the family now, I forget.' She gave an extravagant flap of her fan, then dropped her voice again. 'I am a charitable woman, Niece. Live and let live is my motto. But I tell you, I hardly recognise my own city with all these outsiders moving in. I wouldn't mind if they kept themselves to themselves, but they are always out there shouting about this grievance or that. It is to be hoped that now they have built themselves a temple, they will stay inside it and not spoil things for everyone else.' She sighed. 'But I digress. The point of what I am saying is that Monsieur Boussay always puts my needs above his own.'

'I have observed it.' Minou spoke carefully, though in truth he bullied his wife and never failed to point out her inadequacies and shortcomings.

Madame Boussay seemed on the verge of launching into another circuitous tale when the steward, Martineau, clapped his hands.

'*Mesdames, messieurs, s'il vous plaît.* Pray be silent for Monsieur Boussay.'

Minou hid a smile, imagining how her father would react to such self-important posturing. Her uncle was not even a capitoul, merely the secretary to one, but he gave the impression that he was the most important man in the Hôtel de Ville.

The steward clapped again. 'My lords and ladies, I present to you, Monsieur Boussay.'

Minou's uncle strode into the courtyard, his frame swaddled in official garments, sporting a ruff too tight for his fat neck. Three men were with him. She grimaced at the sight of the Abbot of the order of the Preaching Friars. A weasel-eyed man, with wandering hands, he had pushed her against a wall the last time he had visited and tried to kiss her. Damp hands and wet lips, gasping like a landed fish.

The second wore similar robes to her uncle, another secretary to a capitoul – from the Hôtel de Ville, she assumed. The third was younger, dressed in a yellow doublet and silk hose, with short padded breeches and a Spanish cloak. Minou frowned. He looked familiar, though she could not place him. Sensing her scrutiny, he looked over and nodded a greeting, but without giving the impression that he recognised her in return. All four men looked to be in ill temper.

Monsieur Boussay did not apologise to his wife for keeping her waiting.

'Wife,' he said sharply.

Minou saw the pleasure slip from her aunt's face as she gently put her hand in the small of her back to propel her forward to her husband's side, and felt her wince.

'Is something wrong, Aunt?' she asked.

'No, nothing,' she said, glancing at her husband. 'I am a little stiff this morning, that is all.'

Madame Boussay placed her hand on her husband's arm. The servants opened wide the gates that gave from the courtyard and Monsieur Boussay and his wife led their guests out into the street. Minou could not help glancing over her shoulder in the direction of the university buildings. For the hundredth time, she cursed the modesty that had prevented her asking for the precise address of Piet's lodgings.

CHAPTER TWENTY-NINE

⚜

The letter was written in the same hand with the same wax seal. Vidal had prayed for guidance again and again. God had remained silent.

He had never intended things to go so far. A winter's night six months past. Bare skin wrapped in furs, his blood heated by the wine and the exhilaration of the illicit chase, a kind of madness had come over him.

The following morning, he had woken with regret and shame and swore it would never happen again. For a few days, he kept his word. Then there had been another night, then a third and a fourth. He assumed the affair would finish when the Church summoned him back, though he knew he would miss the comfort she gave him. Mountains, hills, the roads between them. Yet, she had come. She was here in Toulouse, installed within a stone's throw of the chapter house, waiting for him.

He could ill afford any whisper of scandal. What might be kept secret within the walls of a château perched high above a mountain village could never be so in Toulouse. People looked to him. His actions, his words, his presence at every moment of significance – all were under scrutiny. He believed he had every chance of being named as the next Bishop of Toulouse and, though he was young, he was sure he could muster enough support in Rome to be appointed a cardinal soon after that.

No, the affair had to stop, but he had to end it carefully and with propriety. They must remain cordial with one another for, though she was only a woman, she was not an enemy he would wish to have. Indeed, it was her strength that had first attracted him to her. He had decided to go to her today only to tell her that their intimacy could not continue.

Vidal's thoughts slipped to the Shroud, as so often they did. Bonal's suggestion that he might produce the counterfeit Shroud, and challenge any to distinguish it from the true relic, still whispered in his ear.

He shook his head. The imprint of the body of the Son of God was what gave the holy relic its potency, its grace. The fragment he had in his possession, however exquisite a forgery, was a piece of material, nothing more, nothing less. A replica could not work miracles.

Yet, the idea did not entirely leave him.

Vidal summoned his servant, changed into dark robes and a long black cloak that would afford him anonymity, then set off with Bonal at his side, still appalled that she had established herself so close to the Episcopal Palace. Fortunately, at this hour, most of his brother priests would be at prayer.

He knew the house in the Impasses Sainte-Anne by reputation. The lower level fashioned from the usual red brick of Toulouse, with the upper storeys half-timbered and washed pink. There was a small courtyard at the rear of the house where she said she would be waiting.

At the gate, he stopped. 'Keep watch, I shall not be long,' he ordered Bonal.

'You have an appointment with Monsieur Delpech at—'

'I am well aware of that.'

Bonal slipped away and Vidal stood, his hand on the latch, undecided. Then, he saw her beside an apple tree, flowering white with the lightest of spring blossoms at the tips of its branches, and his heart leapt in his chest. With the sun behind her, she was a dark angel, her unbound black hair shining like jet. Vidal knew he should turn back.

But at that moment she looked up and her face was radiant. He felt powerless to resist the summons.

He stepped into the garden.

'I feared you would not come,' she said as he drew level with her.

'I cannot stay.'

He felt the warm tips of her fingers brush against his, then her hands gentle around his wrist.

'Then I ask for your forgiveness for writing to you, when I promised I would not, but I had to see you.'

'Someone will notice us,' he murmured, looking up at the windows overlooking the courtyard.

'There is no one else here,' she said, tightening her grip. He felt her other hand steal beneath the folds of his robes. 'I made sure of it.'

'Blanche, no,' he murmured, trying to push her away.

She tilted her face and he caught the scent of her perfume. He tried to ignore the stirrings of desire.

'Why do you speak harshly?' she said. 'Have you not missed me? Have you not lacked my company, my lord?'

'It is too dangerous. People are not so immersed in their own business in Toulouse that they don't have eyes to see. The situation is delicate,' he rebuked her. 'I cannot be caught in any wrong-doing.'

'How can this be wrong?' she murmured, bringing her mouth close to his ear.

'You know why, I made a vow of chastity . . .'

'An unnatural vow,' she whispered, 'one the early Church Fathers were not obliged to take.'

As always, her theological knowledge took him by surprise. He did not think it was right for a woman to debate such things and yet – she impressed him.

'Things are different now.'

'Not so different.'

Vidal placed his hands on her arms and attempted to put a distance between them. But, somehow, she was pressing against him, so close he could feel the beating of her heart. His blood rose again.

'Have I done something to offend you?' she murmured. 'When last you left me, your words were warm. Full of love.'

'I have sworn my love to God.'

She gave a light and pretty laugh. Vidal tried to bring the old saints to mind, their fortitude in the face of temptation.

'This is a sin,' he tried to say. 'We wrong my vows, and yours to your husband –'

'That is what I came to tell you,' she said, untying the ribbon at her neck. 'My husband is dead and buried, may the Lord God bless his soul.' She crossed herself. 'I belong to no man now.'

Vidal found himself cupping her beautiful face in his hands. 'Dead? This is sudden.'

'It was not unexpected. His health was failing.'

'I am sorry not to have been with you in this time of such grievous loss.'

She dipped her eyes. 'My husband is at last released from his suffering,' she said. 'He is in a better place. I mourn him, but his passing leaves me free to bestow my love where I will.'

'Blanche, you are minded to misconstrue my meaning.' He took a deep breath. 'You may be released from your conjugal vows, but I am not released from mine. My heart and soul are pledged to God, you know it. We cannot meet any more.'

He felt her stiffen in his arms. 'You have no further need of me?'

'No, not that,' he said, pity weakening his resolve. 'Never that. But I made a—'

'What can I do to prove my love for you?' she said, her voice so soft, so beguiling. 'To prove my duty to God. For by serving you, I serve Him. If I have not pleased you, then give me penance. Tell me what I must do to make things right between us.'

Vidal entwined his fingers with hers. 'You've done nothing wrong. You are beautiful and generous, you are –'

The ribbon of her cloak came fully undone and it fell from her shoulders to the ground, the pale blue material pooling like water. He saw that she wore nothing but a shift beneath. The contours of her body, the generous curve of her breasts and waist, the swell of her belly, she was even more beautiful than he remembered.

'This cannot . . .' he murmured, though the words caught in his throat.

In his imagination, Vidal forced himself onto his knees before the grand altar of the cathedral. Again, he tried to fill his head with images of the vaulted stone ceiling and the rose window, the bloodied hands and feet of Jesus upon the cross. He tried to replace the beating of his pulse with the melody of the choir, their voices soaring through the nave and up to the highest rafters. The promise of the resurrection and the life to come for those who followed Him and obeyed God's laws.

She slipped her hand between his legs. 'I wish only to give you comfort. You toil so hard for the good of others.'

Vidal closed his eyes, helpless to withstand the soft whispering of her voice.

'Those days after you had gone,' she was saying, 'I could not sleep or eat or drink. I was sick for the lack of you.'

He wanted to resist, to speak, but his throat was dry. Taking her into his arms, he carried her into the hidden shadows of the loggia.

'In Toulouse, they are talking of you as the future bishop,' she murmured. 'By Michaelmas next, even an archbishop, the youngest in Languedoc for many summers. I can help you be the man you were meant to be,' she said, and he knew he was lost. 'The greatest man of your age.'

He forgot the windows overlooking the courtyard, the sounds of Toulouse coming to life all around them, as he worked her shift up and over her smooth, white skin. He did not heed the rattle of a pail in the street or the bells of the cathedral or the restless presence of Bonal keeping watch outside the gate. He was aware of nothing but the movement of his body inside hers, desire blotting out any thought.

'Did you discover the information that I asked of you?' she murmured into his ear.

Vidal did not answer. He could not. He had lost any sense of where he was. Then he felt his head dragged back and the rough twist of her fingers in his hair, an exquisite jolt of pain as she bit his lip.

'Where is the Joubert family to be found?' she said, pressing her hand across his mouth. 'You promised you would discover this for me.' Vidal did not reply, but Blanche pushed harder until he thought his lungs would burst.

'Carcassonne,' he gasped.

As he came to his end, Vidal called out her name, no longer caring who might hear. He did not see the look of satisfaction in her dark eyes nor the blood – his blood – on her lips.

CHAPTER THIRTY

⚜

A deputation was waiting at the corner of rue du Taur. Minou watched her uncle confer with the arms dealer, Delpech, their heads together. Then, without a word, they swept away in the direction of the Hôtel de Ville, with the young man in the yellow cloak and the friar following in their wake. Madame Boussay offered a half-wave as her husband left, which went unacknowledged.

He was a boorish man, Minou thought, offended on her aunt's behalf, as they continued into the oldest quarter of Toulouse. Here, among the half-timbered houses and narrow passageways, the street names were a living reminder of the medieval trades that had brought prosperity to the city in the past: the money lenders, the cauldron makers, the butchers, the candle makers, the wool merchants and the men of law.

The sun rose higher as they walked slowly into Place du Salin, the site of the old salt market, where the trees were coming into leaf. Silver bark and the shoots budding green. Minou could not help but admire the buildings of the Treasury and Royal Mint, the imposing bevelled windows and ornate carved frames of the Parliament itself, everything speaking of power and permanence. On the corner of the square, the inquisitional court and prison stood cheek by jowl with the modern dwellings built to house the magistrates and clerks, the barristers and attorneys-at-law.

Finally, they went through the gate set deep within the high red walls, across the grassed moat and out into the southern suburb of Saint-Michel.

'Though we are no longer quite within the boundary of the city,' her aunt could not help saying, 'this district is one of distinction. A very good neighbourhood.'

'It seems so,' Minou replied loyally.

The Boussay party joined the crowd waiting outside the parish church of St Salvador. The white surplice of the priest snapped around his legs in the wind. The silver cross, polished and gleaming, caught the midday sun and sent dancing light up and along the red-brick face work of the west door of the parish church. The air was full of sound, of notes finding their pitch, as the musicians made ready. Tabors and gitterns, bagpipes with their fat leather bellies and lutes crafted from box wood. The rattle and shimmer of the mummers' tambourines.

'Did I tell you, Niece, I am named for St Salvador?' her aunt whispered, though there was no need. 'It was my mother's choice, and though I am sure I am at fault, I have always felt blessed to have so distinctive a name.'

'As you should, Aunt. It is a most gracious name.'

Her aunt smiled, dimpling her cheeks. 'I was married at this church. Such a beautiful wedding, everyone remarked upon it. No one could remember such a lavish celebration in this suburb before, not a soul.'

'Do tell me,' Minou said, though her aunt needed little encouragement to do so.

'It was a bright day, not cold, though I was all but dumb with fright. I was younger than you are now. All those eyes upon me, I was not used to it. I could barely utter my marriage vows. But it was such a good match and my mother wept that I had been chosen by such a gentleman.' She clasped Minou's hand, almost dropping her fan. One white feather came loose.

It fluttered in the breeze for an instant, before falling to the cobblestones. 'But I confess it grieves me, Niece, to think you have been robbed of the experience of having your mother there to see you married. My poor sister, taken from us before her time. It fair breaks my heart.'

Minou smiled. 'Please, do not worry. I do miss her company and guidance but, in faith, I do not think the occasion of my marriage will be worse than any other day on that account.' She squeezed her aunt's soft arm. 'And besides, if I marry, you will be there, dear Aunt, and stand for my mother.'

Madame Boussay blushed. 'Well, well, how charming that you would want me . . . and should say so. Well . . .' Her voice fell away, plump with pleasure. 'And, of course, I would be honoured. I dearly would have loved a daughter of my own, but the Lord did not see fit to bless us with the gift of children.' She tapped Minou on the arm. 'But what mean you by "if"? Of course, you will marry. You should marry, every girl should. I had already been married some four years by the time I was your age. Do you not have a suitor?' She dropped her voice lower. 'If it is a dowry you lack, well, whatever Monsieur Boussay might have to say about it, I like to think I know my duty to my own flesh and blood.'

'That is generous of you, Aunt, but I am in no hurry to wed. I am taking great pleasure in my time here in Toulouse and have no desire to bring it to an end.'

Madame Boussay waved her hand. 'No need to thank me, dear, no need at all. It is my pleasure to have young people in the house, though it has to be said Aimeric can be, well . . . his voice, so loud. His boots.'

'I own he has much to learn – and I fear Madame Montfort is rather too strict with him – but my brother is flourishing under my uncle's guidance.'

Another lie. Monsieur Boussay paid no attention to Aimeric except, occasionally, to criticise him.

'He would have liked a son of his own. What man would not?'

Minou smiled. 'Tell me, Aunt, what was my mother like?'

Madame Boussay looked bewildered. 'What was she like? Well, she was taller than me. A mass of black curls, she never could get a comb through them, and –'

Minou laughed. 'I meant in her character, Aunt. What manner of person. I would love to hear your memories of being children together.'

'Oh, oh, I see. Florence was . . . to speak frankly, it is hard to say. There was a full ten years between us and she was blessed with a sharp wit and great intelligence and I was blessed with beauty, well . . . so I am sure I was a trial to her. And, of course, though we had the same dear, dear mother, when Florence's father died and Mother married again, I regret to say my dear father had little interest in another man's daughter and, well . . . not long afterwards, Florence married and was living so far away in Puivert, we saw little of one another.'

'Puivert, you say? Did not my parents live all their married life in Carcassonne?'

Madame Boussay flustered at her hair. 'Well, Niece, I hope I have not spoken out of turn, though I cannot imagine how it would matter after all this time. But they married in Puivert, I am sure of it. Your father at that time was in the employ of Lord Bruyère, the Seigneur of the castle. At least I think that was his title. I do muddle things, I know it and my husband chastises me for it. A large estate, so I was told, with excellent hunting. The wedding was in the château itself for I remember the invitation came with a family seal on it – it depicted a horrible creature, a lion with talons. It made me cry.'

Minou was struck by the description. It sounded very like the seal on the letter now hidden beneath the mattress in her chamber.

'I wanted so much to attend,' her aunt continued, 'but I was only ten years old and my father said it was too far to travel. So I wept again, for I had wanted so to be a bridesmaid.' She frowned. 'A local woman had to stand in her place as matron of honour. Cécile. Though I can't remember her family name, I remember it was Cécile, because I thought the name so pretty and I might have it for a daughter of my own one day.' Her face fell again. 'Well, that's all past now.'

Minou felt the knot of tension in her stomach tighten suddenly remembering her father and Madame Noubel calling each other by their Christian names.

'Might it have been Cécile Cordier, Aunt?' Minou asked in a level voice, though she felt anything but calm.

'Well, do you know, I think it was. Fancy you knowing that. Anyway, to be quite truthful, I cannot remember how long your parents remained in Puivert after the wedding. Certainly, you were born there.'

Minou's throat became dry. 'Forgive me, Aunt, are you sure? I had always thought – assumed – that I was born in Carcassonne, the same as my brother and sister.'

Madame Boussay frowned. 'Again, I might be wrong, but Monsieur Boussay and I had been married some years by then, and God had not seen fit to bless us with children. So when I heard the news of your birth, it stuck with me. I was, of course, so delighted for Florence, but also sad on my own account.'

'I was born in fifteen forty-two. On the last day of October.'

'Well, then, that is right. That's what I remember. My mother was much alarmed. There were such dreadful stories of flooding in the mountain valleys, and landslides. All this at the moment Florence was delivered; my mother was quite alarmed.' She flapped her hands and, this time, dropped her fan. 'But it is such a long time ago now and, of course, life with Monsieur Boussay . . . It is hard to be a wife.' She paused. 'And, then, I am sad to say, there was the disagreement between my husband and your dear mother.'

Out of the corner of her eye, Minou saw Madame Montfort had noticed their private conversation and was pushing through the crowd to join them. Knowing they would soon be interrupted, she pressed hastily on.

'What was the cause of the estrangement between them?'

'It was a misunderstanding, no one can persuade me otherwise.' Her aunt dropped her voice yet lower. 'Though Florence and I rarely – that is to say, never – saw one another in person after she was married, my dear sister sent me the most beautiful present from Puivert to mark your birth.'

Minou frowned. 'How odd that my mother should send you a present. Is it not more customary the other way around?'

'Well, now you say that, of course, I suppose it is. But such a thoughtful gesture. A bible, with the softest leather casing and the most delightful blue ribbon to mark the pages.' She frowned. 'Monsieur Boussay took offence at it, on account of it being in the French language, and forbade me to keep it. Well, though, of course, a wife has a duty to obey her husband in all things, I did think just this once – because it was the only gift I ever had from my own poor sister – I might make up my own mind. It is the only time I've crossed him because, well . . .'

Madame Montfort's shadow fell across them. Her aunt started, like a guilty child.

'How now, Sister?' Madame Montfort said sharply, looking

from one to the other. 'You appear deep in conversation. What is it that you find of such interest, Salvadora, as to keep you talking together all this time?'

'Sister!' Madame Boussay stumbled. 'Well, well. We were . . . That is to say . . .'

'It would be a pity if private matters caused you to neglect your obligations, Salvadora. I wonder what matter has you both engaged so completely?'

Minou bent down and picked up her aunt's fan. 'My aunt dropped this. I was returning it, that is all. One feather has come loose, do you see?'

The communion bell began to toll and a ripple of anticipation spread through the crowd. The priest, in his purple cope, stepped forward. The other clergymen and laity shuffled to his side. The thurible began to swing, sending little gusts of incense, sour and hot, into the air. Banners were lifted and the congregation fell into line, the men at the front and the women and children following behind.

All the animals of the ark, Minou thought, giddy with all that her aunt had told her. Two by two by two.

'Which route does the Saint Salvador procession take?'

'We walk from here, back through the gates to Place du Salin,' Madame Boussay replied quietly, 'then we follow the line of the eastern walls, out through the Porte Montolieu, then round to make our way back to here. I asked the priest particularly. An hour or so, all told, though there are so many here today – so pleasing to see – it will take longer. And are we not blessed with the weather? There have been years, when—'

'Salvadora!' Madame Montfort snapped. 'Try to set a good example. For your husband's sake, if not on your own account.'

Minou saw her aunt shrink into herself. She squeezed Madame Boussay's arm affectionately, and she winced.

'I'm sorry, did I hurt you?'

'It's nothing, nothing, please,' she said, pulling away. Her glove and cuff separated widely enough to reveal an ugly black bruise on her wrist.

'Aunt, what on earth happened to you?'

Salvadora pulled down her sleeve. 'It is nothing,' she said quickly. 'I trapped my hand in the lid of the chest when I was dressing, it is nothing.'

'*Domine Deus Omnipotens . . .*'

Madame Boussay turned firmly towards the priest and closed her eyes. Madame Montfort displaced Minou, forcing her to walk on her own behind them, but she did not mind. It gave her time to think.

'*. . . qui ad principium . . .*'

The words became notes, and the notes became music. The mummers took up the responses as the column, like a creature waking from a winter sleep, slowly began to move forward with a heavy drumbeat marking time.

Minou placed her hands against her chest to feel the beat reverberate deep inside her. Tabor and pipe, the rise and fall of voices, the steady tread of feet. She was entranced.

All around, Toulouse was in bloom. Early geraniums, primroses of yellow and white, and everywhere purple violets. Posies of wild flowers adorned the steps of the churches they passed.

'Is not this wondrous?' her aunt called over her shoulder.

'It is glorious, yes!'

'I do believe Toulouse must be the most marvellous city on God's earth,' she continued, her sweet face pink with delight.

As they continued, Minou allowed her thoughts to fly free. What should she make of the fact that she had been born in Puivert, but that she had not been told? Or that Madame

Noubel – Cécile Cordier as was – had never mentioned she had known her parents for such a long time? Or the gift of a French bible, sent from her mother to her aunt to mark the occasion of Minou's own birth?

And within all the surprises of the day, she had an uneasy feeling there was something of even more importance she had failed to register.

CHAPTER THIRTY-ONE

⚜

Puivert

A little after noon, Bernard Joubert led Canigou into the village. The old mare had thrown a shoe and was lame again on her front leg.

He was taken aback at how familiar Puivert remained after so long an absence. He remembered exactly where the track dipped and fell away, where the orchards fanned out on the southern side of the village, where the clamour and strike of the blacksmith's anvil would be heard and where the baker collected wood for his oven. He saw a thin path, winding up through the woods where, later in the year, acorns would be found.

'Steady, girl,' he murmured, pulling gently at the bridle and Canigou lumbered to a halt. Her neck went down, her head nuzzling the dry earth. Bernard reached into the verge and dragged up a handful of fresh spring grass and offered his open hand to the grateful mare.

Puivert was oddly silent. On a Thursday, the village should have been busy with the sound of gossip and trade, wives carrying midday victuals of bread and ale to husbands working in the fields, but there was barely a sound. He felt a spark of alarm. What if plague had returned?

He glanced around and saw no painted signs on the doors to warn that a house was infected. A little further on, there was a wreath of smoke spiralling white from a chimney, like a twist of cloud. Then the silence was broken with the clinking of bells from a herd of goats on the hillside.

Still, it was strange.

Bernard led Canigou up the main street, which was little more than a track. The earth was dry beneath his feet and the only sound was the scuff of the horse's hooves turning over a stone or two, and the creak of the leather saddlebags.

He tethered her to a tree on the common ground by the well, then headed for the old white cottage at the far end of the single street. The last time he had been inside was at Toussaint in the year fifteen forty-two. On that first day of the harsh November, the single room downstairs had been warmed by a burning fire.

Should he have written to old Madame Gabignaud to warn her of his arrival? He had considered it, but caution stayed his hand. Letters could be stolen. He had not even thought to enquire ahead whether she still lived in Puivert. But she was village born and bred and had seen many winters. Where else would she be?

'You'll get no answer there, Sénher.'

Joubert turned to see an old man peering at him from over a fence.

'Is this not the house of the midwife?'

'It was,' the man replied in Occitan, the sound something between a word, and a cough. '*La levandiera. Mort.*'

'Anne Gabignaud is dead?' Bernard felt his pulse quicken, the possibility of release. If she was dead, that was one less tongue to wag. He frowned, ashamed of such unchristian thoughts.

'When did she die, Monsieur . . . ?'

'Lizier. Achille Lizier, native of Puivert.'

'It is not idle curiosity,' he hurried on. 'I knew Madame Gabignaud once.'

Lizier's eyes narrowed. 'I don't remember seeing you around here.'

'It was some years ago now.'

'I was away fighting in the Italian wars.'

'It must have been about then when I was here,' Bernard lied.

Lizier hesitated, then nodded. 'No one knows how it happened, only that she was found dead in her bed. Beginning of Lent.'

'This March just gone?'

'The same as I stand here.' He put his hand to his throat. 'The life choked out of her.'

'You are saying she was murdered?'

Lizier grimaced, revealing a mouth of rotten teeth. 'That's right. Suffocated. Pillow and slip lying ripped to shreds, like a wild animal had got in there. Pots and pans all over. Oil from her lamp all across the floor.'

Bernard felt his stomach lurch. Who would murder an old woman? What offence could she have given? Then, with the sense of matters spinning away from him, another question.

If she had been killed, why now?

'No family to speak of,' Lizier was saying, 'but she was one of us. We paid for her to be buried.' He jerked his head towards the castle. 'We didn't take a sou from them.'

'Was it a robbery? An intruder?'

'No one knows, though I will say this. She was worrying over something. Even wrote a letter, though she barely knew how to write. On a discarded piece of paper from the castle, bearing the Bruyère seal even. I gave it to my nephew to arrange the sending of it to Carcassonne.'

'Nobody was arrested for the crime?'

Lizier shook his head. 'No, though I say it's the Huguenots.'

'There are Protestants in Puivert?' Bernard asked, surprised.

The man spat again and a fleck landed on Bernard's boot. 'Cockroaches. They get everywhere.' His eyes narrowed suddenly. 'Where was it you said you hailed from?'

'Limoux,' Bernard replied, picking a town at random. He had no desire to announce his presence in the village. Even if Lizier did not recognise him, there could be others who might.

'Limoux,' Lizier grunted. 'Protestants have taken over there too, nothing but vermin.' He jerked his head towards the castle. 'He didn't stand for it. A devil, he was, heart as black as night, but he kept those sewer rats out of Puivert. None of them around here.'

Bernard felt the ground shift from under him. 'Kept them, did you say? He is gone away?'

'He ill-used my daughter,' Lizier ploughed on. 'The daughters of other men besides. What father could forgive him that? And my great-nephew is pressed into service up at the castle, more's the shame. His mother taken by the plague. Two daughters I've lost, it's not right.' He shook his head. 'One of the Devil's own he was, the late Seigneur, no doubt, but he stood firm against heretics. No Huguenots here. Not a one.'

'The Seigneur of Puivert is dead?'

'Didn't I just tell you so? Buried him a month past. Whole village ordered to attend, but not me. I refused. My daughter took her own life, on account of him. A sinner he was, everyone knew it, though we had to bow and scrape. No more right to call himself master of Puivert than me. A villain, none blacker.'

Could it be true? Bernard exhaled. The man he had feared for all these years was dead. Did it mean the secret was finally safe?

'Mind you, his wife is no better,' Lizier continued. 'Another soul as black as night, though her name proclaims the opposite.' He tapped his head. 'Hears voices, they say. Always talking to God.'

And as quickly as Bernard's fears had receded, they flowed back with full force.

'His wife died many years past,' he said carefully. 'That's what I heard.'

'His first wife, yes. Now she was a virtuous lady, too good for this world. The scurvy devil married again with indecent haste. That one ran off and left him, though he kept hold of her money. Then a few years past, he took himself a third wife, less than half his age.'

Bernard turned cold. Who knew what secrets an old goat might whisper to a young bride at night? He glanced up at the castle on the hill above the village, then back to Lizier.

'She's not even local. Comes from an estate somewhere near Saint-Antonin-Noble-Val.' Lizier leant closer. 'She was barely fifteen when she married, having been left destitute when her father died. And needing a husband to claim the bastard she was carrying.'

'She was with child when she married?'

'So they say.'

Bernard's head was spinning. 'Well, how old is the child now?'

'It didn't live, Sénher. There are those who say her own father was the sire.' Bernard's shock must have shown on his face, for Lizier held his hands up in apology. 'Though I don't credit it. What father would be so unnatural?'

Bernard swallowed his distaste. 'Is the widow provided for? Is there a son to inherit these lands?'

Lizier lurched closer. 'There are rumours,' he said.

'What kind of rumours?'

'How old do you think I am?' Lizier suddenly said. 'Go on. Guess.'

'I could not say, Monsieur,' Bernard said wearily. 'Older than me, with, I dare say, more than twice the wisdom to match.'

'Ha! I saw the last century and I won't live to see the next,' he laughed, then dropped a hand on Joubert's shoulder. 'Only one older in the village.'

'I salute you, Lizier.'

He nodded, satisfied with the compliment. 'To answer your question, Sénher, there's no son. No daughter neither, though as the late Seigneur lay dying, they say he talked of a child. But, for good or ill, I'll tell you this for nothing. The Lady Blanche means to be mistress here in her own right, heir or no heir. Mark my words. And then God help us all.'

CHAPTER THIRTY-TWO

⚜

Toulouse

The procession turned into rue Nazareth, then came to a standstill. It was a canyon of a street, the buildings on both sides towering high and narrow. The houses to their right were set into the city wall itself, creating deep shade and cool air.

Quickly, impatience began to whisper through the crowd like a summer wind through a field of barley. People became restless. One of the mummers stepped out of line to see what was happening up ahead.

'It is an outrage,' Madame Montfort said. 'It should not be allowed.'

'Niece, you have the advantage of height, you are so much taller than I am. Can you see why we are stopped?'

Minou stood on her tiptoes and peered over the heads of the crowd. 'There appears to be a funeral cortège, but I cannot—'

'It's a Huguenot funeral,' Madame Montfort interrupted, 'blocking the street. It is a disgrace. They have been granted what they demanded, that is to say a temple of their own. Why do they not stay there? The building is far too close to the Porte Villeneuve in any case. If they had any sense of gratitude for the generosity Toulouse has shown, they would have built a more modest structure and out of sight. Why honest Christians should be obliged to look upon it in the course of attending to our everyday business, I cannot imagine.'

'They don't even dress the same as us for a funeral,' Madame Boussay added. 'Disgraceful, I call it. I own they wear black, but commonplace working clothes: not at all seemly.'

In a rare instance of harmony, Madame Montfort nodded. 'You are quite right, Salvadora. Huguenots do not even bury their dead with propriety. It is quite scandalous how they flaunt themselves within the city walls.'

'Are they really doing anything wrong?' Minou muttered.

The older women ignored her.

'I shall raise this with my brother. He should inform the Hôtel de Ville.'

'As will I,' her aunt echoed, emboldened that her sister-in-law and she were for once in accord.

'There's no need for us both to speak to him, Sister. I will explain clearly, in a way that enables Monsieur Boussay to put the matter before the capitouls. This flagrant behaviour should not be licensed.'

Madame Boussay flushed. 'Very well, if that is what you think is best, Adelaide. I will leave it in your hands. You understand these things much better than do I.'

Minou stepped out from the back of the congregation to get a clearer look. The rue Nazareth seemed to be completely filled with people, perhaps some forty in all. The mourners were dressed plainly, and without ostentation, though Minou did not think they looked the worse for that. Another group were more finely dressed, in black velvet and feathers, accompanied by Catholic clergy.

'What can you see now, Niece? Why are we not moving forward? Are they so numerous that our route is blocked?'

Minou climbed up the front steps of a nearby house to get a better view.

'The street is narrow at the corner,' she said, trying to make sense of what she could see, 'but that is not what stops us. There is some kind of dispute.'

'Dispute?' Madame Montfort demanded. 'What manner of dispute?'

'I cannot hear, but two priests – canons from the cathedral, I think – appear to be remonstrating with the Huguenot pastor. A Catholic gentleman is beside them. Now one of the priests is shouting. The chief mourner is attempting to calm him.'

'Don't be ridiculous, Marguerite,' Madame Montfort interrupted again. 'As if a man of God would be bawling in the street like a common vagrant.'

'Well, the priest is waving his arms around. He looks angry,' Minou said dryly. 'And now – Oh . . .'

She broke off. Four men, each holding a club and with kerchiefs covering their mouths, had moved to flank the Catholic gentlemen arguing with the funeral party.

'Oh no . . .' she said, her heart speeding up.

'What is it?' her aunt said anxiously. 'What's happening now?'

Minou climbed from the steps up onto a low wall.

'Marguerite, really!' Madame Montfort snapped. 'Come down!'

'What can you see, Niece?'

'They are trying to wrest the coffin from the pall-bearers. The pastor is attempting to intervene, but there are too many of them and —'

'What of our own dear priest?' her aunt cried, clutching Minou's skirts. 'Can you see? Do the Protestants menace him too?'

'It is not the Huguenots who are the aggressors,' Minou said. 'They are unarmed. It is the others who have weapons.'

'Weapons?' her aunt wailed. 'Huguenots are not permitted

to carry weapons within the city limits, my husband told me most particularly.'

'As I said, it is not the Huguenots who are armed, Aunt,' Minou replied, fear making her impatient, 'but those who are trying to seize the coffin from the mourners.'

'Don't be absurd. No Catholic would behave in such a matter.' Madame Montfort heaved herself up onto the low wall. 'Let me see, Marguerite.'

Suddenly, the street was full of men. Students, artisans and clerks, Catholics in velvet and wide ruffs, labourers with make-shift clubs coming into rue Nazareth from the far end. Unease murmured through the ranks of mourners and mummers, trapped now between this citizens' army and the glimpse of daylight at the end of the street.

'Like an ambush,' Minou muttered.

The feast-day banners were lowered. The priest handed his thurible to one of the acolytes, who hurried it away. Out of the corner of her eye, Minou saw two musicians put down their instruments and start to push forward.

Minou jumped down from the wall and elbowed her way through the sea of cloaks, until she found the friar who had accompanied them from rue du Taur.

'My aunt is alarmed by the crowd. I wonder if it might be better to take her back to Saint-Michel?'

'Can you not see what is happening?' he hissed, spittle pooling white in the corners of his mouth. 'Are you blind? The well-being of one foolish woman is not my concern.'

'When the "foolish woman" in question is your benefactress, I wonder at how you dismiss her so discourteously.'

To Minou's astonishment, he pushed her away.

'I do not care what you do.'

'My uncle shall hear of this insult to his wife,' she said. 'Do not doubt it.'

Outraged, she turned back, resolved to take her aunt out of harm's way. To her dismay, the space by the steps was now empty.

'Aunt?' she called, casting her eyes around anxiously. Then, in the distance, she spied Madame Montfort hurrying them both to safety.

Minou was on the point of following, when there was a sudden surge of people and she found herself carried forward by the crowd. A foot trod on the hem of her cloak, tightening the ribbon at her neck. An elbow dug into her ribs. She was trapped in a fug of sweat and fear and the sour breath of strangers pressing too close. She tried to find a gap through which to slip free of the seething mass, but couldn't extricate herself. She had been caught in a mob once before, when she was ten years old. She and her mother were leaving the bookshop, when they found themselves swept up in a crowd come to witness a multiple hanging. Minou could remember even now the tightness of her mother's grip on her hand and the roaring of the pack, the hooded faces and the bodies twisting from the gibbet. Then, as now, it was people's expressions that chilled her to the bone. The hatred and malice on the faces of ordinary men and women, transformed suddenly into monsters.

'Excuse me,' she tried to say. 'Please let me through.'

Her voice was swallowed up in the commotion. In the distance, she could hear the sound of horses and the rattle of a cart. Then the sound of metal clashing on metal, and a shrill scream.

For a moment, everyone seemed to catch their breath. Silence, stillness. Then a single word that acted as a call to arms.

'Heretics!'

The street erupted into battle. With a roar, the two tribes pitched into the fray, scattering pennants and flags in all directions. Shoved to one side, Minou saw people running in blind panic, some away from the mayhem and others towards it.

The funeral cortège was now completely surrounded and, though the pall-bearers struggled to lift the coffin above the mob, they were being pushed and jostled.

'Traitors!'

Words, sharp as thorns, baiting, taunting, jeering. The chief mourner still appealed for calm, but his voice was drowned out. A gloved hand shot out and struck him in the face. He stumbled back, blood gushing from his nose.

Minou saw a bearded man with charcoal-black hair leap to his defence, throwing himself between the injured man and the baying mob. He threw up his arm and blocked a second blow, long enough for the Huguenot to scramble to his feet and escape. With a roar, the Catholic launched himself forward, throwing wild punches. They were evenly matched, but then the attacker drew his sword and the atmosphere changed.

Calmly, the Huguenot stepped back, drew his own short blade and stood ready. Minou felt another memory push to the surface of her mind. Another street, in Carcassonne, not in Toulouse, that same stance with a dagger in his hand.

Piet?

The Catholic attacked. His sword glanced away as Piet parried the thrust. The aggressor tried again, this time swinging his sword from the side. Piet jumped to the left, defending himself rather than trying to wound, Minou realised. Then, suddenly, the sword was flying out of the attacker's hand and Piet kicked it away. The man froze, then turned tail.

'Piet!' Minou shouted, but he couldn't hear her over the

cacophony of screaming and battle. She dodged out of the way of two fleeing Huguenot women, and in that moment lost sight of him.

Fists, rocks, stones on the one side; daggers, clubs and swords on the other. The Huguenots were outnumbered ten to one. Their pastor, still shouting, was wounded, blood dripping down his cheek. His cap had been ripped from his head. A kind of wildness was sweeping through the crowd on both sides, each violent act triggering another in its wake.

Minou didn't know which way to turn. Desperately, she tried to catch sight of Piet again in the crowd, but could hardly distinguish one man from another. A heavy stick crashed down onto the shoulders of one of the pall-bearers. He staggered, but did not let go. His attacker drew back his arm and delivered a second strike, crushing his fingers. The pall-bearer screamed, and Minou watched in horror as the coffin pitched forward. A student threw out his arms, trying to get hold of the end, but the angle was awkward and the coffin too heavy.

The front corner struck the cobblestones. The lid shattered and splintered open. The claw-like hand of the dead woman fell out into the light. For an instant, in a gap between the men, Minou had a clear view of her waxy yellow face. Sallow skin stretched over shrunken bones. Black eyes deep in their sockets and the glint of a plain silver cross at her neck.

Minou felt faint. Bile rose in her throat, but she swallowed hard, determined not to give way. Then someone tried to drag the corpse out of the coffin, and she had to turn her face to the wall.

Another gang of men stormed into the street, armed with bill hooks and mattocks. It was becoming increasingly difficult to tell the factions apart. All she knew was that women and children, the infirm, all were trapped, and that she must try to help as many to safety as she could. She looked again for Piet, but he was lost in the crowd.

To her left, an elderly woman staggered and almost fell. Minou threw out her arms and caught her. 'Here,' she said, helping her to the steps to sit, before running back into the fray. A boy was trying to protect his grandfather. With both hands, Minou launched herself at the attacker's back, shoving him forward so that he fell onto the cobbles, striking his head. She gave the old man her arm and, with the support of a young Protestant woman, also took him to the safety of the steps. The boy was mute with shock. Silent tears ran down his cheeks, though he made no attempt to wipe them away.

'Stay here, *petit homme*? Yes? Your grandfather needs you to look after him.'

The boy stared blankly at her, then his whole body shuddered, like a dog shaking the water from its fur.

'Why do they hate us so much?' he whispered.

Minou could not answer. 'What's your name?' she asked quickly.

'Louis.'

She took a kerchief from her cloak. 'Listen to me, Louis. Hold this here.' Minou applied the scrap of linen to the wound on the old man's head. 'It will slow the bleeding. It looks awful, but I do not think he is badly hurt.'

At her side, she felt the young woman tense. 'We don't need your help.'

At first, Minou didn't realise she was addressing her.

'That's perfect, keep the pressure here,' she continued, cupping her hand over the boy's small fingers, 'that's right.'

'I said, get away.' The young woman batted Minou's arm away. 'You're one of them. Leave us alone.'

'What?' Minou said, still not understanding. 'I am not part of any group. I only want to help.'

'What's that on your waist, then?' she said, pointing at Minou's rosary. 'Catholics. You started this. It is your fault. I said, get away from us.'

'I condemn this.' Minou drew herself up. 'I am as much a victim as are you.'

The woman spat in her face. 'I doubt that. Go!'

Shocked by the young woman's hatred, Minou wiped her cheek, and stepped away. A man's voice rang out above the chaos.

'They have blockaded the far end of the street!'

Minou felt another surge of panic swelling through the crowd, sending men, women and children running in all directions. Towards danger or away from it, no one knew. Then came another voice, trying to impose order.

'McCone, take the women and children, anyone who is injured, to the almshouse. There will be people to care for them there.'

'What about you?'

'I will hold things here until our soldiers arrive. Lock the doors and let no one enter, save for those we know as our own.'

In the chaos and the terror of the riot, Minou turned towards the sound of Piet's voice.

'Piet!' she called.

And although it seemed impossible that he should hear her over the cacophony and screaming, Minou saw his eyes dart around looking for her, trying to pick her out in the mass of people.

'Piet!' she shouted again, trying to get to him.

Suddenly, right in front of her, was a child. A girl, no older than Alis, kneeling in the middle of the street, with her eyes closed and her hands pressed together in prayer. Plain clothes, a simple Huguenot bonnet, at the precise point the gangs would collide.

'*Pousse-toi*,' Minou called, trying to reach the child. 'Get out of the way.'

Minou used her hands, her elbows, her knees to force her way through. Closer, closer, nearly there. The rabble armies were almost upon one another, blocking the street in both directions. She hurled herself forward the last distance, and managed to sweep the child up in her arms before the first swords met.

'I have you,' she gasped.

Finally, the girl opened her eyes. Blue, the colour of forget-me-nots. Her tiny hands clasped around Minou's neck.

'I am not afraid,' she said, 'for God will protect me. Trust in Him.'

'We must get away—' Minou began to say, then felt someone behind her.

She spun round as a thick-set man with a black beard swung a club down upon them both. Minou twisted to shield the girl, but as she did so, pain exploded across her shoulder blade and she felt her skin split open, then the warmth of blood. She staggered, but held the child tighter as she started to fall.

All around her, the smell of rage and blood and terror. Fire starting to lick through the shutters of the houses, red flames and blistered paint. Lying on her back, Minou could see a glimpse of the blue April sky over Toulouse above the buildings. All sound seemed to slip away, the shouting and the crying. In the last seconds before she lost consciousness, she was vaguely aware of a pair of strong arms around her.

Then, nothing.

CHAPTER THIRTY-THREE

Puivert

It was sunset and the air was cool. Leaving Canigou in the care of Achille Lizier, Bernard walked away from the village and looked up at the castle.

Occupying the highest point above the valley, overlooking the single road that ran from west to east, it was a grey, squat structure of fortified towers set in rough stone walls. Bernard shielded his eyes and located the beginning of the switchback track that led up from the village, winding steeply back and forth like a snake curled for winter. Bernard had climbed that path so many times, in every season, feeling the tightening in his legs on the sharpest corners, then the relief as the ground levelled out on the approach. He could picture the wooden drawbridge that led under the gatehouse and into the *basse cour*, the lower courtyard, and their modest lodgings in the Tour Gaillarde, where he and Florence had lived as husband and wife. He imagined walking through the archway into the inner courtyard and the oldest part of the castle, from which the medieval Lord of Puivert had held the armies of Simon de Montfort at bay during the Cathar Crusades.

In that time, the business of the estate had been conducted from the keep, the magnificent stone tower built by the de Bruyère family. Their coat of arms was engraved above the main door, set high in the walls atop a steep flight of steps: a lion rampant with a forked and knotted tail, the capital letters of B and P – for Bruyère and Puivert – inscribed on either side.

Despite the character of their master, a man of quick temper and cruel habits, he and Florence had been happy here, at first. He closed his eyes and she was at his side once more. He remembered her dark eyes and black curls, could almost feel the softness of her hand resting in his. Planning their future together and watching the seasons change. The sleet and snow of mountain winters; bursts of wildflowers that covered the ground with colour in the spring; the fierce summer heat; then autumn, Florence's favourite time of the year, when the landscape turned to shades of copper and gold and crimson. Except that last autumn of fifteen forty-two. Then, the rains came and the river Blau burst its banks and it seemed as if the world was drowning.

Bernard rubbed the dust from his eyes and his wife slipped away from him, leaving him alone again. A lonely and old man, forced to return to a place of secrets.

Though it was dusk, sweat soon moistened his brow and his heavy travelling clothes stuck to the small of his back as he trudged on and up the steep hillside. Each step was harder than the one before. Many times, he paused to catch his breath.

Finally, Bernard rounded the last corner and the castle came into view. He stopped. He could hardly walk in through the gatehouse uninvited and demand admittance. Was he being foolish? Was it likely any evidence would still be here after all these years?

Bernard glanced back down to the village below, feeling every one of his sixty years. Then, conscious of being visible on the open ground in front of the drawbridge, he stepped quickly off the main path and into the thicket of trees in the deeper woods on the north side of the castle.

Pushing thin branches back with his hands, he threaded his way gingerly along a narrow path. Footprints in the damp earth, and a few branches snapped at the height of a man's shoulder, suggested poachers had recently come this way.

From the shelter of the trees, he could now make out the outline of the Tour Gaillarde and, opposite, the Tour Bossue, where the dungeons were to be found.

As he drew closer to the keep, he heard the sound of the watch patrolling the perimeter of the castle. He assumed they would withdraw within the walls when night fell. From the highest point of the square tower, a man could see for thirty leagues in every direction: west to Bélesta, north to Chalabre, east to Quillan and, in the distant south, to the great white wall of the Pyrenees.

There was an opening in the walls of the upper courtyard which used to lead into the kitchen gardens. It was little used and, if his luck held and the gate was unguarded, he thought he could steal in and out of the castle within an hour, without anyone ever seeing him. If the object he sought was there for the finding, it would be in the keep.

'There!'

They were upon him in an instant. Bernard cried out in pain as his arms were wrenched up behind his back. Then, the hood of a hessian sack was thrown over his head and a kick aimed at the back of his knees, sending him sprawling, chin first, onto the ground. Bernard tasted blood in his mouth and struggled to breathe, as his hands were bound at the wrist. Rope, strong enough to bind an ox.

'Another poacher. That's the third today.'

'Take him to the Tour Bossue,' came the order. 'He can stay there until the mistress returns.'

'Might be in for a long wait. Our noble lady has gone to Toulouse to pray for her husband's soul, or so they say.'

The soldiers laughed.

'Pray for his soul! More likely she'll pray he stays dead and buried in the ground, the old sinner.'

Bernard felt a rough hand pushing him forward.

'Let's get him inside, the light's fading.'

'Or leave him here for the wolves . . .'

Another stab in his back, perhaps the wooden hilt of a pike. He stumbled forward.

'Get on with it, *paysan*.'

He is snared. I set the trap and it is sprung. Though he has pledged his soul to God, he is a man like any other. His body, his hands, his breath declare it to be so. He is made of flesh and blood and desire.

The keys to the Episcopal Palace will be his if he puts his trust in me. The bishop is old and, so the servants gossip, o'er fond of food and drink. His Excellency's palate can no longer distinguish sweet from sour. I have what is needed to influence a sudden stopping of the heart or an attack of siege sickness. It is simple.

Like other men who aspire to greatness, Valentin seeks to leave his mark upon the world. To be remembered in monuments and stone while common men lie forgotten in unmarked graves. I will help raise him up. He will benefit from a noble patroness.

The disturbance in the streets around the cathedral has quietened, though the night air is alive with the sounds of rioting and looting. My lover will come to me again tonight, however much he tries to resist. His ardour will not let him rest.

So, to my question. Before I take my leave of Toulouse, should I tell him of the child? When his desire is spent, shall I place his hand upon my belly, let him know he has created the new life quickening inside me?

Between now and the setting of the sun, I shall pray for guidance. God is merciful. God loves those who serve Him.

CHAPTER THIRTY-FOUR

⚜

Toulouse
Friday, 3rd April

Minou was floating high above the earth, held by hands as soft as feathers in an endless blue sky, everything full of light. She was weightless and peaceful, no sound and no fear and no pain.

'*Kleine schat.*'

A man's voice, and then a woman murmuring: 'She is waking, Monsieur.'

Minou felt gentle hands arranging a cloth behind her head. As she withdrew, the woman whispered in her ear.

'He has hardly left your side.'

'Take this for your trouble. My thanks.'

Minou felt the curve of a strong arm around her back.

'Can you sit? Take care not to put any weight on your left shoulder, for—'

She put her right hand to the ground, sending a whip-crack of pain shooting up her arm, and yelped.

'– it will be painful!'

'That hurt.'

'Your shoulder is badly bruised, but not broken. You were lucky.'

'Lucky!'

Her eyes flickered open to see her cloak was laid over her legs and her left arm was strapped against her chest in a white triangle of cotton.

Minou turned her head. Piet was sitting beside her on a low chest. Plain clothes, an open jerkin, his hair that peculiar sooty black. So close that she could feel the warmth of his breath.

He smiled. 'I would say so, yes. This far to the left and you would have had a cracked skull. What, in the name of God, possessed you to rush into the middle of the fray?'

She frowned. 'There was a child, kneeling in the middle of the street, the men fighting all around her. Is she . . . ?'

'We have her. She's safe.'

'I have a sister, Alis,' she said, feeling the need to explain. 'She is much the same age . . .'

'Minou,' he said, his tone part exasperation, part affection, and she felt her heart shift.

'You remember my name.'

His eyes sparkled with amusement. 'Of course. You gave it to me as a keepsake, remember?'

'So I did.' Minou closed her eyes. 'She was praying, Piet. In the middle of that chaos and strife, the ugliness of it, that little girl was praying. She believed God would spare her.'

'If it is not heresy to say so, Mademoiselle Minou, it was you who saved her life. Not God.'

'And you, mine. And for that, I thank you.'

'Consider it a debt repaid. Were it not for your assistance in March, I would now be languishing in the Seneschal's prison in Carcassonne.'

Suddenly self-conscious, she pulled herself up to a sitting position. Every muscle in her body, her back, her head, ached.

'My aunt was also caught up in the disturbance this afternoon. I think she was taken away before the worst of it, but I would know that she is safe.'

Piet laughed. 'Not this afternoon, but yesterday,' he said. 'It is Friday. You have been lost to us for many hours.'

Minou felt her head spin. 'That cannot be! My brother, my aunt, they will be desperate for news of me, I must go.' She tried to stand up, but a wave of nausea gripped her, and she sat back again.

'You cannot leave at the moment, even if you had strength enough,' Piet said. 'The streets are too dangerous. We are waiting to hear news of a truce.'

Minou struggled to stand again. 'But I must go.'

'I give you my word, as soon as it is safe, I will take you home. For now, you should rest. Here.' He handed her a goblet of wine. 'This will help. What is the name of your aunt? I will enquire.'

'Boussay,' she replied. 'Salvadora Boussay.'

Piet's face darkened. 'Boussay,' he repeated.

'Do you know her?' she said.

'No, but if it is the same family, I know of her husband. I will be back presently.'

When Piet left, Minou leant back against the wall and took in her surroundings. She was in a small anteroom with plain white-washed walls. A shelf of heavy ledgers ran above a long counter that filled the entire wall, with papers, ink and quills and an accounts book left open beside a wooden abacus. Diamonds of sunlight were filtered through the leaded glass window on the opposite wall.

Piet had left the door ajar, so Minou could see through to the long, wide room beyond, much like a dormitory in a convent. All along one side stood a row of living compartments, divided from one another by heavy red curtains. Each space contained a bed with a small low chair set at the foot and an individual chest. In the middle of the room, makeshift beds had been set, and grey and blue blankets spread on the tiled floor, where the injured lay, many like her sporting bandages or dressings. Women moved in and out of her sight line, carrying pails of water and white muslin bandages.

'Madame Boussay has not been brought here,' Piet said, coming back into the antechamber and closing the door. 'I think it is unlikely she would be, but I have asked to be told if anyone hears something to the contrary.'

'Thank you,' Minou said. 'What is this place?'

'The *maison de charité* in rue du Périgord.'

She smiled, for of course she had walked past it many times. The only Protestant almshouse in Toulouse, next to the humanist college, it was one of the establishments her uncle was trying to have shut down.

'This seemed the safest place to bring our wounded and dead.'

'You are a Huguenot, Piet?'

'I am.'

She held his gaze. 'I am Catholic.'

'I had guessed as much.' He gestured to the rosary at her waist. 'The fact that your uncle is Monsieur Boussay confirms it.'

'Yet someone brought me here.'

'Me.' A smile flickered across Piet's lips. 'I carried you here myself, having first dispatched the man who attacked you.'

'Dispatched! You mean – you did not . . . ?'

'Kill him, no, though I confess I wanted to. I give no quarter to men, be they Catholic or Protestant, who assault women and children.' He frowned. 'Tell me, what manner of man is your uncle? I know he is secretary to a capitoul, but is he a fair man?'

Minou shook her head. 'I regret he thinks any concession given to the Reformed Religion is a concession too many.'

Piet leant forward. 'But what of you, Minou? Do you share his opinions?'

She tilted her head. 'I was raised a Catholic, but with a mind open to the faiths and opinions of others. I think I told you my father has a bookshop in Carcassonne? He stocks texts to satisfy all tastes.'

'The Catholics of Toulouse are not minded to be so tolerant.'

'My father would say a man's faith is his own business, provided he respects the laws of the land. A woman's too, for my sex are as capable of rational thought and devotion as any man. And what I witnessed in rue Nazareth only confirmed what I have long thought, that much of this current conflict is fuelled by a desire for power rather than by any true piety. It is that which caused yesterday's riots, not any love of God.' Minou looked up, then saw Piet staring intently at her. 'I'm sorry. I spoke too forcefully.'

'Not at all,' he said. 'Indeed, I am of the same opinion.' He smiled. 'It seems we are not, in point of fact, on opposite sides at all.'

Minou felt the knot of emotion in her chest untangle. For so many weeks, she had imagined how it might feel to see Piet again. Flesh and blood, not a half-remembered figure in her mind. What she had not expected was that it would feel so normal.

'The funeral was for the wife of a Huguenot merchant,' Piet said, steering the conversation to less dangerous ground. 'A man much respected in our community, a friend of a good friend of mine, and his wife was greatly liked. However, her family are Catholic and wished her to have a Catholic burial. When they came face to face with your procession . . .' He shrugged.

'Everything turned ugly so quickly.'

'It did.'

He started to slide the beads of the abacus back and forth. Minou closed her eyes, taking comfort in the gentle tap, tap of the wood on the frame.

'But, tell me this, Minou. How is it you come to be in Toulouse at all? How long have you been here?'

Minou smiled. In her imagined conversations with him, she had overlooked the fact that he did not know how much her circumstances had changed since they had last been together.

'For almost a month we have been lodging with our aunt and uncle in rue du Taur. My aunt is my late mother's sister and, though there was a long-standing estrangement between the families, I like her very much. She is kind and good-hearted. My father hopes that Aimeric will benefit from Monsieur Boussay's patronage.'

Piet's eyebrows shot up. 'Aimeric, did you say? I met a boy of that name in Carcassonne. Wild black hair, mischievous, sharp.'

'My brother, yes,' she said, then waved her finger at him. 'In fact, I own I was much vexed when I heard how you put him at risk by asking for his help. I mean it,' she scolded, when Piet grinned. 'Bribing him to break into the Fourniers' house, then again to steal out of La Cité to fetch your horse, even though a curfew was declared. You could have had him arrested.'

'Forgive me,' Piet replied, with mock contrition, 'though I venture to suggest Aimeric can look after himself.'

'That is not my point at all,' she said, trying to sound sombre.

'In faith, I do apologise. Truly. But I tell you, I owe my

liberty to your brother. If he had not been so sharp-witted, I would without doubt have been languishing in prison now. It seems I am in your family's debt twice over.'

Minou continued to frown. He nudged her arm.

'But am I forgiven?'

'Are you truly sorry?'

Piet put his hand to his heart. 'Truly, I am.'

'Well, then we will say no more about it.' She smiled. 'Aimeric also claims you promised to teach him a trick with a knife? Some manner of throwing which captured his imagination. He has not stopped talking of it.'

'Indeed, I did. Now I know we are neighbours, I will do my best to keep my word.' Piet ran his fingers through his hair, bringing away flakes of charcoal and black soot. Minou laughed.

'A precaution, though not one that proves long-lasting!'

'As a disguise, it serves. Your true colour would stand out in a crowd.'

He laughed. 'My friend tells me I am as a twin to the Queen of England.'

'May I ask you something?'

'There is no question you might ask that I will not answer.'

'What does *kleine schat* mean? You said it when I was waking up.'

To Minou's surprise, Piet looked away. 'Ah, I did not realise I had spoken out loud.' He smiled. 'It means "little treasure". It's what my mother called me when she tucked me into my bed at night. I lived my earliest years in Amsterdam.'

'It is a city my father much enjoys to visit.'

'It is a wonderful city.'

'Does she live there still?'

Piet shook his head. 'She died many winters past, when I was seven years old, but her grave is there. One day, I will return.'

CHAPTER THIRTY-FIVE

⚜

Minou, remembering how bitterly Aimeric had mourned the death of their mother, took Piet's hand, not caring if the gesture was too forward.

'You loved her very much,' she said softly.

'I did.' He paused. 'Yes, I did. It's a long time ago now.'

'That doesn't mean you cannot still mourn her absence.'

For a long moment, they sat in silence. Then, becoming aware again of the hubbub in the dormitory outside the private chamber, Minou squeezed his fingers, then withdrew her hand.

'Aimeric said the Fournier house was empty,' Minou said, sensing she should change the subject.

Piet cleared his throat. 'That's right. Not a stick of furniture, nothing. On the previous evening, the apartment had been well furnished. A lit fire, tapestries upon the wall, a library.'

'He said there was blood by the windows. Is that true? Aimeric has a tendency to embellish the facts for the sake of his story.'

'Quite true. Aimeric is observant. He has the makings of a fine soldier. A good eye, courage, a sharp wit.'

'My father would rather he was a gentleman or a scholar. It is one of the reasons he sent him here to Toulouse. He cannot accept that it is not Aimeric's nature to spend his life among books.'

'Aimeric must find his own path in the world,' Piet said, 'as must we all.'

A volley of shouting from the room beyond their chamber interrupted their quiet conversation. Piet went to the door and looked out.

'You should go,' Minou said. 'I have trespassed too long on your time.'

'They will manage without me a moment longer. There is something else I would ask of you.'

She hesitated, then gave his own words back to him. 'There is no question you might ask that I will not answer.'

'So, again, we are well matched. That day in Carcassonne, why were you so sure I was innocent? Why did you help me to escape?'

Minou had asked herself that same question many times. Why had she – who kept her own counsel and relied on no one – so completely believed in this stranger?

This Huguenot stranger.

In plain language, she explained about the visitor to the bookshop, about finding his corpse beneath the bridge the next morning before the tocsin was rung, of her father's reaction when he heard of the death.

'So, it seemed all but impossible that you could be responsible. For how could the search for Michel's murderer have begun before he was even dead?'

'This is ill news indeed,' Piet said.

Minou stared. 'I had thought, by my words, to give you comfort. If it is a matter of bearing witness, I will vouch for you. This charge against you should not stand.'

'It is not that,' he sighed. 'I had not known until this instant that it was Michel who was dead.'

'You knew him?'

'Michel and I fought together in the Prince of Condé's army, then our paths took us in different directions. I hadn't seen him for some five years before that day in the Bastide. He was an honourable man.'

'Was it a chance meeting? After so long?'

'It was arranged through a third party. I thought Michel seemed troubled in his spirits, beyond the matter that had brought us into one another's company. Indeed, he took his leave before our business was concluded. I considered going after him, but did not. I deeply regret that now.'

'He came in search of my father that same afternoon.'

'Most likely straight from our rendezvous to your father's shop. He didn't say how he and Michel were acquainted?'

'No. I asked, but he avoided answering.'

Piet gave a long sigh. 'Is it not absurd, Minou, in the midst of everything that has happened in the past twenty-four hours, all this suffering we see around us, that news of the death of one friend should so affect me?'

'It is right you grieve for Michel,' Minou said softly. 'If we harden our hearts against one death, then soon we lose all compassion.'

'I have served as a soldier.'

'You are also a man who mourns the loss of his friend. You are a comrade, a son . . . a husband, too, perhaps?'

Piet shot her a glance, then he smiled. 'No, not a husband.'

Then, they were leaning into one another. His arm resting against the length of hers. Minou felt heat flood through her. She was aware of every sinew, every muscle, almost touching through their dust-stained clothes. Minou closed her eyes and knew this feeling, at last, was desire.

Now his hand was cradling the back of her neck and drawing her to him. Her fingers were entwining through his as they kissed. Chaste at first, then with a force that took her breath from her.

The taste of sandalwood and almonds.

Piet was the first to pull away. 'Forgive me. I should not have taken such liberties.'

Minou held his gaze. 'You took nothing that was not freely given, Monsieur,' she said, willing her heart to stop thudding so hard. She laid her hand on his arm and Piet covered it with his own.

Then, suddenly, they heard raised voices and the tramp of boots coming towards them, and sprang apart.

'I cannot be seen here,' Minou said, panicked.

'Quickly,' he said, handing her the cloak. 'Behind the door.'

Piet waited until she was hidden, then drew his dagger and stepped out, ready to confront whoever was approaching.

'At last. I've been looking everywhere for you.'

'McCone, you should have announced yourself! I have not seen you here before.' Piet sheathed his blade. 'I could have had your eye out.'

'We came to tell you they have agreed to parley.'

'We?'

'These gentlemen,' McCone said, switching from English to awkward French. 'Comrades from Carcassonne. They say they are known to you.'

Peering through the gap between the door and the frame, Minou saw Piet's shoulders stiffen.

'Crompton. I had not heard you were in Toulouse.'

Extraordinary as it seemed, she recognised the young man standing with Crompton. His fresh face, no sign of a beard, and his short yellow cloak and hose – she had seen him in the courtyard of her aunt and uncle's house. And suddenly, she remembered why he'd seemed familiar: this same man, serenading and reciting intoxicated verse on the streets of Trivalle in

Carcassonne before a pail of dirty water was tipped over his head.

'And Devereux, you are here too?' Piet said.

He gave a brief bow. 'Monsieur.'

'Where are the talks to take place?'

'At the Augustinian monastery,' McCone replied. 'As soon as all parties can be gathered together.'

'Who speaks for us?'

'Pastor Barrelles, Saux, Popelinière.'

Piet nodded. 'I will come with you.' He turned and whispered to McCone, 'Might you give me a moment?'

Minou stepped back further into the shadows behind the door.

'What is it?' Crompton jibed, trying to peer into the chamber. 'Have you got a wench in there, a pretty little maid with petticoats around her ears . . .?'

'That's enough, Crompton,' McCone said.

'Wait there,' Piet snapped, stepping back into the room and closing the door.

'I am sorry you should have been subject to such distasteful comments,' he whispered. 'Men's conversation, when unrestrained by a woman's presence, can—'

'I grew up in a garrison town, Piet. I have heard every insult under the sun.'

'Nonetheless, I apologise.'

Minou took his hand. 'The young man, Devereux, I think—'

Piet put his finger to his lip. 'Say nothing, they will hear.'

'But Devereux is a protégé of my—'

A violent banging on the door drowned out her words.

'Reydon! Are you coming or not?'

'J'arrive!' Piet shouted back, then spun back to face her. 'Stay here. Your clothes mark you out.'

Annoyed by his high-handed manner, Minou took a step back.

'I am not yours to command.'

Piet stopped, his fingers on the door handle. 'Have I done something to offend you, I—'

More hammering on the door. 'Make haste!'

'All I was saying is that it would be unwise for you to go out into the streets unaccompanied. The situation is—'

'I am capable of looking after myself,' Minou replied coolly. 'I am not your responsibility. Go. Your comrades are waiting.' Cross with herself, and with Piet, Minou leant back against the wall, listening to the sound of his footsteps growing fainter, and wondered about Devereux. What was the Christian name he had given in rue Trivalle? Minou cast her mind back to that bright February morning, and the memory came.

Philippe. Philippe Devereux. In Carcassonne, he boasted of being a guest of the bishop at Saint-Nazaire. Then, in the courtyard in Toulouse before the procession, he was clearly at home in the company of her uncle, the friar and the Catholic arms dealer, Delpech. Yet here he was, in the Protestant almshouse with the leaders of the Huguenot resistance in Toulouse.

Who was he? Where did his loyalties lie?

The bishop's carriage is fast and his four horses strong. God willing, I will be there by nightfall. I am furnished with letters of introduction and have lodgings arranged suitable to my rank and position.

There are many who talk of Carcassonne with a catch in the breath, as if speaking of a lover. A crown of stone set upon a green hill, a medieval citadel that stands monument to the romance of the past. A symbol of the independence of the Midi.

Traitors, all.

Raymond-Roger Trencavel, Viscount of Carcassonne, was the failed leader of a failed rebellion. An apostate who encouraged heresy to flourish within his lands, who gave shelter to infidels and blasphemers, Cathars and Saracens and Jews? He died in his own dungeons. Was that not the Lord's judgement on a man who turned away from our Holy Mother Church?

Then, as now, what France should most fear is the enemy within.

CHAPTER THIRTY-SIX

Toulouse

Confused by Minou's sudden coldness, Piet stormed through the long dormitory of the almshouse. What reason did she have to be so scornful? He was only being mindful of her reputation and he did not see why that should have so offended her. He was tempted to go back and ask her to explain herself. He hated that they had parted bad friends.

'Have you heard a single word I've said?' asked McCone.

'Forgive me.' Piet jolted back to the present. 'My mind is overcharged with thinking. What did you say?'

'I said that Jean de Mansencal is to preside over the negotiations.'

Piet made himself concentrate. 'Well, that is welcome news.'

'Isn't he the President of the Parliament?' Crompton said. 'Presumably, therefore, he is a Catholic? Why, then, is his appointment good news for us?'

'Because his son, who is at the university,' Piet explained coldly, 'converted to the Reformed Church. Mansencal is also known to be a fair man. I think he will seek to find a workable solution.'

'I agree,' McCone said.

'Who else is to be in the chamber?'

'Four of the eight capitouls,' McCone replied, 'the Seneschal of Toulouse and eight other senior judges from the Parliament.'

They stopped talking as they walked through the kitchens and out into a passageway leading to a little-used door at the back of the building. Piet nodded to the soldier on duty, who let them pass. An unpleasant man, he thought. Too eager to draw his sword and cut others down to size.

They came out into rue du Périgord.

'I still say it's a trap,' Crompton argued. Devereux shrugged, but did not comment.

'Are Saux's men still holding the cathedral precincts?' Piet asked.

McCone shook his head. 'He withdrew most of his forces to protect Huguenot businesses in the Daurade district, where the worst of the looting was taking place. Catholic gangs forced their way into shops, smashing windows, ransacking premises.'

'What of the town guard?'

'They claim they were summoned but did not intervene. The faubourg of Saint-Michel was also attacked. Some twenty or so are said to have died there.'

'All Huguenots?'

'Mostly, yes. Students, legal clerks, artisans.'

'Where else have the bodies been taken? The Hôtel de Ville?'

'Yes, though Assézat and Ganelon attempted to take it back with some five hundred Catholic troops.'

'Five hundred? That many?'

'I imagine the numbers are exaggerated, but I suspect there is truth in the report the capitouls tried to storm the building.'

Piet stopped in the street. 'What of Hunault? He will help us. Is he yet back in Toulouse?'

'I heard he is still in Orléans with the Prince of Condé,' Crompton said.

Piet turned to face him. 'Do you believe that?'

'Who can tell? Too many missives are being intercepted. All I know is that Condé's men in Toulouse are currently under Saux's command. But I repeat what I said before. This is a trap. The Catholics have no need to negotiate with us. They outnumber us ten to one. They want to trick our leadership into gathering in one place, then arrest them all.'

Piet shook his head. 'You do not understand the character of Toulouse, Crompton. This is a city of merchants, of trade. It is the threat of damage to property – to Catholic interests – that forces them to negotiate with us, not the loss of more Protestant lives.'

As they reached the junction, a small boy leapt forward with a note. Crompton held out his hand, but the child sidestepped him.

'Begging your pardon, sir, but the letter is for Monsieur Devereux.'

'I had not realised you were so well-connected in Toulouse, cousin,' Crompton said sharply.

And Piet, suddenly remembering how Minou had been trying to tell him something about Devereux, cursed himself for not listening.

'I know one or two men of influence who are sympathetic to our cause,' Devereux said lightly, opening the letter. 'No more than that.'

'Well?' Crompton said.

Devereux folded the letter and put it in his doublet. 'It seems the negotiations are delayed until four o'clock.'

'Is your informant reliable, Devereux?' Piet asked. 'Someone you trust.'

'In so far as one can be sure of these things, yes. But, by your leave, I will verify it for myself.' He bowed. 'Gentlemen.'

'Where are you going?' Crompton called after him, but his cousin did not answer. He turned on Piet and McCone. 'What are we supposed to do now? Sit around like whores waiting for ships to come into port?'

'Is it a good sign the talks are delayed, Jasper?' Piet asked.

'Hard to say.'

He frowned. 'Do we actually know how many have been injured or killed? Not only our own people, but Catholics, too?'

'You are too compassionate. We cannot expect our people not to retaliate when attacked,' Crompton replied.

Piet stared at him. 'Our people? You are welcome in Toulouse, Crompton, but this is our city, not yours. We do not need outsiders telling us what to do.'

'Outsiders!' Crompton sneered. 'Men of Toulouse, men of Carcassonne, we are all Huguenots. The time for parochial divisions is past. You do not have the forces to withstand these attacks without reinforcements.'

'I am aware of our capabilities,' Piet replied.

'Then you will also be aware that Catholics in Toulouse are stock-piling weapons. They are preparing for war, even if you are not. Did you not hear that the Parliament has again withdrawn the right of Protestants to bear arms within the city walls?'

'Yet you still carry your sword,' Piet said, 'as do I. As do we all. You should not believe everything you hear.'

'There are Catholic soldiers going from house to house, searching cellars and attics for men and weapons. They seek to disarm us and then, when we can no longer defend ourselves, they will round everyone up.'

'Gentlemen, please,' McCone said. 'It helps no one if we fall out among ourselves.'

Crompton jabbed his finger at Piet. 'I don't believe there's any hope of a lasting truce. Royal authority is weak, the Parliament and the Town Council confound one another at every turn. Why should they find common ground for the good of Toulouse now? Of the capitouls, only two have Protestant sympathies, two keep their allegiances hidden and the remaining four are zealous Catholics. If there is truth in the rumour that Condé and his army are marching on Orléans, it seems obvious that the authorities here will assume the same fate will befall Toulouse and act accordingly. It is what I would do.'

Piet kept his voice level. 'You may be right, but I say we have no choice but to give our support to the negotiations. It's our best chance of preventing further bloodshed. If you do not wish to be party to that, that is a matter for you.'

'We came to offer our swords to Toulouse,' Crompton said, offended. 'We will keep our word.'

'In which case, you are welcome to accompany us.'

'Where to?'

'I am going to the quartier Daurade to see what help I might give. McCone, will you come?'

'I will.'

'How can we assist?' Crompton said.

Piet sighed. 'If the damage is as extensive as it sounds, they will need as many hands as possible to help repair houses and shops attacked during the looting last night.' He started walking. 'Are you coming with us, or no? It's all the same to me.'

Crompton hesitated, looking along the empty street as if he expected his cousin to reappear.

'No. I'll meet you at the tavern later.'

Minou was frustrated with herself.

Why, after the sweetness of their last meeting, had she

picked a quarrel with Piet? He had not intended to offend. His failure to listen was no more than a measure of his distraction. Though it was true she hated being told what to do, and that made her peevish, she wished they had not parted bad friends.

At the same time, she had no intention of waiting until Piet returned. Now he knew she was living only a street away, he could find her again if he wanted to.

Minou was light-headed from lack of food, and the muscles in her shoulder and neck were aching, but only a few steps would see her home. She was desperate to see Aimeric and to check that her aunt was safe.

For a moment, the memory of the chaos rushed back into her mind, the horror of it, and she shuddered. The armed mob, the stones and the wooden clubs. The sense of the world spiralling out of control into anarchy.

Minou slipped her arm out of the muslin sling, then examined her clothes. Piet was right, she looked Catholic. Quickly, she untied her mother's rosary from her waist and put the beads into her pocket. She could do nothing about the quality of her expensive velvet skirt, but she removed the lace collar and cuffs to make her appearance plainer.

She stepped out into the long dormitory, which was even bigger than she had first thought. There was even a modest altar at the far end. Women were bustling to and fro with bowls of water and ointments, but it seemed calmer. At the opposite end, was a wide doorway. There, on the ground, Minou could see bodies motionless beneath heavy woollen blankets. Pale squares of fabric covered each face.

She remembered Piet saying she had been lucky; now she understood. She had not realised so many had died.

Suddenly, Minou felt a tug on her skirt, and she jumped.

'Mademoiselle, *s'il vous plaît.*'

Though she was anxious to be gone, she recognised the little boy from rue Nazareth. He was sitting cross-legged on the floor, shivering, his face pale. She crouched down beside him.

'Hello, *petit homme*. Louis, is that right? How goes it with you?'

'I can't find my grandfather. They told me to stay here and not to move. But I have waited and waited. No one has come.'

Her heart went out to him. 'When did you arrive? Was it today? When it was light?'

He shook his head. 'Dark,' he whispered. 'All dark.'

'Louis, I am Minou,' she said. 'You remember me, yes?' He nodded. 'Good. So now we are reacquainted, what say you that we look for your grandfather together?'

Praying the old man would not be found among the dead, Minou took his hand. As they went from cubicle to cubicle, Louis became more confident, his voice a little firmer.

'Are you Louis?' one man asked. He was lying on his side, with his shin in a splint and his right hand bandaged. 'From the quartier Saint-Michel?'

'Yes,' he said eagerly.

'I did see your grandfather, wearing a long black coat with a tear at the back? He was asking for you.'

'Was he all right?' the little boy asked.

'Cross he couldn't find you.'

'When was this?' Minou asked.

He held up his arm. 'They gave me a sleeping draught while they set my fingers, and after that, the time is hazy. I only know it was early.'

'Where is he now?' Louis said. 'Has he gone without me?'

Minou hugged him. 'We shall keep looking until we find him,' she said.

'Could you hold this?' a woman said, pushing a jug at Minou and doubling back through double doors into the kitchens.

'We haven't tried in there,' Louis said.

'So we haven't,' Minou said. 'Shall we go and see?'

Huge, big-bellied pans hung over an open fire, the smell of thyme and haricots filled the air, slices of rough, black bread were stacked in a line of wicker baskets along a long, scored table.

With a cry, the boy pulled his hand from hers and ran.

'You can't be in here,' a woman started to say, then her voice changed. 'Louis! Thanks be to God, you are safe.'

Minou put down the jug, and followed. In amongst the steam and rattle of the kitchen, she saw the boy standing enveloped in the arms of a broad, red-faced woman in a white bonnet and apron.

'This is our neighbour,' he said, his face shining. 'She says Grandfather is quite safe. He was taken home by one of the soldiers. She promises she will take me to him as soon as she can leave here.'

'That is wonderful news,' Minou said. 'There, didn't I say it would all be fine?'

The woman looked at Minou, friendly but also cautious. 'I don't think I have seen you before.'

'I have only recently arrived in Toulouse,' Minou said carefully.

'Oh yes? Who was it who told you about the work we do here?'

She hesitated, then decided to tell the truth. 'A friend, Piet Reydon. It was he who—'

The wariness fell instantly from the woman's face. 'Oh

well, if Monsieur Reydon brought you, you are most welcome. Most welcome indeed.'

'I am?'

'Of course,' the woman said, waving her hand around. 'Without his generosity, we would not be able to keep going.'

'Piet – Monsieur Reydon – owns the almshouse?' Minou said, unable to keep the astonishment from her voice. Nothing Piet had said gave the impression that he came from a family of means. In fact, he had led her to believe the opposite. 'He is the owner?'

'I don't know about that, but certainly it is his generosity that helps keep it going. He comes here whenever he can. He works hard on behalf of those in need or who cannot speak for themselves.' She waved her arm. 'As you can see, there is great need.'

Minou's head was spinning. She had not considered how Piet spent his days or how he made a living, but whatever she had expected, it was not this. How could he possibly afford to support such a place?

'Were all these people brought here after the riots?' she asked.

'A few were here before – refugees from villages outside Toulouse – but most of them came in last night or today, like Louis and his grandfather from rue Nazareth. Many of the worst injured come from Daurade.'

'What happened?'

'You haven't heard? A mob attacked Huguenot businesses and houses down by the river this morning. Many have been left homeless, some have lost everything. Saint-Michel was attacked also. Some two-score are said to have been murdered there. I have never had cause to fall out with my Catholic neighbours in all these years, but somehow now . . .'

Minou flushed with shame. And though she was anxious to be back in rue du Taur, she wanted to make amends.

'What can I do to help?' she asked.

For two hours, Piet and McCone toiled in the quartier Daurade with other Huguenot soldiers, offering their services wherever they were most needed.

They repaired splintered windows and buckled door-frames, shutters ripped from their hinges. They built defensive palisades to protect businesses and workshops overlooking the Daurade church, where the worst of the looting had taken place. The soldiers stood watch on street corners and the walls by the river, looking out for any new sign of trouble. Dazed women and old men sat in silence, contemplating the ruins of their homes.

'Such mindless, pointless destruction,' Piet said, hammering another nail into place with such force that he split the wood. 'Such malice.'

McCone passed him another plank without comment, and helped secure it across the broken shutters of the small, dark shop.

'It will serve for tonight,' Piet said.

The owner, a shoemaker, shook his head. 'Thieves I can understand, but this? Twenty years I have built up my business, and they've ruined me. Everything is spoiled.' He held up a pair of boots, the leather ripped from the soles and the brass buckles hanging on a thread. 'All gone. In a matter of hours, all my leather, needles, lasts, all broken beyond repair.'

Piet's jaw tightened, but he kept his voice light. 'You will build things up again.'

'To what purpose? So they can come back and do such

villainy to us over again?' He shook his head. 'I am too old, Monsieur.'

'And the town guard stood by and let them do it,' his wife said, as angry as her husband was defeated. 'We've lived as good neighbours, served our Catholic and Protestant customers just the same, and never had any trouble beyond the occasional bad debt. Today? People I thought were our friends stood and watched, Monsieur. They stood and watched and never lifted a hand to help us.'

'Our leaders are meeting now to negotiate a truce,' Piet reassured her. 'This kind of thing must not be allowed to happen again.'

She shook her head. 'We are grateful for your assistance, Monsieur, but you are a fool if you believe it. Look around you. When ordinary men believe they can behave like this, without any fear, then it matters little what the judges and the priests have to say. It's too late.'

She threw a furious look at Piet and McCone, then burst into tears. Her husband put his arm around her.

'Thank you, Monsieur. There's no more to be said.'

They went inside their shop. Piet suddenly felt exhausted.

'Do you think everyone thinks the same as them?' McCone asked. 'That it is better to leave Toulouse than stay and risk this happening again?'

Piet's jaw tightened. 'I fear so. There are many Catholics who, though they would not take up arms against a fellow Christian, have let this happen. And for those who resent our presence in Toulouse, they reason that if all Huguenot shops are put out of business, then the Protestants will leave. No one wants to be driven from their home, but who wants to live in a permanent state of fear?'

'The question is where can they go?' McCone said. 'Many are too old to begin anew.'

'To family, friends in larger cities. That's to say, cities where Protestants are not so much in the minority. Montauban has a sizeable Huguenot community now. Montpellier and La Rochelle the same.'

Piet looked around the square with a cold, hard anger. He had been in Daurade the previous day, looking in vain for the tailor who had copied the Shroud for him. Everything had been peaceful, tranquil. He'd seen people going about their business, the shops open, the smell of almonds roasting and soft dappled sunlight beneath the trees. Now this.

He bent down, picked up a cracked earthenware flagon and stood it on the corner of a wall. Everywhere, chairs and stools and tables, shattered beyond repair.

'That's odd,' he muttered, looking across the square.

His eyes narrowed. Painted on the door of the tailor's workshop was a black cross. It had not been there yesterday.

Leaving McCone, Piet ran across the square.

'Mademoiselle, forgive me for disturbing you,' he said to the young woman standing outside the atelier, 'but what has happened? The tailor who works here, was he hurt?'

'He is dead, Monsieur.'

Another death? 'I am sorry to hear it. The looting, was he caught up in the troubles?'

Finally, she raised her dazed eyes and looked directly at him. 'I found my father at his work bench, his needle and scissors still in his hand. A weak heart.'

'He was your father? I am sorry. I knew him. He was a gifted man.'

'Look around you. Look at what they've done. At least he did not live to see this.'

The girl wandered away, leaving Piet with his uneasy thoughts. He wanted it to be true, but he did not trust the timing of it.

'What was that about?' McCone had come over to see what was happening.

Piet was about to speak, then some new sense of caution stopped him. 'Nothing,' he said. 'I thought I knew the girl. That's all.'

McCone dropped his hand on Piet's shoulder. 'You look all in. You should rest. Let's go to the tavern. My throat is parched.'

Piet took a final look around the square, then nodded. 'Very well.'

'*S'il vous plaît, Monsieur*,' Minou repeated. 'Please let me pass.'

The soldier standing guard at the outer door of the almshouse did not move.

'No one is to leave. Orders.'

After two hours of working in the kitchen and helping with the last of the injured, Minou was exhausted and desperate to get back to Aimeric and her aunt.

'Sirrah, let me pass.'

He tapped his ear. 'Didn't you hear? Are you deaf? Orders are that no one is to come in or out.'

'My aunt will wonder what has happened to me,' she pleaded, though she was imagining how her father would fret if he ever learnt she had been caught up in such a riot.

As she tried to step around him, her beads fell from her pocket. The soldier's expression changed.

'And would that be your Catholic aunt?' he said, lifting a corner of her gown with the tip of his sword. 'All this finery comes at a cost, does it not?'

Minou stepped back out of his reach.

'Did they send you to spy on us? We know they use women to do their dirty work.' His hand shot out and grabbed Minou's wrist. 'Is that your game?'

To her horror, he started to paw at the fastening of her cloak.

'Come on, then, if this is what they send their Catholic whores to do, let's see—'

Minou brought her knee up as hard as she could between his legs.

'Bitch!' he shrieked, as he doubled over. '*Putane!*'

Ignoring the pain in her shoulder, Minou clasped her hands together and brought a blow down on the back of his neck. As he fell forward to his knees, she jumped round him, pushed open the door, and ran, terrified, into rue du Périgord.

CHAPTER THIRTY-SEVEN

⚜

The tavern was smoky and dark. A well-known Protestant meeting place, today all the shutters were closed, the atmosphere unsettled. There was a smell of leather, sawdust and spilt ale. Each time the door opened, bringing in a gust of fresh air from outside, all eyes spun round hoping for news.

While McCone and Crompton sat at a table, drinking and playing dice, Piet leant against the wall, trying to still the thoughts in his head. The scene at the atelier in Place de la Daurade had brought the Shroud back to the forefront of his mind. He couldn't shake his suspicion that Crompton's presence in Toulouse, with his cousin Devereux, was more to do with that, than any desire to stand shoulder to shoulder with his Huguenot brothers. For a moment, he even asked himself if Crompton could have been involved in the tailor's death.

'*Per lo Miègjorn*,' he muttered, the password he had been asked to give in the upstairs room in Carcassonne. 'For the Midi.'

Piet pulled himself up. He was allowing his imagination to run away with him. He and Crompton were on the same side, weren't they? He didn't like the man, but that didn't make him a villain.

All the same, Piet couldn't rid himself of the feeling he'd had in the almshouse that something was out of joint. Something said that shouldn't have been said. He glanced across at Crompton, who was rolling his dice.

All the same . . .

The door opened again and a messenger came in. He identified the most senior of the Huguenot officers present, and reported to him. Piet moved closer to hear what was being said.

'There are halberdiers posted at the main entrance to the monastery, the Seneschal's own men. The judges also have a contingent of private soldiers. They assert the town guard is under Huguenot control, so cannot be relied upon to protect them.'

'Ridiculous.'

'It's the reason Parliament gave.'

The captain shook his head. 'Have the talks started?'

'They are about to.'

'And is Jean de Mansencal presiding, as we had heard?'

'Yes, sir.'

'And we have men inside to report back to us what is said?'

'We do.'

He waved his hand. 'Very good. Bring me further word in an hour.'

Piet watched the messenger leave, then sat down next to McCone. They were speaking in English and Crompton, again, was picking a fight.

'Your pastor preaches revolt from the pulpit,' he said. 'He has fire in his belly.' He held up his hand. 'Justified, in my humble opinion. But he is a warmonger, not a man of peace.'

'I agree Barrelles is forthright,' McCone said cautiously.

'He denounces the Duke of Guise.' Crompton swept up his dice from the table and put them in his pocket. 'If these talks go ill, you don't have enough men to take the city without reinforcements.'

Piet leant forward. 'There is no plan to take the city. We want a fair peace, not war.'

Crompton laughed. 'What do you think Hunault is doing with Condé in Orléans, planning an afternoon's hunting trip?'

Piet flushed. 'What have you been doing this afternoon, Crompton, while we were hard at work?' he demanded. 'And Devereux? Where is he? He's not yet back.'

'What are you implying?'

Piet held up his hand. 'An innocent question, Crompton. Why? Have you something to hide?'

'Damn you to hell, Reydon,' he said, standing up. Without another word, he stormed from the tavern, leaving the door juddering on its hinges.

'I know,' Piet said, feeling McCone's quizzical gaze. 'Stupid to bait him, you don't have to tell me.'

McCone smiled. 'Actually, I was only going to ask what was the cause of such ill-feeling between you?'

'He is slippery, his cousin more so. I would know why they are in Toulouse.'

'They say they have come to give their support. You think there is some ulterior motive?'

Piet shrugged. 'Maybe.'

'Spies?'

'In truth, Jasper, I don't know. They may be, but for which side? Us or them? Devereux seems to be able to come and go at will. He is well connected in Toulouse.'

'But you dislike Crompton more.'

Piet reached for his ale. 'There's something about him.'

'Is that why he calls you by another name?' he said mildly. 'Reydon, is it?'

Piet turned hot with shame. 'My friend, forgive me. I meant to tell you, once we got to know one another better.'

'There is no need to apologise.'

'No, there is. When I first arrived back in Toulouse in March, I had reasons not to use my own name. I took another.'

'And that was Joubert. Or is that your real name and Reydon the alias?'

'No, Reydon is my name.' Piet let his shoulders drop, feeling worse because McCone was being so decent about the deceit. 'I truly am sorry, Jasper.'

McCone raised his hand. 'It does not matter. Crompton, for all your distrust of him, is right about one thing. They say the Prince of Condé has raised the standard of revolt at Orléans. I know for a fact Saux received orders requesting arms and money for the prince's campaign a week ago.'

'Do you think there is a plan in place to take Toulouse?'

'Do you?'

Piet lowered his voice. 'I have heard a rumour that the keys to certain of the city's gates, the Porte Villeneuve among them, were taken and copied.'

'When?'

Piet looked up, surprised by the sharpness in McCone's voice. 'I don't rightly know. Last week, perhaps.'

'Who told you?'

Piet shook his head. 'One of the Huguenot garrison at the Hôtel de Ville. It seemed wishful thinking. I paid little heed. There are so many rumours, each more outlandish than the last. All I hope is for common sense to prevail and that our leaders – and theirs – will put the good of Toulouse before their own desire for glory.'

McCone paused, then raised his tankard. 'I'll drink to that.'

Despite his talk of peace, Piet's optimism was fading. He had clung to the hope that the caches of weapons hidden throughout the city, in Protestant as well as Catholic houses, were there as a deterrent. During the course of this long day he had realised he was in the minority.

He thought back to their meeting in the hot, airless house in the Bastide in Carcassonne. For the first time, he realised that more of his comrades thought – like Crompton – that the time for talking was over. The months of waiting had stirred people's blood. They saw injustice at every turn and wanted retribution. Today of all days, after witnessing the devastation inflicted by a Catholic mob on the quartier Daurade, who could blame them?

Piet loosened the chemise at his neck, suddenly unable to bear the fuggy, expectant atmosphere of the tavern a moment longer. He stood up.

'By your leave, Jasper.'

He went outside and filled his lungs with air. He looked up at some of the most beautiful medieval houses in Toulouse and he thought of Minou and how the city, as well as the people, needed to be protected.

A plan began to form in his mind. From where he was standing, Piet could see the red sloping roof and hexagonal bell tower of the church of the Augustinians, clear and sharp against the afternoon sky. He would no longer sit and wait, relying on third- or fourth-hand information, he would steal in and listen to the debate for himself.

The slap took Minou by surprise, sending her stumbling against the stone balustrade of the loggia.

'Madame Montfort!'

She had arrived home to find her with the steward, Martineau, whispering together in the courtyard. Madame Montfort had pulled something from her pocket and had passed it to him. He had looked down, appeared to count, then nodded and vanished into the house. Minou had waited, until she thought Madame Montfort had also gone.

'Madame!' she shouted, deflecting a second blow.

'Where have you been?' Madame Montfort's face was ugly with fury, and something else: guilt, Minou realised. 'Your aunt has not been able to rest for fear something ill had befallen you, yet here you are, skulking back like some kitchen girl on heat.'

Minou stared, incredulous. 'You forget yourself.'

'It is you who forget yourself,' she hissed. 'You are nothing in this house, nothing. You and your uncouth, vulgar brother, poor relations come to leech upon your betters. You bring this fine household into disrepute. Staying out all night, like a common doxy.'

'You cannot possibly imagine—'

'Did you think no one would mark your wanton behaviour? Did you?'

Madame Montfort was shouting so loudly that a serving girl stuck her nose out to see what was happening, and was furiously waved away.

'This is unwarranted calumny,' Minou protested, but the older woman grasped her arm.

'How dare you think you can do as you please? Salvadora might be taken in by you, but I am not and neither is my brother. You need to learn to show respect to your betters. Well, this will give you time to reflect upon your failings.'

Without warning, Minou found herself being dragged down the steps below the loggia. Before she could take in what was happening, Madame Montfort had opened a small wooden door and pushed her roughly inside the basement. Then there was a click of a key in the lock, and Minou realised she was imprisoned.

For a moment, she just stood listening as the footsteps on

the far side of the door grew faint with the clinking of the heavy ring of keys at Madame Montfort's waist. Minou couldn't comprehend what had caused Madame Montfort to so completely lose control of herself. To raise her hand to Minou, to treat her like a servant, that was far beyond her authority.

Was it prompted by what she had been doing with the steward Martineau? The guilt in her eyes when she had turned and seen Minou watching her?

Weary, and with her shoulder throbbing, Minou sat heavily on the top step. Her nose was filled with the sour smell of must and damp wood. The swish of a rat turning tail made her shudder. She felt sorry for herself, but she was determined not to give way. Not after everything she had witnessed and endured and survived.

Slowly, her eyes grew accustomed to the semi-gloom. A criss-crossed lattice of red bricks at ground-floor level allowed both fresh air and daylight into the cellar. She had never noticed the grille from the courtyard. Gradually, she made out that the entire wall opposite was lined with cases, barrels and wooden chests, stacked from the rough earth floor to the brick ceiling.

Minou went over to get a closer look. Many of the crates had the letter D branded in ink upon the side. She realised she was not the only recent guest. Set neatly on top of one of the barrels were two plain cups. She sniffed and smelt the remains of ale. There was also a half-eaten loaf of bread which, although dry and as hard as rock, was not mouldy. Victuals for the men who had brought the barrels down?

Minou traced her fingers over the surface of the nearest barrel and found a fingerhole in the lid. She pulled carefully at the wood, easing it up until she could see inside. She had expected to see grain or flour, but this was something else. Minou pulled up her sleeve, ignoring the ache in her muscles, then wiggled her wrist inside. Her fingers found grit, like coarse sand or the rough dust that caught between the cobbles in La Cité. She held it up so that it caught the light.

A black powder, not the colour of earth.

Minou looked around, at all the other barrels and the long, flat chests. Using a thin piece of wood as a lever, she jemmied off the lid of one of the widest crates. A score of arquebuses laid one on top of another, wrapped in oiled cloth. Inside, the lid was branded the word DELPECH.

She had no need to look inside any other of the boxes to know that she would see other weapons. A private arsenal, but why here? Her uncle was not a military man. Then another thought suddenly struck her. Madame Montfort could not be aware of the cache of gunpowder and weapons, for surely she would not have locked her down here had she known?

A noise above startled her. Hastily, Minou put the lid back into place and straightened the loose cover on the barrel of gunpowder. Listening to the footsteps on the floorboards over her head, she tried to work out which room the sound came from. She counted the steps down, and the orientation of the door in the courtyard, and realised she was beneath the private chapel.

Then she had a more encouraging thought. Was it not probable that there was a way into the cellars from the house itself? Even at night, when there were fewer eyes to see, the commotion of men carrying heavy barrels and crates would have been hard to conceal from the road outside. All the rooms of the house overlooked the courtyard at one aspect or another. Someone would have seen something.

Invigorated, Minou began methodically to work her way along the wall, looking for some inconsistency in the surface of the bricks. She squeezed her hands into gaps between the stacked boxes, rolled the barrels to one side and back, paddling to find a latch or a handle.

At last, the sore tips of her fingers found a beam sitting out proud from the wall. With renewed energy, Minou lifted and dragged and pushed six wooden boxes aside until she could see. She smiled.

Her instincts were right. Set within the wall was a low door. Two metal hinges, clearly oiled and in working order, and an arched keyhole.

There was no key.

Piet stood under the overhang of the houses on rue des Arts, and peered out.

The main entrance to the Augustinian monastery was guarded by the Seneschal's halberdiers, as the messenger had reported, and there were private soldiers patrolling the periphery. The monastery once had been one of the most influential in Toulouse, but fire and a lightning strike on the bell tower had left much of the building in disrepair.

Having watched for a few minutes, Piet decided his best point of entry was through the church. He knew there was a door that gave directly onto the street to allow the civilian congregation to join the monks for services. If he could access the nave, he would have a fighting chance to get through into the cloister itself. In appearance, he looked little different from any of the Huguenot leaders gathered within. If luck was on his side, no one would challenge him once he was inside.

Suddenly he thought of Vidal, their conversation in the confessional of Saint-Nazaire in Carcassonne. A lifetime ago, it seemed.

CHAPTER THIRTY-EIGHT

⚜

Carcassonne

'Your tongue is too sharp, Marie Galy,' Bérenger muttered. 'You'll cut yourself one of these days.'

Marie tossed her head back, and laughed, delighted to have got a rise out of the old soldier.

'You're not my father. You can stop your ears if it's not to your liking.'

She stepped up to the stone parapet around the well.

'Your cheek will lead you into serious trouble,' Bérenger said. 'Mark my words.'

Marie heard his companion whisper how very fair she was on the eyes.

'She's too saucy,' Bérenger grumbled.

'I don't mind it,' the boy said, looking back over his shoulder.

Marie sent him a dazzling smile and a little wave of her fingers, causing him to blush brick red and stumble on the cobbled stones.

'Come on,' ordered Bérenger, continuing his patrol to the Château Comtal.

Marie was on the point of returning to her chores, when she saw an elegant and finely dressed lady walking towards Place du Grand Puits. She put her pail on the ground and watched. Such a graceful walk, her back as straight as a board, her shadow slender and elongated in the late afternoon sunshine.

She had marble-white skin and glossy dark hair, black as a crow's wing, just visible beneath her embroidered hood. And such fine clothes. The crimson cloak trimmed with red satin, the slashes in her sleeves the colour of irises.

The noblewoman stopped and looked around as if trying to find her bearings. Marie took her chance.

'May I help you, my lady?' she said, stepping down from the well. 'I know La Cité well.'

The woman turned. Marie saw how her brows were shaped like crescent moons above her dark, glinting eyes.

'I would know where the house of the Joubert family is to be found.'

Even the woman's voice was unlike any Marie had ever heard. Thick and rich, like honey dripping from a spoon.

'I know it. Aimeric is –' She stopped herself, remembering Madame Noubel had told her to say nothing if anyone came asking.

The woman's expression softened. 'Your discretion becomes you well,' she said, putting her hand into a velvet purse tied with a twisted blue cord at her wrist. 'I see no reason why you should be disadvantaged for that. My thanks.'

She pressed a coin, bright and clean, into her hand. Marie smiled and dropped a curtsey. Surely Madame Noubel did not mean she could not talk to someone such as this? A noblewoman, so exquisitely attired and gracious.

'Tell me about this Aimeric,' the woman said. 'Is there some understanding between you?'

Marie tossed her head. 'He would say so. For my part, I am in no hurry. I would make a better match than a bookseller's son.'

'A bookseller, do you say?'

'Yes, my lady.'

The woman smiled. Marie noted how her teeth were perfectly even, and perfectly white.

'Then that is indeed the house I seek.'

Toulouse

'The lady has quit her lodgings,' Bonal said.

Vidal paused at the foot of the grand stone staircase of the Augustinian monastery. The wide brick corridors and vaulted ceilings were filled with the echoes of men's voices, the rattle of armour and swords and soldiers' boots. The monks moved through their contemplative spaces like black ghosts in their mendicant robes.

'When?'

'Yesterday, shortly after dawn.'

Vidal's grip tightened on the balustrade. 'How is it possible she was able to leave Toulouse? Were not all the gates in the cathedral quarter barred the instant the disturbance broke out?'

Bonal drew closer. 'It appears the lady managed to secure the use of the bishop's own carriage, and since the closest gate to her lodgings, the Porte Montolieu, was under a Catholic guard, they let it through.'

'Without checking who was inside.'

'It seems so, my lord.'

Conflicting emotions battled in Vidal's chest: anger that she had gone without his knowledge; fury at how easily she seemed to have been able to commandeer a carriage from the bishop's palace; finally, and he was ashamed of it, an aching disappointment. Though Vidal had prayed for forgiveness for his human frailty, God had not yet given him the strength to resist her temptation.

Vidal did not doubt the value of her continuing patronage. Though he had the support of men of commerce and law within Toulouse, he had no noble voice speaking in his favour. This was, of course, not the moment to launch his petition to be the next Bishop of Toulouse. The situation within the city was too fragile. But as soon as the next phase of the inevitable conflict began, neither his role, nor the incumbent bishop's negligent inaction, would go unnoticed.

Then he would act.

'Is it known if His Eminence approved the use of his carriage in person?' he asked.

'It is rumoured that he did.'

Vidal raised his eyebrows. 'A story that began with you, Bonal?'

'I thought it was my duty to share what I believed to be true.'

'Quite right,' Vidal said, allowing a brief smile to touch his lips. 'Knowledge of any such lapses of judgement, or transgressions of so grave a nature, must be in the public interest.' He moved towards the staircase. 'I would be informed when she has arrived back in Puivert. Have a messenger sent after her.'

Bonal cleared his throat. 'Forgive me, Monsignor, but the stable boy says he heard mention of Carcassonne.'

Vidal turned again. 'Carcassonne?'

'That was the order given to the driver, so he says.'

'Did you question him yourself? Was he certain?'

'Most certain. The boy seemed trustworthy.'

Vidal hesitated. 'What of our Dutch friend? Where is he?'

'He was in the Huguenot tavern, then went to quartier Daurade.'

'Did he approach the tailor's workshop?'

'Yes.'

'He didn't see you?' Vidal said sharply.

'No one saw me, Monsignor.'

Vidal frowned. 'No one doubts the man died a natural death?'

'No. It was common knowledge that his heart was weak.'

Vidal nodded and moved towards the staircase, then stopped again. 'And, Bonal, find out why the lady has gone to Carcassonne. It may be an innocent arrangement of long standing, but I would know the reason for it all the same.'

CARCASSONNE

Rixende opened the front door to find Marie Galy standing on the step.

'Oh. It's you,' she said, wiping her hands on her apron.

Rixende disliked Marie Galy. Most girls did. She was too fond of herself, considered herself prettier than everyone else and made no attempts to pretend otherwise. Rixende had seen the way even Aimeric looked at Marie, with a mixture of hunger and admiration. She was not alone in resenting the fact that there was always a boy who would offer to help Marie to carry her pail of water or basket of logs when the rest of them were left to struggle.

'What do you want?'

Marie gave a haughty smile. 'I am sure I want nothing of you, Rixende, but there is a friend of Monsieur Joubert who would pay her respects.'

'You know full well the master is not here,' Rixende snapped, starting to close the door. She did not intend to have her afternoon wasted by Marie Galy, making herself important as usual.

Marie's slim foot shot out and blocked the gap. 'I'm sure I don't know anything of the kind. Come, he is always here. Everyone knows he has barely set foot outside the house since the feast of Epiphany.'

'That's where you're wrong!' Rixende was pleased to be able to put Marie in her place. 'He took his leave before Passiontide.'

'Where did he go, Rixende?'

A wine-stain flush spread across Rixende's pock-marked skin when she realised she'd given herself away. Madame Noubel had been quite clear that she was to keep that information to herself.

'I can't say.'

Rixende didn't believe it really was a secret. Everyone knew everyone else's business in La Cité.

'Leaving Alis in the care of Madame Noubel,' Marie sneered. 'I see, that's why she's always here.'

'Well, she's in the Bastide today,' Rixende snapped. 'Now, if you don't mind, some of us have things to do.'

She slammed the door. Any encounter with Marie always left her with the sense she had been judged and found wanting. Then, turning back to her chores, she smelt burning.

'No . . .' Rixende wailed.

The pan of milk she had left on the fire had boiled over. The only way Alis would take her medicine was if it was mixed in milk with a little honey. Rixende seized the handle, hoping to save a little of it, then let out a howl. The pan slipped from her scalded fingers and clattered to the ground, spilling what little remained over the tiles.

'Minou?'

Alis, curled upon her father's chair, jolted awake and the

kitten leapt off her lap. Rixende was alarmed to see the girl's colour so high.

'No, it's me,' she said, fussing to tuck the blanket around the girl's legs. 'It's nothing. I dropped the pan and the noise woke you. Go back to sleep.'

Alis stared up at her. 'Minou hasn't come home?'

Rixende's heart turned over. She hated to see the little girl getting more sickly, thinner, by the day. In truth, though she would lose her daily wage, she was starting to hope Madame Noubel would return to the Bastide and take Alis with her. The little girl's sadness was too much to bear.

Alis closed her eyes. Soon, her troubled breathing became steady again. Without Aimeric and Minou to play with her, she rarely went out. She was tiny, all skin and bone. Her black curls lay damp and flat on her cheeks.

Rixende bustled about, clearing up the mess on the floor, opening the door to let the acrid smell out. She could do very little to ease Alis's suffering. The only thing she could do was make sure she had what she needed to soothe her cough. Another root of liquorice. Warm milk, honey, and the linctus.

She looked out of the window, at the light of the early evening dancing along the top of the wall at the rear of the house. It would only take a moment. Alis was sleeping again, Madame Noubel was not due back until dusk. If she went quickly, she could run home and borrow a quart of milk from her mother and be back within the half-hour.

Rixende took an earthenware jug from its hook, made sure the fire was safe, then slipped out the back door into the yard and into the street beyond.

No one would ever know she had gone.

CHAPTER THIRTY-NINE

⚜

Toulouse

High above the debating chamber, Piet balanced his way along the narrow stone ridge at the top of the staircase, then vaulted the balustrade and dropped down onto the balcony out of sight.

Far below him, he saw a mass of faces. The room was cavernous. Red brick walls soared to a vaulted ceiling. On the south side, six tall arched windows of plain glass, many times the height of a man, overlooked the colonnades of the cloister and the refectory. On the north side were rows of wooden stalls where the monks were accustomed to sit.

At the west end of the chamber, a raised dais had been installed and furnished with five high-backed ecclesiastical chairs. A pass door led directly from the dais into an antechamber, shielded by a tapestry of St Augustine himself. Below the stage, at a long oak bench, two scribes sat, their heads bowed, white quills and inkhorns set before them, waiting to record the words of the discussion.

Piet was too high up to distinguish any man's expression below, but their style of clothing marked their allegiance. A huddle of men in the red and purple of the cathedral chapter; the black and grey of the lawyers and attorneys-at-law; the gold-trimmed robes of the judges and the green and military blues of the town guard. Piet cast his eye around until he saw the Huguenot leaders, Saux, La Popelinière and the pastor, Jean

Barrelles, amongst them. A day and a half since the riots had started, tempers were still high.

'We will not agree to that,' someone declared.

An explosion of complaint, everyone talking at the same time. Fingers jabbing at the air, a priest raising his hands, the Seneschal of Toulouse summoning a servant to bring him more wine. Presiding over the whole was the President of the Parliament, Jean de Mansencal.

The sharp rap of a gavel. 'I will have silence!'

'You insult the King by refusing to honour the statutes of—'

'And you offend God by your . . .'

Piet saw Saux turn away, his fists clenched.

'Order! I will have order,' one of the judges shouted. 'My lords, gentlemen all, please. Let us put this issue to one side for now, and instead address –'

His suggestion was drowned in another wave of angry shouting. Piet sent his eyes around the chamber, noticing Toulouse's most notorious dealer of weapons and arms, Pierre Delpech, standing in the Catholic corner with a corpulent man, whose forehead glistened with sweat.

•

'There is no key,' Minou said out loud.

Her voice echoed in the dank, vaulted cellar. But then, what else should she expect? If this was the concealed way in and out of the cellar through the house, it was obvious the key would be on the far side of the door.

All at once, she heard a different tread above her head. Moments passed, then she heard a scuffling.

'Minou?' hissed a voice. 'Are you there?'

Her heart leapt with relief.

'Aimeric,' she said, pressing both hands to the door. 'Is

there a key on your side?' She heard the latch turn, then the door was pushed open and her brother was standing there, grinning in triumph.

'You brilliant, brilliant boy.'

He threw his arms around her.

'I thought you were dead,' he blurted out. 'When they came back yesterday without you, I thought you'd been killed, even though old witch Montfort said you'd run away.'

'Run away! You could not think I would go anywhere without you. As if I would ever leave you behind.'

Awkward about his show of affection, Aimeric stepped back.

'I didn't believe it, but she claimed she saw you in the arms of a soldier – a Huguenot – and that you had gone with him.'

Minou's colour rose. 'Madame Montfort is a vile and unpleasant woman, who lets her imagination – and her tongue – run away with her.' She frowned. 'What of our aunt? Did she believe Madame Montfort's lies?'

Aimeric shrugged. 'No one tells me anything, but she's been in her chamber crying all the time.' He paused. 'I am glad you are safe.'

Minou hugged him tight. 'As you can see, all is well, even if I am a little dusty. Come.'

She pulled the door to the cellar shut, and they began to walk along the passageway that led back up into the main house.

'Madame Montfort said that the Huguenots attacked the St Salvador procession. Is that true?' Aimeric asked.

'No. It was the Catholics who attacked a Protestant funeral cortège, nothing to do with the procession. We were caught in the middle of the fighting.'

'Why didn't you come home with them?'

'We became separated and I was struck.' She dropped her voice. 'Madame Montfort was right in one particular. It was a Huguenot who came to my aid. It was Piet, Aimeric. He took me to safety in the almshouse in rue du Périgord, and stayed with me until I recovered consciousness this morning.'

'Piet!' Aimeric's eyes blazed. 'I knew he would make it out of Carcassonne. Did he speak of me? Did he say how I helped him?'

Minou laughed. 'In point of fact, he did. And, for my part, I scolded him for putting you at risk. He intends to make amends by teaching you to throw a knife, as he promised.'

'When?'

'We'll have to see.' The smile faded from her face. 'The fact of it is that Piet is a Huguenot. Our uncle is one of the leading Catholics in Toulouse, and nurses a profound dislike of Protestants. At the moment, with everything so unsettled, it will be difficult.'

'But I'm not Catholic,' Aimeric exclaimed. 'I mean, I am, but it makes no difference to me. I like Piet.'

'These days, *petit*, it makes every difference, whether we like it or not. But, from what I overheard, the two sides are meeting this afternoon to negotiate a truce. God willing, everything will be resolved. Toulouse will return to normal.'

They had climbed the last step and come out in the private chapel. It was calm, everything still and quiet. The unlit candles, the silver offertory plate, the hassocks with the Boussay crest on them neatly placed before the altar. Minou brushed a cobweb from her hair, then shut the small cellar door behind them. She ran her hand over the wood. The door was completely flat, designed to fit precisely into the section of the wainscoting. From this side, save for the keyhole, it was hard to see there was a door there at all.

'How did you even know this was here? Or even to come looking for me in the cellar?'

'The kitchen maid saw you arguing with Madame Montfort in the courtyard and ran to tell me. When I came looking and there was no sign of you, I guessed what had happened.'

Aimeric sat himself down in the narrow, straight-backed pew and stretched out his legs. 'Nicer here when there's no one around,' he said. 'Peaceful.'

Minou frowned. 'Madame Montfort's behaviour was extraordinary. She was talking to Steward Martineau in the courtyard. The next thing I know, she struck me and locked me down there.'

'They are always conspiring together. She steals things, and Martineau smuggles them out of the house when they think no one's watching.'

Minou sat down beside him. 'You can't be suggesting she is a thief? I dislike her too, but you're letting your imagination get the better of you.'

Aimeric shrugged. 'I've seen her. They meet here in the chapel, or sometimes Uncle's study in the afternoon when everyone is sleeping. She has the keys to every cupboard, every chamber. Sometimes it's something small, other times I've seen him sneaking out through the kitchen yard carrying a flour sack. A candlestick went missing last week.' He gestured to the altar and Minou noticed that the two bases did not match. 'One of the chambermaids was blamed, but I'm sure Madame Montfort took it. And Aunt Boussay is always losing things. A brooch, a necklace. I heard Uncle shouting at her again last week for being careless.'

If Aimeric was right, Minou thought, it might well account not only for Madame Montfort's panic earlier, but also why she had always so resented their presence in the household.

'There's a quantity of barrels and crates being stored in the cellar,' she said, glancing at the door. 'Gunpowder, guns, shot.'

Aimeric's dark eyes blazed. 'That's what they've been doing at night.'

'You knew?'

He shrugged. 'Not what it was they were bringing into the house, but I knew they were up to something. When I can't sleep at night, I sometimes go outside to the balcony.' He sighed. 'It reminds me of sitting with Bérenger on the battlements of La Cité, watching the stars.'

Minou squeezed his hand. 'I'm sorry you are so unhappy.'

He shrugged again. 'I'm getting used to it. Anyway, half the houses in the city are being used to store weapons now.'

'I was not aware of that. And I cannot believe Madame Montfort is either, otherwise why would she have put me down there in the first place?'

'I wager she does, but she and Martineau are becoming careless now Uncle is so rarely here.' He paused, then looked down at his feet. 'But you are all right, aren't you? No one hurt you, or . . .'

Minou put her arm around his shoulder. 'All is well, my brave little brother. Is Uncle here now?'

'No. He went out at midday and has not returned.'

'I need to speak to our aunt, to put right any falsehoods Madame Montfort has put in her head. Can you keep watch? It will not take long.'

'At your service,' Aimeric said with a flourish. 'Leave it to me.'

Delpech was signalling to someone at the far end of the chamber, out of Piet's line of vision, beckoning for him to join him.

Others, soldiers and monks, were slipping in at the back of the room to hear the verdict.

The scribe passed a parchment to a servant, who took it to Jean de Mansencal. He read it, nodded his approval, then rose to his feet. The chamber fell silent.

'By the authority invested in me,' he pronounced, 'and in the presence of honourable capitouls of the Hôtel de Ville, his noble excellency the Seneschal of Toulouse, and my fellow judges of the Parliament, these are the terms of truce as agreed on this, the third day of April, Friday, in the year of grace of our Lord fifteen hundred and sixty-two.'

Piet realised he was holding his breath. Would the decision be just? Would it be fair? Was this to be the moment when Toulouse turned away from civil war or marched towards it? There was a price to be paid, but who would be called upon to pay it?

'This day it is decreed,' de Mansencal read, 'that the powers and rights set down in the Edict of Toleration of January last shall be upheld. Thereby, under said conditions, it is agreed that the Huguenot community of Toulouse shall be permitted to maintain, at its own expense, a force of no more than two hundred unarmed militia to protect their persons and property.'

A bellow went up from all sides of the chamber. It was both too much, and yet not enough.

'With equal consideration and' – de Mansencal had to raise his voice to be heard – 'and with equal consideration and under the same conditions, as set down in the Edict of Toleration, the Catholic community shall be allowed to recruit a force of similar number and to serve under four professional captains, responsible for the levy of the town militia, these four to be under the control of the Town Council.'

Another uproar of complaint. They were like schoolchildren, Piet thought with disgust, objecting for the sake of it. The lives of innocent people were at stake, yet they behaved as if it was a game.

'All other soldiers,' de Mansencal continued, all but shouting the verdict now, 'whether their presence within the city limits is by invitation, as part of a private militia, or as a volunteer – save those retained by the conditions hitherto laid down – shall withdraw immediately from Toulouse. It will be considered a breach of the terms of this truce for the tocsin bell to be rung or for any other call to arms to be issued. Finally, it is agreed by the leadership of both parties as set down here this day, that my officials – together with those of the Hôtel de Ville – shall undertake an investigation into those responsible for the damage to property and loss of life from midday on the second of April until noon today and punish those deemed culpable.'

One of the judges banged his gavel and de Mansencal raised his hand.

'Hear ye, in the sight of God and in the name of His Royal Majesty the King and her most noble Excellency, the Queen Regent, this is the decision of these here assembled. It is the duty of every man to uphold the terms of the truce for the good of Toulouse. *Vive le Roi.* God save the King.'

At a signal, the trumpeters played a flourish, forestalling any questions, and the President exited the chamber, followed by the other judges, the Seneschal's entourage and the eight capitouls.

For a moment, there was silence. Then, pandemonium. Men headed for the doors, pushing and elbowing one another aside in their haste to return to their own territories and report the decision.

High in his eyrie, Piet leant back against the pillar. Was there any chance of a fair investigation to identify the true perpetrators of the disorder, Catholic as well as Huguenot, or would innocent men hang for the sake of re-establishing public order? Each side would pretend to honour the terms of the peace whilst shoring up its own defences. If Toulouse had been flooded with weapons before the riots, from this moment on it would get worse. Men like Delpech, he thought bitterly, would profit.

Piet peered down, looking to see if the weapons dealer was still there. He saw Delpech walking through the chamber flanked by a clutch of lesser officials from the Town Council and several churchmen, including a canon from the cathedral. He saw a tall and imposing man who, in the stuffy heat of the chamber, briefly removed his biretta, smoothed down his hair, then replaced it. Black hair with a white streak.

Vidal.

At first, relief surged through him, then a rat-a-tat of a myriad images assaulted his senses, flashing in and out of his mind as in a drug-induced dream: Vidal's red robes sweeping into the Saint-Nazaire cathedral at dawn; the Fournier house like the setting for a masque, a sleight of hand of make-believe and mirrors; the drugged wine; lying cold on the ground in the shadow of the medieval Cité walls.

So much trouble, and for what? For the Shroud of Antioch?

Piet knew the answer was yes. It was an object of great and holy significance for the Catholic Church, a relic said to be able to work miracles. Vidal would do everything he could to get it back.

And then, as always, the same question like a splinter beneath his skin: why would Vidal go to such trouble to catch him, to question him, only to let him go? There could only be one answer. Piet could no longer deny it. It was because, for now at least, he was more use to Vidal at liberty than in prison. And Vidal had arranged to have him followed. It was not his overcharged imagination, but the truth.

Piet felt cut adrift, exhausted by the days of fighting and suffering, the lack of sleep and living on his wits. He had no choice but to accept that the man who had been his greatest friend was now his most dangerous enemy. Vidal, alive not dead. Not imprisoned, but here, clearly a man of influence and power in the heart of the beast.

His relief at Vidal's deliverance died, leaving in its place the cold, bitter taste of betrayal.

CHAPTER FORTY

Carcassonne

Blanche pressed another coin into Marie's hand. 'I have no further need of your assistance.'

'If there was a position in your service, my lady, would you consider me? I am a hard worker, I would travel anywhere, the further away from Carcassonne the better, and I—'

'Enough.' Having gathered the information she needed, Blanche wanted rid of the girl. 'I have no need of a lady's maid.'

Marie flushed. Blanche waited for the girl to vanish into one of the alleyways leading from the square. She then summoned her manservant, who had been following at a discreet distance since they had left the bishop's palace.

'Prepare the carriage for immediate departure. We will continue to Puivert as soon as my business here is concluded.'

He bowed and took his leave.

Blanche walked to the Joubert house. A wild rose trailed, uncut, above the lintel. From Marie, she knew the household was made up of Joubert himself – his wife having died in the last plague epidemic some five years previously – and his three children: a nineteen-year-old called Marguerite, known as Minou, who was unmarried and still lived at home; a thirteen-year-old boy by the name of Aimeric, and a younger girl called Alis.

Blanche considered the possibilities. It was frustrating to discover the two oldest were currently in Toulouse. At seven years old, Alis was too young to be of interest. If only Blanche had known this, she would not have come to Carcassonne.

No matter. God was at her side. All things happened for a reason and in accordance with His plan.

Blanche crossed herself, then knocked on the door. Marie Galy had a low opinion of the Joubert maid, dismissing her as dim-witted and clumsy. She did not therefore anticipate any difficulty in gaining access. Beyond that, she had no plan. She waited. When the maid did not come, she tried the handle and discovered the door was unlocked.

Her first impression was of a well-kept house. The maid was clearly not as much of a slattern as Marie had led her to believe. The hooks in the passageway shone, a wooden chest polished as bright as a looking glass. Blanche opened the lid, releasing the familiar smell of beeswax. A pile of neatly folded linen lay inside, threadbare but carefully stitched. A possible hiding place for a document of value? She lifted the cloth, but her eye saw nothing of interest.

She followed a smell of burnt milk to the kitchen, prepared to confront the maid at work, but that room was empty too. The blackened pan stood just outside the open back door. Beyond the small yard, a gate to the street was swinging. Had the maid been in her service, Blanche would have had her beaten for such slackness.

She opened the dresser and started to search through the drawers, finding nothing of note. She regretted not going first to the Joubert bookshop in the Bastide. It was more likely any legal documents would be kept there, rather than in the family home. Then again, it was Minou she wanted.

Only when she turned towards the fireplace did Blanche see a sleeping child was curled in a chair with a kitten on her lap.

Was this Alis?

Blanche took a step forward, startling the cat. It shot from the girl's lap, a streak of tabby fur, out into the yard.

The girl jolted awake, her black eyes wide. 'Who are you? Where is Rixende?'

TOULOUSE

Piet quit his hiding place, and lost himself in the throng of men streaming out of the monastery. His thoughts were buzzing like flies in a jar. Angry, relentless. Was it Vidal who had drugged his wine that night? He had tried to ignore his suspicions, needing to keep faith with his friend and their friendship. For weeks Piet had told himself that though he and Vidal saw the world through different eyes, they both were guided by decency and honour.

He didn't even know where he was going. Back to the tavern to find McCone and to apologise to Crompton for losing his temper? He couldn't bear the idea of it. Back to his lodgings in rue des Pénitents Gris? What purpose would that serve?

Piet had little faith the truce would hold. Both the Catholic and the Protestant leaders were aggrieved, believing too much had been conceded to the other side, with too few assurances given to them in return. The city was swamped with weapons and aggression. He did not think either faction would disarm, whatever the terms of the truce. Toulouse was on borrowed time.

He turned his mind to the almshouse. There, at least, he could do some good. He thought of Minou and, suddenly, he felt a sense of purpose, a sense of possibility. How many hours had passed since he had left her? Time had run fast and slow during this long day. He kicked a stone and heard it bounce away along the cobblestones. Just to see her would give him pleasure.

For a moment, Piet allowed himself to dream, then he pulled himself up. There had been a kind of wild liberty during the strange hours of the riot and its aftermath, allowing them to be together. Now, though he doubted the peace would last, things would return to normal for a while. Minou was a Catholic, he was Huguenot. What would be the cost to her character to be seen in his company?

He decided to go to the Eglise Saint-Taur, and tried to put his swirling thoughts in order: Vidal's surveillance, Michel's murder, the presence of Crompton and Devereux in Toulouse, and now the opportune killing of the tailor in Daurade. They were each connected to the Shroud.

If the truce held, well and good. If not, this might be the only chance Piet would have to retrieve the precious original from its hiding place.

CARCASSONNE

'Rixende has gone to fetch more milk.' Blanche pointed at the spoilt pan. It seemed her guess might be right.

'From her mother's house?' Alis asked.

'Well, she said she would not be long.'

Alis sat up and threw the blanket off her lap. 'Then she spoke false. Rixende often goes out when Madame Noubel is not here, then she starts chattering and the hours pass. I don't mind. She talks too much. It wears me out.' Suddenly, she remembered she was talking to a stranger. 'Who are you?' she asked again.

Blanche smiled. 'A friend.'

The child looked at her fine clothes and gown, and frowned. 'You do not look like one of Rixende's friends.'

Blanche laughed. 'I am not a friend of your maid, silly, but of your sister. I have come from Toulouse.'

The girl's demeanour transformed. 'You've come from Minou? Are you to take me to her?'

How easily the child was duped, Blanche thought, sending up a silent prayer.

'Your sister pines for your company. She would have you join her. Aimeric misses you also.'

Alis frowned. 'I cannot think he cares. He says girls are dull, a nuisance.'

Blanche folded her hands in front of her. 'Ah. It is a truth you will learn as you get older, that men say one thing and do another.'

'Aimeric's not a man,' Alis giggled. 'He's a stupid boy. Are we to go today?'

'Indeed, yes.' Blanche was aware that the maid, or this Madame Noubel, might return at any moment. On the other hand, she could see how Alis was still cautious and could not be hurried. It was essential she came of her own accord. The streets of La Cité were crowded at this time of evening and there were many who might see them. 'My carriage is waiting in Place Saint-Nazaire.'

'What did Minou say I should bring with me, Madame?'

'Your sister has arranged everything for you in Toulouse. Clothes for the city, toys.'

'Toys? But she knows I do not care for—'

'I jest,' Blanche said quickly, realising she had struck a false note. 'When I suggested we might purchase a doll for you, Minou said you had never been one for such pastimes.'

The girl nodded. 'I prefer to read.'

'Indeed. She also has told me how advanced you are for your years. She has many new books waiting for you. But look at us, talking the afternoon away. We have the entire journey to become acquainted.'

'Might I bring my kitten? If I call, she'll come straight back.'

'It would be unkind to confine the creature within a carriage.' Blanche clapped her hands to distract the child. 'Come, fetch your things. The sooner we take our leave, the sooner we will be in Toulouse.'

'I shall bring only my best cloak and gloves, and my medicine. Madame Noubel will be back at dusk. She can prepare a batch for me to take with us, then we will go. Is it a grand carriage?'

'It is, and pulled by two pairs of horses, but it is a long way. Much as I would like to make Madame's acquaintance – Minou talks so fondly of her – I fear we cannot wait. We must leave immediately.'

Alis frowned. 'But I need my medicine. I am not supposed to go anywhere without it.'

'Minou knows about your medicine, better than anyone, does she not?' Blanche risked putting her hand on the girl's thin shoulder. 'When you are with her, you will not need Madame Noubel.'

Alis's expression lightened. 'That is true.'

'And if we leave now, you will be in Minou's company before the sun rises tomorrow. Imagine her joy at waking to find you there. On the other hand, if we delay our departure, we will not arrive in Toulouse until tomorrow afternoon at the earliest.'

'But Madame Noubel said I wasn't to leave the house.'

Blanche pretended to think. 'We shall leave a letter, explaining our haste. Then she will have no cause to worry. These are Minou's wishes, after all.'

'That is true,' Alis said, though still doubtful.

'Good, then we are resolved. Fetch your travelling clothes, while I prepare a note. Then we shall be on our way. Quickly now.'

While Alis dressed, Blanche looked around until she found a scrap of paper on which to write. There was a faded drawing propped on the mantle above the fire, a rough sketch in chalk. The reverse side was blank.

With a piece of charcoal from the fire, Blanche wrote 'Madame Noubel' on the outside, folded the sheet and put it back on the mantel.

'There, that is done,' she said, as Alis came back into the room. 'Are you ready?'

'Yes, Madame.'

Blanche held out her hand. After a moment's hesitation, Alis took it.

CHAPTER FORTY-ONE

⚜

Toulouse

'Ready,' Minou whispered. 'Whistle if anyone comes.'

At the bottom of the wide staircase, Aimeric put his thumb up. 'Be quick.'

Minou ran along the corridor on the first floor to her aunt's chamber and knocked on the door.

'Aunt,' she whispered. 'Aunt, it's me, Minou. Will you let me in?'

The door opened a crack and a maid peered out.

'Madame Boussay is not supposed to receive anyone,' she said. 'Madame Montfort's instructions.'

'But it was Madame Montfort herself who sent me,' Minou lied.

The door opened a fraction. The maid had been shut up with her mistress for much of the day and she was bored. 'I don't want to get into trouble. Madame Montfort's like a bear with a sore head today.'

'You won't,' Minou said.

At that moment, there was an explosion of laughter in the courtyard and then they heard the sound of Madame Montfort shouting. As the maid stepped out further to see what was happening, Minou slipped past her and into the room.

'Five minutes at the most,' she said, and firmly shut the door.

*

Hands shackled behind his back, Oliver Crompton was led blindfolded down the subterranean tunnels. His bare feet plashed on the damp ground. Through the hessian hood, he could smell blood and the stench of the sewers, sulphur and river weed, and feel the chill of the brick walls dripping with moisture.

He knew he was in the inquisitional prison, the notorious labyrinth of vaults and chambers beneath Place du Salin. The *oubliettes*, a place where a man could vanish from the face of God's earth. Few who were incarcerated here were ever released. Those who were, it was said, were so ruined by what they had suffered that they might as well be dead.

As the ground sloped down, the stench worsened. A poisonous stink of fear and excrement, nausea and humiliation. Prisoners who had spilled their guts, and those who had not, were incarcerated in the same cells as a reminder of what the torturer's craft might do to fragile human flesh and bone.

Crompton did not understand how he came to be here. It had to be a mistake. A matter of hours ago, he was pounding the streets, cursing himself for having let Piet's sanctimonious disdain provoke him. He regretted storming out of the alehouse. He disliked the fellow and the antipathy was mutual but, all the same, they were on the same side. Crompton had swallowed his pride and retraced his steps, intending to apologise and to share the information he had discovered in the quartier Daurade. But by the time he returned to the tavern, Piet was gone.

He had waited a while, then left in search of his cousin, Devereux, instead. As he had turned the corner into rue des Arts, he had been set upon. A hood was thrown over his head, he was tossed into a cart and taken across town.

Crompton stumbled up a step, then was shoved forward.

His arms were dragged up behind his back, then the hood was ripped from his head. He blinked, trying to get his bearings, in the flickering light of the torches on the wall. Then his breath froze and his heart pounded.

He was in the rack room, the evidence of previous torture all around. Bloodstains – some fresh, some dried brown – splattered and pooled on the floor, the walls. To his left, the iron chair with its seat of nails, the straps hanging loose from its arms, the spikes bloodied. On the wall to his right, manacles and a choke pear, the vilest of contraptions. Gauntlets that could hold a victim suspended for hours until his own weight pulled bone from socket. Straight ahead, he saw the ropes and the rack itself.

To fight in the streets, to look a man in the eye and face him fairly and square, that Crompton understood. Not this.

In the furthest corner, he saw a desk, an ink horn and a quill. The jolt of seeing such benign commonplace objects in this hellish place made him sick to his stomach. Three men, heavy felt hoods concealing their features, sat ready to record his every word.

'Why am I here?'

From the shadows, a counter question. 'Why do you think you are here?'

'You have the wrong man.'

'Try again.'

'I tell you, you have the wrong man,' he said, trying to steady his voice. 'I am English, a visitor to Toulouse.'

The inquisitor laughed.

'By law, I have a right to know on what charge I have been brought here.'

'Do you know where you are?'

'Identify yourself, Monsieur, and tell me why I am arrested.'

'Do you think you are in a position to bargain, you Huguenot dog? No one knows you are here.'

Crompton forced himself to stand tall. He had heard that no man knew how he might react, how his body might resist if stretched or pressed, but he thought himself valiant.

'I do not know why I am here.'

'You are a traitor. You are part of a conspiracy against the King.'

'No! I am loyal to the King.'

The inquisitor waved a sheaf of papers. 'It is all here. The meetings, the plotting, the traitors with whom you are known to consort.'

'I have done nothing wrong. You have the wrong man.'

The inquisitor came out from behind his desk, holding a single piece of paper. 'It says here that, on the twenty-ninth day of February last, you and your fellow conspirators met with another in Carcassonne to buy a relic sacred to the Catholic faith – a priceless relic – in order to fund rebellion against the throne. Do you deny it?'

Crompton's answer caught in his throat. Whatever he had expected, it was not this. All this over a scrap of material? Indeed, he had all but forgotten about the Shroud. It had left his hands almost as quickly as it had come into them and at a better price than he'd paid.

'I don't know what you are talking about,' he blustered. 'Who accuses me?'

'Furthermore,' the inquisitor continued, 'it is alleged that you, a traitor to your own cause – as well as a blasphemer – arranged for the true Shroud to be exchanged for a counterfeit, the monies raised thereof to be contributed to the levy raised by the Prince of Condé.'

'Impossible,' Crompton protested, 'I saw it myself and—'

He turned cold. He should not have spoken. He should have admitted to nothing.

The inquisitor drummed his long fingers on the table.

'There are questions I shall put to you. If you have any sense, you will answer freely. If not, my colleagues here will be obliged to jog your memory.' The tapping got quicker, faster, then stopped. 'Do you understand?'

'On my life, I am not a traitor. I swear I know nothing of a forgery.' His voice tailed away. 'You have the wrong man.'

'You are a fool to yourself, Crompton,' the inquisitor said, then turned to the gaoler. 'Strip him.'

Crompton fought back, trying to get free from the soldiers, but it was no use. He was dragged naked to the rack, still kicking and jerking as they strapped him down.

'From whom did you buy the forgery? How was the transaction set up? What are the names of those who aided you in this?'

'I do not—'

His denial was lost in a scream as the first of the levers was turned, wrenching his arm from its socket.

'Now, shall we try again? What do you know of the man known as Piet Reydon?'

Aimeric felt Steward Martineau's hand on the back of his neck, dragging him up from the steps to the cellar into the courtyard itself.

'I might have known,' Madame Montfort said, advancing upon them. 'What are you doing down there? Snooping? Keeping the servants from their work? You are a vile and disobedient boy.'

Aimeric was about to protest when, out of the corner of his eye, he saw Minou step out into the courtyard. Knowing she was all right, and that Madame Montfort had not discovered her in their aunt's room, he smiled with relief.

'How dare you? How dare you make light of the situation? Do you think you can behave like a peasant in a household such as this? Wait until Monsieur Boussay returns. He will give you such a hiding, I warrant you will not be able to sit down for a week.'

'Madame!' Minou said.

The older woman spun round, shocked to see Minou standing there. Madame Montfort glanced at the cellar steps.

'How did you . . . ?' she began, then clamped her lips shut.

'By some ill fortune, the wind blew shut the cellar door and I found myself trapped. I am surprised you did not see it.' Minou saw the uncertainty in Madame Montfort's face. 'However, by luck, my brother heard me cry for help and released me from inside the house. There, through the chapel.'

'The chapel?' Madame Montfort exchanged a glance with Martineau. 'In which case, what is he doing outside now?'

'I imagine he had gone to check if there was some fault in the lock that the door should have shut with such force, so that another should not suffer the same fate as I. Is that not the way of it, Aimeric?'

Her brother nodded. 'It is.'

Minou turned back to Madame Montfort. 'In other circumstances, I would suggest an apology was in order. But since I am certain you acted in good faith, I am sure it will not be necessary. Aimeric?'

'No harm done,' he said.

Minou could hardly believe that they would get away with such defiance, but their plan was working: Madame Montfort kept her temper in check.

'Let the boy go,' she said dully.

Martineau released his grip, then wiped his hands, as if touching Aimeric had contaminated him.

'Now,' Minou said, 'if you will excuse us.'

Hooking her arm through her brother's, she walked them up into the house expecting at any moment to be summoned back. The instant the front door was closed, her legs seemed to turn to water.

'We will pay for that,' Aimeric said eagerly, 'but it was worth it! Did you see her face?'

'Her expression could have frozen the Aude in summer,' Minou laughed. 'But why were you in the courtyard? You were supposed to be keeping watch inside.'

'I know, but moments after you'd gone, Madame Montfort went into the chapel. To check the door, perhaps, I don't know. She was in there hardly any time at all. She stormed out and headed towards the stairs. I feared she'd catch you, so I ran out into the courtyard and dropped a pail of water down the steps, to make as much noise as possible, hoping to draw her away from the house.'

'Well, it worked. You did excellently well.'

He gave a flamboyant bow. 'Did you have enough time to talk to our aunt?'

'I think I have put things right between us,' she said. 'She had not wanted to give credence to Madame Montfort's lies, but she is so easily influenced. I have promised we will accompany her to Mass in an hour. She always goes on Friday, but Madame Montfort had refused to allow it in light of the troubles. She feared to defy her sister-in-law.'

'I'm not going to church,' Aimeric protested.

'I would have you with me,' she said. 'There is another reason for it. I have learnt that our mother, on the occasion of my birth, sent our aunt a French bible.'

'So?'

'A French bible means a Protestant bible,' she said, stressing each of the words. 'Monsieur Boussay refused to allow her to keep it. For once, our aunt defied his wishes. She was too scared to hide it in the house, so she concealed it in the Eglise Saint-Taur.' Minou paused, then gave a wry smile. 'Where better to conceal a bible than within a church?'

CHAPTER FORTY-TWO

⚜

Carcassonne

The carriage was waiting in Place Saint-Nazaire, the black horses pawing the ground in their eagerness to be gone. Blanche lifted Alis up into the cab, settled her and untied her bonnet.

The girl ran her hands over the soft upholstered seats in delight.

'I have never been in such a carriage before. It is beautiful.'

Blanche took her place beside her and the manservant closed the door, then they felt the carriage lurch as he climbed up beside the driver. A crack of the whip, the heavy jolt of the wheels beginning to turn, and they were on their way.

'May we have the curtains open?' Alis asked.

'Not until we are out of La Cité.' The child might not recognise the crest of the Bishop of Toulouse on the doors of the carriage, but others would and Blanche did not want Alis to be seen inside. 'When we are on the open road, then you may look out.'

Alis sat back patiently with her hands in her lap. The high carriage wheels rumbled under the Porte Saint-Nazaire, then the ground became smoother as the horses trotted through the lists between the inner and the outer walls.

At the Porte Narbonnaise they were stopped by the guard. Blanche heard the muttered conversation between a sergeant-at-arms and her driver, praying the watch would not ask to check the identity of his passengers.

'That sounds like Bérenger,' Alis said.

'Stay still,' Blanche hissed.

Then, to her relief, the thump of a hand on the side of the carriage, and they were on their way.

'Hope you have a good run of it,' Bérenger called after them. 'The weather's set to turn tonight.'

'I only stepped out for an instant,' Rixende cried. 'I meant no harm.'

'If I told you once, I told you a hundred times. Never let Alis out of your sight. I warned you. Not only did you go out, but you left the house with all the doors unlocked.'

'It was only a moment. I needed to fetch some milk and—'

'She's gone,' Madame Noubel said heavily. 'Alis is gone.'

'She will only be out for a walk, or with a friend, or . . .'

Madame Noubel gestured to the chair where the kitten sat on the untenanted blanket. 'Alis never goes anywhere without taking her pet with her.'

'When Marie came to call,' Rixende said, 'I sent her away with a flea in her ear. I give you my word. I didn't do anything wrong. I didn't let anyone in. I was only gone for a quarter of an hour.'

'And what business, pray, did Marie Galy have coming here? She knows Aimeric is in Toulouse.'

'I don't know.' Rixende was twisting her apron into knots. 'I sent her packing, I told her nothing.'

Madame Noubel looked around the kitchen, noticing how little things were out of place – a drawer left open, the basket of kindling too far back on the hearth, books on the shelf in the wrong order, Bernard's chair pushed against the wall. And there was the old map drawn by Florence, except now her own name was printed in block capitals on the reverse side.

She picked it up. No message. Nothing. Yet proof someone had been here.

'Did Marie come into the kitchen?'

'No! I told you, Madame, I sent her away. She didn't set foot inside, I swear.'

Cécile Noubel sat down and patted the bench beside her. 'Come here, Rixende. Start at the beginning. Tell me every single thing that happened this afternoon from the instant I left the house.'

In no time, Blanche and Alis were out on the open road, the land rising and falling as the horses picked up speed.

'You may look out now,' Blanche said.

Alis set her hands on the rim, watching as the outskirts of La Cité gave way to a few solitary houses and farms. Then, the endless fields of the Aude valley – wheat and vines and orchards. In the distance, she saw the white-capped mountains of the Pyrenees. Soon the dust of the road, thrown up by the horses' hooves, swirled into the cab and Alis settled back on the bench.

'It feels as if we are flying like birds,' she said.

Blanche drew the curtains shut. 'Tell me about your father, Alis. Why does he not take you with him to the bookshop? A clever girl like you, I am sure you would be a great help to him.'

'I would,' she said in her solemn little voice, 'but Papa is not there at the moment.'

'No?'

'He left Carcassonne shortly after Minou went to Toulouse with Aimeric. That's why Madame Noubel is looking after me.' She paused. 'I thought Papa would have written to my sister to tell her so.'

'Perhaps the letter went astray.'

Blanche produced a blue glass phial from beneath her cloak. She did not think the child would know they were travelling in the wrong direction for Toulouse, but soon the road would fork and there was no sense taking the chance.

'Here,' she said, 'this is something to help us with the journey. It is always better to drink before the nausea can take a hold.' She removed the stopper and handed the bottle to Alis. 'Don't drop it.'

'It is beautiful.'

'It comes from a place called Venice.'

'I know about Venice,' Alis said. 'The streets are all made of water there. Even the poorest people travel from place to place in special boats. Minou told me.'

Blanche watched her sip the sleeping draught, disguised by a tincture of honey and rosemary.

'It's horrible!'

'Dutch sailors take this remedy before they set out into open water, to counteract the swell of the sea at the harbour mouth.'

Alis emptied the phial and handed it back. 'Papa goes sometimes to Amsterdam. Minou says it is much like Venice, though she has not visited there either.'

'Perhaps your father has gone to Amsterdam this time?'

Alis shook her head. 'No, not this time.' She paused. 'He said he was travelling south. Amsterdam is not to the south, is it?'

'No, Amsterdam is a long way north. You are a clever child.'

Alis blushed red. 'I wasn't eavesdropping, but Madame Noubel was talking in a very loud voice. I couldn't help but hear.'

Blanche allowed the music of the road and the sleeping draught to take effect for a minute. The drumming of the horses' hooves, the rattling wheels on the carriageway, the hiss and sigh of the air.

'So, do you remember the name of the place Madame Noubel said?' she asked quietly.

'It began with a P,' Alis murmured, her eyelids closing. 'I had not heard of it, but it made me think of spring. Something green . . .'

'*Vert*?' Blanche felt a fluttering in her chest. 'Might it have been Puivert?'

'Puivert, yes,' Alis said, her words blurring together. 'Like springtime.'

CHAPTER FORTY-THREE

Toulouse

In the time between Minou leaving her aunt's chamber and returning with Aimeric to escort her to Mass, Madame Boussay had changed her mind.

'Perhaps it is better to stay here,' she said. 'My husband so values my company. He is always vexed if he returns home to find me absent without his permission.'

'Keeping you prisoner,' Aimeric muttered under his breath.

Minou shot a warning glance at him.

'I see that,' she said patiently. 'However, if you do wish to attend your usual Friday service, Aunt, then there is no choice but to leave the house for a short while. However, if you prefer, I could ask the priest to come here instead and . . .'

'No! Monsieur Boussay would not like that. He prefers his own confessor. He says Valentin will be the next Bishop of Toulouse. He has already contributed significant alms to his campaign.'

Minou glanced again at the door, listening for the sound of Madame Montfort's footsteps. It would only be a matter of time before she discovered they were here.

'I am sure God will understand if you do not attend,' Minou said. 'He knows what is in your heart, Aunt.'

'Though I always go to Mass on Friday,' she fretted. 'And today of all days I would give thanks for our safe deliverance from the mob and to praise God for sparing you, Minou, from

. . . well, from I do not know what. They are like animals, these Huguenots. They have no respect for –' She drew in her breath. 'If I do not show my gratitude, then next time the Lord might turn away from us in our hour of need.'

Behind her aunt's back, Aimeric was pretending to hang himself with an imaginary rope. Minou frowned at him to stop.

'Perhaps if I ask my sister-in-law to come with us, Monsieur Boussay would have no reason to be angry with me.'

It was the last thing Minou wanted. 'I am sure my uncle is proud to have a wife of such piety,' she said, trying another tack.

Madame Boussay's expression lightened. 'Do you think so?'

'I do.'

'What can be keeping him?' she said, wringing her hands. 'He works every hour God sends, but this is very late for him not to be home. Perhaps something has happened . . .'

Minou shook her head at her aunt's naivety. It was extraordinary that she did not realise that the terrible events of yesterday and today's attempts to negotiate a truce might interfere with Monsieur Boussay's usual routines.

'Since we know all the leading men of Toulouse are in council, trying to broker peace between the Catholic and Protestant factions,' she said, 'it is possible he might not even come home until after dark.'

'I do not know, Niece, really I do not,' she said, shaking her head. 'Everything is upside down. They say the Huguenots looted all the houses in Saint-Michel and the cathedral quarter too.'

'They did not,' Minou said.

The bell began to ring from the church. Her aunt turned

towards the sound, hesitated for one last moment, then stood up.

'You are right, dear Minou. I should pray. For God will know if I am not there. Fetch my cloak, Aimeric. I am so pleased you are to come with us too.'

'The pleasure is mine, Aunt,' he said politely.

'We could be there and back again before my husband comes home, do you not think? I really do not want to anger him. That would not do.'

The bells were ringing for Mass as Piet hurried the few steps from rue du Périgord to the back entrance to the church.

He was disappointed not to have found Minou at the almshouse. At first, the only evidence she had been there at all was the triangle of muslin used as a sling left folded on the counter in the antechamber. Then a woman from the quartier Daurade – who often helped in the kitchens – described someone matching Minou's description having helped for some hours. And a little boy confirmed the same lady had helped him look for his grandfather.

'She has different-coloured eyes,' Louis said. 'One was blue, and one was brown.'

It gave him pleasure to think that she had stayed.

Piet approached the vestry door, still in two minds as to whether to retrieve the Shroud or leave it be. Perhaps things were not so pressing? News of the truce had reached the almshouse and people were inclined to trust in it. Many had left already to return to their homes.

He lifted the latch on the small arched door, and stepped inside the vestry. The smell of incense and the voices of the choir greeted him, both as familiar as the pattern of his own breathing. Mass would be over in a little while. He would wait and rest, ready to act once the congregation had gone.

The evening service was short but, when it ended, Aunt Boussay did not stir.

Minou glanced at her – still on her knees, with her head bowed – and wondered how much longer she intended to continue at prayer. A few other worshippers also remained. She was aware of two nuns behind them and others in the side chapels. The curate was walking through the body of the church snuffing out each of the candles in turn, leaving a lingering scent of wax and smoke.

'When can we go?' Aimeric mouthed.

'Soon,' she whispered back.

Before Minou could prevent him, he had slipped out of the pew and was heading up the side aisle to the three chapels behind the altar. 'Aimeric,' she hissed, trying to fetch him back, but he pretended not to hear.

He slipped out of sight. Though it was becoming darker, Minou felt a strange sense of peace, despite the exhausting events of the past two days. The last rays of twilight were glinting through the mitred windows above the east door, sending blue and red and green ladders of light into the nave.

She wondered where the bible might be hidden, then glanced again at her aunt and thought of her mother. Though they had different fathers, Minou fancied she could detect a family resemblance. They were of different build and colouring, but Salvadora's eyes were dark as Florence's had been. Aimeric and Alis were the same, eyes as black as coal.

The sound of an offertory plate falling to the ground brought Minou back to the present. Her first thought was to wonder what Aimeric was up to, and she half rose from the pew to see. Her aunt clasped her hand.

'Stay with me, Niece,' she whispered.

'Of course,' Minou said. 'Though, I wonder, if soon we should return home? The time is passing. Soon it will be dark and—'

'Please.' She seemed to be gathering her thoughts. 'Until I confided in you, Minou, I never told a soul I kept the christening gift Florence sent to me.'

'The French bible?' Minou said, her interest quickening.

'Monsieur Boussay would be so angry if he knew. He does not like me to be disobedient and, though I do try so hard not to provoke him, I know I am a trial.' She opened her eyes, but kept her gaze fixed on the Cross. 'I think of your dear mother often. In the blackest hours, I try to imagine what she would do. She would not endure such . . . well, no matter.'

'No one could be a kinder person than you, dear Aunt. No harm will befall you.'

'If something does happen to me,' she continued, as if Minou had not spoken, 'I would be glad if you should have it.'

Minou squeezed her aunt's hand. 'Nothing will happen to you, to any of us. The events of yesterday, terrible as they were, are over. A truce will be agreed and life will return to normal. This is Toulouse. Everything will go back to the way it was before, you'll see.'

A trill of nervous laughter slipped from her aunt's lips. 'You are young, Niece. It is not what lies outside the walls of the house I fear, but –' She stopped, and levered herself awkwardly off the kneeler and up onto the pew. 'Promise me this,' she said. 'If anything does, well . . . Promise me that you will retrieve the bible and keep it safe, in memory of my beloved sister. I owe her that much.'

Minou nodded. 'I will do whatever you want.'

'You're a good girl, Minou. It is hidden within this church. Did I tell you?'

'Yes, though not precisely where.'

Madame Boussay smiled. 'An old priest showed me the place. He is dead now, God bless his soul. No one knows of it.'

Minou's heart sank. She could not help wondering if the story was quite true. In the short time she had been living in the Boussay house, Minou realised her aunt often said one thing, then days later would claim the exact opposite to be true.

'Just knowing the bible was here,' her aunt continued, 'even though I could not touch it with my own hands – has been a comfort to me during the darkest times. A link between me and Florence.'

'I could fetch it for you?' Minou asked. 'I could keep it within my chamber.'

'Not yet, dear Niece. I will keep my secret a little longer. It is the only special thing I have. But, as I said, if something happens to me . . .'

'Nothing is going to happen to you,' Minou insisted, not knowing what else she could say.

A movement behind the altar caught her eye. She looked up and saw Aimeric beckoning her to join him.

'Not now,' she mouthed.

Then, in the fading light of the afternoon, a man stepped out to stand beside him. Minou watched him put his hand upon her brother's shoulder and saw Aimeric look up at him.

Minou caught her breath.

'Aunt, might you excuse me for an instant?'

Fighting her every instinct to run, Minou walked up the

side aisle and along the flagstones until she had reached her brother.

'Look what he's given me.'

Minou looked down at the plain silver dagger in her brother's hands. 'It is a fine dagger,' she said, in a voice that seemed to come from a long way away. She turned to his companion. 'Monsieur Reydon, you are too generous.'

'I made a promise, my Lady of the Mists, and I always keep my word.' Piet took her hand and kissed it. 'I am pleased to see you. It grieved me we parted on such ill terms.'

'He says he will start teaching me the trick with the knife tomorrow, provided I can get away,' Aimeric said brightly. 'Can I go?'

'We'll see,' Minou said carefully, but she was smiling too.

CHAPTER FORTY-FOUR

⚜

Toulouse
Tuesday, 12th May

Five weeks passed. A stormy April gave way to a gentle May. The winds blew from the south and the sun shone. On the plains of the Lauragais between Carcassonne and Toulouse, lily of the valley and mimosa, violets and primroses blossomed, the colours of spring tipping into summer. Poppies and forget-me-nots blazed red and blue.

Within the city the truce was still holding, though there was a simmering undercurrent beneath the surface of daily life that threatened to erupt into violence at any moment.

Minou looked up at the decaying body hanging in chains from the gibbet in Place Saint-Georges, and her stomach clenched. The balls of the victim's feet were livid where the blood had pooled, the jaw hung loose. His eyes were gone, the sockets picked clean by the carrion birds. Tufts of hair, tipped with dried blood, had rotted free from the dead man's scalp and dropped to the ground below. There were three identical scaffolds in each of the other corners of the square.

'They should cut them down,' Aimeric said. 'The bodies stink.'

'They're leaving them as a warning to others.'

'But it's been more than a month.'

Minou suspected that leaving the corpses in plain view had achieved the opposite effect. Rather than act as a warning, they served more as a Huguenot call to arms. The rotting corpses were a constant reminder of how the Parliament was partisan and could not be trusted to protect all of its citizens. For, although more than a hundred people had been charged with incitement during the riots, and six condemned to death, at the last moment the Parliament had pardoned the Catholics. Only the four Huguenots had been executed.

In the early weeks of May, disturbances had broken out in different quarters of the city. A series of small fires around Place Saint-Georges were quickly doused. A Catholic priest was found dead near the Porte Villeneuve, his hands and feet bound and his throat cut. In Place du Salin, a young nobleman in yellow hose and cape, was discovered propped up against the door of the inquisitional prison with his tongue cut out. Few ventured out without a weapon concealed beneath their cloaks, in defiance of the terms of the truce. Women did not walk alone in the streets after dark. There were conscripted soldiers and mercenaries everywhere.

Reliable information about the state of affairs outside the Midi was scarce. It was rumoured the Prince of Condé and his Protestant army had taken Orléans and the mighty eastern city of Lyon. His supporters, either at his command or acting of their own volition, had seized and garrisoned towns along the valley of the Loire – Angers, Blois and Tours among them – and attacked Valence on the Rhone. Condé claimed his sole aim was to liberate the King from the pernicious clutches of the Duke of Guise and his allies. The Queen Regent was said to have applied to the King of Spain for military assistance to bring the Huguenots to heel. Another rumour was that letters had been issued stating the Edict of Toleration did not apply to Languedoc as it was a border province. That, in fact, it had never done so.

'Minou, look,' Aimeric said. 'Over there.'

She turned and saw a band of soldiers, in full battle armour, walking into the square.

'I overheard Uncle say Parliament had changed the terms of the truce Sunday last, with the result that more than two hundred Catholic noblemen and their retinues have been allowed to enter the city.' Minou frowned. 'Uncle is delighted, of course.'

'No, not them,' Aimeric said, pointing. 'Beneath the trees in the middle.'

Minou shielded her eyes, then her heart shifted. There, framed by the green branches of the plane trees, stood Piet, his attire sombre, his red hair still muted and his beard grown out. At this distance, he looked rather thinner and his face more finely drawn. She felt a smile come to her lips.

'He's seen us,' Aimeric said. 'He's coming this way.'

'Go to him,' Minou said, glancing at the soldiers and a flock of black-robed Jacobins who had swept into the square from the Augustinian monastery. 'I cannot be seen talking to him in so public a place.'

Aimeric ran across the square and Minou lost sight of him and Piet for a moment, her view blocked by the Catholic battalion.

After their accidental meeting in the Eglise Saint-Taur in April, she had seen little of him. Her aunt had been demanding of her company and, more anxious than ever, kept Minou by her side. And whenever she did consider trying to arrange a rendezvous, mounting evidence of how dangerous the streets were held her back. There had been many rumours of soldiers treating any woman out alone as fair game. Blood and petticoat attacks, as they were becoming known.

It was different for Aimeric. Piet had kept his promise to

teach her brother how to throw a knife with skill. Sometimes at dusk, if the light was good and the streets quiet, Piet would steal her brother away to the quartier Daurade and there set up a straw man, drilling Aimeric until his shoulders ached and the palms of his hands were sore. He claimed now to be able to hit any target at a distance of several *toise* – at least three lengths of a man. His devotion to Piet was now equal to that of any medieval squire to his lord, and Minou teased him for it, but she was also grateful that he would carry notes between them. Inoffensive and innocent, unsigned messages of goodwill and remembrance. The crumbs of their conversation in the *maison de charité* had sustained her through these long weeks.

As for the happenstance that had found them both, on that April evening after Mass, Minou often thought of it. About the great good fortune that should have brought them to the church at the exact same time. Piet had not told her why he was there – any more than she had confided in him – but she couldn't help seeing it as another sign that their lives were destined to entwine.

'What did he say?' she said, when Aimeric returned. 'Is all well with him? Is Piet –'

'He wants you to meet him in the side chapel in the church at four o'clock.'

Minou frowned. 'That's impossible. I can't possibly leave the house at that time without being seen.'

'Piet said to tell you how he would understand if you couldn't accept the invitation, but that he would not ask if it wasn't a matter of life or death,' Aimeric said.

'Life or death? He used those actual words?'

Aimeric shrugged. 'Not exactly, but it's what he meant.'

She glanced over to where Piet was waiting in the green shade of the trees. Minou didn't really know truly what manner of man he was, yet instinct told her he would not make such a request without good reason.

'What answer shall I give?' Aimeric asked.

She took a deep breath. 'Tell him that I will be there.'

CHAPTER FORTY-FIVE

⚜

Carcassonne

The hours, and then the days and weeks after Alis vanished, blurred into one endless and desperate search. Cécile Noubel barely slept. She walked the streets of La Cité and the Bastide, asking friends, neighbours, strangers if they had seen the little girl. No one had.

'About so high, with wild black hair and eyes as dark. A clever child, serious in her manner.'

She had scoured the dark alleyways where the cutpurses and doxies plied their trade, had worn down the paths along the river and pressed coins into the hands of the bargemen and fishermen. No body had been washed up and, though Cécile could not account for why she was so certain, she remained sure in her heart that Alis was still alive. She believed she had gone with the noblewoman, the lady who had bribed Marie Galy to point out the Joubert house. But whether Alis had gone willingly or been taken by force, she could not bear to consider and had been unable to ascertain.

Under threat of being sent before the Magistrate as an accessory to a kidnapping, Marie had confessed and at least provided a detailed description of the woman and her clothes. Poor Rixende's account of the afternoon was inconsistent and changed with each telling.

Cécile had written to Minou, to tell her of the tragedy, but had heard nothing back. She intended to send another letter as soon as she had something more to report. Until now, there had been no further news.

Finally, though, there was something. The garrison had been sent away from Carcassonne, to deal with reports of copycat uprisings in the villages of the Midi after confirmation of the massacre at Vassy had been received. Bérenger's unit had been dispatched to Limoux and had only returned this afternoon. Cécile had gone immediately to find him and for the first time in more than a month, she felt a glimmer of hope.

'You are absolutely sure it was that same day?' she asked. 'Friday the third day of April?'

'Yes, Madama,' Bérenger replied. 'I remember it particularly because it was only a little later that evening we were dispatched to Limoux. It is why I did not hear about how little Alis—'

Madame Noubel held up her hand. 'You are not to blame, my friend. You have been away from La Cité. But, please tell me clearly what you saw.'

The old soldier nodded, though his face was grey with guilt. 'I recognised the carriage as that of the Bishop of Toulouse, because I had seen it recently – around about the time of the murder of that Michel Cazès – carrying a visitor staying in the Episcopal Palace.' He shook his grizzled head. 'Strange business. The whole Cité barricaded, the entire garrison set to hunt down the villain, then – pouf! That was that. Orders to forget all about it. Then it turns out to be a local matter after all. Fellow by the name of Alphonse Bonnet, a Bastide man, hung for the crime. Or so they claim. It's my belief he had nothing to do with it. I think the powers that be needed someone to swing for it and Bonnet was the scapegoat. It's all very strange.'

'We discussed Bonnet's case and I am sorry for his family,'

Madame Noubel said impatiently, 'but can we return to Alis? I want to be clear. On that Friday afternoon, you saw this carriage leaving La Cité.'

'At a little after five o'clock, it was. I was on duty at the Porte Narbonnaise. The occupant of the carriage was a dark-haired lady, though I caught only a glimpse of her. Very finely dressed. We remarked on it, because we thought it peculiar that there should be a lady travelling in the bishop's carriage.'

'Think, now.' Her voice cracked. 'Might Alis have been with her?'

'I wish I could help, Madama, but I couldn't see inside. The curtains were drawn.' He sighed. 'Isn't it a bad business? And Madomaisèla Minou and Aimeric still in Toulouse.'

'Can you remember in which direction the carriage turned out of La Cité?' Cécile pressed. 'Did the driver give any clue to their destination?'

He shook his head. 'Not towards the Bastide, that's all I can say. They went over the drawbridge, then turned to the right.'

'Towards the mountains?'

'Not in the direction of Toulouse, I can say that, though who knows which road they took when they were out of sight?' He gave another weary sigh. 'I'm sorry I cannot be of more help.'

'You have done your best,' Cécile said, turning away to walk home.

'I'm sure you will find her,' Bérenger called after her. 'Things have a habit of working themselves out. Don't they? Isn't that what they say?'

Cécile Noubel did not answer. She was sorely disappointed at how little Bérenger knew. As she made her way back towards rue du Trésau, she asked herself the question that had gnawed away at her for these long, dreadful weeks of not knowing. The

Jouberts were not a rich family, so why kidnap Alis? And why no ransom note? The obvious answer – that the child was already dead – she refused to entertain.

'What news?' Rixende asked, as she walked into the house. 'Did Bérenger see anything?'

'No,' she replied, sitting down in the chair.

'Nothing?'

Madame Noubel sighed, weary to her bones. 'Well, he saw a carriage leave via the Porte Narbonnaise and turn towards the mountains rather than the Bastide, but . . .' She shrugged. 'He noted the crest of the Bishop of Toulouse, though swears the passenger was a woman.'

'The noblewoman who talked to Marie?'

'It is possible.' Cécile Noubel shrugged. 'Bérenger had the impression she was not alone in the carriage, but could not swear to that.'

'Oh,' Rixende said, her face falling. She hesitated. 'Has there yet been word from Mademoiselle Minou? Does she know little Alis is . . . not here?'

'No, and I had expected an answer before now.'

'Perhaps your letter did not reach her?'

Madame Noubel frowned. 'It is true things take their time these days.'

'Any word from the master?'

Madame Noubel shook her head. Bernard's silence worried her too, though it did not surprise her. There were fewer people travelling at present who might deliver a letter. She didn't know what more to do. She had considered journeying to Toulouse in person, but Bérenger told her large numbers of troops were on the march on the plains of the Lauragais, many without clear command. Besides, if Minou *had* received her letters, she might even now be making her way back to Carcassonne.

'Here,' the maid said, handing her a cup. 'This will warm you.'

She accepted the drink gratefully. Rixende had done everything she could to make amends and Cécile no longer blamed her. She blamed herself.

Madame Noubel could not share her fears with Rixende – with anyone – but Cécile feared the past had caught up with them. Secrets, in the end, could not remain hidden: Alis's disappearance; Bernard's ill-advised expedition to the mountains and his continuing silence; Minou and Aimeric sent away to Toulouse to stay with Florence's sister – all of it could be traced back to what happened in Puivert those many years ago.

Old crimes cast long shadows . . .

Cécile sat in the kitchen a while longer, watching the mellow afternoon light dance along the top of the wall in the yard. She turned Florence's old sketch of a map – with her own name now printed on it – over in her hand. The bells of the smaller churches in La Cité began to chime the half-hour, followed by the louder carillon of the cathedral.

She came to a decision. Quickly, she got to her feet.

'Where are you going, Madame?' Rixende asked.

'The reason Bérenger was certain the coach was that of the Bishop of Toulouse was because he had seen it at Place Saint-Nazaire some weeks previously. What if this noblewoman was also a guest at the Episcopal Palace?'

'You are going to request an audience with the Bishop of Carcassonne?'

For the first time in weeks, Cécile laughed. 'No. I cannot imagine he would be prepared to receive me. But someone will have heard something. And if we at least discover this woman's name, then we might know where to start looking for Alis. Don't you have a cousin who works in the kitchens?'

'Yes,' Rixende said, brightening at the thought of being useful.

Madame Noubel pulled her shawl over her shoulders. 'Come. We'll go together. You can make the introduction.'

CHAPTER FORTY-SIX

⚜

Toulouse

Vidal looked down at the broken body of Oliver Crompton, slumped ragged on the spiked chair. His arms were still shackled to the wooden arms of the interrogation seat, metal hoops holding his wrists in place. A thick leather strap around his forehead kept his chin from falling forward to his chest. The tip of a shattered collarbone jutted at a grotesque angle through grey skin.

'He was more resilient than I expected,' said the other man. 'I did not think he would survive so long.'

'The Devil protects his own,' Vidal said, unwilling to concede either the courage or the strength of the man. To endure five weeks of intermittent torture was exceptional.

'His cousin, on the other hand, sang like a bird.'

'Oh? What did Devereux say?'

'That, as we thought, plans to embed Huguenot spies within Catholic households throughout the city were well advanced. That the *maison de charité* in rue du Périgord is indeed being used to store weapons and harbour soldiers. That they are aware that the spate of recent assaults on lone women, alleged to be perpetrated by Huguenots, are in fact being orchestrated by Catholic militias.'

Vidal paused. 'It was unwise to dispose of Devereux's body so ostentatiously.'

'I disagree. It is a lesson to any other who might attempt to benefit from selling intelligence to both sides that we, at least, will not tolerate it. However highly born the man, he will be brought to account.'

'You should know.' Vidal turned back to Crompton. 'Did he speak?'

For the first time, the man looked uncomfortable. 'I concede it is possible Crompton did not know he had purchased a forgery.'

'We were acting on intelligence supplied by you.'

'The information was from a reliable source.' The man held Vidal's gaze. 'But if he was not guilty of that charge, he was still a heretic. God will punish him hereafter, is that not your belief?'

Vidal fixed him with a wintry look. 'It is not ours to reason or speculate on the ways of the Lord.'

The other man snorted. 'I do not see the Lord's hand in any of this, only our very urgent need to identify the traitors within our midst who are in the pay of Condé.'

'And that', Vidal said, dropping his voice so the guards could not hear them, 'might be said to be heresy.'

The man laughed. 'You don't believe that, so save your sermonising for the pulpit.' He glanced at Crompton, then back to Vidal. 'Whilst we are on the matter of our need for accurate information, I still do not understand your continuing reluctance to arrest Piet Reydon. I know you were once boon companions, but in these final hours surely the time for such sentiment is over. He is – by his own admission – a Huguenot and, as such, a traitor to the Crown. Bring him in.'

'He is more use to us at large.'

'So you have repeatedly said, yet nothing has come of it. If it is true the Huguenots intend to attack tonight, then time has run out.'

Vidal clenched his fist. 'If we had left Crompton free to come and go, we would have learnt more of this Huguenot plot than by these means.'

'Perhaps. I intend to leave Toulouse tonight, before the trouble begins. I assume you will be taking similar precautions?'

'I will withdraw to the quartier Saint-Cyprien across the river.'

'In which case, even more reason to arrest Reydon now while you still have the chance. Not least that if you continue to protect him, some might begin to question your loyalty to the King.'

Vidal suddenly grabbed the other man by the throat, surprising them both, and shoved him back against the wall of the rack room.

'None could doubt my loyalty to the Catholic cause,' he said in a cold voice. 'You, on the other hand? You, McCone, are a man who, by your presence here and with your every breath, betrays the land of your birth and your Queen. So, do not dare to lecture me.' He held him for a moment longer, then released him. 'Guard!'

The soldier leapt forward. 'Yes, Monsignor.'

'This gentleman is leaving. Escort him to the gates of the prison.'

McCone straightened his clothes. 'You are making a mistake.'

Vidal made the sign of the cross and raised his voice. 'May God go with you,' he said. 'Rest assured that I will share your concerns with His Excellency, our noble Bishop of Toulouse, and indeed with our friends at the Parliament.'

McCone hesitated, then bowed and left the cell, the guards following at a respectful distance behind.

Vidal held himself erect, listening to their footsteps echoing along the chill corridor that led from this hell into the light. He had expected to be challenged, but not that the challenge would have come from Jasper McCone.

He realised McCone was in the pay of the arms dealer Delpech, like so many others. And, like Delpech, he was driven by money and a desire for power. But Vidal's interest lay more in retrieving the Shroud and in his own ambitions to become the next bishop. Moreover, he believed it would strengthen the Catholic position if the Protestant uprising went ahead. Those liberal Catholics, those who still believed compromise was possible, would be forced to retract their support and the city would be cleansed of the Huguenot contagion for good.

For a moment, he heard his lover's voice in his mind, and he flushed at the memory of her. When all this was over, Vidal would perhaps permit himself a last visit to the mountains. He would be pleased to know she fared well in her widowhood.

'What do you want us to do with him?'

The guard's voice brought Vidal back to the present.

'What's that?'

'This prisoner,' he said, prodding Crompton's shoulder. Crompton moaned weakly, before slipping back into unconsciousness.

'Will he talk more?' Vidal asked. 'He has withstood much.'

The guard's eyes were red and worn. In the dim light of the cell, Vidal could see the bloodstains beneath the man's fingernails. They were loyal servants of God and were as exhausted as he was himself.

'The evil is burnt so deep into this one, he no longer knows truth from false. We would better spend our time elsewhere.'

'In which case, let the river have him,' Vidal said.

'He no longer has the use of his arms or his legs. He will drown.'

'If the Lord in His mercy sees fit to save this poor sinner, He will do so.' Vidal made the sign of the cross on Crompton's forehead. 'In any case, we will pray for his soul.'

How much longer am I condemned to wait?

I continue to believe that Minou Joubert will come. She must. Her devotion to the girl makes it so. When I think of how I might have spared myself the trouble if only I had known that we were but streets apart in Toulouse.

Does God seek to try me? To punish me? What is it that I have done, or left undone, that He seeks to test my resolve in a such a way? In the city, it would have been simple. A sleeping draught, the blade of an assassin in the dark or my own hands around her neck. The watery embrace of the Garonne.

The child asks endless questions and will not be mollified by my answers. I reassure her that her sister will come to join us here in the mountains because there is a threat of pestilence in the city. She no longer believes me.

I must not lose faith. I trust in God, in His guidance and His wisdom. Is it not written in the scriptures that to everything there is a season, a time to reap and a time to sow?

As for the girl's belief that her father was headed to Puivert, there have been no reports of a stranger in the village by the name of Joubert. Otherwise, save poachers – an habitual problem at this time of the year – my lands are quiet.

I have finally been obliged to let out my bodice and add pleats to my skirts. By my reckoning I am some seven months gone. I care nothing for it, any more than I did for the bastard my father sired upon me. But I need this creature growing in my belly to be born and survive long enough to secure what is mine. Then, living or dead, Minou Joubert will no longer matter.

But, better dead . . .

CHAPTER FORTY-SEVEN

⚜

Puivert

Bernard Joubert rubbed the sore skin on his ankle. Tonight, his right leg hurt more than his left. He was shackled by both feet to an iron hoop set in the stone wall, and the heavy cuffs had worn his flesh raw.

All the same, the chains were long enough to allow him to stand up and move about the cell, some three paces in all directions – and though his left hand was also chained, his captors had allowed his right hand to be free. This prison, inhospitable as it was, was not the *oubliettes*. All the same, sometimes he still thought he heard the nightmare screaming of dying, tortured men. He feared he always would.

With a nail retrieved from beneath the straw covering the beaten earth floor, Bernard had been scratching the days of his captivity on the wall. A calendar to mark the passing of time, he hoped it would not make another month.

By this reckoning, he had been held in the tower for some five weeks. Passiontide had come and gone. Now it was May. The river Blau would be flowing in the valley and the hillside below the castle dotted with hundreds of tiny meadow flowers, pink and yellow and white, and the air would carry the scent of wild garlic. There had been one year – perhaps their first as man and wife – when Florence had woven a garland of springtime blooms and worn it in her hair. Bernard smiled, remembering how her black curls had tumbled, unbound, around her face and how he thought his heart would burst with joy at the sight of her.

When recollections of Florence became too painful, he imagined himself instead in the comfortable lodgings he always used on the Kalverstraat in Amsterdam. He thought of Rokin and his favourite herring house behind the Oude Kerk, where the sound of the rigging on the tall ships moored on the Amstel, snapping against the masts when the wind was high, filled the chamber.

Joubert heard the cell door being unlocked. He opened his eyes as a young soldier put down his daily dish of black bread and ale on the straw. Some of the guards felt the need to taunt him, to boost their own courage. This boy was not one of those.

'Thank you,' Bernard said.

The soldier looked over his shoulder, to check he was unobserved, then stepped a little further into the damp cell.

'Is it true you understand the French writing?' he whispered in Occitan.

'I do,' Bernard replied. 'Is there something you would like me to read to you?'

The boy began to walk away, but stopped half in and half out of the cell, undecided.

'I often do this service for soldiers in my home town. There are many men like you who never had the gift of schooling.' He beckoned the boy to come closer. 'No one need know of it.'

The guard hesitated, then took a burning sconce from the tower wall and stepped inside again. The flame sent shadows dancing up the dripping walls and Bernard saw how violently the boy's hand was shaking.

'Will you tell me your name?'

A pause, then, 'Guilhem Lizier.'

'That's an honest name,' Bernard said, remembering the old man he'd met outside the midwife's house.

'My family is from Puivert.'

Bernard held up his chained left arm. 'There is no need to fear me. I can do you no harm.' He held the boy's gaze. 'But to make sure, you can put the letter on the floor and push it towards me, then I can read it aloud for you. It is a letter, I suppose?'

'Yes.'

'Well, then.'

Guilhem produced a creased and battered paper from within his clothes, and did as Bernard suggested. Gently, so as not to startle the boy, he shook the letter open, smoothed it on the rough ground, and read. Then he went over it again, to be sure in the dim light he had not misread the words, then handed it back.

'It is bad news,' the boy said, his face collapsing. 'I knew it.'

'Why would you think that?'

'From your face, Monsieur. I have lain awake these past days, knowing that it was, and—'

'No, Guilhem,' Bernard said gently. 'This is good news, the news you hoped for. Your offer is accepted. Her father gives his permission. I congratulate you.'

'He gives his permission,' Guilhem repeated, then sank to his haunches with his head in his hands.

Bernard smiled. 'I have a son, a few years younger than you as yet, but I hope he will find someone he loves as much as you clearly love your girl.' He paused. 'I must ask, how comes it that you should have written to –'

'Jeannette?'

'How did you write to Jeannette's father to ask for her hand, but yet cannot read the answer received?'

'I wrote in Occitan,' Guilhem explained, 'but he wishes the family position to rise. He believes that only peasants speak the old language. He wants his daughter to have a better life.'

'So you can read and write?'

'A little, Sénher, but not French. I can speak well enough, but I was never taught from a book, so I –'

'You asked someone to write to him on your behalf,' Bernard said.

'The priest, but he has been arrested since and taken away.'

'I see.'

The boy frowned. 'My intended father-in-law has a smallholding, some two leagues south of Chalabre on the banks of the Blau. He swore on the Bible that, if I was released from my service here, he would sign over the farm – that is, bequeath it to Jeannette and her future husband – provided he might make his home with us.' His voice dropped. 'But there are accounts to be settled, the ledger of livestock, and Jeannette is not one for letters. He wants her to take a husband who can write.'

Bernard's heart went out to the boy. He would not be the first, so much in love, to promise more than he could deliver.

'It says here that the marriage is set to be the fifteenth day of August.'

'Assumption Day is much celebrated in Chalabre,' Guilhem explained. 'Jeannette's father is a devout Catholic. I thought he would approve the choice of the date.'

'Assumption,' Bernard muttered. He prayed he would not still be imprisoned by the time August showed her face.

He looked at Guilhem. The boy seemed sharp and it would help to pass the unforgiving hours. 'If you would like it, I could teach you to read and write. In time for your marriage.'

Lizier's expression lightened for a moment, then he remembered himself.

'We are not allowed to talk to prisoners.'

'No one will know,' Bernard reassured him. 'This is what we shall do. On days where you are dispatched to watch over me, I will show you how to shape letters and how to read them. Enough, at least, for you to persuade your father-in-law to allow the marriage to go ahead.'

Guilhem stared at him. 'Why would you do this, Monsieur? I am your gaoler, your enemy.'

Bernard shook his head. 'You and I are not enemies, Guilhem. Ordinary men like us, we are cut from the same cloth. It is those whom we serve who set us against one another.' He held the young man's gaze. 'Tell me, do you wish to stay in service here? Do you love your mistress? Did you love your late master?'

Guilhem hesitated, then dropped to his knees in front of Bernard. 'God forgive me, I hated him and, though I know she is what he made her – and what her father made her in turn, if the rumours are true – I cannot feel any love for her. They say she talks to God, but she is cruel. I would be free of my service to Puivert if I could.'

'Does the lady know I am here?' Bernard asked, hoping to gain a scrap of information now the boy's guard was down.

'When first she returned some three weeks ago –'

'Three weeks . . .' Bernard murmured.

'Yes, Sénher, at the end of April. Then, our commander was summoned to make his report. He told her some poachers were being held in the dungeons awaiting her orders.'

Bernard smiled. 'I am taken for a poacher?'

Guilhem flushed. 'You are not the only one, Monsieur, who took advantage of her absence to trespass on her lands.' He hesitated. 'The maids say she is with child. Some months along. Also, that she has brought some changeling back from Toulouse with her, whom she keeps out of sight in the old house. The keep is being prepared for other visitors, the linens bleached, the upper rooms turned out.' He looked down at Bernard with hopeful eyes. 'But do you think you might help me to read?'

Bernard smiled. 'When next you are sent to guard me, conceal a board and piece of charcoal beneath your surcoat. We will have you writing and ready to wed your Jeannette before the month of May is out.'

CHAPTER FORTY-EIGHT

⚜

TOULOUSE

'What are you intending to do, Aimeric?' Minou asked again, full of misgivings.

'What you asked of me,' he said innocently. 'To create a diversion, so you can leave the house without anyone noticing.'

'But not in such a way as to put yourself in trouble,' she said.

He grinned, then shot off down the passageway towards the kitchen yard. A moment later, Minou heard a wild squawking of hens and the cook bellowing. Shutting her ears to the commotion, she slipped across the courtyard and out into rue du Taur.

She gave a coin to the old woman selling violets on the steps of the church then, when she was sure she was unobserved, slipped inside just as the bells began to strike four.

'Catch it!' Madame Montfort was shouting, waving her arms.

Smothering a laugh, Aimeric ducked down onto the steps below the loggia. He had kidnapped a chicken from the coop and tied a wooden spoon to its leg, before setting it loose in the main courtyard. The chaos was everything he had hoped.

'Do something!'

The hen was blundering around, knocking things over with

the spoon. Now it had got itself trapped behind the wheels of the butcher's delivery trap.

Madame Montfort waved her arms. 'Drive it into the corner, fool!'

A kitchen boy descended upon the hen, sending the creature flapping in the opposite direction. A groom tried to sweep the bewildered bird up into his arms, but failed to notice the full pail of water until he stumbled over it and fell, soaking Madame Montfort's skirts.

'Idiot,' she shouted. 'You dolt! Throw something over it. A blanket, a cloak!'

Aimeric looked up through the green canopy of ivy and the turn of the wall beneath the loggia. Most of the household was now either outside, or watching from the balconies and windows. Aware he had to keep the diversion going until Minou reappeared, he reached up and prodded the chicken with the broom handle, to set it flapping back into the courtyard again.

Minou and Piet were standing close together in the shadows of the smallest of the side chapels of the Eglise Saint-Taur.

'I cannot stay for long,' she said, taking back her hand.

'I know,' he said softly. 'I wish you had brought Aimeric with you to keep watch.'

'I could not. I had to ask him to create a diversion so I could leave the house unobserved. Monsieur Boussay has come home unexpectedly, and the household is anxious and watchful because of it.'

'I am grateful you came,' Piet said quickly.

It was the first time they had been alone since their strange interlude in the *maison de charité* on the day of the riot, and Minou could see how he had changed. Though his beard and hair were not returned to the colour nature intended, his face was freckled from the sun, and there was a new sense of purpose in his eyes. A resolve.

'I want you and Aimeric to leave Toulouse tonight,' he said.

His words momentarily stole her breath from her. 'Would you not grieve for the lack of me?' she teased, then she marked the expression on his face and became sombre. 'Why now? The streets are quieter than they have been for some days.'

'Tonight . . .' Piet began, then stopped.

'You should know that you can trust me.'

'I do know, though they would hang me if they knew I was warning someone like you.'

Minou narrowed her eyes. 'Someone like me? A Catholic, do you mean? I have ever been so, and that has not mattered before.'

Piet ran his fingers through his hair. 'Not just any Catholic – Boussay's niece,' he said. 'Your uncle, who is so deeply involved in this matter, and who is one of the chief persecutors of Huguenots within Toulouse.'

Minou considered the ill-tempered, corpulent man who was so rarely at home. She disliked him, thought him boorish and unpleasant, but had never before thought of him as dangerous. Someone to be feared.

'Surely not.'

'He is in the pay of Monsieur Delpech, Toulouse's most powerful dealer of arms and men. He is also known to have associates within the cathedral, factions allied to the Duke of Guise, people who do not even bother to hide the fact that they want to expel all Huguenots from Toulouse. From France.'

Minou thought of the barrels of powder and shot in the cellar and the many visitors who came and went at night. Then she spoke quietly.

'There is a churchman who often comes to the house. Red

robes, a tall man and young for his office. Distinctive, black hair with a white streak.' Minou watched Piet's eyes sharpen and his face set rigid.

'You know him.'

'Yes.' He ran his hands through his hair again. 'He was once my dearest friend. His name is Vidal. We were students here together in Toulouse, as close as brothers once. It was with him I spent that evening in Carcassonne.'

'Oh,' Minou said gently, seeing how the mention of Vidal had pained him. 'And now? You are no longer friends?'

'No. That night he said things I chose not to hear. Yet, I still believed it was possible for us to have taken different paths to God, and to remain friends. I was naive. I realized that when I saw him in the negotiating chamber as the truce was being decided in the company of your uncle and Delpech. Then, finally I knew.'

'He goes by the name of Valentin now,' Minou said. 'My uncle promotes his petition to be the next Bishop of Toulouse.' She thought for a moment. 'The only other frequent visitor of this cabal, though I have not seen him of late, is Phillipe Devereux.'

'Nor I,' Piet replied, 'and good riddance. A man who plays both sides, I have nothing but contempt for him. You were right to try and warn me. I should have listened.'

'He is also a spy?'

'He was. His body was found in Place du Salin. How I wish I had trusted my instincts.'

'It is your nobility of spirit that leads you to see the best in all men.'

Piet shook his head. 'Would that I deserved your high opinion of me, but it was an English friend, Jasper McCone, who counselled me to hold my tongue.' He sighed. 'Devereux's cousin, Oliver Crompton, has disappeared too. Jasper says he has left the city to join the Prince of Condé's forces advancing from the north.'

Late afternoon light was shining through the high windows, sending a rainbow of patterned light into the nave. Calm and peaceful, it was impossible at this moment to imagine anything disturbing this timeless tranquillity.

'Why did you ask me to meet you, Piet?' Minou asked. 'Not simply to ask me to go, for you could have sent Aimeric with that message.'

'I knew you would refuse to leave.'

Minou gave a brief smile. 'Maybe. I can't see that the situation now is any different from these past weeks. The truce is still holding. Besides, I can't leave Toulouse. My aunt relies upon me, I cannot leave her.' *Or you*, she thought. *How could I leave you?* 'And what would my father say if we arrived back in Carcassonne without warning?'

Piet drew her further back into the shadow of the side chapel and lowered his voice.

'Minou, listen to me. At first, after the riots, I held to the hope that both the Catholic and our Protestant leaders wanted to find a compromise for the good of Toulouse. I no longer believe that. With each week that passes, there is more evidence of the prejudice of the Parliament against Huguenots. Every miscarriage of justice comes at a cost. Now there are too many of our number whose spirits, heated by news of the success of the campaigns in Orléans and Lyon, want conflict to come.' He took a deep breath. 'Condé has levied troops in Blagnac, and other villages around his estates. They plan to enter the city tonight.'

'What do they intend?'

'To force Toulouse to implement the Edict of Toleration

and treat Huguenots and Catholics the same under the law and in the eyes of God.'

'By means of an army?'

'What other way is there now?' he said. 'Strength speaks unto strength. There are now thousands of Catholic soldiers in the city. We need to match them in order to bring them back to the negotiating table.'

Minou felt suddenly cold. The idea that a Huguenot army would enter the city by stealth tonight for the sole purpose of forcing a debate seemed the stuff of a child's game. But she could see Piet wanted to believe it.

'This is not another rumour?'

'No.' Piet took her hand. 'I beg you, my own love, leave today before the gates are closed for the night. After that, it might be too late.'

'I cannot leave. I have no means of transport, I have –'

'The graveyards of history are littered with the bones of those who delayed too long, Minou. I will arrange a horse and carriage to take you out of the city, then an escort to take you across the border into the Aude. You should be safe then.'

'Why are you doing this?' she whispered. 'You put yourself at risk.'

'My sweet love,' he said fiercely, 'return to Carcassonne. I will fear nothing in the battle to come, and be better able to protect all those whose lives are in my hands, if I know you are safe. As soon as all this is passed, I will come to you.' He cupped her face between his hands and brought his lips to hers. '*Lieverd*. My own darling.'

And hearing those words Minou realised then that he did not expect to survive the battle. She felt a fierce courage surge through her. She put her arms around his waist and held him.

'Though I hesitate to put you into any danger, there is

something else I would have you do for me,' Piet said, finally pulling away.

'Anything,' Minou said.

'God willing, tonight will pass with no loss of life.'

'What would you have me do?'

'There is something of great value I would like to be taken to safety in case, for whatever reason, I cannot later retrieve it. There's no one else I dare ask.'

'What is it?'

'I'll show you,' Piet said, quickly drawing her to the back of the narrow chapel and crouching down in front of the wall. 'See? It is hidden here.'

'What is it?' she asked again, watching as he eased a loose brick out of the wall and set it to one side.

'A fragment of the Holy Shroud, said to have been brought back by Crusaders from the Holy Land.'

'The Shroud of Antioch.'

His eyes widened. 'You know of it?'

'My aunt told me it was taken some years ago, that's all I know.'

'It was stolen. Later, it found its way into my possession. When the time came, I found I could not bring myself to let it be bartered away.' He flushed. 'It is an object of exceptional beauty.'

Minou smiled. 'I understand.'

'I had a replica made and hid the original where it had always been. Here, in this church. I cannot bear the thought of it being damaged, or destroyed, if things tonight should go ill.'

Frowning, she crouched down and peered into the dark cavity at the base of the wall. 'How long ago did you discover this hiding place?'

'Four winters past,' he said. 'Why?'

Many years after her aunt had gone looking for somewhere to conceal her treasured gift within this same church.

'Are there other such hiding spaces left within the walls?'

'I don't know of any. I learnt of this place from the old priest who was affiliated with the Collège de Foix when I was a student.'

Minou watched, as Piet gently drew out a square of rough grey cloth.

'I wrapped the Shroud in a scrap of my old military cloak for safe-keeping,' Piet said, holding the material softly in his hands.

Minou hesitated. 'Is there anything else inside the cavity?'

He looked up at her. 'Should there be?'

'There might be a book.'

His eyes sparked with enquiry, but he reached his hand back into the darkness. 'I can't find anything.'

'To one side, or further back perhaps?'

Piet lay down and worked the full length of his arm into the dust and the cobwebs.

'Hold fast, there is something here. I can feel some kind of cord and . . . a small bag.'

Minou hardly dared breathe, realising how much she wanted her aunt's story to be true, as Piet slowly pulled out a black velvet drawstring purse.

She smiled. 'I had no real expectation it would be here. My aunt told me she had, some years ago, hidden something within the church.'

'What is it?'

'A bible, which was sent to her by my mother as a gift to mark the occasion of my birth. Of course, there should be no reason for you to have both found the same place of concealment, except that it was the same old priest who had told her of it.'

'And in my urgency, I didn't think to look to see if the space was empty or not.' Piet passed her the bag. 'Will you open it?'

Minou picked away the cobwebs and dust, untied the drawstring at the neck and took out the bible.

'Well,' Piet said, glancing up to heaven. 'Someone was watching over her.'

Minou nodded. It was just as her aunt had described. Blue leather boards with a brighter blue silk ribbon to mark the pages.

She opened it. 'And the text is in French.'

The sound of the outer church door silenced them. Sounds of the street filtered in from outside. The rumble of the wheels of a cart, the whisper of the door to the church shutting again, the air slipping out.

'Can you see anyone?' Piet hissed.

Minou peered out of the side chapel, then darted back into the shadows.

'No one. Perhaps it was the old woman with her violets. She was on the step when I came in.'

They were both nervous now and feeling the pressure of time passing. Piet quickly pushed back the brick into place, placed the Shroud carefully into his satchel and handed it to Minou.

'You are sure you are willing to do this?'

'It will be safe in Carcassonne,' she said, then put the bible inside the bag as well. 'This too, treasures both.'

He stroked her cheek. 'Thank you.'

'All will be well, I am sure of it.'

Piet nodded, though his expression told a different story. 'A carriage and horse will be waiting for you and Aimeric in the stables on rue des Pénitents Gris at seven o'clock this evening.'

Minou looked down at the battered leather case, then slung the strap over her shoulder beneath her cloak. 'What if you find yourself trapped here in Toulouse? What then?'

Piet smiled. 'I have been finding ways in and out of this city for many years. I give you my word I will find you again.'

The bells in the high tower above began to ring for the fifth hour, and they stood side by side, their hands clasped, until the echo had died away in the shimmering air.

CHAPTER FORTY-NINE

⚜

Some half an hour after he and Minou had parted, Piet was standing in the stables in rue des Pénitents Gris confirming the arrangements.

'But you understand that it is essential they leave the city tonight,' Piet said again.

'Yes, Monsieur.'

Piet placed his hand on the withers of a bay mare tethered in the corner of the stables, as if to anchor himself.

'And that—'

'There will be two passengers,' the groom interrupted, repeating the instructions he had been given. 'You said. A lady and a young gentleman. Escort them to Pech David, where a second carriage will be waiting to take them on to Carcassonne.'

'Do not leave them. Stay until you are sure the next escort is there, ready to take them on. And heed this. Take them out of the city via the covered bridge. Do not pass by the Porte Villeneuve.'

Piet knew he should be more circumspect in what he said, but if Condé's troops did attempt to enter via the Porte Villeneuve at nine o'clock this evening, he wanted to be certain Minou was nowhere near.

The boy's eyes narrowed with suspicion.

'The covered bridge would be the customary route out of the city to the south. For my own safety, is there some particular reason to avoid the Porte Villeneuve tonight?'

'It's a private matter,' Piet said quickly, vexed that he was handling the situation badly. He was finding it hard to think. 'An argument. In the quartier Villeneuve, there is a Catholic relative who might cause trouble.'

'There is nothing illegal in this matter?'

'Not at all,' he said, trying to make light of things. 'A family dispute, nothing more.'

He pressed a second coin into the boy's hand. 'There will be another such when you return.'

Piet feared the groom might be a coward, but it was too late to find another to take his place. Troubled in his spirits, he walked back out into the late afternoon sunshine and crossed the road.

Piet thought it a mistake to attempt to take the city, especially now the coup had been brought forward by one week for fear the plan had been discovered. As Crompton had said, the Catholic forces outnumbered them ten to one, and that was some weeks back. He had no hope the citizens of Toulouse would heed their call to arms and protect their Huguenot neighbours. Above all, he wished fervently he could take Minou to safety himself. But he knew that was impossible. Rightly or wrongly, his first duty lay with his comrades. Tonight, he would stand beside them.

God willing, he would not fall beside them.

Deep in thought, Piet pushed opened the door to his lodgings and walked quietly up the stairs. Then, on the second landing, he stopped, alerted by some sixth sense. Something was different, something was changed.

He pressed himself back into the shadows and carefully drew his sword. Could it be McCone waiting for him in his chamber? He dismissed it. Surely Jasper would have heard his footsteps and called out?

Then Piet caught the breath of an old but familiar scent – the oil Vidal used upon his hair. Vidal. Yes, of course. But why had he come?

Piet tried to harden his heart. Vidal was on the opposite side of the door, he knew it. His erstwhile friend, who had drugged his wine and framed him to be hung as a murderer. Who else could it have been?

But what if Vidal was the solitary voice among his comrades wanting, even at this eleventh hour, to halt the bloody conflict?

Rather than turn away, Piet found himself moving towards his chamber, unable to resist seeing Vidal one last time. He reached out with his left hand and slowly pushed open the door.

There, sitting in his red robes in a chair in the middle of the room, was Vidal. He appeared to be alone and unarmed. Piet hesitated, then sheathed his sword.

'What are you doing here, Vidal?' he asked, unable to keep the hope from his voice.

'Seize him,' was the response. And the guards waiting in the blind spot behind the jamb, leapt forward.

CARCASSONNE

'What are you doing?' Rixende wailed as Cécile Noubel came back into the kitchen carrying a travelling case. 'Are you going away?'

'Fill the pewter flagon, Rixende,' she said, 'the one with the lid that does not leak. Ale not wine. And wrap the last of the bread and goat's cheese.' Her calm voice belied the chaos of emotion she was feeling. 'And the fresh root liquorice, all of it. It might be hard to come by further south.'

'What did you learn at the bishop's palace?' Rixende said, firing the question like an arrow. Having made the introduction to her cousin, Madame Noubel had firmly shut the door on their conversation. 'Did anyone know anything about the visitor, where she came from? Would anyone speak to you? And what of the bishop himself? My cousin says he has been unwell these past two weeks, and—'

'Rixende, be quiet.'

The maid's doleful eyes filled with tears. 'I am sorry, I don't mean to let my tongue run on, but I just –'

Cécile put her hands on her shoulders. 'Rixende, listen to me. I need you to do what I ask without question, else I will forget something of importance, or . . .' She broke off, trying to calm her own nerves. 'Or I will lose the courage to go through with what needs to be done. Do you understand?'

Rixende looked at her dumbly, but she nodded. A drab streak of a girl, Cécile thought, but well-meaning. She had become fond of her, despite everything.

'Good. Now, do you know where Monsieur Joubert kept his compass?'

'Did he not take it with him?'

Madame Noubel sighed. 'I don't know. Could you look?'

Rixende fished in the long, shallow drawer of the kitchen table. 'It is usually kept in here,' she said, finding the small walnut box and handing it over.

Cécile held the box flat in the palm of her hand for a moment, then opened it. She took it to the doorway, knowing how easily a compass could lose its bearings, and held it to the sun.

'A quarter past five, and south-south-west,' she said, 'which seems about right.'

'I wonder why the master left it behind.'

Cécile sighed again. 'I dare say because he knew where he was going.'

It took another quarter of an hour to settle the arrangements. She shuttered the windows and had Rixende lay a fire in the hearth ready to be lit. Plates, bowls and jugs were put clean and in their place. If Minou should come back, she wanted it to be a familiar homecoming, even though no one would be there to greet her.

She hesitated, then stretched up and took Florence's old map of Carcassonne from the mantle. It was this, more than anything she had learnt at the bishop's palace this afternoon, that gave credence to the story. She pulled from her pocket a purloined note Rixende's cousin had given her, and compared the handwriting.

A perfect match. Identical.

The cousin had been delighted to gossip about the noblewoman who had come to stay in April and had set the palace on its heels. The lady had come furnished with letters of introduction from a Monsignor Valentin, a canon from the cathedral in Toulouse who had himself been a guest of the Bishop of Carcassonne in March.

'I don't know, Madame,' she had said, diverted into another story. 'Some say he was here to investigate the murder back in the spring, though he arrived before that. Alphonse Bonnet was hung for the crime, though no one really believed he'd done it, and now it seems he was in the stocks in the Bastide in plain view, so how he could have been cutting Michel Cazès's throat at the same time, I don't know. I heard the reason the Monsignor was in La Cité was to do with some relic.'

'The lady?' Cécile had prompted, interested only in Alis.

It seemed the noble guest had arrived from Toulouse on the first Friday of April, the intention being she would stay in the palace for a few days before returning to her estates in the foothills of the Pyrenees. The cousin remembered the day particularly because a banquet, suitable for the lady's high position, was being prepared when, without warning, she took her leave.

'What was the noblewoman's name?' Cécile asked again. 'Where does she come from?'

'Puivert,' had come the answer. 'Blanche de Bruyère, widow of the late Seigneur. Do you know the place?'

Cécile's heart skipped a beat. 'I knew it once.'

'Well, there's a thing. She left this,' she added, handing her a piece of paper with a family crest and insignia. 'In the middle of writing a letter, I suppose, when she was called upon. And I tell you something else for nothing. Though she took pains to hide it, the lady was with child. Odd, we thought it, that she should be travelling so far from home at such a time.'

And at that moment, Cécile knew where Alis had been taken and why; she knew Bernard's suspicions were justified. She understood that all the strange, seemingly unconnected events could be traced back to the last day of October nearly twenty years ago.

Old secrets cast long shadows . . .

TOULOUSE

Whispering to one another through the locked door of Aimeric's chamber, where Madame Montfort had again confined him, Minou finished telling him what she and Piet had agreed. And though she grieved for having to leave Piet, her brother's joy at learning they were going back to Carcassonne cheered her.

'If we are going home,' he hissed back, 'I don't mind anything.'

'I will get hold of the key to let you out of here.'

Aimeric laughed. 'No need. The latch on the casement window is loose. It's easy to climb out onto the ledge, along the roof of the grain store, and down. I've done it plenty of times.'

'Be careful,' she said sternly. 'Bring only what you cannot bear to be parted from. I will do the same. We will meet just before seven o'clock in the stables in rue des Pénitents Gris.'

'Will Piet be there?'

She wished she could tell him yes. The truth was, she didn't know.

'Don't be late,' she whispered. 'We have this one chance.'

Minou hurried back to her own chamber. She dragged the nightstand across the floor and wedged it under the handle of the door. At any moment, Madame Montfort might take it upon herself to storm in and demand to know where she had been all afternoon. Minou tilted her head to one side, listening, but the house was oddly quiet.

Aware of how little time she had, she fetched her old woollen travelling cloak, and a needle and thread. She padded her fingers around the hem of the cloak until she found the fold in the material concealing a hidden pocket, then worked the opening wide enough for her hand. Next, she took the grey square of fabric from Piet's satchel and laid it out on the table. Though raised a Catholic, she disliked the cult of relics, seeing it as a throwback to superstitious times when women and men knew no better. What holy or transcendent significance could possibly be found in an old splinter of wood or a fragment of torn cloth? But when Minou unwrapped the binding and lifted out the antique material with its unfamiliar stitched lettering, the beauty of the Shroud's long and deep history moved her to tears.

She imagined it in the hands of a grieving woman in the Holy Land, or being transported across the sea on a Crusader ship sailing home from Antioch to Marseille, or carried along the old Roman road from Narbonne to Carcassonne to its final resting place in Toulouse. Now, in the glister and shifting of the late afternoon light, Minou understood why Piet, a Huguenot and a man who lived in the modern world, had not been able to bring himself to let this fragment of cloth be bartered or destroyed. He had kept it safe, and had now charged her to do the same.

She would not fail him.

Minou removed her hairbrush and glass from their leather casing, rolled the Shroud carefully inside and sealed the lid with melted candle wax. Easing the narrow tube into the seam of her cloak, pushing it round as far as she could, she sewed up the gap in the hem. In her haste, she pricked her fingers, leaving two drops of blood on the green wool.

Finally, she turned her attention to the bible, comforted by the idea that her mother had once held this same book in her hands. Minou ran her fingers over the leather binding, wrinkled like the skin on the back of an old man's hand, and smoothed the thin silk ribbon, cornflower-blue, set to serve as a page mark. The painted silver leaf around the bible's edges seemed to sparkle and shine and, inside, diaphanous pages carried the imprint of a delicate black and red script. The edition looked as if it might be valuable. Her father would know. Distracted from her task for a moment, she again wondered at his silence. She comforted herself that tomorrow, when she and Aimeric arrived back in Carcassonne, she would be able to ask him all the questions that had filled her mind these past weeks. Not least to find out if he had known about this beautiful Protestant bible sent by Florence to her sister.

Minou held the book up to the light, tilting the pages so that the light fell on them through the window. She turned to the frontispiece and looked at the dedication and the name of the translator – Jacques Lefèvre d'Étaples – as well as the year and place of its printing: 1534 in Antwerp. The page was bordered by simple black and white etchings, all scenes from scripture.

Then she noticed, tucked in a pocket at the back, a folded sheet of parchment. Her heart sped up. Might it be a letter from her mother to her aunt? Hardly daring to open it, for fear it might crumble to dust, Minou placed it on the table and carefully unfolded it.

No, it was not her mother's handwriting.

This is the day of my death.

And not a letter at all, but a Will.

As the Lord God is my witness, here, by my own hand, do I set this down. My last Will and Testament.

Minou's eye skipped ahead to the name inscribed at the foot of the document: Marguerite de Puivert. Beyond the coincidence of it being her own given name, it meant nothing. Then she saw the two names written below it, and the date, and she turned cold. The thirty-first day of October in the year fifteen forty-two.

The day of her birth.

CHAPTER FIFTY

⚜

Minou folded the Will back inside the bible and pushed it into the lining of her cloak.

She cast around the chamber. She spied her birthstone, a pink tourmaline brooch, and pinned the hem with it. Then she lifted the mattress, and took the letter with the red seal from its hiding place.

A sudden hammering on the door made her jump.

'Who's there?' she called.

'You must come,' Aimeric shouted, struggling to open the door.

'Wait a moment,' she said, dragging the nightstand out of the way and Aimeric burst into the room. 'Why are you here? We agreed to meet at the stables –'

'Come now,' he said, grabbing her arm. 'I swear he has gone mad. He's trying to kill her.'

Monsieur Boussay took his cane from its usual place behind his chair. His wife took a step away from him.

'No. Please, no. I give you my word. I said nothing, husband.'

'You disobeyed me.'

'I did not.'

'The boy wanders as he wills through the streets, like a common urchin, and now I discover the girl has been meeting with a known Huguenot in our church in rue Saint-Taur. Aided by you.' He advanced on her. 'How do you think that makes me look? That I cannot even control the women under my roof.'

'I am sure you are mistaken,' she said, backing away from him even though she knew it would do no good. 'Minou is an honest girl. A dutiful niece. She would not meet a man unchaperoned. I'm sure you are mistaken.'

'Are you questioning my judgement?'

'No, no, of course I would not,' she stammered.

'You lie. My sister, acting upon my orders, saw them. While you pretended to pray, she was meeting with this heretic in a side chapel.'

'I do not believe it,' Salvadora said, her voice trembling. 'Indeed, my sister-in-law, virtuous as she is, does not like Minou and will say—'

'Be quiet, you pathetic hag.' He brought the stick sharply down on the desk. 'In these times, when everything is under such scrutiny, you have encouraged your whore of a niece to defy me. You have made a fool of me.'

Salvadora shrank further back, taking tiny steps as if he would not notice, until she could go no further. He whipped the air with the stick, as if it was a sword, then within three strides he was standing in front of her.

'Husband, I do not. I do everything I can to –'

He poked the skin beneath her chin. 'You not only encourage your niece and your nephew to defy me, but you spur them to laugh at me behind my back.'

'Never,' she said. 'I would not.'

He ripped the ruff from her neck, then tore her partlet open so her flesh was exposed.

'You need to learn what it means to be a loyal wife. An obedient wife.'

*

'We have to stop him!' Minou shouted.

Though Madame Montfort looked shaken, her eyes were bright with defiance.

'She is his wife. It is his right to discipline her in the way he sees fit.'

'Discipline her? How can you stand by and let anyone be treated so vilely, not least such a sweet and gentle woman?'

Minou made another attempt to get past, but Madame Montfort stood firmly in front of the study door. 'This is not your business.'

Freed by the knowledge that they were to leave the Boussay house, Aimeric flew at her. Every punishment, every humiliation he'd suffered at her hands, spurred him on. He knocked her off balance and pulled her hood over her eyes.

'Get away from me, you devil!' she cried, staggering forward into the wainscoting.

Minou darted past and tried the handle.

'It's locked from the inside,' she said. 'Give me your keys.'

But Madame Montfort was already hurrying away down the passageway.

'Shall I go after her?' Aimeric said. 'More likely than not she's gone to fetch Martineau.'

'There isn't time,' Minou cried in desperation, rattling the handle again. 'We can't get in.'

'I can,' Aimeric replied, doubling back along the passageway and out to the courtyard.

'Please husband, no . . .' Salvadora pleaded, then cried out as Boussay brought the stick down across her bare shoulders.

'You allow them to take liberties,' he said, striking again. 'You are careless of my reputation with your pitiful gossip, your stupidity.' He brought a third blow down, this time catching her cheek.

Salvadora was sobbing, crouched on the floor with her hands over her head, for fear of where the next blow might land. For fear of how long the beating might last.

'Get up,' he said, kicking her with his foot, 'you disgusting, foul, feeble-minded hag. Whimpering like a bitch in heat, you disgust me.'

Minou was astonished none of the servants had come running. She banged on the door, trying to drown out the pitiful sounds of her weeping aunt's desperate pleas for mercy.

Then there was a crash, and an ominous silence.

'Aunt,' Minou shouted, banging louder. 'Aunt!'

It seemed an eternity before she heard the turn of the key in the lock. Moments later Aimeric pulled open the study door.

'Brilliant boy,' she said, rushing into the chamber.

'I think I might have killed him,' he said, ashen faced.

She glanced to where their uncle lay slumped over the desk in front of the open window, a trail of red blood dripping down his temple and shards of white pottery scattered around him.

Minou rushed to her aunt, who was curled in a ball on the floor, her face and chest a mass of bruises, and her arms and hands marked with red stripes where she had tried to protect herself.

Minou picked up the cane and snapped it over her knee. She cast her eyes around, saw her uncle's cloak on the back of the door, and put it around her aunt's shoulders to cover her injuries.

'Dear Aunt,' she said, 'it is all right. You are safe now.'

'No,' she was sobbing, 'no, you should not be in here.

Monsieur Boussay will be angry. It was my fault. I am sure I deserved it, for I should not have provoked him.'

'We must go,' Minou said, refusing to allow herself to be angry. Not yet. 'Can you stand, Aunt?'

She beckoned Aimeric to shield their aunt from the sight of her husband, unconscious and bloodied.

'Monsieur Boussay is so relied upon,' she muttered in a high, childlike voice. 'It is to be expected. He always did have a fierce temper. I learnt that soon enough . . .' Her eyes suddenly flared wide with terror. 'Where is he? Has he gone? Has the capitoul come to ask his counsel? Is that it? He is so important. In these treacherous times, ever more so.'

'Yes,' Minou replied, understanding her aunt's wits had frayed with shock. 'That is right. He has gone to the Hôtel de Ville with his colleagues. Aimeric brought him the message.'

'So, he is gone away? My husband is gone? He is not in the house?'

Minou heard the hope in her aunt's voice and her heart clenched. She saw one of her eyes was swollen and there was a clear crimson scar, a mark of the cane, from her temple to her jaw.

'Monsieur Boussay has gone. He will not need you this evening.'

'Oh.' Her aunt seemed to collapse in her arms. Aimeric leapt forward, and together they walked her towards the door. 'If he is gone, then I might rest a while? That would be allowed, I think? No one could blame me.'

They helped her from the room and into the window seat in the long corridor.

'It is your house, dear Aunt,' Minou said. 'You can do whatsoever you wish.'

'What about him?' Aimeric mouthed, jerking his head in the direction of the study.

She could see the lace of her uncle's cravat was rising and falling with each breath and, though Minou wished him dead for his cruelty, she was relieved for all their sakes that he was not.

'Did you take his keys?'

'I did.'

'Then we will lock him in and take the key with us.'

'What about Madame Montfort. She knows we were here.'

Minou frowned. 'I don't know where she's gone. Help me take Aunt to her chamber. We need warm water and cloth, a little wine. Don't tell anyone. She would not want her servants to see her like this.'

'There's no one else here,' Aimeric said. 'I was on my way to let you know when I heard Boussay shouting.'

'What do you mean?'

'I saw the carts being loaded in the kitchen yard. Everyone has gone.'

Minou stopped. 'Are you saying that, apart from us, the house is empty?'

'I don't know about Martineau, but all the other servants have been sent away. I watched them go. Madame Montfort is the only one left. Uncle ordered her to wait to give the soldiers entry to the basement, then she was to follow to a safe house in the quartier Saint-Cyprien across the river.'

Minou felt a stillness seep through her. 'Then it's true. It's tonight.'

'What's tonight?'

'It's why Piet made arrangements for us to leave Toulouse so urgently. There is a Huguenot plan to take the city.'

'So Boussay sent everyone to safety but us. The treacherous, vile, pox-ridden –'

'Never mind that.' Minou frowned. 'But it suggests the Catholics know of the planned attack. They will be waiting for them.'

'More than anything, I want to go home. But if what you say is true, I want to stay here with Piet in Toulouse and fight.'

'I will not let you,' Minou said quickly.

'Don't you understand, I hate them! Our uncle, the witch Montfort, all the overfed hypocrites who come to this house. I'm ashamed to be a Catholic.'

Minou sighed. 'I understand, *petit*, and your courage and sense of honour do you credit. But Piet has arranged for us to leave, and that's what we are going to do.'

On the window seat, their aunt suddenly started to mutter.

'Is he here? Is my husband coming back?'

Minou quickly moved to her side. 'No, he's gone. You are quite safe.'

Aimeric joined them. 'What are we going to do? We can't leave her here.'

'We will have to take her with us,' she said.

'To Carcassonne? She'll never come.'

'For the time being, let's just concentrate on getting her away from the house. Are your belongings packed?'

Aimeric pulled a face. 'There is nothing of this house that I would keep, not a single thing.'

'Good, then can you take her to rue des Pénitents Gris. I'll join you there. There is something I must fetch from my chamber.'

CHAPTER FIFTY-ONE

‘Seize him,’ Vidal shouted again.

But Piet was quicker. He grabbed the door and smashed it back on its hinges as hard as he could, catching the first soldier flush in the face. He heard the crack of bone and saw blood spurt from his nose as he fell, cursing, to the floor.

A man was advancing towards him. Dark hair, with a vivid scar on his cheek. Piet stabbed his dagger into the top of his hand, disabling him for long enough to get out of the chamber.

As he took the stairs two by two by two, Piet realised why the man had seemed familiar in the Fournier house in La Cité. He was also the captain who had raided the boarding house in the Bastide.

Vidal’s man.

If he’d had any illusions of his former friend’s intentions, they had been torn to shreds. Thinking of their last conversation in the borrowed house in the rue de Notre Dame, Piet was shocked by how much his own need to be reconciled with Vidal had blinded him.

He flung open the door to the street, hoping to gull his pursuivants into thinking he had fled into rue des Pénitents Gris, but then doubled back to a door set beneath the stairwell that led down to the series of tunnels beneath the buildings. Vidal knew the university quarter of Toulouse as well as Piet did himself. It was their old stomping ground, these narrow streets and alleyways around the Collège de Foix and the alleyways that linked the humanist college and the *maison de charité* in rue du Périgord. But the escape tunnels were new. He was relying on Vidal not being aware that the cellars beneath the street were now connected.

Pushing the spiders' webs away from his face, Piet made his way down the subterranean passageway. He felt only a cold desire for retribution. Until now, whenever Jean Barrelles had preached from the pulpit that Huguenots should rise up against oppression, Piet had argued for calm. Whenever his comrades had spoken of persecution, he'd responded that not all Catholics were the same. No longer. Now, when the battle started, he would stand on the barricades alongside his Protestant brothers and fight.

His breath was burning in his throat, from betrayal as much as from exertion. The ground began to slope upwards and he extended his pace, running his hand along the wall to ensure he did not overshoot his destination in the gloom.

He found the rope ladder and climbed up, stepping onto a ledge and sliding the bolt on another door. Silently, he stepped into the rear room of the Protestant bookshop in rue des Pénitents Gris and hoped there would not be another welcoming committee.

Minou watched Aimeric lead Madame Boussay, still dazed and stumbling, through the gate in the kitchen yard and out towards the street. Then she slipped back into the main house.

Despite everything, she felt strangely calm, as if all the events of the past few months had been leading to this moment. The stillness of the city outside the deserted house spoke of the anticipation of what was to come. As when a summer storm came down from the mountains, black clouds bearing down upon the walls of La Cité, Minou felt the approaching cataclysm in her bones.

Everyone waiting. Everyone holding their breath.

She ought to be afraid, she knew it. But Minou also felt free. No longer cooped up in the airless domesticity of the women's quarters, but determining her own fate out in the world. So long as they could get away from Toulouse before the fighting started, all might still be well.

'And may God protect and save Piet,' she said out loud, though she was no longer sure to whom she prayed.

Piet wiped the blood from his hands, leaving a red smear on his breeches. Once more, he peered through the gap in the shutters of the bookshop window. The rue des Pénitents Gris was still empty. No sign of Vidal or his men.

'All is well, Monsieur?' asked the bookseller anxiously.

Once plump as a woodcock, the old man's skin now hung loose on his bones. His long grey beard had grown unkempt.

'When I go, bolt your doors. Admit no one,' he said.

Hope died in the old man's eyes. 'It is true, then, that the Huguenot army is coming tonight? I have seen many leaving their homes, but had hoped it was another false alarm.'

'Stay inside,' Piet repeated.

'Will it be over quickly, Monsieur?' he said. 'They say that Orléans fell in a matter of hours. The Catholics surrendered and the civilian population was little harmed.'

'It is in the Lord's hands now,' Piet said, looking out towards the stables at the opposite end of the street. Praying, hoping, for a glimpse of Minou.

Instead, he saw a solitary figure, Jasper McCone, approaching his lodgings. He sighed with relief. Two swords would be better than one.

'Monsieur, I will take my leave of you. I am in your debt. Lock your doors.'

'May God go with you. And may God save Toulouse.'

CHAPTER FIFTY-TWO

⚜

Aware of the weight and bump of the bible and the leather cylinder, both stitched within the hem of her cloak, Minou walked as quickly as she could through the silent house.

She had Piet's satchel over her shoulder, containing the few items of sentimental value she had brought with her to Toulouse: her mother's rosary, her hairbrush and glass, two books. She intended to leave Toulouse with nothing belonging to Monsieur Boussay.

The study door was still closed, but as she crept along the passageways, she heard voices. Aimeric said all the servants had gone. Had her uncle woken?

As she got closer to the front door, the voices got louder. She realised they were coming from the private chapel, where the door stood slightly ajar.

'I won't ask again, Adelaide,' the steward said. 'Give it to me or I will take it.'

'I have as much a right to this as you,' Madame Montfort replied.

He laughed. 'It is I who have taken the lion's share of the risk, and now it's over.'

'It was I who hazarded my reputation, not you. Altering the books, disguising the figures, ensuring no blame could be laid at your door.'

'Sliding an object or two into your pockets,' Martineau said with contempt. 'You have grown rich sitting on your fat arse doing nothing. This is my last warning, Adelaide. If you do not hand it to me now, I will take it by force.'

Minou heard footsteps, then a shout and the sounds of a struggle. And though she hated how vilely Madame Montfort behaved to Aimeric, and to her sweet aunt, she could not bring herself to walk on by.

'No!' Madame Montfort screamed. 'I will not let you have it.'

Minou pushed open the chapel door. Madame Montfort spun round, her expression a mixture of desperation and guilt. Martineau took his chance. He grabbed the wooden chest from her hands and turned.

Madame Montfort hurled herself at him. He threw a blow, sending her crashing back into the altar. The candlesticks clattered and fell to the ground. Martineau charged out of the chamber.

Minou ran to the fallen woman, but she pushed her away.

'This is your fault,' she hissed. 'You and your peasant brother. Until you came, everything was fine. Under my control.' She staggered to her feet. Minou stepped back out of her reach. 'This is your fault. Do you hear me? You bitch. Coming here, sniffing for scraps. Parasites. You ruined everything and what am I left with? After all I've endured and put up with? Nothing.'

Shaken by the naked hatred in her eyes, Minou took another step back. Her face red with failure and loss, Madame Montfort raised her hand, as if to strike her, but instead turned and stumbled to the door, and out into the passageway.

'Where are you going?' Minou called after her. 'Everyone has gone.'

The only answer was the sound of the front door opening, and crashing shut.

Stunned, Minou stood for a moment in the chaos of the chapel. The evidence of the altercation was all around: the cloth ripped, the two prie-dieux lying on their sides and the hassocks, with the embroidered Boussay crest, thrown into a corner like a pair of old boots. The gold cross that usually sat on the altar was gone and the panelled doors beneath were open.

Minou bent down, then noticed a sheaf of papers and letters on the shelf. With a jolt, she saw her own name. Her pulse racing, she reached in and pulled out three letters she had never seen, each addressed to her.

She knew she should take them and leave. Every second she remained in the house was a second lost. But Minou recognised her father's handwriting, and she could not wait. She felt relief, followed by fury that Madame Montfort – she had no doubt it would be her – had kept these letters from her. It didn't even appear she had opened them, but she was a woman for whom everything was a matter of power, of negotiation.

'Hateful, hateful woman.'

Minou slid her finger under the flap of the first letter. It was from her father, dated a few days after she and Aimeric had left for Toulouse in March. She scanned its contents, full of local news of Madame Noubel, of the reluctance with which the Sanchez family were packing up to leave the Bastide and how Charles's behaviour was more erratic by the day.

The second letter, dated the fifteenth day of March, acknowledged receipt of her letter to him, but it was more sombre in tone. In it he begged her forgiveness, explaining he intended to put matters right. Forgiveness for what?

To that end, he was intending to journey to a place called Puivert. He gave his word he would tell her everything when next they were together but, in the meantime, she should not worry. Alis was content to be left in the care of Madame Noubel.

There it was in black and white – Puivert.

Everything her aunt had told her rushed back into her mind. Minou pressed the letter to her chest, haunted by the fact that all the time she'd been imagining him in his usual chair by the fire in their little house, he hadn't even been in Carcassonne at all.

She turned to the last letter, only now seeing the form of address was different: MADEMOISELLE MARGUERITE JOUBERT. She recognised the seal from the letter delivered to her in her father's bookshop: the two initials, a B and a P, set either side of a mythical creature with talons and a forked tail.

The seal might be a match, but the handwriting was different. This was sophisticated writing. Elegant and cursive letters, written with a thin quill and expensive ink.

Minou cracked the seal. Her breath seemed to turn to ice in her lungs.

I shall expect your company, Mademoiselle Joubert. You must do me the honour of coming in person. Your sister will be released only into your care.

The letter was dated the third day of April and signed Blanche de Puivert.

She read it, and read it through again, then screwed the paper in her fist. If this communication was to be trusted, for five entire weeks, her little sister had been alone, far from home. Minou could not bear it. And hard on the heels of her anger, a burning hatred not only for the author of the letter, but for Madame Montfort too. By keeping the ransom letter from her, she had ensured her sister was left at terrible risk.

Was Alis dead? Minou shook her head. She wouldn't entertain it. She'd know it, she'd feel it.

Then, like a glint of winter sun on a December day, she suddenly understood how everything fitted together. It was as if she had been looking at the reverse side of a piece of embroidery, seeing all the bright colours and loose threads and uneven stitches, but failing to see the picture. Now, turning the tapestry around the right way, the true image was revealed.

Minou left the chapel, hurried across the courtyard and stepped out into rue du Taur. She was resolved. Aimeric would take her aunt to Carcassonne, where Madame Noubel could care for her. She would go to Puivert, not only to find Alis, but perhaps also her father. He had lived in the shadow of the past for too long.

'*Si es atal es atal*,' she said, an old phrase of her father's coming to her mind. 'What will be will be.'

Was that where she had first heard it said? In Puivert?

Minou paused at the steps to the church. The flower seller was gone and the streets were silent.

'*Kleine schat*,' she murmured, the Dutch words clumsy in her mouth. His little treasure, that's what Piet had called her. He spoke of Amsterdam with the same affection she felt for Carcassonne. She would like to see the streets made of water. She would like Piet to meet her father and talk of the city so dear to them both.

For a moment, Minou smiled, imagining them in one another's company. Then the bells of Saint-Taur began to ring and the picture faded. Her father was not in Carcassonne, but in Puivert. And Piet? Minou caught her breath. Who knew what would happen once the sun had set and the Huguenot attack began?

Minou locked her dreams away and hurried to meet her brother at the stables in rue des Pénitents Gris.

CHAPTER FIFTY-THREE

⚜

'Where is my niece?' Madame Boussay asked again. 'She cares for me, my niece, and she would know I would be better indoors. The sun is not good for my complexion. My husband likes my skin to be white.'

'The sun has gone down,' Aimeric said, though he realised she was not listening.

Madame Boussay was sitting on a hay bale at the back of the stables, talking to herself. She held out her hand in front of her. Livid scratches, where she had tried to defend herself. Her shoulders were a mass of red and purple bruises and her left eye was swollen shut.

'That's the secret to keeping your husband, pure skin. A wife should have white skin if her husband is not to stray.' She suddenly turned on Aimeric. 'I want my niece. She will care for me.'

'Minou will be here soon,' he replied, embarrassed. He thought her wits had gone. She seemed unaware of her surroundings and her words were strange and made no sense.

Aimeric glanced at the groom, who pulled a face. He didn't know him well, but they had drunk a gage or two together on nights where Aimeric had crept out of the house in search of companionship in the taverns of Saint-Taur.

'She fell,' he said.

'If you say so,' the boy replied.

Madame Boussay was trying to stand up again. 'I must go,' she said, slurring her words as if drunk. 'Monsieur Boussay will be displeased to find me gone, and it will go the worse for it. Far better to go back now.' She gave an eerie trilling laugh. 'But then, if I am not there, then he cannot be angry with me, can he? He will be pleased. He will be pleased and everything will be quite all right again. Like it was, like it was . . .'

Aimeric wondered how they were possibly going to persuade her into the carriage. He looked out into the street again, as the seven o'clock bells echoed into silence, willing Minou to come.

Piet and Jasper McCone strode down rue des Lois, chased by the ringing of the bells.

'But where the devil has Crompton been? I thought you said he'd gone north to join Condé's army?' Piet repeated, trying not to glance over his shoulder for a glimpse of Minou. He would meet the carriage at the covered bridge and see her safely away there. 'I do not trust him.'

'It seems he's back,' McCone said casually, putting out his hand and steering them towards the Hôtel de Ville. 'This way. After he left the tavern that afternoon, he was caught up in some disturbance, was hit on the head, and lost his memory.'

'Convenient for him,' Piet muttered.

'As he tells it, a widow in the quartier Daurade took him in and cared for him. Little by little, his senses have come back to him. Finally, but a few hours ago, he realised where he was, and sent word.'

Piet shook his head. 'I still don't understand why he wants to see me. God knows, there is little love lost between us.'

McCone shrugged. 'He may also have sent word to Devereux, but don't forget he does not know his cousin is dead. The message came to the tavern and I said I would deliver it and bring you to him. I was waiting in the street outside your lodgings for some hours.'

'I see,' Piet said, then he stopped.

Was it likely that tonight, of all nights, McCone would be sitting drinking ale in the tavern? And was it his own anxiety making him see danger in every single thing, but if McCone had been waiting outside his lodgings for hours, why had he not seen Vidal and his men?

'How long?' he asked, throwing a glance at his friend.

Were there beads of perspiration on McCone's temple?

'An hour, perhaps more.'

'A little more than an hour,' Piet countered, keeping his voice steady.

He was racking his brains, trying to remember what – if anything – he had told McCone of his friendship with Vidal, but he could not remember. So many conversations, so many lies.

Only two people knew where he was lodging in Toulouse, Minou and the man standing beside him. Even the good ladies who worked in the *maison de charité* knew no more than that he lived nearby. Yet Vidal had been waiting for him, not without the building but inside his very chamber.

'Then surely you must have seen them?' he said.

This time there was no mistaking McCone's reaction. His shoulders tensed and his left hand balled into a fist as he decided what to say.

'I saw nothing out of the ordinary,' McCone said eventually. 'Not even that girl, the one with the unusual eyes.'

Piet forced himself not to react. How could he possibly know about Minou? They had arrived at and left the Eglise Saint-Taur separately. He would swear no one had seen them together.

They were now in the heart of medieval Toulouse, with its labyrinth of tiny streets and overhanging buildings. The air smelt of the detritus of the day and the metallic tang of old blood in rue Tripière, where the butchers and their boys sluiced the ground outside their shops with water stained pink. They were certainly not heading towards the quartier Daurade, where McCone claimed Oliver Crompton was waiting.

'Tell me what should I have seen?' McCone asked.

'An hour ago, maybe less, two men attacked me in my chamber. They are, I believe, in the service of a canon at the cathedral. If you were waiting outside, I am surprised you did not see them enter.'

Piet slipped his hand to the hilt of his dagger. Everything was falling into place: the theft of weapons from stores known only to a few, the sense of his always being watched, the leaking of Huguenot plans into Catholic hands.

The spy within their ranks was not Crompton, but McCone.

Was he also working for Vidal?

'This is a circuitous route you are taking, McCone,' he said, as they passed another of the grand houses built by the capitouls. 'We could have been in Daurade in half the time if we'd gone via the embankments.'

McCone gave a taut smile. 'There are patrols on the river, protecting the bridge. Safer this way.'

They turned into a narrow alleyway, and Piet was suddenly pierced by a memory of them toiling side by side to repair the houses destroyed in the rioting. Could he really have misjudged the Englishman so badly? He had trusted him. Liked him. He had thought they had much in common.

'Jasper . . .' he began, but as he turned, he realised McCone had drawn his sword.

'You have worked it out. Finally.'

Piet stared at him. 'Why?'

'Why do you think?' he sneered. 'You're not so wet behind the ears as to not understand? Money, Piet.' He rubbed his fingers together. 'Power. That's what drives the world, not faith. Same in England, same in France, all over the Christian world.'

'I don't believe it.'

McCone pressed the tip of his sword against Piet's throat. 'Then you are a bigger fool than I took you for. Turn around, Reydon. Put your hands where I can see them.'

'Who told you about her?' he said, unable to stop himself.

'There are spies everywhere in Toulouse,' McCone laughed. 'You of all people should know that.'

'Who?' Piet demanded.

He laughed. 'No one can live by selling violets. Everyone's got their price.'

'Thank God you're here,' Aimeric said, rushing to meet her. 'I think her wits have gone.'

'Minou,' her aunt wailed. 'Dear Niece. Has he sent you? Is he angry with me? I must go back. I cannot have the sun on my face. My skin should be white, always white.'

'He paid me to take two,' the groom complained. 'A lady and a young man. And definitely not a lunatic.'

'I will pay extra,' Minou said quickly. 'Is it you who is to drive us?'

'Got any complaint?'

Minou held up her hand. 'I meant nothing by it. How old are you?'

'Old enough to manage a carriage and horse,' he said sullenly, kicking the straw with the toe of his boot. 'Besides, it's only as far as the Roman hill fort some five leagues south.'

Minou turned to Aimeric. 'Piet has organised for a second carriage to meet at us Pech David and take us on to Carcassonne.'

'We should get going. It is already a quarter past seven. The gentleman was most insistent that we leave the city tonight.'

'Is he here?' Aunt Boussay suddenly said again. 'Don't let him see me, don't let him—'

'You're quite safe,' Minou told her. 'Aimeric and I will look after you. Come, we are going on a journey.'

Whether it was shock, or that the beating had inflicted some lasting damage, Minou could see her aunt was very confused. She had intended to drive directly to Puivert, but Madame Boussay would not be able to cope in this state. She needed rest. She needed ointment for her wounds.

'If we're going, we must go now,' the groom said again, 'else the gates will be shut.'

Minou took a deep breath. There was no choice. For now, they would go to Pech David, as Piet had arranged, and then she could decide what to do next. She glanced at her brother, realising she would have to tell him about Alis soon.

And then she thought of Piet, and the precious cargo she was carrying for him, and her courage returned.

'Dear Aunt,' she said, using the same voice she had used with her brother and sister when they were little, 'Aimeric is going to help you up into the carriage. Will you take his arm?'

'We're going away? Does Monsieur Boussay know? He does not like me to go anywhere without his permission.'

'It is he who has bid me take you out of the city, dear Aunt, for the sake of your health.'

'Didn't I tell you?' A strange, lopsided smile came across her bruised face. 'He always puts me first. Monsieur Boussay is a good husband, always thinking of me, always . . .'

'Come, Aunt,' Minou said, guiding her onto the bench seat with Aimeric's assistance.

'Will dear Florence be there too? Will my sister be waiting for me? I would so love to see her. It has been so long.'

'We are all going to look after you, dear Aunt,' Minou said softly. 'You won't ever have to be afraid again.'

He will be here any day now.

This letter, written in his own hand and with his personal seal, attests it. In it, he speaks of impending chaos and the final battle to save the soul of Toulouse. The date set is for the thirteenth day of May and he considers it prudent to remove himself until the worst has past. Until every last heretic has been burnt or expelled and the cancer of Protestantism extirpated. Only then will he return to Toulouse and provide the leadership the Church needs.

Until that time, Valentin will find sanctuary with me in Puivert.

He writes, too, that he knows the whereabouts of the true Shroud. God willing, he says, by the time I have his letter in my hand, it will be in his possession.

The most welcome news is this. He has discovered where Minou Joubert is lodging and is taking steps to have her taken into his custody.

From his hands, to mine.

CHAPTER FIFTY-FOUR

⚜

Toulouse

'Why are we stopping?' Minou asked, as the carriage came to a standstill in Place de la Daurade.

Madame Boussay had slipped into a stupor. Her eyes were open, yet she seemed insensible of her surroundings. Minou was concerned, but did not want her to come to at this moment.

'They've set up a checkpoint before the tollhouse on the bridge,' the groom replied, half standing on his platform.

'Why?' Aimeric said.

'Searching everyone trying to leaving the city, by the looks of it.'

Minou squeezed Aimeric's hand. 'We must not be alarmed. There are often checks on the bridge.'

'But what about her?' he said, jerking his thumb towards Madame Boussay. 'What if they think we are responsible?'

Gently she pulled her aunt's hood further across her face, to hide her swollen eye and the bruising around her jaw.

'Leave it to me,' Minou said, with a confidence she did not feel. 'All will be well.'

McCone had sheathed his sword, but Piet felt the point of the Englishman's dagger sharp against his side and hidden from view. The slightest pressure would drive it into his guts. Meanwhile, they were walking close together as if boon companions, across Place de la Daurade.

As they drew level with the steps of the church, Piet's eyes darted around, trying to decide how and when to make his move: if he allowed himself to be taken to the dungeons of the Inquisition, that would be the end of it.

'There is no point thinking of running,' McCone said. 'We have men everywhere.'

It was true, there were soldiers on every corner. A checkpoint had been set up at the entrance to the covered bridge, and there was a bottleneck of wagons and carriages waiting to cross over to the fortified suburb of Saint-Cyprien. Some belonged to Huguenot families, part of the general exodus since the rioting in April, but others were clearly those of wealthy Catholics. Expensive livery and decorated carriages. He hoped to God that Minou and Aimeric had got safely away before the searches began.

McCone's dagger jabbed him again in the ribs.

'This way,' he said under his breath. 'Don't want to keep the noble Valentin waiting.'

'What ails her?' the guard asked roughly, pointing at Madame Boussay.

'She suffers with her nerves,' Minou said quickly, 'not contagion. We are taking her to the country for her health.'

'Remove her hood so I can see her face.'

'Sirrah, she is unwell. It would not be seemly for her to unveil.'

'Unless I see her face, you will not pass.'

Minou hesitated, then stepped down from the carriage. 'This is the wife of an associate of Monsieur Delpech. No doubt you know his name. I have been ordered to take her out of Toulouse with the minimum of fuss.'

The soldier laughed. 'The wife of a high-ranking official, in a carriage like this with a single horse! You expect me to believe that?'

'So as not to draw attention,' Minou said, producing a sou from her purse. 'My master wishes his wife to have the privacy appropriate to her station. He believes it would be regrettable if attention was drawn to her presence.'

The coin vanished. 'Who's the boy?' he said, pointing at Aimeric.

'The son of her physician,' Minou said, 'in case my mistress needs one of her tinctures on the journey.'

He looked doubtfully at Aimeric, who had the sense to hold his tongue.

'Get on with it,' a man shouted from a wagon behind them. 'What's the hold-up?'

'Come on, hurry up.'

'Are you Catholic?' the guard said.

'Of course,' Minou said, producing her rosary. He seemed undecided and the moment stretched thin, until to her relief, he waved them through.

They quickly caught up with the slow-moving caravan crossing the bridge, trundling forward between boarded-up stalls, and Minou started to breathe more clearly. This is where she had come on her first outing with her aunt in Lent. She had lost the stone to her favourite ring and they took it to be reset. And this stall on the right was where her uncle had founded the business that was to make him so rich, using money from her aunt's dowry to buy his stock.

A shout went up behind her. 'Wait a moment. You.'

Minou glanced back over her shoulder and saw that the soldier who had let them through had been joined now by another, who was pointing at her. She turned cold. After all this, were they going to be stopped now?

'Mademoiselle!' he called.

The bridge was crammed with people and animals. There was no way of evading the sentries.

'I say, you there. Pull up.'

Minou had no choice. She had to protect her aunt and brother. She had to protect the Shroud. The only way to do so was to separate herself from them. Without drawing attention, she untied her cloak and let it fall down to the floor beneath the seat.

'Are they shouting for us?' Aimeric asked.

'I fear so,' she said in a low voice. 'I'll see what they want. You carry on without me.'

'No! I'm not leaving you here.'

She clasped his hand. 'You must. There is more at stake than you know. God willing, this is nothing and I will soon join you at Pech David. Most people will be travelling that way.' She glanced over her shoulder again, to see the two soldiers now pushing their way through the crowd towards them. 'But if I do not arrive tonight, then you must instruct the driver to take you to Puivert. In the mountains. There's money enough in my purse. Here, take it.'

'Puivert?' Aimeric's eyes widened. 'But we're supposed to be going to Carcassonne.'

'The plans have changed,' Minou said urgently. 'All you need to know is that both Father and Alis are there.'

'What! Why? How do you know?'

'You remember? Aunt told me our parents lived there before you were born.'

'Yes, but what's that got to do—'

'Aimeric, there's no time to explain now. Go, and take this with you. Guard it well.' Minou slid the cloak across the floor with her foot. 'In the lining, there is something of great value that belongs to Piet. Also, something of our aunt's that I am keeping safe for her.'

'Of value? Then why—'

'You must keep it concealed and safe in the cloak – keep both objects hidden.'

Aimeric frowned. 'Is Piet coming to Puivert to retrieve this whatever it is?'

'If he can, yes. Courage, *petit*. I am relying on you. We all are. *A bientôt*, my favourite brother.'

'Come soon,' he said in a small voice, but Minou was relieved to see resolve in his eyes.

'I will.'

She let go of his hand, climbed down from the carriage and walked towards the soldiers.

'Were you speaking to me, sirrah?'

'I told you.' He addressed the guard who had allowed them passage. 'It is her, don't you see her eyes? They don't match.'

Minou had no idea if Madame Montfort had reported her to the authorities or if Monsieur Boussay had recovered and sent men after them, only that she had to both draw them away from the carriage and try to avoid being taken herself in the process.

Minou leapt forward, catching them off guard.

'Hey!'

She ran straight between them, zigzagging in and out of the mass of wagons and traps, past the tollhouse and off the bridge.

'In the name of the Seneschal, stop!'

Minou made it to the square, moments before the sentries on the bridge realised what was happening. She kept running towards the Eglise de la Daurade, where the congregation was just spilling out onto the church steps after Vespers.

God willing, she could lose herself in the crowd.

*

Piet heard a cry go up down by the bridge. Out of the corner of his eye, he saw two soldiers chasing someone through the crowd. McCone heard it too and half turned.

Piet took his chance.

He threw himself backwards, sinking his elbow into McCone's belly and using his other to knock the stiletto dagger away. Then he bolted back towards the church, where the evening service had just finished.

God willing, he could lose himself in the crowd.

CHAPTER FIFTY-FIVE

Puivert

Once Alis was sure the nurse was asleep, she put down her book, tiptoed past the cold fireplace and out of the chamber. Full of ale, the nurse had left the key in the door again.

The building where Alis was being held had once been the main living quarters of the château de Puivert. The estate offices were on the top floor. The middle floors – where she lived with the woman who was guarding her – were given over to the sleeping and living quarters, with the kitchens on the ground floor. The rooms were stacked one upon the other like in a medieval castle and older houses, connected by ladders.

In the weeks of her imprisonment, Alis had watched and listened, and come to learn the routines of the household. When she first arrived in April, she had been confined within one room. Then she had been given the run of the middle floor and accompanied into the courtyard for a little air each afternoon.

Everything in the castle revolved around the Lady Blanche, her mercurial moods and her shifting demands. Alis did not know if it was the baby she was carrying that made her so changeable, only that the servants feared and disliked their mistress.

Alis was lonely and she missed her tabby kitten, but the mountain air suited her. Her cheeks were pink and plump, her long curled hair shone as black as a crow's wing and, after more than a month in Puivert, she rarely coughed. Her lungs were strong now.

She was taller by a *pouce* and there was more skin on her bones. When Minou came to take her home, she would be pleased.

She hoped the kitten would remember her.

The days were long, however. To pass the time, Alis read and read. She wanted to have plenty to tell Minou when she came about the history of the château de Puivert and the village. She was collecting dates and stories and scraps of information, like a magpie feathering its nest. When she was bored with reading, and the nurse was snoring, she quietly went exploring.

Alis stepped into the upper courtyard, which was the oldest part of the castle. She had never been allowed to go through the arch into the main courtyard, and had never risked trying to creep through on her own. It looked as large as the Grande Place in the Bastide, with four defensive towers to house the garrison, including a prison in the base of the Tour Bossue and the counting house in the Tour Gaillarde. It was like a small town in its own right. She would tell Minou all about that too when she came.

If she came?

Alis still didn't know why Lady Blanche wanted to entice Minou to Puivert, though she understood she herself was the bait. Though she often cried herself to sleep at night and hoped desperately someone would come to take her home, she also prayed Minou would stay away.

In Toulouse, Minou was safe.

Toulouse

Vidal nodded to Bonal, who closed the door, then returned his attention to McCone.

'You let him escape.' He held up his hand. 'Just to be clear,

McCone. You are telling me that you had him, but you lost him. You are telling me Piet Reydon is not in your custody.'

'It was unfortunate that—'

'Unfortunate! It is unfortunate that we did not obtain the information we needed from Crompton, I agree. It is unfortunate for Devereux that he was discovered and someone saw fit to cut out his tongue. But failing to bring Reydon to me is not unfortunate, McCone. It is a very grave error on your part.'

'In my defence, I say—'

Vidal took a step towards him. 'You have no defence, McCone. It was on your urging that I decided to arrest Reydon, having explained my reasons for not having done so previously. I gave you charge of following out my orders. You failed. And because you failed, he is now well aware he is being hunted and will most likely vanish.'

'Your men also failed,' McCone protested. 'Reydon claimed you attempted to arrest him at his lodgings. It was you who put him on his guard.'

Vidal ignored him. 'Tonight, a Protestant army will enter the city. We are expecting them and it is what is necessary – to bring this pernicious stalemate to an end and for Toulouse to be wholly, properly Catholic again – but it means we have but a matter of hours to recover the Shroud.'

McCone threw up his hands. 'The Shroud. Why do you fix such attention on a ragged piece of cloth? You are a sophisticated man, Valentin. You can't possibly believe it means anything?'

'You are talking like one of them, Jasper. All that time in the company of Huguenots. Have they got you? Have they converted you?'

'You insult me.'

'I chose you because you appeared to believe only in money. Not so grave a sin as heresy, but a sin all the same.'

'I have not been converted. I am still at your service.'

Vidal clicked his fingers. Bonal opened the door, and two armed soldiers entered. 'I have no further need of you, McCone.'

'Monsignor! I beg you. I will—'

'Here we have another heretic who should be given the chance to confess the error of his ways. Take him away.'

McCone tried to run. Bonal stuck out his foot, he stumbled, and the guards seized him.

'I have served you well,' he shouted. 'I have served your cause well.'

Vidal made the sign of the cross. 'May God be merciful and receive you into His presence.'

As the guards dragged McCone away, struggling and still protesting his innocence, Vidal removed his official robes. He wanted nothing that would mark him out as a priest.

'Have the carriage made ready and fetch my travelling clothes, Bonal,' he said. 'I would not be in Toulouse tonight.'

'Very good, Monsignor.' The servant hesitated, then asked: 'Might I ask where we are going, in order to know what best to pack for your comfort and safety?'

'We will go first to Carcassonne. It is the obvious place for the girl to make for.'

'You think it was her the soldiers failed to apprehend on the bridge?'

'Unfortunately, I do.'

'And that Reydon gave the Shroud to her?'

Vidal frowned. 'If the flower seller's evidence can be trusted, then yes.'

Bonal's fingers stole to the bandage wrapped around his hand. 'He is a dangerous opponent.'

'He is nothing,' Vidal snapped.

'Very good, Monsignor.'

'After Carcassonne, we will continue to Puivert and remain there until Toulouse is safe once more.' Vidal smiled. 'The air is clear in the mountains.'

PUIVERT

Alis's spirits were low.

It had been weeks and weeks, and still no word. Minou loved her – was she not her favourite sister? – but Alis was starting to lose hope. Lady Blanche was losing patience, too. The maids said she spent endless hours at the top of the keep looking out for signs of a visitor.

In the logis, Alis heard the sound of a door opening and she ran across the grass towards the keep. For weeks now she had wanted to see the musicians' gallery. When she was in her cups, the nurse talked of the old days when singers and players came from all around to perform for the household. Of how the candlelight flickering on the vaulted ceiling and the delicate carvings on the corbels and pillars were a marvel to behold. Alis wanted to see for herself. She ran up the long, steep flight of steps. The Bruyère coat of arms was engraved above the main door with some ferocious beast. She thought it was ugly.

Alis pushed open the wooden door and stepped into the lowest room of the tower. All was quiet. There was no noise, no sign that anyone else was in here at all. She looked up at the spiralling stone stairs, going up and up. They were steep and dark. The chapel was on the first floor, with the musicians' gallery on the floor above. She knew where she was going. There was a final flight of stairs up to the roof.

Putting her left hand on the wall to guide her, Alis started to climb. Round and round, higher and higher. At regular intervals, narrow windows were carved into the thick walls, like the arrow slits carved deep in the bastions of La Cité. The steps were uneven beneath her feet, worn away in places by generations of soldiers and members of the Bruyère family, but Alis was careful and did not slip.

On the first level, she stopped to look into the chapel. On the keystone at the centre of the doorway was a carving of a saint wrestling a lion. Beyond the threshold into the square room, she could see the high vaulted ceiling and a small altar, lit by a glancing ray of sunshine.

She stepped inside.

There were two large windows on either side of the chamber with inbuilt stone benches. From the northern window, Alis could make out the woodlands and valleys that lay beyond the castle. The southern window looked down towards the village of Puivert, the glass coloured a delicate pink by the rays of the setting sun.

Alis crossed the room. On the wall behind the altar hung an embroidered tapestry. She stepped forward and stood beneath it, the words in gold thread telling verses from the Book of Ecclesiastes.

'"To every thing there is a season, and a time to every purpose under the heaven",' Alis began. '"A time to keep silence, and a time to speak; a time to—"'

'How dare you come here!'

Startled, she spun round. To her horror Alis saw Blanche de Bruyère sitting on the stone bench in the southern window, holding a letter in her hand.

'I— I meant no harm,' Alis stammered.

'You are supposed to be confined to your quarters.'

'I'm sorry,' Alis babbled, taking small steps backwards. 'I only wanted to see where the musicians—'

'Yet here you are in the chapel,' Blanche said in a hard voice. 'Have you come to pray? Are you a good girl? Do you honour God? Fear God?'

'I don't know,' Alis said, taking another step backwards.

'Come here.'

Alis was too scared to move. She could see Blanche was very angry. Her face was drained of colour and there were dark shadows beneath her eyes. She had loosened the collar of her gown and her forehead was bare and slick with sweat.

'Are you unwell?' The words were out of Alis's mouth before she had a chance to check them.

'How dare you be impertinent. Where is the nurse? Where –'

Blanche tried to stand up, but suddenly she clutched her stomach and fell back to the bench. Alis saw a ribbon of bright red blood trickling down from the stone seat to the floor.

'Are you hurt?'

'Damn you.'

Blanche's curse was lost in cry of pain, then she pressed her hands to her belly as another bloom of red cascaded onto the chapel's stone floor.

No longer caring if she was doing wrong, Alis turned and ran to fetch help.

CHAPTER FIFTY-SIX

⚜

Toulouse

The first explosion was heard at nine o'clock in the evening. The sound echoed briefly through the night air, the rumble of masonry falling, but the charge did little damage. No one was hurt.

Toulouse was holding her breath.

Under the cover of the ten o'clock bells, Captain Saux and a small band of Huguenot soldiers came into Toulouse via the Porte Villeneuve. There were no Catholics waiting to ambush them, only allies and comrades assembled inside the walls. Piet Reydon was among them.

With little noise, they moved through the streets to the heart of the city. Within an hour, they took control of the Hôtel de Ville, taking three capitouls and their staff hostage. Saux decided to set up his campaign headquarters there. No blood was spilt.

Toulouse gave a sigh of relief.

Minou, who had fled back to the Boussay residence in rue du Taur, knew none of this. Her gratitude at discovering the house still deserted had gone, leaving her with a deep sense of dread. There was at least food enough and, when she went down to the cellar, she discovered the barrels of powder, shot and crates of guns had gone. If the house was no longer being used to store weapons, then perhaps Monsieur Boussay would have no reason to return. In truth, she had no way of knowing what the next hours might hold.

Minou sat at the window of her chamber and waited, a watcher in the darkness. She thought of Aimeric, hoping he and Madame Boussay had made it safely to Pech David and that, when she did not arrive, he would remember her orders and head south. There was great danger in the expedition, and her aunt's condition would make it more challenging still, but they were safer away from Toulouse. She wished she had kept the bible with her, but there had been no time.

She thought of Alis, a prisoner for five weeks in Puivert, her mind tortured with the blackest thoughts of her sister terrified and alone, believing she had been abandoned. What if they never found her? What if Alis was already dead? She took a deep breath, fighting the tears that had been threatening ever since she had taken her leave of Piet in the church some six hours ago.

Minou blinked them away. She would not give in.

PUIVERT

'Is she going to die?'

The nurse, stinking of ale and sweat, tried to pull Alis away from the apothecary, who had been summoned from the village. They were standing outside the chamber where Blanche lay sleeping.

Cordier shook his head. 'A scare, that is all. Your mistress must rest.'

'She's not my mistress,' Alis said.

'That'll do,' the nurse said sharply.

Alis tried again. If she could make him listen, might he not take her away with him when he left the castle? 'You don't understand, I'm not a servant. She made me—'

'That's enough,' the nurse said, pinching her. 'Stop your mouth.'

Alis flinched. The nurse was always harsher when she woke after drinking.

The apothecary observed them both with distaste. 'The Lady Blanche has lost a lot of blood,' he said, 'but she is otherwise in good health. If she rests and does not tax herself, there may be no further danger.'

'Are you sure?'

'No one can be sure in such matters.' He ran his tongue over his lips. 'When will her own physician be returning to Puivert?'

Alis suddenly saw the beads of perspiration on his temples and realised he was scared too. Hopes of him helping her faded a little.

'Out of the goodness of her heart, my lady sent him to tend to the priest in Tarascon,' simpered the nurse. 'A hunting injury that is taking too long to heal. She is generous to the clergy serving God within her lands.'

By the way she was speaking, Alis realised it was something the nurse had overheard and hoped to receive credit for repeating. The apothecary waved her words away.

'When is her own physician expected? That is the question I asked you.'

'Tomorrow, maybe the day after. Why should I know?'

'What about the baby?' Alis asked, expecting another pinch. When it didn't come, she understood the nurse also wanted to know but didn't dare ask.

'The baby is alive, I felt it move,' Cordier said, closing his bag in his haste to be gone. 'Everything is in God's hands.'

Knowing this was her last chance, Alis grabbed his sleeve. 'Monsieur, I beg you, take me with you. I was brought here from Carcassonne against—'

The slap knocked Alis almost off her feet.

'My name is Alis Joubert!' she shouted, as a greasy hand was clamped over her mouth.

'She's a silly, spoilt girl, that's what she is,' the nurse said. 'Disobedient. My lady will have something to say about it when she wakes up, mark my words.'

'Domestic matters are none of my business.'

'No, indeed. But I would be grateful if you might mention how valuable my assistance was to you, Monsieur? That it was I who called for you?'

'As I understand it, it was the child who summoned help,' he said coldly, 'and by so doing, perhaps saved her mistress's life. Good day. I will see myself out.'

Toulouse

Minou jolted awake.

For a moment, she didn't know where she was. Not in her bed in their little house in La Cité with roses around the front door. Not in the bookshop in the Bastide. She was cold, sitting on the ground in the dark.

Where was her father? Where were Aimeric and Alis? Piet?

Then, she remembered. It was Tuesday, the twelfth day of May – or was it now Wednesday? She was alone in her aunt and uncle's house in rue du Taur. Everyone else had fled. Minou put her hand to her cheek, and found it was damp with tears.

But something had woken her.

She listened and heard voices in the street below. Her heart started to beat faster. Standing close to the wall, so as not to be noticed, she looked through the casement. A group of men, kerchiefs covering their mouths and noses, were rolling barrels along the street towards the junction with rue du Périgord to form a barricade.

Huguenots or Catholics?

Reason said the former. The university quarter was considered to be a Huguenot enclave. The colleges of Saint-Martial, Sainte-Catherine and Périgord had all been raided for seditious material in the past weeks. Minou turned cold. If so, would they know this for her uncle's house? Would they attempt to break in?

She tried to still her mind, watching as the barricade was stacked higher and higher. Rue des Pénitents Gris was closed off, dividing Piet's lodgings and the stables from the *maison de charité*. Were the residents in the almshouse safe? Piet had told her they were evacuating the residents, but where had they gone? There were said to be some ten thousand Catholic troops mustered in the city, as against fewer than two thousand Huguenots. Though the student bands were well armed, and there were weapons caches in Protestant safe houses, Piet had admitted that the odds were against them. And she remembered the tail-end of a whispered conversation with Aimeric in the carriage as they cantered, fearful, towards the covered bridge.

'But if you love Piet,' he had asked, 'which side are you on? Catholic or Huguenot?'

Standing, watching in the dark from the Boussay house, her brother's question echoed in her head. It was time to choose.

*

Piet and some twenty comrades-in-arms – a few trained soldiers but mostly students and artisans – stood in the shadow of the barricade on rue du Taur. A young man with blond hair was cleaning his gun.

'We must secure Daurade and the area around the Basilica,' the commander said. 'The Porte Villeneuve is protected and we have men ready to take the Matabiau and Bazacle gates. The priority now is to ensure access for Hunault's troops advancing from Lanta.'

'When are they expected?'

Piet glanced at the questioner, the young man with fair hair.

'God willing, by Friday.'

'That's two days hence. Do we have forces enough to withstand until then?'

'We'll have to,' the commander said sharply. 'Meanwhile, Captain Saux is in charge. His orders are that we should concentrate on seizing monasteries and churches, taking their occupants prisoners. He wants as little bloodshed as possible. We are to avoid private houses.'

He paused to let his words sink in. Piet looked at his new band of brothers, their faces lit by the flickering flames from the fire burning in the middle of the blocked street.

'Of course,' he said. 'Our fight is not with ordinary citizens.'

He caught the eye of the young man, who held out his hand.

'Félix Prouvaire.'

They shook. 'Piet Reydon.'

'We have men ready to take the Jacobins and Cordeliers,' the commander continued. 'Each unit to hold its own section. The Couteliers and Daurade districts are well fortified. There are cannons in place on the tower of the Hôtel de Ville.'

'For what purpose?' Piet asked. 'General defence, or is there some specific target?'

The commander met his gaze. 'The great pilgrimage church of Saint-Sernin. If we could destroy it, it would demoralise their troops. Those are my orders.'

Piet opened his mouth to protest, then had second thoughts. It grieved him to think of so magnificent, so ancient a building as the Basilica being destroyed, but what did he expect? That there could be fighting and yet Toulouse would remain untouched?

'Who leads the Catholic troops?' asked Prouvaire.

'We believe it is Raymond de Pavia from Narbonne,' the commander answered. 'Their base is within the Chancery buildings.'

'Parliament has ordered the awnings of all the shops in Place du Salin to be taken down,' Piet said. Then, recalling it was Jasper McCone who had told him, he added, 'It may not be true.'

'Fewer places for us to conceal ourselves,' Prouvaire said.

The commander grunted. 'They want to prevent us being able to muster enough of our troops to besiege Parliament.'

Piet nodded. 'It's also said they have told people to wear white crosses, or paint such upon their doors, so that their troops can identify Catholic households.'

He thought of the notorious words said to have been spoken at the start of the massacre of Béziers, one of the worst atrocities of the crusade against the Cathars. Every boy and girl of the Midi knew them.

'*Tuez-les tous. Dieu reconnaîtra les siens.*'

Some three hundred and fifty years ago, those words had given papal licence to the slaughter of thousands of men, women and children in the space of a few hours. It had been the brutal first step in a conflict that was to last decades and turn the green lands of the Midi red with blood.

Piet sighed. God willing, Toulouse would fall to them as quickly as Orléans had, and with few civilian casualties. If God was on their side, this would not be another Béziers.

The commander finished giving his orders.

'Now, rest. When the sun rises, we must be ready. Prouvaire, you take the first shift. Reydon, you relieve him at six.'

'*Oui, mon capitaine.*'

Piet sat by the fire and tried to sleep. He watched Prouvaire climb to the top of the barricade, musket in his hand, but he couldn't shake the infamous words of the papal legate from his mind.

'*Kill them all. God will know His own.*'

CHAPTER FIFTY-SEVEN

⚜

Puivert

The land surrounding the château de Puivert was in darkness. Pinpricks of light in one or two of the houses in the village below broke the blackness, and the single bobbing lamp of the shepherd minding his flock. There were wild dogs in the hills, becoming bolder by the day, and several animals had been killed.

In the soldiers' mess in the Tour Bossue, a small fire warmed the midnight of the room and the faces of the two men sitting at the table. They were flushed with ale and two empty trenchers spoke of a meal well eaten.

Paul Cordier wiped his fingers on his kerchief, shook the crumbs from his beard and doublet, then sat back.

'Good cheer,' he said.

'The hour is late. You will stay here until daybreak?'

He nodded. 'In case the Lady Blanche has need of my services again, yes.'

Cordier's pleasure at being summoned to the castle had swiftly become fear: if the baby died, would he be blamed? When young Guilhem Lizier, on guard at the main gates, had invited him to stay and share his supper, he had been grateful to accept. His nerves were shaken and, in any case, he had no reason to rush home. He had no wife or child, there was nothing but a cold hearth waiting for him.

'You think the mistress will live?' the boy asked.

Cordier nodded. 'Unless her blood goes bad, which it still might. But her general health is good and the pregnancy has caused her no difficulties until now.'

'What about the child?'

'It is a dangerous time, there's no doubt. If the baby decides to be born now, it would be unlikely to survive. But it's in God's hands.'

Guilhem nodded. 'There are many rumours, Sénher. Hitherto, the Lady Blanche gave her orders in person, but we have not seen her in the lower courtyard for weeks. It is said she is waiting for someone. I have seen her myself at the top of the keep, looking out. Do you observe this behaviour in her?'

The apothecary looked over his shoulder, as if fearing to be overheard. 'I am not one to gossip –'

'Of course not.'

'But this I can say. In her fever, the lady kept saying "he" would be here soon.' He took another gulp of ale. 'Other times, it seemed to be a woman she was expecting.' He shrugged. 'I have no doubt a visitor is expected.'

'It was not the delirium talking?'

'I think not.' He leant further in. 'She was holding a letter in her hand.'

'Who was it from?'

'I could not see and, even if I had, I would not have presumed to look.'

'It is the lady's great good fortune that you were on hand, Sénher Cordier.'

Pleased, Cordier nodded. 'In truth, she was more vexed by her situation than fearful. Most mothers-to-be would worry for their child, for their own health after such a scare, but she never asked a thing. Shows a lack of maternal feeling to my mind but then, what do I know?'

'Hearts of stone, the late Seigneur and her both,' Guilhem said.

The apothecary wondered if the boy was thinking of his aunt, driven to take her own life by the violence visited upon her by the Lord of Puivert. He himself had pulled the Lizier girl from the river Blau. Cordier hoped never to see such a sight again.

'Though truth is,' he slurred, 'whatever the Lady Blanche might say of the matter, if the girl hadn't fetched help when she did, the outcome might have been very different.'

'I thought the child was confined to the logis,' Guilhem said.

'Confined? Why so?'

'The mistress brought her back with her from Toulouse in April. No one knows who she is or what she's doing here.'

'The nurse was rough with her, so I took her for a servant. Then again, the nurse is a sot.' He took another gulp of ale. 'If what you say is right, Guilhem, and the girl was roaming around the castle unchecked, it might explain why the Lady Blanche was in such a rage.' Cordier drained his cup. 'The little one begged me to take her with me, said she didn't belong here. I dismissed it all as fancy at the time.'

'How old is she, think you?'

'Six years of age, perhaps seven? She told me her name.' His brows furrowed deeper into his forehead. 'Alis Joubert, that was it. And I tell you something else for nothing. She said she came from Carcassonne, not Toulouse.'

'Carcassonne?' Guilhem said, refilling their cups in the hope of loosening the apothecary's tongue further.

Cordier was Puivert born and bred. His uncle Achille did not like him, and he was not popular in the village, but he had done their family a good turn in the past and Guilhem was hungry for information. The apothecary was known to trade in other people's secrets. He never missed a thing.

He couldn't wait to lay all this before Bernard. When he finished his lessons, and if there was no one else about to see them, Guilhem had fallen into the habit of staying to talk. He and the prisoner were now on first-name terms, though he still knew little more about his friend or where he had come from. When he last was sent out of the castle on patrol, and had stolen a few hours courting in Chalabre, he had told Jeannette all about his mysterious prisoner.

'I am learning to read and write French,' he now confided to Cordier. 'I want to prove myself worthy of Jeannette's hand.'

The apothecary nodded. 'I heard she had accepted you. Congratulations.'

'We have set the date for August. By then, I hope to be as good at letters as any in Puivert.'

'Who is teaching you?'

Guilhem hesitated, but then why would it matter? Dropping his voice, he told him about the educated man being held in the Tour Bossue, taken for a poacher, and who – like the child – seemed to have been forgotten by everyone.

CHAPTER FIFTY-EIGHT

Toulouse

The killing started at dawn on Wednesday, the thirteenth day of May.

As the sun rose over Toulouse, Catholic soldiers opened fire and killed Huguenot students as they attempted to cut down the rotting corpses of their friends from the gibbets.

At first, the fighting was concentrated in Place Saint-Georges, but it quickly spread to the cathedral quarter and the medieval heart of the city.

The spark was lit.

Huguenot strongholds were established around the Hôtel de Ville and the districts of Villeneuve, Daurade, Couteliers and the university quarter. The Protestants were well armed, but included many artisans and students in their ranks. The Catholic forces were stronger and better trained. They were supported by the Town Guard and several dozen private militias retained by rich Catholic households, outnumbering the Huguenots some ten to one.

A twelve-year-old was lynched for failing to recite his *Ave Maria*. When the boy was proved to be Catholic after all, the mob turned on Protestant shop keepers in Daurade and accused them of provoking the killing. Two Jewish servants in the medieval heart of the city were attacked and their beards ripped out with blacksmiths' tongs. A Catholic maid was raped and left for dead in rue du Périgord.

Blood and bone and dust, order falling into ruins.

By the time night fell, the prisons were already full. Men stripped and beaten, chained to the wall, dragged before the inquisitors in Place du Salin to face invented charges of heresy or treason. In the Hôtel de Ville, Catholic prisoners were bound together and locked inside the council chambers.

In an attempt to deter looters, Catholic families painted white crosses on their doors in the wealthy quarters of the city. They glowed in the moonlight like polished bone.

By dawn on the second day, the numbers of dead ran into many hundreds.

Huguenot civilians who had taken shelter in the mighty Roman sewers that ran into the Garonne were discovered and betrayed to Parliament by their neighbours. Hours later and without warning, huge quantities of water were flushed into the system. Many drowned, swept out into the river and dragged under by the weight of their cloaks and heavy skirts. Old men, and children in their mothers' arms.

Soldiers lined up along the bank and shot at the survivors. The number of dead rose into the thousands.

In the afternoon of Friday the fifteenth of May, all the bookshops around the Palais de Justice were raided and their owners, regardless of allegiance or professed faith, arrested. If they did not agree with the heretics, then why stock material sympathetic to their views?

As the sun began to set, Catholic siege engines were positioned to defend the cathedral quarter. Defences were constructed in rue des Changes, paid for by Pierre Delpech himself, to protect the financial heart of the city. Whichever side won, he was in profit. His weapons killed without discrimination.

On the barricades in rue du Taur, Piet watched with despair as the bombardment of the Basilica of Saint-Sernin began.

Minou remained within the Boussay house. Like a spirit in an old story, she moved unseen from room to empty room. The street remained blocked three quarters of the way along. She watched the palisade being reinforced with wooden chests, tables and chairs.

Occasional shots were fired.

She ate a little and, from time to time, drifted into a light sleep. The cupboards were bare and the fine linen stripped from the family chambers on the first floor, making it clear the departure of the household had been long planned. Had their uncle intended to abandon them to whatever horrors lay ahead? Was that why he had not immediately sent men after them when he recovered consciousness and found them gone?

All that night and the early hours of the next day, Minou heard sounds of battle getting closer. Silence, followed by bursts of shouting and cannon shot. As the temperature rose, the sickly smell of rotting bodies filled the air.

At dusk, fires lit the night from the direction of Place Saint-Georges and a relentless thud of battering rams against the northern walls could be heard.

There was nowhere to flee.

From her lookout, Minou soon noticed that there were in fact others in her neighbourhood, hiding like her, in their houses until the fighting drove them into the streets.

The first to come seeking refuge was the old bookseller from rue des Pénitents Gris. From her lookout on the first floor, she saw him stagger bewildered onto the steps of the church. Had his shop been ransacked? Was he fleeing Catholic soldiers or Protestant looters?

Minou opened the gates and let him inside.

Piet helped the messenger climb over the barricade, then sent Prouvaire to fetch their commander.

Piet had returned to the barricade at dusk, having gone to inspect the districts north and west of the Basilica. He had come back via the *maison de charité*. The almshouse buildings bore evidence of recent looting. Wandering through the empty rooms, he wondered who had taken in the refugees when they left here. From his childhood, he knew how quickly men hardened their hearts. When first his mother became sick, people had helped. But as the weeks passed and their money ran out, they were forced to move on, and on again. In her last days, it was only the English nuns in the Protestant convent in Amsterdam, refugees themselves, who had found a bed for a destitute woman and her young son. Every other door had been closed to them.

Piet pressed a cup into the messenger's hand. 'What can you tell us?'

'I've come from Place du Salin. Raymond de Pavia, leader of the Catholic troops from Narbonne, intends to launch an attack on rue du Taur at first light tomorrow.'

'Cavalry or foot soldiers?' asked Prouvaire.

'I don't know. He has both under his command.'

There had been no concerted attempt yet to breach their barricade, though it was only a matter of time. Piet had hoped they could hold out until Hunault arrived with his troops. Too many in the Huguenot ranks were, like Prouvaire, students not soldiers. Without the men promised from the Lauragais and

Montauban, there was no hope of them holding the university quarter, let alone advancing into Catholic-controlled areas.

Their commander appeared at their side. 'What news?'

'Nothing good.'

The commander heard the messenger's report, then turned to Piet. 'And what more can you tell me, Reydon? What's the situation to the north?'

'I found out what I could. The streets are unsafe and many of our safe havens no longer accessible. Our tavern is behind the Catholic cordon. Saux's men still have the Matabiau and Villeneuve gates, but the Porte du Bazacle has fallen. Most of the gates to the east of the city are also in Catholic hands.'

'So even if Hunault's army does arrive soon, access to the city is compromised.'

'I would say access now – without being sighted – is nigh on impossible.'

Piet saw his commander's shoulders sag.

'And what of the rumour that Saux tried to negotiate a ceasefire last evening,' he asked. 'Is that true?'

Piet nodded. 'It seems to be. The story is he was given safe passage to parley with Delpech. They failed to agree terms and Saux withdrew to the Hôtel de Ville.'

'The advantage is all on their side.' Prouvaire shrugged. 'What need do they have to agree to a truce?'

'Saux is said to believe there are more than a thousand dead already,' Piet replied, steel in his voice. 'Not only soldiers, but women and children. In my opinion, he underestimates the numbers slaughtered. There has been widespread looting and atrocities unconnected with any fighting. A settling of old scores.'

The commander shook his head. 'And they intend to attack us tomorrow.'

'I believe so.'

'Then we are on our own,' Prouvaire said.

'What are your orders, sir?' Piet asked.

'Reinforce the barricades,' the commander said grimly. 'We shall be ready for them.'

In the grey hour just before dawn, Minou was jolted awake by the sounds of wooden wheels on cobbled stones.

Still half asleep, she ran to the window. At first glance, nothing had changed. The barricade three quarters of the way up the street was quiet and there was not a soul about. Minou thought of Piet. Was he at the *maison de charité* or fighting to defend the city he loved, manning some barricade? And what of her family? Were Aimeric and their aunt safely on their way to Puivert? How fared her little sister?

As always, when she thought of Alis, Minou shut the doors on her imagination. The pictures her mind painted were too painful to bear.

Then, from the chapel below, Minou heard a child crying. She took a grim pleasure in the fact that her uncle's house had become a place of refuge for so many: Protestants as well as Catholics. Women, children, old men of tolerance and learning. When – if – Boussay returned, she hoped the spirits of all those who had passed through the house would haunt him.

Minou set her shoulders, then prepared herself to face the challenge of the day ahead. Though there was wine and a little ale, they were now very low on food. Was it possible that there was still bread in Toulouse? Meat? Fruits? In other parts of the city, might the bakers and butchers and cheese makers still be working? Did she dare venture outside the house? She sighed. Even if there was still food within the city, everything would be requisitioned for the armies. Thousands of soldiers needed to be fed.

Minou suddenly remembered her mother telling her the story of Raymond-Roger Trencavel and the siege of Carcassonne in the Cathar times. The blistering heat, the wells running dry, not enough food for those packed cheek by jowl into the narrow streets. Below the city walls, on the banks of the Aude, Simon de Montfort and his Catholic soldiers bathing in the cool river water, eating and drinking their fill while La Cité was starved into surrender.

How was it that, in more than three hundred and fifty years, so little had changed? So much suffering, such waste and cruelty. And for what?

Minou shook her head, then headed downstairs to the kitchens to see what could be done.

As the sun came up and the mighty dome of the Basilica shone against the pale blue sky, the bombardment began once more.

Rocks and stones rained down on the streets surrounding the pilgrims' shrine, sending tiles hurtling from the roofs in rue du Périgord, a splintering and shattering of glass, blasting holes in windows and the red-brick walls. A stray spark, caught by the wind, set light to a pile of dried leaves. The flames licked up one side of the almshouse, charring the sun-baked timber beams.

Soon, the whole building was burning.

Piet saw the flames, and realised that all he had worked for as a way to honour his mother's memory was being destroyed. The money he had tricked out of Crompton and Devereux in

Carcassonne for the counterfeit Shroud was all wasted now. But he kept his position, eyes trained on the street ahead. Waiting. He could sense it on his skin, the short hairs on the back of his neck, the taste and smell of battle approaching. Prouvaire stood beside him, tense and ready, as once Michel Cazès had been his comrade-in-arms. All along the barricade, he heard the sound of muskets being prepared, hands testing the strength of swords, the tightening of belts and gloves, adjusting helmets.

Waiting.

As the sun came around, and the first rays touched the façade of the Eglise Saint-Taur, Piet heard the sound of hooves on the cobbles, the snort and whinny of horses. A unit of cavalry, in full battle armour, appeared at the far end of the street. Light glinting on silver helmets, feathers dancing in the air, the livery of Narbonne on the cloth beneath their saddles. They stood six abreast, the heavy animals jittering and plunging, their solid haunches blocking the light from the street.

The battle cry went up and the charge began.

'France! France!'

The cavalry came thundering along rue du Taur towards them.

Piet took aim and fired. His first shot hit a lancer in the shoulder, finding the gap between armour and breastplate. The lancer's pike flew out of his hand and his horse reared, sending him down to the ground to be pounded by hooves and iron. Piet reloaded, and fired again. And again.

'To your left!' Prouvaire shouted.

Piet swung round. Two soldiers were attempting to push into place a flaming siege engine to set the barricade alight. Prouvaire fired and one went down, but the heavy oak machine kept trundling forward.

Desperate to prevent it reaching the barricade, Piet fired

again, but the flames were already licking the timber frames of the houses and catching at the wooden layers of the palisade. A gush and shattering, as the heat found glass and an oil lamp, and the far end burst into wild fire. Women and children ran screaming out into the street to escape the inferno. Someone was shouting for sand or earth, anything to dampen the flames, but it was too late.

In their panic, the civilians ran towards the soldiers. Piet saw an old man punched through with a sword, front to back, dead before he reached the ground. Piet reloaded and fired again, but could no longer get a clear shot. He felt powerless to prevent the bloodshed, watching sickened as a woman clutching a child in her arms was slashed across the throat. Crimson blood pumped bright red from her neck, soaking the white bonnet of her screaming baby.

Minou was watching the carnage from her lookout as the horror unfolded. Saw the houses at the end of the street begin to burn. Saw the civilians being driven out by the fire into the roaring street, and couldn't stay still a moment longer.

She had to help. She had to do something. Taking the stairs two by two, she rushed downstairs and out across the courtyard to the gates. She didn't know if the civilians were Catholic or Protestant, only that they were now trapped between the barricade, the fire and the lances and swords of the cavalry. Aware she might be about to risk the lives of everyone inside for the sake of those trapped in the street, she dragged the wooden bar from its fixings and opened the pedestrian door.

'Here,' she cried. 'In here.'

In the mêlée, only a few heard her voice over the screaming and shouting. Gathering their children, they ran towards her. One soldier saw what was happening and pulled his horse round to come after them. Another shot rang out from the barricade, and he spun in his saddle, blood coursing from his thigh.

'Hurry!' Minou shouted, dragging in as many as she could through the gate. 'Get inside. *Vite.*'

Finally, there seemed to be no more. With shaking arms, Minou levered the wooden bar back into place, then took her latest refugees into the safety of the Boussay house.

The attack continued, but Raymond de Pavia's men were being pushed back. Their heavy armour inhibited the cavalry's movement. As the sunlight crossed rue du Taur, the order was given to withdraw.

Piet slumped against the barricade, exhausted. On the ground below him, two of his own comrades – friends now – lay dead, and three others wounded. Prouvaire was unscathed, save for a burnt hand where he had struggled to put out the fire.

On the street in front of the barricade, the cobblestones ran red. Blackened scorch marks defaced the brick walls of the burnt-out houses. The air was heavy with the smell of blood and flesh, powder shot and fire.

A bay stallion lay on the ground beside its dead rider, its black eyes wild with pain and distress. It struggled to get to its feet, but its belly was ripped open, like the seam on a piece of cloth. Each time it moved the wound widened. The animal's desperate bellowing grew louder as its flesh unfolded pink against the bloodied brown of its coat.

'Cover me,' Prouvaire said. 'It's not right to let it suffer.'

Piet watched him jump down from the barricades with a thin blade in his hand. He crouched and made his way to the wounded animal. He ran his hand along the animal's neck, whispering until the horse became still. Then, gently and with care, he delivered a sharp upward thrust and slipped the knife straight into its heart. The horse shuddered, as if shaking water from its coat, then lay still.

'I grew up on a farm,' Prouvaire said, when he climbed back to safety. 'I couldn't leave it in such pain.' He wiped his hands, then his eyes. 'Will they be back?'

'The cavalry? I doubt it,' Piet said. 'The street is too narrow for them to be effective and their losses were worse than ours. But infantry, yes. They will want to re-establish access to the Basilica.'

'So, we wait?'

'We wait,' he said.

Prouvaire waved his arm. 'When I was down there, I heard the almshouse in rue du Périgord had burnt down, but with no casualties. That's something, is it not?'

Piet glanced at him, wondering if he was aware he had a particular interest in the place. 'It was evacuated on Tuesday evening,' he said. 'It's a known Huguenot refuge, so would have been a target.'

Prouvaire nodded. 'Do you think, there are any other civilians left in the district?'

'Those that escaped the fire, I think, took shelter at a house further along the street. Hard by the church, I couldn't see which one.'

For a moment, rue du Taur was silent. Then, like a rumble of dry thunder in the mountains, a bombardment began again somewhere else in the city.

When Minou had finished dressing the wounds of the new arrivals and had allocated everyone somewhere to rest, she went back to her lookout at the top of the house.

She could see the Huguenots shoring up the barricade, preparing for the next attack. From the ruined houses, they carried tables and chests that had survived the fire, rolling out more barrels and filling them with earth. She wondered how much longer they would be able to hold out.

The final attack came at eight o'clock in the evening.

The harsh voice of a trumpet, then the standard-bearer of Raymond de Pavia and a battalion of foot soldiers marched into rue du Taur and took position in front of the barricade.

'They have a cannon,' Prouvaire muttered, seeing the cart wheeled into place. 'There's a hundred or more of them.'

'Take them one at a time,' Piet said, reloading his musket.

This time, their opponents' tactic seemed to be to try to pull down the barricade. Grappling hooks were hurled up to the top of the wooden walls, quicker than they could be cut down, scaling ladders too.

'Take cover!' Piet shouted, as the cannon fired into the heart of their defences, blasting a hole the width of a man, and the first of Raymond de Pavia's soldiers swarmed through.

Piet threw his gun to one side – there would be no time to load and reload – and drew his sword.

'*Courage, mes amis.*'

At his side, Prouvaire also raised his sword. 'Ready.'

Piet nodded. '*Per lo Miègjorn,*' he roared, the battle cry of Raymond-Roger Trencavel at the siege of Carcassonne. 'For the Midi.'

With a shout, they charged forward into the street, cutting their way through the forces coming towards them. Lances and swords, the cannon recoiling back on its cart with a heavy thud. Beside Piet, a student was shot in the chest, his thin body thrown up into the air from the barricade, knocking Prouvaire off balance. He lost his concentration, only for a moment, but long enough for an attacker to stab at him with a lance. Piet watched Prouvaire try to raise his sword in defence, but he had no strength in his arm. He took a second blow, this time in his side, and went down.

Piet ran to him, put his hands under Prouvaire's shoulders, and dragged him out of the line of fire. Rue du Périgord was blocked and there was no way through to his own lodgings. His only choice was to try the house further up rue du Taur where the civilians had fled, not far from where Minou's aunt and uncle resided.

'Leave me,' Prouvaire was saying. 'There's more to be done.'

'I'll see you safe first.'

As they stumbled out of hiding, one of de Pavia's soldiers launched himself on them from behind. Prouvaire was now barely conscious, a dead weight in his arms, but Piet managed to land a blow on his assailant, cutting his hand. The soldier shouted and jumped back out of reach as Piet prepared to strike again.

Using the whole of his weight, Piet heaved against the wooden legs of the burnt-out siege engine, pushing against it with his shoulder once, twice, a third time. The structure teetered on its wheels, then went over, trapping their attacker on the far side.

He did not look back. Picking Prouvaire up in his arms, he staggered along the street – he prayed to safety.

There was a hammering on the gates. Minou spun round. More civilians seeking refuge, or soldiers?

'They're going to break in,' the old bookseller babbled. 'They'll kill us all.'

'Monsieur, hush,' Minou said, with more confidence than

she felt. 'We are a household of women, old men and infants. Even if it is the soldiers, I do not believe they will slaughter civilians in cold blood.'

'But if they are looters come to take—'

'Go back to the chapel and blockade the door,' she said. 'And, forgive me, Monsieur, but please control your tongue. You will spread panic. For the sake of the children, try to remain calm.'

This was the moment of reckoning. She would either succeed in pleading their case and they would be spared, or she would not.

It was in God's hands now.

Minou felt a stillness go through her. A pure, untrammelled, fear. Yet her heart was beating a steady rhythm and her palms were dry. She pictured Aimeric and Alis squabbling in the kitchen in rue du Trésau and Madame Noubel sweeping her steps, Charles talking to the clouds and all their other friends and neighbours who had filled her life. Then she thought of all those sheltering here and in the *maison de charité*, put from their homes by the hatred of others.

She thought of Piet.

Piet was staggering under the weight. Blood was gushing from the wound in Prouvaire's side, red turning to black. Piet's breeches were soaked.

Confused, he looked up at the gates with the Boussay crest carved into the wood. Piet would have sworn this was where the fleeing civilians had been taken in, but would such a man as Boussay give sanctuary to Huguenots?

Had he mistaken the house?

Piet looked down. He saw a child's bonnet, lying caught in the doorjamb, and remembered the woman fleeing from the barricades with her child in her arms. A white bonnet spotted with ash and blood. This had to be the place.

He kicked at the gate with his boot. 'I need help. Someone. For mercy's sake, let us in.'

Standing in the courtyard, Minou heard the harsh sounds of the battle even more clearly. The clash of swords, the fear in men's voices, the screaming.

Then, in the silence between, the sound of knocking and a voice.

'Is somebody there? I have a man injured. He needs help.'

Minou could barely make out the words over the renewed cacophony of battle outside.

'Please, I beg you. Let us in.'

Minou put her eye to the spy hole and saw a soldier, his face covered by his visor, holding a fair-headed man in his arms. There was a gash in his shoulder, in which a fragment of lance was embedded, and the entire left side of his body was drenched with blood.

'Please. Whoever you are, will you let us in?'

Students from the barricade, Minou realised; the injured boy was the one who had put the horse out of its misery. She no longer hesitated, but quickly removed the bar, unlocked the gate.

'My thanks,' the soldier muttered as he stumbled in. 'He's hurt badly.'

He laid his wounded comrade carefully on the ground, before sitting back on his haunches and removing his helmet.

Minou's eyes widened. 'Piet.'

His head shot up, her shock now mirrored in his face. '*Jij weer.* It's you, Minou. But how?'

She grasped his hand. 'Our carriage was stopped at the

bridge. To make sure Aimeric and my aunt got away, I ran back into the city.'

'I cannot believe you are here,' he said.

'I couldn't think of anywhere else to go. There was no one at the almshouse.'

A moment of stillness and calm in the chaos, then Minou smiled. For despite everything, Piet was here in front of her. Battle worn and bloodied, but here.

CHAPTER FIFTY-NINE

⚜

As the hours passed, the air in the Boussay chapel grew stale. More had come seeking sanctuary and Minou could not find it in herself to turn anyone away.

The bells rang out for midnight, then for one o'clock, two. Minou carried on working, administering what tonics and medicines remained, dressing wounds with whatever came to hand, until her eyes ached and her hands were caked hard with blood. Though Piet was at her side, for the most part they laboured in silence.

Prouvaire's injuries were serious. He had been struck several times. His left shoulder was broken and a pike had pierced his flank, shattering several of his ribs. Minou feared he had lost too much blood and the risk of infection was high, but she kept trying.

'How goes it with you, Monsieur?' she asked, as the first fingers of light started to pierce the darkness of the night.

He tried to answer, but words were abandoning him. Minou lifted the cloth that covered his fighting arm, then let it drop again. She had bandaged his crushed shoulder, but blood was ebbing steadily through the muslin, turning the dressing red.

'This will help,' she said, dropping a pearl of valerian between his lips to ease the pain.

For the next few hours, Prouvaire drifted in and out of consciousness. Minou kept returning to him, monitoring the plash of his breathing in his chest. But each time, there was a little less colour in his face.

QUARTIER SAINT-CYPRIEN

From the far bank of the river Garonne, Vidal watched Toulouse burn.

'It was Parliament that ordered Place Saint-Georges to be set alight, Monsignor,' Bonal said. 'They felt our losses were too heavy in that district. Better that it was destroyed than taken by the enemy.'

Vidal gave a thin smile. 'But then the wind changed direction, so Catholic property was also destroyed. Yes, I see.'

He pressed his fingers together, not dissatisfied by the turn of events. The greater the chaos, the better for his ambitions in the longer term. All he had to do was be patient.

'And the bishop has been asking for you,' Bonal added.

Vidal opened the casement. From the safety of their quarters in the fortified suburb of Saint-Cyprien, the skyline of Toulouse burning on the far side of the river had turned the dark of the night to fiery day.

'Has he indeed. Then it is regrettable that, in these dangerous conditions, his summons did not find me. Since there is nothing more to be done here – and I would not wish for the bishop to think I was ignoring his commands – we will leave Toulouse tonight.'

'For Carcassonne, Monsignor?'

'No. After their carriage was stopped at the bridge, the Joubert girl fled back into the city. She might survive, she might not. Either way, there is no need for us to go to Carcassonne at this point.'

'What if she does have the Shroud?'

Vidal closed the window. Even though it was late and the air cooler, the stench of the dead and dying lying untended within the city walls could be clearly smelt on their side of the Garonne.

'God will keep the Shroud safe from harm, if He wishes it. The matter is in His hands. It is not what I wanted, but the counterfeit is fine enough to deceive most, and those who know it to be a copy are either dead or cannot speak out.'

'Like Reydon.'

Vidal nodded. 'Who might, by now, also be dead.'

An image of Blanche, the last time he had seen her, came into Vidal's mind. He smiled. Her absence had strengthened his resolve. He would resist carnal temptation, but was it not right, after all she had done for him – and would surely do in the future – that he should tend to her spiritual needs? That he should offer comfort and guidance in the safety of the château?

'Prepare the horses. We leave for Puivert.'

By five o'clock in the morning, most of the refugees were sleeping. Minou and Piet stole out into the courtyard and sat side by side, their backs against the rail of the loggia. From the quartier Daurade, the sounds of the bombardment continued and the fires in Place Saint-Georges were still burning, but the streets around the Basilica had fallen quiet.

'There is some news I should have given you earlier,' Piet said, 'but in my concern for Prouvaire, I forgot it.'

'What is it?'

'It's your uncle,' he said. 'He was one of those taken hostage in the Hôtel de Ville at the beginning of the battle. Captain Saux agreed to release the women and children who were being held, but not the men. Your uncle tried to leave with them. When he was discovered, he attempted to steal the guard's sword. I'm afraid he was killed, Minou.'

Minou sat with her hands in her lap. 'I am glad of it,' she said eventually, 'though it is unchristian of me to say so. My aunt suffered greatly at his hands. I will not pretend to mourn his passing.'

In the hours since his arrival with Prouvaire, Minou and Piet had spoken only of the needs of the present moment. Now, knowing they were on stolen time, they began to talk of everything that had happened since their parting in the church in rue Saint-Taur on the eve of the battle: he told her of how Vidal had been waiting in his lodgings and McCone's treachery; she told him how she had been forced to give the Shroud into Aimeric's safekeeping at the bridge, about the letters withheld from her by Madame Montfort. Finally, about Alis held hostage in the mountains.

'The idea of subjecting an innocent child to such unkindness, I cannot comprehend it. Alis is so young, so fragile. Her lungs are weak. The thought of her alone, without the medicines she needs . . .' Minou broke off and struggled to compose herself. 'But I will find her and take her home. My father's second letter informed me he had gone there, too. God willing, Aimeric will arrive safely in Puivert and they will find one another.'

Piet's head snapped up. 'Puivert?'

She turned to look at him. 'You know it?'

'I know of it.'

'The ransom letter was signed in the name of Blanche de Bruyère.'

Piet was frowning. 'Vidal served as a priest-confessor to a noble family in the Haute Vallée. I wonder if it might be the same woman. It is widely believed that Vidal – Valentin – intends to be the next Bishop of Toulouse. They say he has a powerful and wealthy benefactress supporting his suit.'

Minou thought for a moment. 'But how does that have anything to do with Alis? With me? Even if it is the same woman, are these things connected?'

'The only way to find out is to go there.'

'You intend to come with me?'

He smiled. 'Since you have given the Shroud into Aimeric's keeping, and since he is headed for Puivert, what choice do I have?' His face grew serious. 'Besides, you cannot think I would allow you to make such a journey alone?'

She raised her eyebrows. 'Allow?'

'Want, wish, desire, allow, what does it matter? I'm coming.'

Minou felt a lightness come over her. For a moment, she forgot her newly acquired responsibilities and her aching back. She no longer heard the constant noise of suffering and bombardment and shot. Instead, she was riding across the plains of the Lauragais, the peaks and crests of Canigou and Soularac in the distance.

Too soon, the image faded and Minou was back in the courtyard of her aunt's house, the smell of death and ash and a city in ruins. She took Piet's hand, and he put his arm around her shoulder and drew her towards him.

'Close your eyes,' he said. 'Put everything and everyone from your mind. All this misery and slaughter, the good you are doing here, your love for your family. For a moment, think only of yourself. Imagine you were free to go anywhere or do anything. Now, tell me Minou, what do you see?'

For a moment, she was silent.

'A library,' she said quietly. 'Myself at a desk. If I had the liberty to choose, without the restrictions placed upon me by my sex, I would study. Yes. Here at the university in Toulouse, or Montpellier. I would keep my candle burning all night, without a care to the cost. I would read and read, with no care to the strain upon my eyes. I would learn to debate and to think, to . . . well, such things will never happen.'

Piet cupped her face in his hands. 'Isn't this what we are fighting for? The right to want change or to be allowed to do things in a different way, our way.'

'This is a war of faith.'

'A war of faith is always about more than faith,' he said. 'And why shouldn't women study? In our temple, women are encouraged to read, to speak out. The best minds, without prejudice.'

Minou laughed. 'If this is what Huguenots preach, no wonder many are drawn to your ranks.'

Piet flushed. 'It might be that I make freer with my own opinions than reflecting common Protestant thinking, yet I still believe history will prove me right.'

'We'll see.' She leant forward and kissed him, knowing that whatever did happen in the hours ahead she would not want to exchange a single moment of this night.

'Mademoiselle?' A child was standing in the doorway beckoning to Minou. 'It's the student, Prouvaire. He's worsening.'

Minou and Piet scrambled to their feet and went back into the chapel. She bent down beside Prouvaire, listened to the plashing in his chest, then looked up at Piet and shook her head.

'His lungs are filled with blood. We did all we could, but his injuries were too bad. It won't be long now.'

Piet knelt down beside him. 'I'm here, friend.'

Prouvaire opened his eyes.

'Is that you, Reydon?'

'I'm here.'

'What if we are wrong? What if there is nothing waiting for us on the other side? Only darkness?'

'God is waiting for you,' Minou said. 'He is waiting to bring you home.'

'Ah . . .' he said, the word slipping between his lips like a sigh. 'Would that it was all true. Such wondrous, wondrous stories . . .'

His face drained of colour and his eyes flickered shut.

'He's gone,' Minou said, gently placing a kerchief over his face. 'I am sorry.'

Piet bowed his head and said a prayer.

'Does he have family?' she asked. 'Is there anyone we should tell?'

'No. His family were his fellow students at the Collège de l'Esquile. They are either fled or dead, like him.'

'What is going to happen to us?' Minou said, looking around at the huddled groups of women and children and old men. 'What's going to happen to them? Even if the fighting stops, they have lost everything. Their homes, their possessions, everything.'

Piet shrugged. 'The killing will continue until the talking starts. Tomorrow, or the day after that, or the day after that.'

'There will be a truce?'

He nodded. 'There were too few of us, they were better armed and prepared. We were fighting for the right to be left in peace, but –'

'By attempting to take the city, you became the aggressors not the defenders.'

Piet smiled.

'Why do you look at me so?' Minou asked. 'Is that not what you were going to say?'

'It was exactly what I was going to say, and that's why I'm smiling. This is the argument I had with Vidal, with my comrades in Carcassonne, in the taverns here in Toulouse. Only Michel Cazès understood. He said that if we took up arms in attack, we would lose.'

'Will you return to the barricade?'

'One last stand?' Piet said. 'No. Our commander is a good man. I have no doubt he will negotiate and lay down his arms. He knows it is pointless to continue.'

'Will you return to the almshouse?'

He shook his head. 'It's razed to the ground. Everything is gone.'

'Oh, Piet.'

'With no loss of life, we must be thankful for that.'

'Then, what?'

He looked her in the eye. 'If you are prepared to leave the safety of this house, Minou, then I will find a way to take you across Toulouse and away. If you will let me.'

She met his gaze. 'To Puivert?'

'Yes, but it will be dangerous. Many are being slaughtered outside the walls, as within the city, as they attempt to leave.'

'Alis needs me,' she said simply. 'My father and Aimeric also. I would rather try to reach them, and fail, than stay here and do nothing.'

What Minou did not say – for fear of sounding sentimental or assuming more than Piet might want to give – was that she would rather die at his side than be parted from him again.

'There is someone who can take charge of the house?' Piet asked, cutting into her thoughts.

Minou nodded. 'The bookseller from rue des Pénitents Gris. He is old, and not a man of courage, but he has a care for his neighbours, Catholic and Huguenot.'

'I know him. A good choice. He will take no risks.' He exhaled. 'We agree, then? We must attempt to get out of the city?'

Minou swallowed hard. 'We are agreed.'

The ceasefire between Catholic and Huguenot forces came after six hours of vicious fighting on Saturday, 16th May. Antoine de Resseguier from the Parliament acted as mediator between Captain Saux for the Protestants and Raymond de Pavia, commander of the Catholic troops.

Toulouse was exhausted. Whole districts were burnt to the ground or left in rubble. The city was a charnel house, more than four thousand left dead, massacred in the streets or in their beds. The air was black with flies. Corpses floated down the river Garonne.

By then, Minou and Piet were gone. Stealing out of the Boussay house at first light, creeping past the blackened shell of the *maison de charité*, she spied the broken body of Madame Montfort, her clothes torn and her eyes blank to the world, still clutching a few fragments of stolen jewellery to her chest.

Minou averted her eyes from the suffering as they travelled on to the Porte Matabiau to the north of the city, one of only two gates remaining under Huguenot control.

Too many dead. Too many souls to pray for.

As the terms of the truce were being negotiated, Minou and Piet were already at Pech David agreeing a price for two horses capable of covering the distance between the Lauragais and the mountains. Piet had a few coins, and Minou some trinkets taken from the Boussay house.

By the time the sun set that night, as Mass was being said in the Carmelite church for the deliverance of Toulouse back into Catholic hands, Minou and Piet were crossing the boundary of the lands of the Lauragais into the hills of the Razès.

Following the old Cathar trail, they rode south, passing other refugees on the road. Bedraggled columns of oxen and carts, traps loaded high with meagre possessions, Huguenots fleeing Catholic troops and neighbours who had once been friends.

When their horses could go no further, Minou and Piet stopped. In the silence and deep blackness of the night, where there was no one to see them, they fell asleep in one another's arms.

PART THREE

PUIVERT

Summer 1562

CHAPTER SIXTY

⚜

PUIVERT
Wednesday, 20th May

The altar candles, flickering either side of the silver crucifix, shone a pool of light over the white cloth.

Blanche bowed her head, her glossy black hair falling forward across her face as she recited the act of contrition.

'God, I am heartily sorry for having offended You, and I detest all my sins because I dread the loss of heaven and the pains of hell; but most of all because they offend You, Lord, who are good and deserving of all my love. I firmly resolve with the help of Your grace to confess my sins, do penance, and to amend my life.'

She felt a pressure on the top of her head as the priest gave her the blessing, then his hand on her elbow helping her to her feet.

'Amen.'

Carefully, as if she was a priceless and fragile creature, Vidal guided her to the stone bench. The servants had scrubbed, and scrubbed, but the dark lines of dried blood were still visible between the cracks.

'How goes it, lady?' he said.

'The better for having you at my side, Monsignor,' she replied, dropping her eyes. 'I have missed your wise counsel these weeks.'

Blanche let him take her hand. 'I would that I had been here sooner. To think of what you have suffered – and with no one at your side.'

'I put my trust in God,' she said piously. 'This is His will. That He saw fit to save me, and to spare our child, I am blessed.'

Vidal moved his hand to her belly and the baby moved. Blanche thought it a disgusting sensation, but she was pleased at the power it conferred on her. Last time she had been with child, fifteen years ago when she was no more than a child herself, it had been different. Of course, it would have been impossible to hide her condition from him now. The moment he arrived at Puivert, she had confessed. His pride was immediate, he could not have been more solicitous. All the same, Blanche detected a measure of distaste when he touched her.

To her surprise, he had expressed no concern about his reputation. Many Catholic priests had clandestine families. Provided they lived quietly, there was no reason for anyone to object. Then again, Vidal was preoccupied with his own legacy. He was ambitious for power and wealth in this world, yes, but he also wanted his memory to live on after he had gone. A son, bearing his name, would give him something of the immortality he craved.

Blanche's remaining problem was Minou Joubert. Even if the Will was never found, the precariousness of her own claim to the estate had been laid bare. The child she was carrying might be born dead, might not survive past infanthood. And if she gave birth to a girl, the title of Seigneur of Bruyère and Puivert would not be hers.

Minou Joubert had to die.

'Do you think Piet Reydon survived the siege?' she asked.

'Impossible to say. He is clever and shrewd, he knows Toulouse well, but the fighting was fierce. Whole districts were destroyed and one cannot blame pious Catholics for seeking vengeance for the horrors visited upon the city by the Huguenot attack.'

'The Joubert girl fled back into the city too?'

'Yes. The sentries recognised her by her mismatched eyes, one blue and one brown.'

'She must be found, do you agree?'

'I have people searching for them both. If they are still within the city, and alive, my orders are for her and Reydon to be held until I return. I will interrogate them myself. Experience has taught me to be wary of the heavy-handedness of certain inquisitors.'

'You are convinced Reydon handed the Shroud into her safekeeping?'

'He commissioned the copy to be made, he sold the counterfeit to the Huguenots of Carcassonne, he kept the original and, yes, I believe, on the eve of the attack, he retrieved it and gave it to Minou Joubert.'

He paused and Blanche, recognising his thoughtful expression, wondered what new scheme he was considering.

'There is something that might be done in the interim,' he began. 'It is an excellent replica. Few would know it to be false and—'

'Tell me.' Blanche nodded her encouragement. 'I would help in any way that I can.'

Vidal's hand hovered over her, but this time he withdrew it without touching her.

'You understand I am thinking solely of what is better for our Mother Church and the devout Catholics of Toulouse. So many were murdered, or forced to witness the destruction of their holiest icons.'

'It is the greatest tragedy.'

'With that in mind, it could be said that at this moment in time it would be of great value to the common people if they believed the true Shroud had been found. It would be a sign of our deliverance. I made a vow to return it to its reliquary in the Eglise Saint-Taur. Its miraculous properties are beyond compare and I shall, of course, continue to search. But in the meantime –'

'I understand.' Blanche smiled. 'In the meantime, for the comfort of your flock, you might do this kindness and put the substitute in its place.'

'If they think the Shroud has been found and see it returned to its rightful home, it would be a sign that God was on our side.'

'It would be a simple matter, as soon as you do have the true Shroud in your possession, to effect an exchange. No one need know.'

'No one *would* know.'

Blanche looked at him, his face in shadow and the rogue streak of white hair almost silver in the candlelight. She wondered if his manoeuvring had been as sure-footed as he claimed. He had made little secret of his ambitions. What if the current bishop had taken steps to block him?

Time would tell.

'It is an excellent idea, Monsignor,' she said.

Alis heard the bell in the village striking for noon.

Since the incident in the chapel, the nurse had been more careful with her duties. She had moderated the amount of ale she drank, had confiscated Alis's shoes, and the child was locked in the chamber day and night.

But two days ago, the tall priest arrived – she had glimpsed him striding through the upper courtyard – and the household was turned on its head. Lady Blanche had withdrawn to the keep, taking all meals there, with her priest-confessor from Toulouse. No one was allowed to disturb them.

Finally, for the first time in some days, thinking her asleep, the nurse had gone to gossip with the other servants in the kitchens. Alis threw her blankets off, jumped out of bed and ran to the window.

She had given up expecting anyone to save her. It was on her shoulders. She had decided to run away and find a way home to Carcassonne on her own. Or perhaps to Toulouse to find Minou. She hadn't decided. She wasn't sure which city was closer.

Just after sunset, Alis opened the casement and looked out into the dark. It was an awfully long drop to the grass slopes below, and rough stones jutted sharply out from the fortified walls. She wasn't sure she could do it. But then she heard Aimeric's teasing voice in her head, telling her girls were useless, and was determined to prove him wrong.

Alis thought back to all the times she had watched him misbehaving on the battlements of La Cité, begging him to come down before he was caught. He could climb anything from the highest trees on the banks of the Aude to the sheer walls of the barbican below the Château Comtal. So, what would Aimeric do?

Aimeric would pick out the strongest rocks in the wall to anchor his feet and the surest gaps to fix his hands. He would plan in his mind, only then work his way down from the window to the ground. His arms and legs were longer, of course, and he was stronger. But Alis thought she could do it.

In the woods to the north of the château, she heard the screech of an owl out hunting and the baying of a pack of dogs further away towards Chalabre. Alis shut the casement. It was too dangerous to attempt an escape in the dark, but tomorrow?

She would be ready.

'I have one more sin to confess, Monsignor,' Blanche said. 'I pray you will not be angry with me.'

'Angry, how so?' Vidal said.

'I should have confessed to it too, for I know it to be wrong.'

Vidal reached out and raised her chin. 'What have you done?'

'I will accept any punishment or penance you impose.'

'Come, Blanche, let's have no talk of punishment. But, tell me.'

She looked at him meekly. 'You remember I have an interest in the Joubert family.'

'I remember,' he repeated cautiously.

She smiled. 'Suffice to say that, on the strength of my interest, when I took my leave of Toulouse I went to Carcassonne.'

'Yes?'

'I was most keen to make the acquaintance of Minou Joubert and to invite her to Puivert. In order to accomplish this, I brought the younger girl, Alis, back from Carcassonne with me.'

Vidal's expression grew still. 'I see.'

'The child was there alone in La Cité, in the care of a most inadequate servant. I thought she would be happier here.'

'Did anyone see you?'

'I was careful,' Blanche said, injecting as much contrition into her voice as she could. 'I used the carriage of the Bishop of Toulouse, which he had graciously loaned to me.'

'Do you realise what you have done? To take a child against her will?'

'She came willingly enough, though I admit under false pretences. It was only when she realised Minou was not in Puivert waiting for her that she became difficult.'

'Where is she now?'

'In the logis, where do you think? I'm not a monster. There is a nurse with her, though by rights I should have dismissed her. She's a drunkard and allows the girl to roam ungoverned.'

Blanche hesitated, remembering she owed her life to Alis. It was something else she had not told Vidal. So much blood. The voices in her head had warned her not to. They were quiet now.

'I am astonished you took such a risk.'

'There was no risk. No one saw me in Carcassonne, I made sure of it. I wrote to Minou Joubert in Toulouse straight away, but heard nothing in reply. No one here knows the child's name, no one knows who she is.'

'Has it occurred to you that the letter might not have reached her?'

'I sent it in April. Long before the current disturbances.'

'Is that how you describe it! Thousands died.'

Blanche reached out for him, but Vidal shrugged her off.

'*Deus vult*. If God wills it. Isn't that what the Crusaders cried as they attempted to take back the Holy Land from the Infidel? I am only accomplishing His purpose.'

'How long has the child been here?' he asked sharply.

Blanche recoiled, unable to read his mood. 'Don't raise your voice to me.'

'Answer me! How long has the girl been held here?'

'Several weeks,' she said, holding her voice steady. 'I own, it is taking longer than I anticipated. I have soldiers patrolling the local villages, as far away as Chalabre, searching for strangers in the district. In Puivert itself, there are several whose tongues I have bought. When she comes, I shall know it.' She stared at him, her black eyes glinting. 'And Minou Joubert will come for her sister. That I know too.'

The air seemed to crack between them. The flames from the candles sent elongated shadows dancing across the vaulted ceiling, and glinted on the crucifix in the middle of the altar.

Suddenly, Vidal was striding towards her and, despite herself, Blanche's hand went to her belly. She took a step back. Then she felt his hand on the back of her neck and his mouth greedy on her lips.

'You are magnificent,' he said, breaking away. 'If Minou Joubert is alive, she will come to Puivert. And she will bring the Shroud with her. Reydon will follow and, this time, there will be no mistakes. In the meantime, I will speak to the child. She might have more to tell.'

'So, you are pleased with me, my lord? There is no penance to be made?'

'None,' he murmured, easing her chemise from her shoulders. 'We will absolve one another of our sins.'

CHAPTER SIXTY-ONE

⚜

Chalabre

Minou woke before dawn, for a moment not sure where she was. Then she reached out and her hand found Piet, sleeping in their humble, chaste bed of straw, and she remembered.

They had been travelling for three days and nights, resting the horses when they could, sometimes joining other refugees on the road, at other times keeping themselves to themselves. After a day, noticing the sideways glances, Minou had twisted a piece of twine around her ring finger and introduced Piet as her husband. They looked too unalike to be brother and sister.

This barn on the outskirts of Chalabre, on the banks of the river Blau, was the most comfortable place they had yet stayed. Piet had persuaded the farmer to let them rest for the night. He had asked no questions, and they had offered no explanation, but he had sent his daughter Jeannette to offer them fresh milk, bread and slices of salted ham. A pretty, plump girl, she had been glad of their company. As they ate, she talked about her forthcoming marriage to a soldier in the neighbouring village of Puivert, in service at the castle, and of a prisoner who'd been teaching Guilhem to write French words, so they could take over the smallholding from her father.

As Minou listened, she had not been able to stop herself wondering if it was possible that Guilhem's teacher was her father. In the second of the letters Madame Montfort had kept from her, he had written that he was travelling to Puivert. And she remembered how faithful Bérenger, and so many other soldiers of the garrison in La Cité, had come to their little house to learn how to read. Minou tried not to let her imagination run away with her, but in her heart, she felt a spark of hope.

God willing, she would know soon enough.

Careful not to wake Piet, Minou crept quietly out of the barn and down to the river. She splashed her face with the cold water, then cupped her hands and drank. In the distance, she could hear the sound of goats, their bells ringing light in the early morning air. The hillside was dotted with hundreds of tiny meadow flowers, pink and yellow and white, and when she breathed in she caught the scent of wild garlic on the air. It was the most beautiful landscape she'd ever seen and, for a moment, she forgot why she came to be here at all.

Puivert

The bells were striking ten o'clock, a thin single note.

'I tell you, Aunt, that is my father's mare, Canigou,' Aimeric repeated. 'I'd know her anywhere. She has a bald patch on her withers, from an accident when she was a foal.' He pointed. 'Look, can't you see? And grey whiskers around her mouth, like an old lady.'

The old horse was tethered, grazing on common ground at the edge of the village beyond the church, beside a low, white-washed cottage. Two oxen and a small herd of goats in a makeshift wooden pen shared the land.

Madame Boussay looked at him. 'You are quite certain, Nephew?'

'Certain,' he said. 'It's the only horse my father ever owned.'

'Well, then, help me down.'

While Aimeric offered his hand, he marvelled at the change that had come over their goose-brained, chattering aunt.

When they had parted company with Minou at the covered bridge in Toulouse, Aimeric had dreaded being responsible for Madame Boussay. At Pech David, while they waited in vain for Minou to join them, she had been bewildered. Weeping, demanding to be taken back home, terrified of her husband coming after her, making plaintive enquiries about her dead sister.

But although it had been a battle to persuade her into the country carriage-and-pair that Piet had arranged, once they were on their way into the Lauragais, the open land to the south-east of Toulouse, she had become a different person. Like a caged bird offered liberty, Madame Boussay was at first cautious, but then curious. And the light came back into her eyes.

On the second night, they had reached Mirepoix and found a comfortable inn with the money Minou had given him. They remained there for a few days, to allow his aunt's bruises and cuts time to heal. On the third morning, she was awake before him, and she proved to be an amusing and witty companion. He had even taught her Piet's trick with the knife. By the time they set off again – though he was loath to admit it – Aimeric was enjoying being in her company.

'In which case, Nephew,' Madame Boussay said, 'let us go and discover how this gentleman comes to have possession of your father's horse.'

They walked the length of the street and knocked on the door of the white cottage closest to the common land. There was no answer there, so Madame Boussay tried the adjacent house. She rapped sharply on the door.

'Ah. And what might your name be?'

Aimeric could only assume the man was so surprised to find such a finely dressed lady on his step at ten o'clock in the morning that he blurted out his name without question.

'Achille Lizier, Madama.'

'Good morrow, Lizier. This is my nephew, Aimeric Joubert. Now, what I would like to know, is how you come to have possession of my brother-in-law's mare.'

'*Caval*? The horse, Canigou?'

'Told you,' Aimeric said.

'The horse, yes,' Madame Boussay replied. 'It belongs to my brother-in-law.'

'Joubert?' another voice called sharply from inside the house. A young man in guard's livery appeared on the threshold. The family resemblance was evident. 'Joubert, did you say?'

'And you are?' she asked.

'Sorry, Madama. This is my nephew, Guilhem. He is in service in the garrison in the castle, much against my wishes.'

'Uncle,' Guilhem muttered in Occitan.

Madame Boussay took no notice of the interruption. 'You recognise the name Joubert? How so?'

'He looks much like her,' Guilhem replied, gesturing at Aimeric.

'Who looks like me?'

'The lady hasn't come to listen to your gossip, Nephew,' Lizier interrupted, 'she's asking about the horse. Madama, I swear I came by the mare honestly. Back a few weeks, before the spring had rightly come, a man arrived looking for the midwife.'

'The midwife,' Madame Boussay echoed, bewildered.

'Old Anne Gabignaud, who was murdered some weeks ago now. The point is, the gentleman asked me to look after his horse for a few days. Wouldn't say where he was going, only that he'd be back. Haven't seen hide nor tail of him in six weeks. Old mare's been pining.'

'You never told me about this,' Guilhem said.

'When would I, Nephew? You're never here to tell.'

'I can't come and go as I please, Uncle. You know that.'

Aimeric pushed himself forward. 'What do you mean, I look like her? Look like who?'

Guilhem nodded up towards the castle. 'The little girl up there. A mass of black curls, same as you.'

'About seven years old. So high?'

'I'd say taller, but then I've only seen her from a distance. There's no mistaking that hair, though. The apothecary saw her when he was called to treat Lady Blanche a week ago.'

'Here's something you never thought to tell me,' Lizier interrupted, 'so I reckon that makes us equal.'

'Lizier, please,' Madame Boussay said. 'Let Guilhem finish.'

'It's Cordier's opinion the little girl saved her mistress's life, though she got no thanks for it.'

'Cordier!' Aimeric cried. 'But that's what Madame Noubel—'

'The point of what I'm saying,' Guilhem continued doggedly, 'is she told apothecary Cordier her name was Joubert, Alis Joubert. Lively little thing, he said. Tried to persuade him to take her with him when he left the castle.'

'It's her,' Aimeric said, spinning round to face his aunt. 'Alis is here.'

'Less haste, Nephew,' she murmured, then returned her attention to the old man. 'Lizier, though I would not want to trespass further on your time – nor yours, Guilhem – might we continue this conversation in private? It seems there is much to discuss.'

CHALABRE

'Minou, wake up!'

She felt the pressure of a hand on her shoulder. The last thing she remembered was coming back from the river to find Piet still sleeping in the barn. She had lain down beside him again, only for a moment.

'What hour is it?' she asked, quickly sitting up.

'Past midday,' Piet said. 'You were so weary, I couldn't bring myself to wake you.'

'Oh no.' Minou scrabbled to sit up. 'We should have left at first light. We promised.'

'Don't worry, Jeannette knows we're still here. Her father doesn't mind. A couple of soldiers came by and he sent them on their way.'

'All the same, I wish we had gone earlier.'

'It is better we waited. Jeannette says the castle is set at the highest point overlooking the valley, as you'd expect, but there is open land all around. There are woods to the north. If we want to approach unobserved, we'll have to wait until dusk.'

'Unobserved? But I have the letter inviting me to Puivert. We would be given safe passage.'

'You call it an invitation!' Piet gave a low laugh. 'The letter is precisely why we must plan to get into the castle without being seen.'

Minou shook her head. 'I must go to Alis. I cannot delay.'

Piet put his hands on her shoulders. 'You seem to think that Blanche de Bruyère will behave with honour. That if you present yourself to her, she will hand Alis into your care and allow you both to leave. But why would she, Minou? A woman who kidnaps a child and holds her hostage has no honour. You cannot trust her. If you walk unprotected to her gates, where's the guarantee that she won't then imprison you as well? Or worse. We've got to find a way of smuggling Alis away before Blanche knows we have ever been near Puivert.'

'I'm not a fool.' Minou shook off his embrace. 'I know it's dangerous, but I can't risk her hurting Alis. If I offer myself in place of my sister, there is a chance she will be set free. It's me Blanche wants, no one else.'

'I beg you to reconsider, Minou.'

'I have to try.'

'At least hear me out. We will go directly to Puivert. Jeannette says the chatelaine is hated in the village, as was the late Seigneur, so there might be people prepared to aid us but we must proceed with care. Her soldiers regularly patrol her lands, looking for heretics and poachers, and are known for their harshness.'

'But what's to be gained –'

'Jeannette also says that her betrothed, Guilhem, might be able to help, depending which of the soldiers are on duty at the castle. He is part of the garrison and says there are some more loyal to their mistress than others. Before we do anything, I will reconnoitre the castle and find out where Alis is being held.'

Minou touched her finger to his lips.

'Piet, please. Everything you say is true, but I have no choice. The thought of Alis, alone, haunts me. I can't stop thinking that she might have no medicine, that she's being held in terrible conditions. But the worst is imagining her believing I have forsaken her.'

'I cannot believe she would ever think that.'

'I don't care what happens to me, so long as she is safe.'

Piet sighed, the fight going out of him. 'But what of me, Minou? I care what happens to you. Does that not count for anything?'

Minou pressed her hand against his cheek. 'Of course, but she's only a child. She needs me.'

'I need you too.'

Flushing a deep crimson, he suddenly strode away from her.

'Piet, I'm sorry. Please understand.'

He pushed open the barn doors, as if seeking solace in the world outside, then turned back.

'Minou –' he began.

'Come back. Sit with me.'

'I cannot. I will lose the courage to speak.'

Minou's heart stumbled. Why was he suddenly so nervous?

'What do you mean, courage? Please, Piet, come back inside. Someone might see you.'

'Let them.' He sighed. 'I would rather have wooed you like a true suitor. The fact of the matter is I was intending to wait until a sweeter time.'

She frowned. 'You are talking in riddles. A sweeter time for what? Your words obscure your meaning.'

'Forgive me. What I want to say is this . . .' He rushed his words like a tongue-tied schoolboy. 'I would have you for my wife.'

Minou caught her breath. 'Are you asking me to marry you?'

'On— Only if it pleases you,' he stammered. 'I would ask

your father for your hand, as soon as this is over and, God willing, we are safe. And I don't have much to offer, and he might hold that against me. Everything I owned was destroyed in Toulouse, but . . .' Piet stopped again, his face as pale as previously it had been flushed. 'That is, if you would have me for your husband. Do you, could you, love me?'

The question was so unnecessary, Minou almost laughed. 'Can you doubt it?'

The look of agony started to fade. 'You do?'

'I do.'

'And you would consider taking me . . .'

'My answer is yes, *mon coeur*. Of course.'

And now Minou could see every true emotion – joy, desire, hope, love – lighting his face. Then his arms were around her, too tight, but when finally he did release her, she laughed and so did he. Their expressions mirrored one another.

Two halves of the same coin.

'And I give you my word, *lieverd*,' he said, touching the scrap of twine on her finger, 'my own love, that when we speak our vows before the altar it will be with a ring worthy of you.'

'I don't care about finery, it means nothing.'

'And when I've put my petition to your father – and if, God willing, he looks kindly on me – we can live in Carcassonne, perhaps even Toulouse, wherever you wish. Alis and Aimeric, your father too, should make their home with us, if that pleases you.' He hesitated. 'From everything you told me, I do not think he would baulk at a Huguenot for a son-in-law.'

She met his gaze. 'Or even a daughter.'

'What do you mean?' he said slowly.

She laughed, emboldened by something she had not known she was going to say until the words were in the air.

'I don't know, only . . . My mother and father raised me to respect those who took another path to God from my own. After what I saw in Toulouse, I am not sure I can stand with those who believe God is found at the tip of a sword.'

'There was evil done on both sides,' Piet cautioned.

'I know. Even so, to pray in French, would not that be wonderful?'

Piet stepped back. 'I would never ask you to change your faith. We would find a way.'

On the rare occasions Minou had imagined herself a bride, she thought she would be married in their local church in La Cité. Nothing grand or important. But now? She had never even stepped foot inside a Huguenot temple.

Then she heard the goat bells on the hillside, and their horses pawing the ground, restless, and thoughts of marriage faded.

'We have many hours ahead of us,' she said, reaching for his hand.

In gentle silence, they packed the saddlebags and bridled the horses, then set out on the road south from Chalabre.

'Will you agree to what I propose?' Piet asked. 'To go to the village of Puivert first?'

'There is a great deal of sense in what you say – there might be news in the village about my father and Alis, but . . .' Minou's voice cracked. She took a deep breath. 'But yet I fear we would be seen, and our presence quickly reported to Blanche de Bruyère. Then we lose any chance of approaching the castle unseen.'

'You are still determined to go directly to the château?' Piet asked.

'To the woods to the north of the castle, yes. We can wait

there until the sun sets,' she said. 'Once there, I'm sure it will become clear what to do for the best.'

Minou smiled to reassure him, but she felt as if there was an iron band around her ribs.

CHAPTER SIXTY-TWO

⚜

Puivert village

'Lizier,' Madame Boussay said, with a courteous bow, 'my nephew and I are most grateful for your time.'

Aimeric stood beside his aunt, impressed at how she had established a fellow feeling with the old villager and his nephew so swiftly. All the same, his nerves jangled. Not only did it seem that Alis was still alive, but, possibly, they had found his father too. Guilhem knew the prisoner only by his Christian name – Bernard – but who else could he be?

If only Minou would come. She'd be proud of him.

Aimeric pushed away the ugly thought she might never know how well he'd done, that she and Piet might not have survived the battle for Toulouse.

'Accept this for your trouble,' his aunt was saying, pressing a coin into old Lizier's hands. 'Not least for the stabling of my brother-in-law's horse.'

'Most generous, Madama.'

'Your discretion will also be much appreciated.'

'Of course. I am glad to have been of service.'

'I will not forget your assistance. Now, I will take my leave. There are things to be done. I'm sure it is all a mere misunderstanding. Perhaps Bernard was taken unwell visiting the château and is being cared for there.'

Aimeric pulled a face. 'In the dungeon, Aunt?'

She took no notice. 'Or perhaps it was he who requested little Alis be sent for, to keep him company in his distress.'

Achille Lizier tapped his nose. 'Most likely.'

'In fact,' Madame Boussay continued, 'it also seems possible to me that this apothecary – Paul Cordier did you say? – misunderstood the situation. You said he only saw the child fleetingly?'

Guilhem nodded. 'Yes.'

'But—'

She turned to look at him. 'Yes, Nephew?'

Aimeric shrugged. 'Nothing, Aunt.'

'Very well, then.'

'Madame Boussay,' said Guilhem, addressing her directly for the first time, 'I am due to return to the château by sunset this evening. If that might be of help.'

She tilted her head to one side. 'Are you indeed?'

'Are you certain I can't give you something to drink before you go?' Achille Lizier said, resenting the attention his nephew was receiving.

For the first time, his aunt's composure cracked and Aimeric grinned. The small house was dark and filthy, showing clearly the lack of a woman's touch. He could not imagine his aunt accepting even a cup of wine from Lizier's dirty hands.

'You are most kind, but no. You are quite sure you do not mind continuing to watch Canigou for a while longer?'

'It is my honour,' he said, with a crooked half-bow.

Madame Boussay smiled. 'As a final request, Lizier, might you spare your nephew for a few minutes to accompany us back to our carriage? Having not been blessed with a son of my own, though of course Aimeric is a great comfort to me, I am interested to hear about life as a soldier in a household such as Puivert.'

Lizier puffed his chest with pride. 'Of course, of course. Guilhem, you heard what she said. Go with Madame Boussay to her carriage.'

CHÂTEAU DE PUIVERT

'And don't get up to mischief today,' the nurse threatened, 'else I'll take a rod to you. Do you hear me?'

The instant Alis heard the key turn in the lock, she rushed back to her bed and plumped her pillow beneath the blanket, so it looked as if she was still sleeping. It wouldn't fool anyone for long, but it might delay the discovery of her disappearance for a while.

Alis removed her stockings and hid them under the mattress, remembering how Aimeric always told her that bare feet were best for getting a good grip when climbing, then tucked her skirts into her undergarments and clambered up onto the sill.

In the daylight, the drop looked worse.

Alis sat with her legs dangling out of the window, willing herself the courage to go through with it. She inched closer to the edge, trying not to imagine what it would feel like if she slipped and fell. She was about to let herself go, when everything went wrong. The door opened and the nurse returned.

'I forgot—'

She saw Alis balanced on the ledge, screamed and rushed across the chamber. Alis felt a sharp pain in her scalp as she was grabbed by her hair and pulled down off the sill. Then she heard heavy footsteps on the stairs and the chamber was suddenly full, as the priest, his manservant Bonal and Blanche de Bruyère appeared in the doorway.

'How many times must you be told not to leave the brat alone?'

'Forgive me, my lady, I—'

'Silence!' Blanche shouted. 'I will decide what to do with you later.'

Alis was trying to slip out of the chamber, but Bonal caught her round the waist and threw her roughly onto a chair.

Blanche crossed the room. 'You had your chance to be treated civilly. Now you will stay like this until your sister comes. Tie her hands.'

'No!'

Bonal pulled Alis's arms through the wooden struts and tied her wrists. Alis bit her lip until she tasted blood, determined not to cry.

'Minou will come,' she shouted defiantly, then cowered back as the manservant raised his hand.

'Leave her,' the priest commanded.

Alis looked at him. Long red robes, tall. He was wearing a biretta, but she could see his black hair was slashed through with a streak of white.

She had seen him before. Where? She ran through her memory, like rooms crowded with images, until she found it. Standing on the doorstep in La Cité, looking out for Minou in the cold February mist. Minou had been late that night coming back from the bookshop, and Alis was worried. This priest had walked past and into rue Notre-Dame, then into the garden of the Fournier house.

The Fournier house, where Aimeric had met the man accused of murder, where blood had been smeared all over the walls. He had told them all about it. Alis shivered, terrified for the first time since arriving in Puivert.

And as if sensing it, the priest took a step towards her. He was so close she could smell the oil on his hair and the faint scent of incense in his robes.

He bent down and put his hands on her right shoulder, his thumb and forefinger pressing uncomfortably between the joints.

'Answer me truthfully and no one will hurt you. But if you lie, God will know and I will know. It is a sin to lie and sinners must be punished. Do you understand?'

Alis could not speak. Her breath felt as sharp as pine needles in her throat.

'Do you understand?' Blanche said. 'Answer.'

Alis nodded.

'Tell me,' the priest continued, 'did your sister talk about what would happen when she was rich? When she came into her inheritance? Did she promise you a pony, perhaps, or a new gown?'

'I don't know what you mean, Monsieur.'

'Or robes for your father? A carriage?'

'My aunt and uncle are wealthy, but we don't have anything.'

Alis saw him glance at Lady Blanche.

'Very well. Tell me instead about your sister's friend, Monsieur Reydon. Have you heard of him? Piet Reydon.'

She shook her head. 'I don't know who you mean.'

'If we catch him, he will hang, and your brother with him. Do you understand?'

'No,' she cried, struggling to get free.

'No one is angry with you yet, Alis. If you tell us what you know, no one will hurt you.'

Alis tried not to give anything away. Aimeric always teased her for having too honest a face. She tried to think of something else. Her tabby kitten and the otters on the river bank, gentle things that didn't hurt at all. But now the priest was squeezing her face between his fingers and forcing tears into her eyes.

'Do you know this Reydon?'

She couldn't help answering truthfully. Minou had told her the name of the man she had met, the same man whom Aimeric had helped.

'Yes,' Alis answered.

'You see, that's better. God loves you when you tell the truth. Is he with your sister?'

'Why would he be with Minou?'

'Where do you think they are? Has she forgotten you?'

'She loves me,' Alis said in a small voice.

'Then perhaps it is time for you to remind her of it,' he said, clicking his fingers. 'Bonal, fetch paper and ink. Do you know your letters, Alis?'

Alis was going to lie, then she saw the nurse out of the corner of her eye and knew she would be punished for pretending. The nurse had seen her writing often enough. She nodded again.

'Good. I shall tell you what you are to write. While we're waiting for Bonal to return, shall we try again with some of my questions? You might answer better than before.'

'I don't know anything.'

'Did your sister tell you about a Will? You understand what a Will is?'

'It is to say who has your belongings when you die.'

'Clever girl. Think hard before you answer. Did Minou tell you where she had hidden the Will? Do you know where to find it?'

'I don't know what you mean.'

Alis felt she was trapped inside a nightmare. She didn't

know what the priest was talking about, but he kept asking the same question.

Why wouldn't they believe her?

'Where did Minou conceal the Will?' Vidal pressed, his voice silky with persuasion. 'Did she show you? Or does she carry it with her for safekeeping? Nothing bad will happen to you if you tell us the truth.'

'Please, I have never heard anything about a Will. Never.'

'Did she promise you beautiful things when she was rich? Is that why she went to Toulouse? Think carefully before you answer, Alis. God commands us to tell the truth. He sees everything. He will know if you lie.'

Puivert Village

'Do you not know me, Paul?' Madame Noubel asked again.

She was dismayed by her cousin's stained hose and threadbare doublet, the fastenings hanging loose on a snagged thread. A stink of stale wine hung about him, as if he had not washed for days. Beside her, Bérenger shuffled his feet, clearly also embarrassed by the dissolute state of her kinsman.

'Cécile Noubel. Cordier, as was. I was married to your cousin Arnaud, a long time in the past now. Surely you remember?'

The apothecary swayed on unsteady legs, staring with eyes blurred by drink.

'Cécile?' he slurred. 'You left. Went to Carcassonne.'

Madame Noubel glanced at Bérenger. 'That's right, when Arnaud passed on.' She took a step forward. 'We have come in the hope of some information about the village, Paul. I hoped you might be able to help.'

'Me? I know nothing. Better to know nothing. I can't help you.'

Madame Noubel looked doubtfully about the cottage, its windows in a state of disrepair and tiles missing from the roof.

'You've done well for yourself,' she said. 'An apothecary now, and your own house.'

Her first husband, Arnaud Cordier, had been older than her by some twenty years and in poor health. She had spent most of her married life as a nurse not a wife. The Cordier family was large, lots of cousins and half-cousins and in-laws, but she remembered Paul, an unpopular child, a gossip, always telling tales and betraying secrets. She knew she could coax him to talk.

'What ails you?' she asked kindly.

'Nothing,' he mumbled, attempting to shut the door. 'Why do you torment me? It's none of your business. You left Puivert, you got away. You don't live here now, you've got no right to judge. You don't know what it's like.'

Cécile's curiosity sharpened. Why was he so frightened? Why was he inebriated at this hour in the morning? Was it habitual, or had something in particular caused him to take solace in the bottle?

'I've not come to cause trouble,' she soothed.

'Leave me alone! A man has to think of himself. What was I supposed to do?'

'No call to take on so, Sénher,' Bérenger intervened, stepping between them.

Several times on their tiring journey from Carcassonne to Puivert, Madame Noubel had been grateful of his solid presence, but there was no need here.

She put her hand on his arm. 'It's all right, Bérenger,' she said mildly, 'Paul and I are kin. Listen to me, Cousin, we are seeking a child. A girl of seven years old called Alis. We have reason to believe she was brought to Puivert some weeks ago. Her father is possibly somewhere in the district also. Arrived at Easter, or roundabout. Have you heard anything? Talk of strangers in the village? Or the château?'

From his pallor and the violent shake of his hands, the way he glanced up at the hill behind them, then away, she knew he did.

'Might I come inside?' she said. Before he had another chance to prevent her, she stepped past him into the house. 'We will talk of the old times, Cousin, then you can tell me what you know.'

CHAPTER SIXTY-THREE

⚜

'Bérenger!' Aimeric shouted with delight.

Leaving his aunt and Guilhem Lizier staring after him, he ran the length of the street to where his old adversary was standing outside the house at the far end of the village.

'Steady, boy, you'll have me over.'

'Bérenger, I can't believe it's you. Why are you here? How?'

'I might ask the same of you,' Bérenger replied gruffly, discomfited by the affectionate greeting. 'Last I heard, you were in Toulouse, causing havoc there no doubt.' He looked along the street. 'Is Madomaisèla Minou with you?'

Aimeric's face fell. 'We were separated trying to get out of the city before the fighting began, and Piet . . .' He stopped, suddenly remembering the previous time when Bérenger had been pursuing Piet through the streets of La Cité, assuming him to be the murderer of Michel Cazès. 'Our carriage was stopped at the checkpoint on the bridge in Toulouse,' he said sombrely. 'Minou ran back into the city to draw the soldiers away from us. I don't know what happened to her after that.' He swallowed hard. 'She is supposed to meet us here.'

'I see you have your sister's cloak, though,' Bérenger said, pointing at the green woollen garment. 'Grown out of everything of your own, have you?'

Aimeric coloured. 'She asked me to take care of it for her, that's all. But in faith, Bérenger, why are you in Puivert? The Seneschal's authority can't stretch all the way down here.'

'Happen it does, in a manner of speaking. We're still within the boundaries of Aude.'

'The garrison's been sent here?'

'No.' Bérenger held up a hand. 'Look, it's not my place to say. Bide a while until Madame Noubel comes out. I warrant she won't be much longer.'

'She is here too?'

'Madame Noubel has family here. Cousin of her late husband. Her first husband, that is. Drab excuse of a man, Cordier is, though he's supposed to be educated.'

Aimeric's eyes grew wider, remembering the conversation between Achille Lizier and his aunt. 'This is Paul Cordier's house?'

Bérenger frowned. 'How do you come to know of him?'

Aimeric was saved from explaining by the breathless arrival of Madame Boussay. Guilhem was with her.

'You should not run off, Nephew. It is most discourteous.'

'I'm sorry, Aunt.'

'The fault is mine,' Bérenger said. 'The boy was so taken aback to see me here I dare say he forgot his manners. Not for the first time, I should add.'

Madame Boussay looked suspiciously at him. 'Who are you?'

'Bérenger,' Aimeric jumped in. 'From the garrison in La Cité. We are old friends. He came with Madame Noubel, who's inside – this is Paul Cordier's house.' He turned back to Bérenger. 'This is my noble aunt, Madame Boussay, from Toulouse. And Guilhem Lizier, who's in service at the château. From what Guilhem tells us, we think Alis is there. Possibly my father also.'

Bérenger looked him in the eye. 'You know your sister is missing?'

Aimeric nodded. 'Minou received a letter from—'

At that moment, Cordier's door opened and Cécile Noubel came out.

'Aimeric? Can it be?'

'Madame Noubel!' Aimeric cried, beginning the introductions all over again. 'And this is my aunt, Madame Boussay.'

For a moment, the two ladies stared at one another. Neither wished to be the first to speak, neither was sure what to say. Then, Cécile inclined her head.

'Madame Boussay, I heard a great deal about you from Florence. Your sister always talked fondly of you.'

Aimeric watched his aunt's face soften. 'Cécile Cordier. You were a dear friend to Florence, her matron of honour, I believe.' She held out her hand. 'It is a pleasure to meet you.'

CHALABRE

Minou and Piet rode in single file along the green valley of the Blau, keeping to the shade of the overhanging trees, the gentle rhythm of the horses' hooves on the stone and earth track soothing them. Nearby, the river sang its ancient song, flowing over the rocks and roots in flecks of silver and white. Sparrows dipped in and out of hedgerow nests, making the leaves shiver, and there was a steady humming of bees and a chorus of cicadas on the grasslands above the banks.

Minou felt a curious mix of tranquillity and apprehension. From time to time, aware of Piet's eyes on her, she turned and smiled at the man who would be her husband.

Then she thought of what lay ahead.

For all her fighting talk, she was terrified. She was haunted by thoughts of how poor a condition Alis might be in, that none of them would ever see their little house in rue du Trésau again.

They might not even survive the night.

'How goes it with you?' Piet called. 'Shall we rest a while?'

Minou smiled over her shoulder at him. 'No. It can't be much further.'

He pressed his horse forward and drew level as the path widened out. 'If you are sure, my Lady of the Mists.'

'Your Lady of the Glades wishes to keep going,' she teased.

The path came to a dead end at a low waterfall, so they turned their horses onto a farm track that sloped steeply alongside a field of barley.

'I still don't understand why Blanche de Bruyère is so desperate to get you to come to Puivert that she would take Alis hostage,' Piet said. 'Your father is not a rich man. What can she possibly want?'

Like light shining through a winter window, Minou suddenly had an image of herself holding the hidden Will in her hands in her bedchamber in Toulouse, the faded black ink on the yellow parchment.

This is the day of my death. As the Lord God is my witness, here, by my own hand, do I set this down. My last Will and Testament.

With a jolt, she realised she had never told Piet about what she had found concealed within the bible, nor what she thought it signified.

'Minou? Do you know what she wants?' Piet said.

'I think I do,' she said. 'It is not even anything to do with me as myself, but rather the threat I represent to her position.'

'Now it is you who speaks in riddles,' he teased, echoing her words to him in Chalabre. 'What do you mean?'

Minou waved her hand, taking in the hills and the woodlands, the crops and the road winding into the distance to Puivert.

'I mean this,' she said. 'All of this.'

Château de Puivert

Blanche stretched her arms above her head, letting her black hair fall away from her white skin.

She had arranged the sheet across her belly, to shield the baby from his gaze. Though Valentin liked to feel his child moving beneath the velvet and lace of her clothes, she suspected the sight of her belly swollen and uncovered would please him less.

And he had changed. He seemed consumed by ambition for its own sake, not for the glory of God. The voices in her head whispered that he was turning away from the Lord, almost constantly now.

'Come back to bed,' she said. He was solicitous of her condition, but Blanche knew there were still many ways for pleasure to be given and accepted. 'I would have you beside me.'

Instead he walked to the window and looked down over the lower courtyard.

'A man approaches,' he said.

Blanche pulled on her shift, feeling dizzy and light-headed, then joined him at the casement.

'Do you know him?' Vidal asked.

Blanche frowned. Did she? She tried to concentrate. Images, thoughts, slipped in and out of her mind. Blood, a violent stabbing sensation in her abdomen, the cold of the stones and blackness. Alis shouting and shouting for help. For a fleeting moment, she felt a pang of guilt for the girl, but she killed it. There was no room for sentiment. It would make her weak.

She nodded, relieved she could remember. 'It is the apothecary from the village.'

'Who attended you?'

'The same. Paul Cordier.'

'Did you send for him?'

'I did not.'

Vidal laughed. 'Another of your spies?'

Blanche found a smile. 'That's right.' She slipped her hand beneath his robes and heard him sigh. 'I told you, everyone can be bought at the right price.'

PUIVERT VILLAGE

The long narrow village street was in shadow as the setting sun sank behind the houses. On the hillside above, only the château de Puivert remained bathed in golden light.

Madame Boussay, Madame Noubel, Aimeric and Guilhem were in the midwife's old house, next to Achille Lizier's cottage. They had set up camp there, after leaving Cordier's dwelling, needing somewhere to wait out of sight of prying eyes. The cottage was damp, with the melancholy air of a place abandoned, but once they had opened the back shutters and lit a fire of hawthorn wood in the grate to take the chill from the room, it had served them well enough.

Bérenger was standing watch outside. Inside, the conversation had been heated. They were like knights at the joust, Aimeric thought. First one point scored, only to be knocked down by a different suggestion. Finally, after many hours of talking, a plan had been agreed.

At dusk, Madame Noubel would go to the château with Guilhem. He would help her through the guardhouse at the main gate, before attending to his duties in the Tour Bossue. He would try to find a way to speak to Bernard and tell him what had happened.

While Guilhem was talking to Bernard, Cécile Noubel would make her way to the logis to find Alis, with a view to getting her away under cover of darkness. Though Cordier's words became more slippery with drink, her cousin had been useful. She was confident she knew in which chamber the child was being held and how best to get in and out. Her principle worry was for Alis's health. If she was sick, and too ill to be moved, then she would have to think again.

In the meantime, Bérenger was to take up position in the woods to the north of the castle to be on hand ready to bring Bernard and Alis back to the village.

Aimeric was to remain in the village with Madame Boussay and hold the fort.

'I tell you, I should go with you,' Aimeric repeated. 'It's not fair.'

Madame Noubel shook her head. 'We have been through this a dozen times. The fewer of us there are, the less the chance of us being seen. I know the castle and grounds well. It will be easier for me to blend into the background.'

'That's ridiculous! The servants will know you don't belong there.'

'I did once belong,' she said mildly. 'Servants come and go. And besides, one old woman looks much like another to young eyes.'

Madame Boussay chuckled. 'How right you are, Cécile.'

'If by ill fortune I am challenged,' Madame Noubel continued, 'I will claim I was sent by my cousin to deliver medicine to the castle.'

'Cordier's an idiot,' Aimeric said. 'I wouldn't trust him as far as I can spit.'

'That's enough, Nephew. I need you here with me. We must make sure the cottage is ready for when your father and sister come back. Or if, God willing, Minou should arrive.'

Aimeric frowned. 'You don't think she is trapped . . .'

'Your sister is a resourceful, courageous person,' Madame Boussay said firmly. 'I have no doubt she will have found a way to get out of Toulouse and is, even now, making her way to Puivert. The only question is when she will arrive, not if.'

'You truly believe that, Aunt?' he said, clutching his sister's green woollen cloak. He had barely let it out of his sight since Minou had entrusted it to him on the covered bridge.

'I do believe it. And when Minou does come, I will rely on you to explain everything. I so often get in a muddle and say the wrong thing. My husband—' She broke off. 'Well, that's as no matter now.'

Aimeric grinned. 'I don't believe you get in a muddle at all. I think you know everything, but pretend not to.'

Madame Boussay stared at him, then a glint of mischief sparkled in her eyes.

'Is that so? Well, who's to say? It is sometimes safer to be taken for a fool and to be overlooked, than be considered wise and have your every word examined.'

Madame Noubel stood up suddenly. 'This endless waiting plays on my nerves.' She turned to Guilhem. 'You are sure Bernard will still be in the Tour Bossue?'

'He's been held in the same cell since April, Madama. I have been away from the castle on patrol this past week, but I see no reason why he would have been moved.'

'I still don't understand why Father was arrested in the first place.' Aimeric said. 'What was his crime?'

'He was taken for a poacher,' Guilhem replied. 'Lady Blanche was away in Toulouse – so we were told – and all matters of security were placed in the hands of the captain of the guard. A couple of other poachers were arrested that same night. They were charged and released with a fine but, because Bernard refused to give his name, the captain wouldn't let him go.'

'And Bernard couldn't give his name,' Madame Noubel said, thinking out loud, 'for fear Blanche de Bruyère would learn of it and realise who he was. I thought it odd I received no word from him, but then I was so worried for Alis.'

'And nobody knows who he is, even now?' Aimeric asked.

Guilhem shook his head. 'Only us four, and, of course, now my uncle.' He turned to Madame Noubel. 'Or perhaps also your cousin?'

'I did not speak to Paul of Bernard, only of Alis.' She sighed. 'It is odd, though, to be back here in this cottage after so long. Twenty years.'

Madame Boussay looked at her. 'You know a great more of this matter than you have so far said, Cécile.'

Madame Noubel hesitated, then she nodded. 'I do. But it is Bernard's story to tell. I cannot break a confidence.'

At that moment, they heard the single bell tolling the dusk, and everyone fell silent. Bérenger reappeared in the chamber, his solid bulk in the doorway blocking the light.

'It is time,' he said.

CHAPTER SIXTY-FOUR

⚜

Château de Puivert

As the last of the blue slipped from the sky, a nightingale began to sing in the woods behind the castle. The air was sharp with the smell of pine and sweet, damp earth.

There was a flickering glow of candlelight in the keep, like fireflies piercing the velvet blue. Bolder, stronger torches flamed at the gatehouse, sending elongated moving shadows scattering across the grassy courtyard. Lamps burnt above the stone doors in the towers of the lower courtyard. Not a soul appeared to be stirring, either within or without the walls. But the night was alive with those secretly waiting.

Breaths taken in short, shallow bursts. Caps and hoods pulled low over faces. The muffled tread of those wanting not to be heard, the crack of a twig or a stone dislodged seeming as loud as any rumble of thunder.

Eyes watching from the woods.

Madame Noubel and Guilhem approached the drawbridge.

'You are sure you wish to go through with this?' she said, putting her hand on the young soldier's arm. 'If your role is discovered, it will go ill for you.'

'It won't be,' he said, though she heard the snap of fear in his voice. 'Villagers come regularly to the castle, bringing food or wares to sell.'

'At this time of night?'

'At any time.'

'If you are certain.'

'Don't worry. There's no reason for anyone to suspect you of anything,' he said. 'You are a Puivert woman, one of us.'

'What was that?' Piet hissed, drawing his sword.

'It's nothing,' Minou said quickly. 'The high notes of a nightingale, can you not hear her? The woods are full of birdsong at this time of night.'

Piet let his hand drop back to his side. 'After the barricade, even the most innocent sound now speaks of some threat.'

They settled back against the base of the beech tree, its twisted trunk glowing silver in the light of the moon. Minou turned over a leaf in her hand.

'It is the shape of a teardrop, do you see?'

He laughed, then picked another from the carpet of leaves on which they sat.

'I prefer this, for it looks like a heart.'

'That's from an alder,' Minou said. 'When I was little, my mother taught me to recognise trees from their leaves and flowers. We would walk in the woods, the marshlands down by the river, the orchards on the slopes of La Cité.'

Piet smiled. 'My childhood in Amsterdam was about waterways and dams. The sound of the wind in the rigging of tall ships and the merchants unloading cargo. All noise and bustle, not the peace of the countryside.' He froze again. 'What's that?'

This time, Minou had heard it too. The sound of a branch snapping underfoot.

'It came from that direction,' she whispered, pointing towards the deeper woods to the north of the château.

'I'll go and look.'

'No, wait.'

'I won't be long. Best to be certain.'

'Piet, better we stay together,' she said, but she was already speaking to the moon. He had vanished.

Minou waited, listening out for his footsteps in the darkness. The nightingale's song gave way to the cry of an owl going out to hunt. Then the bells of the village church struck for eight o'clock. Should she follow? What if there was someone there and Piet needed help?

She looked up. At that moment, the candles that had been burning in the tall rectangular castle tower were extinguished. It was very early for the household to retire for the night, but maybe that was the way in the mountains.

'Piet?' she whispered into the night, thinking she heard something.

There was no answer.

Minou stepped out of the shelter of the beech tree.

Without warning, a hand was clamped across her mouth. A man's hand, smelling of ale and metal. She struck out, punching and kicking and trying to pull herself free, but she was overpowered.

'Here's another one,' he said. 'Looks like that old sot Cordier got his facts right for once.'

Minou made another wild effort to get away, but her arms were dragged up behind her back and a hessian hood thrown over her head. She felt herself being half marched, half carried uphill towards the castle. Moments later, the sound of a gate.

'What are we supposed to do with her?'

'Put her in the dungeon in the Tour Bossue.'

'Goodnight.' Guilhem addressed Madame Noubel in a loud voice, for the benefit of the guards on duty.

They were playing dice and paid no attention. Too little attention, perhaps? Was it odd no one had asked who his companion was? He had told Madame Noubel not to worry, but the atmosphere in the gatehouse seemed as sharp as a knife. Still, there was nothing he could do about it now. So long as Bérenger was safely in position in the woods, all should be well.

'Thank you for your kindness, Sénher,' Madame Noubel replied in Occitan. 'I am much obliged. Goodnight.'

'*Bona nuèit,* Madama,' he said again.

Guilhem took the keys for the Tour Bossue, then walked out into the night. He saw Madame Noubel pull her shawl around her face, then hurry into the blackness of the courtyard beyond.

As Guilhem turned to go back into the gatehouse he found two soldiers blocking his way. A third man, a stranger with a vivid scar on his face, was with them.

'Is something wrong?'

The first blow took his breath from him, the second connected with his jaw, and his head snapped back. Then he was pushed hard in the chest.

'Friends, what is it? What's happening?'

Guilhem felt his arms gripped, one on either side of him, before being dragged out of the gatehouse.

'Am I under arrest?'

At the last moment, in the lamplight, he caught a glimpse of a familiar face, someone who should not have been there.

'Cordier?' he shouted, struggling to free himself. 'Cordier!'

Then the door was kicked shut, a hand was clamped over his mouth, and he was dragged across the drawbridge and into the woods behind the castle.

*

'No,' Guilhem tried to say, as he felt the point of a knife against his side. 'You're making a mistake.'

'No mistake,' Bonal said.

Guilhem tried to shout for help as the blade slipped in between his ribs. Clean and expert, final. For a moment, there was no sensation at all. Then the point of the knife went home. Guilhem felt the first spreading of blood on his skin and his jerkin, a terrible cold like a winter's frost reaching right to the tips of his fingers. He fell down to his knees. He tasted blood in his throat, his mouth. Why couldn't he breathe?

In his last moments of life, he thought he saw his Jeannette on the river bank, so proud that he had learnt to write in French. How he would never now be able to thank Bernard for the gift of his teaching. He thought of Madame Noubel – betrayed, as he realised they had all been, by her own cousin – and prayed Bérenger would at least have a chance to defend himself, that he would die like a soldier.

Guilhem reached for his sword, but it was too late.

Noises filtered in from outside his cell, and Bernard jolted awake.

'Guilhem?' Bernard said. 'Is it you?'

Holding the weight of the chain that tethered him to the wall, Bernard shuffled to the narrow window and looked out.

The night air was cool on his face. Clouds moved fast across the face of the moon, sending beams of silver light over the tops of the trees, illuminating fragments of ground around the edge of the woods.

He could see little, but he could hear the beat of the wings of a bird, folding into the air and away. Rustling in the undergrowth. A wild boar perhaps? Was it more poachers he'd heard? Though the penalties could be harsh, the hunting was good.

Then, the sound of men talking. Muttering, but unafraid to be heard. Not poachers. The jolt of swords and armour. Soldiers? It was unusual for them to patrol outside the castle walls at night.

Bernard tried to twist his head, but the chain wouldn't stretch further and he couldn't see. He heard the click of a gate – into the upper courtyard, he thought – and wondered who was coming into the château at this time of night.

Not wishing to be caught looking, he quickly hurried back to his bench and sat down to wait.

Piet held his fingers to the man's neck and found no pulse.

The body was still warm, the life had barely left him. Piet ran his hands over his jerkin, found the hilt of a dagger and his shirt sodden with blood. He ran his hand over the man's pockets, taking a knife and a set of keys, then stood up. He hid the keys in his own pocket, then out of the corner of his eye, he saw a movement.

Piet drew his sword and spun round, but he was too slow. He saw the stick come down, felt the club connect with the side of his head.

Then, darkness.

Bernard heard someone drag open the outer door of the Tour Bossue, then the tramp of several pairs of boots in the passage and the key in the lock.

Two soldiers, neither of whom he recognised, appeared in the doorway holding a person between them. Bernard held up his hands to shield his eyes from the blinding light of the lantern.

'Stay where you are.'

'Where's Guilhem?' he asked.

'We've brought company for you.' One of the soldiers pushed the prisoner forward.

To Bernard's distress, he saw the prisoner was a woman. Tall and slight, her skirts were stained wet at the hem. One of the soldiers crouched down to untie her hands and then pulled the hood from her head. 'The first of many new arrivals this evening, I warrant.'

The door was locked again and the air settled. The woman kept her head bowed, but he knew. Bernard could not breathe, dared not speak for breaking the spell. Was it a dream? A spirit sent to taunt him?

The cell was dark, but the ribbon of moonlight through the narrow window was all he needed. A tear rolled down his cheek.

'Daughter . . .'

CHAPTER SIXTY-FIVE

⚜

Blanche de Bruyère stood in a long grey gown, buttoned high at the neck and artfully tailored to conceal her condition. Her underskirt and the slashes of her sleeves were ivory white, shimmering in the light of the candles, and her black hair was braided and arranged beneath a grey cowl. At her neck, she wore a string of pearls. Pinned to her waist hung an exquisite rosary of silver and carved ivory beads.

Vidal stood behind her in his red robes, a silver crucifix heavy around his neck. Standing guard on the landing outside the open door to the musicians' gallery, Bonal stood listening to every word the captain of the castle guard was saying.

'What news?' Blanche said.

'We have located them all, my lady,' he replied. 'There are four of them, as the apothecary reported, though he was not accurate in his descriptions.'

'What do you mean?'

The captain shuffled. 'Their ages, clothing, he—'

'Tell us who you do have,' Vidal interrupted.

'An old woman and a soldier, who arrived in the village this morning from Carcassonne. Also, another woman and a young boy from Toulouse, who travelled from Chalabre this afternoon. Both the women are already in our custody.'

'What name did the younger woman give?' Blanche demanded.

'She refused to speak. We found her just after eight o'clock outside the château walls on the woodland side of—'

'Alone?' Vidal interrupted again.

'Yes, Monsignor.'

'Did she have anything with her? A leather satchel, say?'

'No, though we have reason to believe the pair arrived from Chalabre on horseback. My men are looking for the horses now.'

'If you do not have her name, tell me what she looks like.'

The captain stumbled. 'Of more than average height, with straight brown hair. Neither a great beauty, nor, on the other hand, plain.'

'What colour were her eyes?' Blanche asked.

The captain faltered. 'Forgive me, my lady, but it was dark. I did not notice.'

Blanche turned to Vidal. 'It is her, I am sure of it. Who else? I want her brought here immediately. I shall—'

'Patience, my lady,' Vidal said, throwing her a warning look. 'Let us hear the rest of the good captain's report.'

Her colour rose but Blanche waved her hand. 'Very well. Proceed.'

'The old woman goes by the name of Noubel. Originally from the village here, she was married to one of Cordier's cousins. She moved away some years ago after she was widowed.'

'The child had been left in her care in Carcassonne,' Blanche whispered to Vidal, before turning back to the captain. 'I did not know she came from Puivert. When exactly did she leave the village?'

'The apothecary said it was some nineteen years ago, my lady. Or twenty, he was not certain.'

Vidal waved at the captain to continue.

'Madame Noubel was given admittance into the castle by one of my own men, I regret to say. He has been punished.'

Vidal nodded. 'Where was this Noubel creature found?'

'Caught trying to enter the logis.'

'Looking for the child, no doubt,' he muttered. 'What of the men?'

'Cordier described an old soldier and a boy. They are not yet in our custody. We could not find them in the village, so we believe they have taken refuge in the woods. There is a search party, with a pack of dogs, looking for them now. They won't get far.'

Vidal raised his hand. 'I want them taken alive, Captain.'

'Yes, Monsignor. I gave orders accordingly.'

Blanche seemed to have recovered her equilibrium. 'You have done well, Captain. I shall see you are rewarded for it.'

He bowed. 'Thank you, my Lady. What of Monsieur Cordier? He is waiting in the gatehouse.'

'He too should be rewarded for his service,' she said, glancing at Vidal.

'Bonal,' Vidal called, 'go with the captain. Escort Cordier out of the castle. The road can be perilous at night.'

Blanche waited until Bonal and the captain's footsteps had faded away on the winding stone steps before she spoke again.

'Something is not right,' she said. The voices were insistent in her head again. 'What have we forgotten, misunderstood, what?'

Vidal looked at her in surprise. 'What do you mean?'

'What do I . . . ?' She blinked. 'Nothing.'

'We must proceed carefully,' he said. 'If it is Minou Joubert—'

'It is, it must be. Though how Madame Noubel comes to be with her, I do not understand.'

'And assuming the man with Minou Joubert is Reydon,' he muttered.

'He said a young man. Could Cordier have been mistaken in the number of people he saw? The captain said the descriptions were not accurate.'

'What, that there are more than four of them?' Vidal frowned. 'And if it is Reydon, why would he leave her and go into the woods?'

'To hide the Shroud?'

'Why would he hide it here? On your lands? Safer to keep it with him.'

Blanche put her hand to her head, willing the voices to quieten.

'Does something ail you?' Vidal asked.

She quickly smiled. 'Not at all. I think we should have Minou Joubert brought here now. Find out what she knows.'

Blanche started towards the door, but then felt Vidal's hand on her arm.

'Not yet. Let the captain finish his work, Blanche. When he has them all in his custody, we will begin. I have some experience in these matters. It will be easier to persuade each of them to speak if they know we have the others in our care too.'

Blanche frowned. 'But we have Alis. That will surely loosen her tongue. I cannot wait until morning.'

'You should rest.' Vidal started to stroke the back of her neck. 'I promise you, Blanche, if you question her now, she will hold her tongue. And we will not discover where they have hidden the Shroud. Nor, indeed, where the papers you seek are hidden.'

Blanche leant back against him and felt him stir. The priest stepped back into the shadows and the man took his place.

She sighed. 'Very well, we will wait until dawn. But if Reydon is not caught by then, I will have her brought to me.'

CHAPTER SIXTY-SIX

⚜

PUIVERT

In the gloom of the cell in the Tour Bossue, Minou sat holding her father's hand.

All the distance of the past months, the silences and shadows, had been banished by the joy of finding one another again. They had talked and talked of what had happened since they had parted at the Porte Narbonnaise in La Cité on that chill March day. Stories laced with guilt and regret. Minou spoke of life in the Boussay household, the horror of the massacre, and how his letters had been withheld. She decided not to tell her father about Blanche's letter, or Alis's kidnapping, yet. She did not want to cause him more pain, and knew she would have to choose the right moment to tell him. In his turn, Bernard talked of his capture and long captivity. Why he had come to Puivert in the first instance was still not clear to her, but as she was on the point of pressing him, the cell door had opened again and Madame Noubel was pushed roughly inside.

They all felt the same confusion of delight and anguish at how they came to find themselves in one another's company. Madame Noubel explained what had happened to Alis and how Bérenger had accompanied her to Puivert. Minou, of course, knew her little sister was a hostage. But for Bernard to learn his younger daughter had been held for so many weeks in the same castle that was his prison, distressed him into silence, as Minou had feared it might.

The hourly chiming of the bell in the village marked time as they talked. Every now and again, they caught the echo of a shout in the woods beyond the compound, the baying of hunting dogs which chilled the blood.

'They are still searching,' Minou said.

'If something ill befalls Bérenger, I will never forgive myself,' Cécile Noubel said. 'None of this is his fault.'

'It's no one's fault but the author of it,' said Minou.

'Bérenger is a good friend to our family,' Bernard said. 'Has always been.'

Minou nodded, but she was thinking of Piet. Though she had told them in Toulouse how her path had crossed with Madame Noubel's erstwhile lodger – and how much Aimeric admired him – she had not confided more to her father here in the cell.

Minou traced a pattern in the straw with the toe of her boot, occasionally glancing up. Bernard stood beneath the narrow window. She could not but notice how thin he had grown. At the same time, Minou detected a new stoicism, even resolve, in him.

'To think Aimeric is with Salvadora Boussay in the village,' he said suddenly. 'To think of it, Cécile.'

'They seemed at ease with one another. Fond, even.'

Minou smiled. 'He hated living in Toulouse. So to learn they both got safely away, but have also found some pleasure in one another's company, is a great relief.'

'Where are they now?' Bernard asked.

'They are waiting in Anne Gabignaud's cottage,' Cécile replied. 'If we do not come by morning, they will raise the alarm.'

'What alarm?' Bernard said. 'The village and the soldiers here are in the employ of Blanche de Bruyère.'

Madame Noubel frowned. 'I know, but Madame Boussay is not without influence.'

'Who is Madame Gabignaud?' Minou asked.

'She was, for some thirty years, the midwife in Puivert. She died last winter.'

'Was murdered, in fact, old Lizier told me,' Bernard said. 'She was worried about something in the days before her death. She gave him a letter to be taken to Carcassonne.'

'To whom?'

Bernard shook his head. 'Lizier didn't know. He cannot read.'

Minou caught her breath. 'It was for me. A warning, though I didn't realise it at first.'

'To you!' Cécile exclaimed.

'Tell us,' her father said quietly.

When she finished explaining about the strange note delivered to her in the bookshop, with what she now knew to be the Bruyère seal, Minou saw a glance pass between the two old friends. The three of them had filled the hours with talk about the present and the future, but no one yet had had the courage to lay bare the past.

'Each of us knows we might not survive the night,' Minou said. Her voice sounded too loud in the confined space. 'Even if we live to see the sun rise, we cannot know what Blanche de Bruyère intends to do.'

'Guilhem will help,' Bernard said quickly. 'You say you came to the castle with him, Cécile?'

'That's right.'

He frowned. 'He must have been sent on duty elsewhere. Normally, he would come to the Tour Bossue.'

'Perhaps he's part of the search party in the woods,' Madame Noubel said, though her expression was rigid. They had caught her and, given that she had been brought into Puivert by Guilhem, she feared for the boy. 'I'm sure that's it.'

Minou nodded. 'Anything might happen. Our friends might be able to help us, they might not. But, at this moment, we have to assume we are on our own.' She smiled at her father across the silver light of the cell, hoping to reassure him. 'The time has come. All those weeks ago, in rue du Trésau, you would not confide in me.'

'I could not.'

'I tried to respect your decision.'

'I regret my caution now. If I had trusted you, as Cécile counselled me, we might not find ourselves in so grievous a situation now.'

Still he hesitated. Minou could see the habit of keeping his own counsel ran so deep in him that it was hard to break.

'It is what Florence would have wanted, Bernard,' Cécile said.

'No more secrets, Father.'

In the woods, a crescendo of barking from the hunting dogs shattered the silence. Bernard jolted and looked to the window, then back to his daughter.

'Very well,' he said, his voice a mixture of defeat and relief. Minou waited. The only sound was the hiss of the torches burning in the passageway and howling from the dogs, more distant now, in the woods.

Finally, he began.

'Some twenty years ago, I was engaged as scribe to the Seigneur of Puivert. Florence was employed as lady-in-waiting to his young wife. Florence and I were recently married and had moved to quarters within the castle. Straight away, we realised our master was a hard man. He was not pious, though he made great show of being so. He imposed higher taxes than any of the other landowners hereabouts. The penalties for poaching or trespassing were harsh. I had to record the fines and punishments meted out, so saw it all at first hand. The women of the village knew to keep out of his way. He was also obsessed with having a son to inherit the estates and secure his legacy, even though it was believed he had bought the title from another.'

'He was a vile, damnèd man,' Cécile said.

'He was. When Florence and I first went to the château, we knew none of this. We learnt quickly enough, though. All I ask, Minou,' he said, 'is that you understand that I was only ever trying to do what I thought was best.'

Minou took his hand. 'You have always done your best for us all – me, Aimeric and Alis.'

'I made many mistakes. Too many.' Bernard leant back against the wall. 'Though I think much of what I am about to say will not come as a surprise to you.'

Through the window, the clouds scudded across the face of the moon. A single band of white light shone through the narrow opening, turning the straw on the ground to silver. Bernard put his hands on his knees, as if to anchor himself, then he began again. This time, his words were soft and elegant and Minou realised he was telling a story he had told himself many times before.

'You were born at dusk on the last day of October. The Eve of All Saints. It was a cold day in a wet autumn, grey showers trailing on a bitter wind. The air was thick with the smell of wood fires burning. To mark the feast day, sprigs of box wood and rosemary had been tied to the doors of the village houses to ward off evil spirits. At each road crossing and mountain track, informal shrines had sprung up. Posies of flowers wrapped in bright ribbon, invocations and scribbled prayers in the old language on scraps of cloth. The Seigneur was in the chapel. I may wrong him, but I doubt if he was at prayer. He was waiting for news to come down from the logis.'

He glanced at Minou. 'The thirty-first of October in the year fifteen hundred and forty-two.'

The atmosphere in the cell seemed to sharpen, as if the room itself was holding its breath.

'Do you understand, Minou?' he said quietly, his question rippling the surface of the silence like a stone falling into water.

'I do,' she said, astonished at how calm she felt. 'I didn't understand what it meant when I was younger, only that I knew I was different from my brother and sister. Aimeric and Alis, everything of their character and appearance spoke of a family resemblance. And when they stood next to Mother, they were like reflections in her glass: short and strong, where I am tall and thin; their skin dark, where mine is pale; all three of them with a mass of black curls, where my hair hangs as straight as a rod.'

She felt her father's eyes fix on her. 'And what of me?'

'I was not sure if you were my blood father or not,' she said. 'But even if not, it makes no difference. You raised me and taught me to love books, Mother taught me how to think.' She caught her breath. 'You both loved me. That is what matters. Not blood.'

In the pale moonlight filtering into the cell, she saw him smile.

'Florence and I loved you as much as if you were our own child,' he said, his voice cracked with emotion. 'Sometimes it felt as though we loved you more, though I am ashamed to admit it.'

Minou reached out and squeezed his hand.

Cécile Noubel chuckled. 'And didn't I say you were a fool

for imagining Minou would think anything else?' she said gruffly, a catch in her throat. 'You have been a good father, Bernard Joubert.'

Minou turned to Madame Noubel. 'And you were there,' she said, a statement not a question.

'Yes. I was Cécile Cordier then.'

'Tell me,' she said.

Bernard nodded. 'But you will help me, Cécile? If I forget anything, or my memory betrays me. Might we tell the story together?'

'We will.'

Now the atmosphere in the cell seemed to shift, to settle. Then, as they began to talk – a duet of their memories – Minou was taken back nineteen years. To the day she was born.

CHAPTER SIXTY-SEVEN

⚜

CHÂTEAU DE PUIVERT
31st October 1542

In the main bedchamber in the logis, the fire had burned low. The flames cracked with the last of the dried hawthorn taken from the valley of the river Blau in summer. Fresh straw lay on the floorboards around the bed, perfumed with dried herbs – rosemary and wild thyme – gathered from the hills around Puivert.

The bed curtains held the scent of winters past and the echo of the voices of all the women who had laboured in this chamber to bring Catholic daughters and sons into the world, their secrets kept safe in the embroidered folds of the hangings.

For hours, the servants had gone to and fro carrying copper pans of warm water up from the kitchens below, replacing the stained cloths with fresh strips of cotton. It was taking too long, the servants whispered. So much blood and yet still no child. They knew if their mistress was delivered of another daughter it would go ill for her. The master wanted a son. If it was a boy and did not survive, it would go ill for them all, especially the midwife, Anne Gabignaud.

The Seigneur had stationed the captain of his guard inside the chamber. A thin, birdlike man, with hooked face and craven manners, he was both disliked and feared. His master's spy. The scribe had also been ordered to be present. Unlike the captain, Bernard Joubert knew a birthing chamber was no place for men. He had set himself in the furthest corner to preserve the chatelaine's modesty.

Joubert's wife Florence, lady-in-waiting to Marguerite de Puivert, was at the bedside. Another woman from the village, Cécile Cordier, was also in attendance.

'How much longer?' the captain demanded, restless with waiting. His future was dependent on the fortunes of the de Bruyère family and his master's goodwill.

'Nature will take her course,' the midwife replied. 'These things cannot be hurried.'

Marguerite de Bruyère cried out as another contraction racked her weakened frame, and the captain stepped back in disgust.

Anne Gabignaud's expression had not altered during the twelve hours of the labour, but the truth shone clear in her eyes. She had seen more than fifty summers – and assisted at the births of many daughters and sons of Puivert – and did not believe the lady would survive her ordeal. Her will was spent, her body torn. The only question now was whether or not the child might be saved.

Florence Joubert was stroking Marguerite's head. Cécile Cordier passed to the midwife the things she needed – olive oil to help move things along, clean cloths, a tincture of warm honey and garlic to soothe the lady's dry lips.

'You are showing great fortitude,' Florence whispered, her face flushed with concern. 'You are nearly there.'

Marguerite cried out again and, this time, Madame Gabignaud made a decision. If she could not save her charge, she could at least afford her privacy and dignity at the hour of her departing. She drew Florence to her.

'The lady will not survive. I am sorry.'

'Is there nothing we can do?' Florence whispered.

'She has lost too much blood and, after the tragedy of her last confinement, she never fully recovered. But the child might.'

Florence met her eye, then nodded even though she knew she was going against the Seigneur's wishes.

'The chamber must be cleared,' she called out. 'The midwife asks for it.'

Bernard Joubert instantly stood up and gathered his papers. The captain stood his ground. 'I refuse,' he said. 'My express orders are to remain throughout.'

Florence took a step towards him. 'If your presence influences things for the ill – as well it might – and it becomes known that you went against the advice of the midwife, your master will not thank you.'

The captain hesitated. Even he would not deny that, in the matter of childbirth, a woman's word carried more authority than that of a man. He turned on the scribe instead.

'On your head be it, Joubert,' he said. 'This is your wife's doing. You are to remain outside the chamber and the door is to be open.'

'As you wish,' Bernard answered mildly.

'I am to be summoned the instant there is news,' he said, turning back to Florence. 'I insist upon it, the very instant.'

She met his gaze. 'I will summon you when there is something for you to tell your master, not a moment sooner.'

'The door is to remain open, do you hear me?'

'I hear you.'

When she was sure he was gone, Florence breathed a sigh of relief. She glanced at Cécile Cordier, both of them wondering what price would be paid for this small victory. Then another pitiful cry drew them back to the bedside.

'Close the curtains,' Florence said.

After twelve long hours of labour, the three women worked in silence around the bed. The sheets were changed again, the soiled straw was cleared from the floor and fresh laid, but the smell of blood lingered. The scent of death. When the next run of contractions came, Marguerite barely made a sound.

The Tramontana wind was blowing harder, rattling through the gaps in the shutters and gusting in the hearth, sending flurries of ash like black snow into the room. Suddenly, Marguerite opened her eyes and stared ahead. Her eyes were extraordinary and opposite, one the colour of cornflowers and the other like leaves in autumn. Growing dim now.

'Florence? Florence, my dear friend, are you here? I cannot see.'

'I'm here.'

'I must write . . . can you fetch me –'

Florence nodded and, without a word being exchanged, Cécile crossed the room to the escritoire where Bernard Joubert had been stationed. She took a quill and paper bearing the Bruyère seal, and rushed back to the bedside.

'Shall I write something for you?' Florence asked.

Marguerite shook her head. 'This I must do for myself. Can you help me sit?'

'She should not move,' the midwife said, but Florence and Cécile moved to either side of Marguerite and placed a pillow beneath her right hand.

'*This is the day of my death*.'

Marguerite half spoke, half mouthed the words out loud as she wrote, as if to remind herself of what she wanted to set down.

'*As the Lord God is my witness, here, by my own hand, do I set this down. My last Will and Testament*.'

They could all see how much effort it cost her, witnessed

the painful and slow scratch of the quill, the black teardrops on the page.

'*Merci*,' Marguerite said when the document was done. 'Will you witness my words?' Florence quickly signed her name at the bottom of the paper, Cécile too.

'There,' Marguerite said. 'Keep it safe, Florence. If the child lives, it should not lack for anything.'

She sent a whisper of breath across the surface to dry the ink, then sank back exhausted on her pillows.

Madame Gabignaud smoothed away a strand of brown hair from Marguerite's face. She pressed a cold compress to her brow as another contraction gripped her, then receded.

'Beneath the mattress, Florence,' she whispered. 'I would have it with me.'

Despite knowing they could all be hung for heretics should this act of rebellion be discovered, Florence reached down and pulled out the forbidden Protestant bible she knew Marguerite kept hidden there. She placed it into her mistress's hands.

'Here,' she said.

'You will look after my child. Don't let—' Her words were lost in the pain of another contraction.

'This time, try to push,' the midwife said.

'You will look after the child,' Marguerite gasped.

'There will be no need, for you will be there,' Florence said, though she knew she was lying. 'Once more, then you can rest.'

Obedient to the last, Marguerite found the strength.

At that moment, the last of the light slipped from the sky, plunging the bedchamber into shadow. She cried out again, not in pain or sorrow this time, but release.

'It's a girl,' the midwife whispered, sweeping the child up and quickly tying the birth cord.

'Alive?' Florence whispered, fearful because the baby had not made a sound.

'Yes. She's a good colour and has a strong grip.'

The midwife cleaned and swaddled the baby, handed her to Florence, then turned her attention to Marguerite.

'You have a beautiful, healthy daughter,' Florence said, leaning over the bed. 'Look.'

Marguerite's eyes fluttered. 'She lives?'

'She is the image of you.'

'Thank God,' she murmured, then her eyes widened in panic. 'Do not let him take her, not like my other little ones. Keep her safe.'

'You must save your strength,' Madame Gabignaud was saying, though she knew it was no good. The bleeding could not be stemmed. 'It will be best if you lie still.'

'Florence, promise. Don't let him take her.'

As the bells began to ring for five o'clock, Marguerite gave a long, low sigh. Her expression was serene. She murmured a French prayer as her soul took flight. She had no need of an intermediary. She believed her God was waiting to welcome her home.

The chamber was quiet at last.

'She's gone,' Cécile said, bowing her head.

'The pity of it,' the midwife said. She had seen death many times, but this loss touched her greatly. 'Why is it always the good who are taken before their time? If there is a God, then tell me that.'

Florence kissed Marguerite on her forehead, already seeming to be growing cold, then pulled the sheet up over her sweet face. She would not let herself cry now. She would not grieve yet. There was too much to be done.

Five o'clock on the Eve of All Saints.

CHAPTER SIXTY-EIGHT

⚜

Château de Puivert
Friday, 22nd May, 1562

'The Eve of All Saints,' said Cécile quietly. 'Nineteen years ago, though it could be yesterday.'

Bernard nodded.

Lulled by their voices, Minou blinked, surprised to find herself still in the cell. It was not yet dawn, but there was a gathering light in the sky that suggested morning was not far away. Their words hung heavy in the air, colliding with myriad questions in her head. She hardly knew where to begin. She looked to her father, then back to Madame Noubel.

'I understand the kind of man Lord Bruyère was, but to deny him his own child? Why was it so important that he believed I had not survived?'

'You were a girl,' Bernard said simply. 'Marguerite had, a year previously, given birth to twin girls. Taken from her hours after their delivery to be examined by a physician, on her husband's orders. She never saw them again. Both were found dead in their cradles.'

'Both? At the same time?' Minou asked.

Cécile nodded. 'The common belief was that he had ordered them to be killed. Everyone thought so, though there was no proof.'

'His own children . . .' Minou murmured, horrified.

Bernard shook his head. 'He wanted a son. Was desperate

for an heir to inherit his estates. He had no interest in supporting daughters, who would grow up to require dowries or take his lands into another family.'

'He was a wicked man,' Cécile said.

'That is more than wickedness,' Minou said. 'A mortal sin.'

Bernard leant forward. 'And Florence was certain the same thing would happen to you, which is why she gave her word to Marguerite.'

Minou shook her head, thinking more about what Marguerite must have suffered.

'There was no time to talk about it before it happened. Suddenly, I heard the door below slam and the captain shouting at the servants to get out of his way. I could hear him on the stairs. There was no time to think.'

'I have no doubt,' Cécile said, 'that the only consideration in Florence's mind was how to protect you. She took charge and, without a word being spoken, she selected the most stained of the delivery cloths and handed them to the midwife, who understood. Madame Gabignaud wrapped the foul material around you, to discourage attention, and held you tight. I rushed to replace the quill, paper and ink on the escritoire.'

'And still you didn't make a sound,' Bernard added, 'as if you knew your life was at stake.'

'We were only just in time. The captain stormed into the room and dragged open the bed curtains, setting the rings rattling on the rail, demanding to know what was happening. Florence stepped back to allow him sight of the bed and told him how the Lord had not seen fit to grace the Lady Marguerite with His mercy. At this, the captain turned white.

'"She is dead?" he demanded. Florence pulled back the edge of the sheet to reveal her marble face and, for a moment, the captain was silent. Then he asked about you. Florence crossed herself and explained that, to the great sorrow of us all, the child was born dead.

'"But I heard a cry," he said.

'Now Florence looked him in the eye, as if defying him to contradict her, and told him it was not the cry of a child, but rather our poor lady at the moment of her departing.'

Cecile Noubel smiled. 'It was pitiful at how eagerly the captain clutched at this, Minou. Stumbling over his words, asking if it was true that the child had been another girl. Florence gestured for Madame Gabignaud to come forward and asked if he would like to see the baby for himself. Of course, Minou, if you had cried then all would have been lost.' She shook her head. 'But the captain's stomach was not strong enough. He, who signed the warrants for those the Seigneur condemned to a flogging or hanging, in truth could not endure the sight of blood.'

'Like so many who are bullies, he was a coward at heart,' Bernard said. 'He hid behind his authority. By now, the church had struck the half-hour and it was dark outside. Since the dead child was a girl, the captain persuaded himself that what he had seen was proof enough.'

Cécile nodded. 'He told Florence to dispose of the body. She immediately stepped away from the bed, drawing him with her, and pulled the curtains shut, leaving me and the midwife, holding you inside. "If you would offer your master our condolences on the tragic loss of his wife and child," I heard her say, "I would be in your debt. There are things we must attend to here."'

'I have no doubt he heard the rebuke beneath Florence's words,' Bernard said, 'but the captain was the kind who thought only of his own situation. He did not want to be the bearer of bad news and decided I should act as his shield. "Come with me, Joubert, we will go together. You are the other witness." I had no choice but to comply but, as I left the chamber, Florence whispered we should meet at Madame Gabignaud's house later that night.'

'When the men had gone,' Cécile said, 'at first we did not speak at all. Any stray word might have given us away. But we knew you would not sleep for much longer – and when you did wake, you would cry for food – so we had to act quickly. It was agreed I would stay and lay out the body, in case the Seigneur came to pay his last respects to his wife.'

'You did not fear he might wish to see the body of his child as well?' Minou asked.

'We did,' Cécile said, 'but it was a chance we had to take. We knew he had no interest in a daughter, and feared if he had sight of you, well . . .' She broke off.

'I understand,' Minou said quietly.

'We could not risk your life. Florence smuggled you out of the castle in a panier, and down to the village.'

'Over the course of the next week,' Bernard said, 'Florence and I visited when we could. Madame Gabignaud found a wet nurse, who asked no questions. Cécile looked after you.'

Minou smiled. 'It was you who sang the lullaby to me.'

'Fancy you remembering,' Madame Noubel said, and sang the first few lines:

'*Bona nuèit, bona nuèit . . .*
Braves amics, pica mièja-nuèit
Cal finir velhada.'

Minou nodded. 'Even though I couldn't understand the words, I never forgot them. They stayed in my memory.'

'It is an old Occitan song.'

Bernard smiled. 'Anyway, you thrived. You grew stronger each day and we tried to decide what to do in the longer term. Cécile had her own husband to attend to, I had my responsibilities at the castle. Only Florence was relieved of her duties now her mistress was gone.'

'Marguerite was buried a week after her death, with little ceremony, in the grounds of the castle,' Madame Noubel continued. 'Then at Advent, it was given out that the Lord Bruyère was to marry again. The village disapproved of his haste, but he cared nothing for the good opinion of his subjects. The girl brought with her a substantial dowry and her own household servants.'

Bernard nodded. 'Florence and I saw our chance to leave. In December, I asked to be released from my duties. The captain, for once, spoke on our behalf. He was scared of Florence, in truth, and wanted to see the back of us.' He smiled. 'By the following spring, Florence and I were settled with our young daughter – you – in Carcassonne. A little house in La Cité, modest premises in the Bastide. We put the past behind us.' He raised his head. 'And you know, we never regretted what we did for a moment.'

'Nor should you,' Cécile said.

'Six years later, we were blessed with Aimeric and then, another six years later, with Alis. You doted on your little brother and sister. We always said we would tell you the truth of your origins when the time was right. Somehow that day never came and when Florence died, I lost heart. Besides, until then, everything was fine. Our business was doing well, we were content. We had all we needed. I suppose I put it all from my mind. Florence had told me the Will was in a safe place. I assumed she had concealed it within the château itself. That is why I came back to Puivert, to search for it.'

For a moment, Minou was silent, thinking of the great risks taken to save her life and how the three old friends had guarded the secret for nearly twenty years. Then, her darkening thoughts brought her back to the present.

'How did Blanche de Puivert find me?'

Anguish flooded her father's face. 'It was my fault.'

'Tell her, Bernard,' Cécile said.

He nodded. 'In January, on my way back to Carcassonne, I was arrested in Toulouse and taken to the inquisitional prison there.'

'Dearest Father,' Minou murmured in distress, 'why did you not tell me?'

'I could not.' Bernard shook his head. 'I was held in a cell with Michel Cazès. He suffered more terribly than did I. At night, we talked – to keep the fear at bay – and I spoke of this. Of the truth of your arrival into the world.' He dropped his head. 'He was stretched, I heard it. He must have told the inquisitors. It is my fault he is dead.'

'It is not,' Cécile said briskly. 'You take too much responsibility on your shoulders, Bernard. It was the death of the old sinner here that set things in motion. From the moment he died, Blanche de Bruyère was desperate to shore up her own position. She had heard the rumours about a child who had survived.'

'But how?' Bernard cried.

'From everything I have heard, it's my belief that Madame Gabignaud was forced to talk before she was murdered. You said the letter you received in Carcassonne had the Bruyère seal on it, Minou?'

'Yes.'

'Is it not likely that Blanche had been in communication

with Madame Gabignaud? How else would she have access to a piece of Blanche's writing paper?'

Minou nodded. 'Then, when Blanche had got what she wanted, she murdered her.'

'I fear so.' Madame Noubel paused. 'Or the captain who was there on the day of your birth might have admitted to someone he had never actually seen the baby. Even old Lizier's wife in the cottage next door might have seen our comings and goings, and put two and two together. The point is, Bernard, there are many ways the rumour could have spread. We will never know. All I do know is that it is not your fault.'

Minou's head was spinning with conflicting thoughts, her heart knotted with warring emotions. It was hard to absorb the tragedy of Marguerite's death and the courage of her parents. But what did any of it actually matter in the long term? Was she a different person because of the circumstances of her birth?

Suddenly, Minou felt an intense longing to talk to Piet. Wouldn't he help her to make sense of things? Then, she thought how pleased he would be to learn that her birth mother had been a Huguenot.

She glanced at the window where a pale dawn was giving shape to the ghostly outline of the trees. Was he still out there in the woods? Was he looking for her? Or had they caught him too?

She pushed the thought from her mind.

'Florence's intention was always,' her father continued, 'that once the Seigneur of Puivert was dead, you should have the right to decide whether you wished to claim your inheritance.'

'There are no other children?' Minou asked.

'None, though Guilhem told me Blanche de Bruyère is expecting. No one believes it is the late Seigneur's child, but if it is a boy, it would be first in line to inherit. As for the question of your claim, I don't even know whether the Will is still in existence.'

Minou sighed. 'It does exist, I have it. Mother concealed it within Marguerite's bible, and sent it to her sister in Toulouse.'

'To Salvadora?' Cécile said. 'How extraordinary.'

'Does Madame Boussay still have it in her possession?' asked Bernard.

'Yes, at least she did until a few days ago. My aunt also lived in terror of her husband. When the gift arrived, Monsieur Boussay refused to allow her to keep a Protestant bible. For once, she defied him and hid it in the church opposite their house in Toulouse, where it remained until I retrieved it no more than a week ago. I sewed it into the lining of my cloak, along with . . . something else of value, and gave the cloak into Aimeric's care when we were stopped trying to leave Toulouse.' She paused. 'I pray he still has possession of it.'

Madame Noubel clapped her hands. 'That green woollen cloak, I thought I recognised it. Aimeric was wearing it when we met yesterday in the village, and very odd it looked on him. A silver dagger at his waist too.'

Minou smiled, remembering how proud her brother had been when Piet gave him the gift of the knife.

'The pity of it is that I would never have made a claim on the estate. I would have been content to sign over my rights to her.'

There was a noise in the passageway, and they all turned towards the door of the cell.

'Someone's coming,' Cécile whispered.

'It could be Guilhem,' Bernard said hopefully. 'Or the changing of the guard at first light.'

'Or she has finally come for me.' Minou stood up. 'I am ready.'

It is dawn. I have ordered her to be brought to me in the forest.

I have left Valentin sleeping in my chamber – and he will sleep a while longer. He dreams of power and majesty and glory. He imagines himself on the bishop's throne. Toulouse today, then Lyon tomorrow, perhaps even Rome. He sees himself interpreting Holy Scripture and leading our Mother Church.

He has raised himself higher than God.

The voices in my head are loud, persistent now. They tell me I should no longer trust him. Valentin says if he can barely tell the replica from the original, then what chance any other will? He says once the counterfeit Shroud is placed behind glass, none will know it for what it is.

An illusion.

But God will know. He sees everything.

It has taken me a long time to see it, but now I understand. For all his talk of serving God, it is actually the man he wants, not the recovery of God's precious relic. Piet Reydon has become an obsession with him. Valentin cannot bear that he was outwitted – and by one once so close to his heart. When love turns to hate, it is the strongest and most violent of emotions. I knew this when I killed my father. My late husband knew this when I murdered him, too.

Minou Joubert is my enemy.

Were it not for Valentin staying my hand, I would have killed her at the moment of her capture. He spares her only because he thinks she will bring him to Reydon. He would play the inquisitor until she gives him the information he wants.

What I want is her death. God has told me to do this. He speaks to me, and I listen. It is He who guides my hand.

It must be death by fire. The burning chambers, the purification of the soul. If her spirit is pure then it will fly to heaven. If it is not, then the Devil will take her.

Is it not written that there is a time to weep, and a time to laugh; a time to mourn, and a time to dance?

This is where it ends. In fire and in flame.

CHAPTER SIXTY-NINE

⚜

'It's nearly light,' Piet said, drawing up his knees and wrapping his cloak around his legs. 'Something must happen soon.'

'Maybe.' Bérenger yawned. 'Maybe not.'

They had spent the night hiding in the woods. It was Bérenger who had knocked Piet down – assuming he was part of the Puivert garrison – and Piet who had swung at Bérenger, thinking him the killer of the young soldier he now knew to be Guilhem Lizier.

As the dogs and the flaming torches of the search party had come closer to their hiding place, then closer still, they had been forced deeper into the wood, lower down the hill. In the end, they had decided to wait until morning before trying to find out what had happened.

'I've seen a fair few mornings,' Bérenger said, 'though none as fine as this. This is wonderful country.'

'You're a man of the city?'

'Carcassonnais born and bred. Travelled around with the garrison, of course. I spent six months in the Italian Wars, but otherwise never stayed anywhere longer than a month or two. In the end, La Cité always called me back.' He coughed, expelling the night air from his lungs. 'What about you? A city boy yourself?'

Piet nodded. 'My father was French, from Montpellier. I never knew him. My mother never said a bad word about him, though the truth of the matter is he abandoned her in Amsterdam.'

'She was Dutch?'

'Yes. She died when I was seven, but I was lucky enough to be taken up by a Catholic gentleman, a rare Christian who carried the teachings of the Bible into his daily life. He paid for me to study and I was quick at lessons, so later he sent me to college in Toulouse. He even left me a generous legacy in his Will.'

'But you are not a Catholic,' Bérenger said.

'I was then.'

'A Huguenot now, though.'

'Yes.'

Silence fell between them.

'And what does Madomaisèla Minou think her father will have to say about that?' Bérenger asked eventually.

As the extent of the old soldier's admiration for the Joubert family had become clear during the course of the night, Piet had found himself confiding in Bérenger about his love for Minou.

'I don't know,' he said honestly. 'What do you think, Bérenger? You know what manner of man he is. Do you think Bernard Joubert might look favourably on me, even though I'm not Catholic?'

Bérenger gave an earthy laugh. 'If we survive this, my friend, and bring Minou home, I warrant he will grant you anything.'

Piet stared at him, then laughed. 'Well said, my friend. I hope you're right.'

Then suddenly, he stopped.

'Did you hear something?' Piet drew his dagger and got to his feet. 'Coming from over there.'

Bérenger stood up and drew his sword, then stepped

silently into the shadow of the tree on the opposite side of the woodland track.

For a moment, they heard nothing more. Then, the creep of footsteps on the dry leaves at the fringes of the woods, a stone kicked out of place and the sharp snap of a dry branch.

Piet held up one finger.

They waited until the stranger drew level with the trees, then Piet leapt out and had the flat of his dagger against the man's throat before he had a chance to cry out.

'If you make a sound, I'll kill you.'

Alis heard the dogs outside, and saw the flickering of the torches in the woods through her window, and cried to be released. No one came and finally she fell asleep on the hard chair, her head lolled back against the top rail and her wrists still bound to the seat.

A noise woke her. She opened her eyes and saw the sun was rising, filling the chamber with pale yellow light. She was stiff and cold, her neck hurt and she was in desperate need of the pot. She was also hungry and realised that, although she was still frightened, things did not feel quite so bleak as they had in the dark of the night.

She was alone in the room now. The nurse was gone and there was no sign of Monsignor Valentin's manservant, the one with the scar on his face. Then Alis remembered he had been sent to escort the apothecary back to the village.

She shivered. What if no one came back? What if they forgot all about her and she was left to starve to death? Would someone find her here in years to come, a pile of bones? Quickly, to push the dark thoughts away, Alis shut her eyes and thought of her tabby kitten. It wouldn't be a kitten anymore. She hoped Rixende and Madame Noubel were being kind and that it wouldn't have forgotten her. She could no longer bear to think of Minou or Aimeric or her father. The pain of being separated for so long pulled too hard at her heart.

She heard a noise in the passageway outside. Her heart leapt with relief.

'Hello?'

The door opened. Alis blinked. Blanche was dressed all in white – white gown, with a silver *fleur-de-lys*, and a white cloak with a satin trim. She looked like an angel. How strange someone who was so beautiful could be so bad.

'It is time to go,' she said.

'Where are we going?'

Blanche didn't answer. She tied a cord around Alis's neck, like a noose, to stop her from running away, before cutting the ties on her wrists with her knife.

'If you try to run away, I will kill you,' she said, her voice strange and flat. Then she looked up to the sky. 'I will kill her.'

'Who are you talking to?' Alis asked.

Blanche did not answer.

'Where are we going?' she repeated.

Blanche gave a slow, strange smile. 'Didn't I tell you your sister would come for you? Well, now she is here. God has brought her to me. Minou is here. She is waiting for you in the woods.'

Caught between hope and terror, Alis felt her stomach lurch. She wanted it to be true, at the same time prayed it was not.

'I don't believe you.'

'I'm going to take you to her,' Blanche said, in the same dead voice.

Alis feared Blanche was mad. Her eyes were so bright, but yet she did not seem to be looking at anything. Her hands kept clenching and unclenching, then fanning out across her swollen belly.

'Why can't Minou come here to the logis?' Alis managed to say.

'She is in the woods. I'm going to take you to her.'

'For pity's sake, boy,' Bérenger said, 'keep your voice down.'

'Aimeric,' hissed Piet, 'by all that's holy! What the Devil are you playing at!'

'Piet. You got out. You're alive!'

'So are you, though you were seconds from being dead. What are you doing skulking about the woods like this? Are you trying to get yourself killed?'

'Madame Noubel and Bérenger were supposed to come back to the village with Alis. They didn't. I was getting worried, so I thought I'd come to see. Aunt Boussay didn't want me to go.' He raised his eyes and fixed Piet with a stare. 'But is Minou with you, Piet? Is she safe?'

Piet felt instantly guilty for being so harsh. 'I don't know. We left Toulouse together and followed you here. You have Minou's cloak, I see.'

'She told me not to let it out of my sight, so I haven't. But where is Minou? She's all right, isn't she?'

Piet put his hand on Aimeric's shoulder. 'We were together last night until it got dark. I heard something in the woods and went to investigate. There I found a man dead. He'd been stabbed.'

'Guilhem Lizier,' Bérenger said quietly.

'Oh.'

'Bérenger and I found one another,' Piet continued. 'He was waiting for Madame Noubel. By the time I returned to where I'd left Minou, she had gone.'

'They are both taken?' Aimeric said, his face falling.

'We don't know that,' Bérenger said.

'Perhaps,' said Piet.

All three looked back through the pale dappled light of the woods in the direction of the castle walls.

'In there, do you think?' Aimeric said.

'We don't know, but we intend to find out.' Piet hesitated, then held out his hand. 'Will you help us?'

'You're going to let me come with you?' Aimeric said.

'Better than leaving you out here on your own causing trouble,' Bérenger said gruffly.

'I will do my best.'

Piet shook his hand. 'I think you've earnt it. You're not a bad swordsman now.'

Bérenger cuffed him on the shoulder. 'Though mind you do as you're told. None of your usual tricks.'

Aimeric's hand went to the silver blade at his waist. 'One day, I'll be as good as you, Piet. Maybe better.'

'Where are you taking me?'

The two soldiers had led her from the cell in silence. In the watery morning light, they had walked into a large courtyard, ringed by grey stone walls set with high lookout towers. They crossed the courtyard to the squat gatehouse that stood at the main entrance to the castle.

Minou didn't understand. She could see the keep, towering high into the air behind them. Her father had said that was where the family's lodgings were. Where Blanche de Bruyère had her chambers. Why wasn't she being taken there?

They pushed her forward over a wooden drawbridge. They seemed to be heading back to the woods where she and Piet had taken refuge last night.

Then she saw two other soldiers standing at the edge of the forest. One had a coil of rope over his arm, the other what looked like a pile of rags. Both also held flaming torches. As they got nearer, Minou picked up the smell of oil on the still morning air.

'What's happening?' she said. Her voice sounded as if it was coming from a long way away. One of the men looked like he wanted to speak, but when she met his eye, he looked away. 'Tell me. Please, I –'

Her courage wavered. She had expected to be questioned. To be taken before Blanche de Bruyère. To be allowed to see Alis.

But this? Was she to be executed? No chance to speak or defend herself? No chance to say goodbye to those she loved?

She tried to gather her strength. The dew was seeping through her boots and her feet were wet, but the light was dappling through the green canopy of leaves and the forest was beautiful. For a fleeting moment, Minou imagined herself with Piet, side by side, and thought how wonderful it would be to live their lives together in a place such as this.

CHAPTER SEVENTY

⚜

Madame Boussay was sick with worry. Not only had Bérenger and Madame Noubel failed to return with little Alis, but she had woken to find Aimeric had vanished, too.

'I didn't see him go, but I wager he's gone to the castle,' Achille Lizier said, when roused from sleep. 'The young gentleman didn't appreciate being left behind last evening. He made no secret of it.'

'He is a restless boy,' she said.

She had carefully listened to everything Cécile Noubel, Bérenger and Guilhem Lizier had discussed the previous evening. On balance, she had come to the conclusion that they had all been too quick to assume the worst. The facts spoke against their interpretation of things. Blanche de Bruyère was a devout and pious Catholic, on that everyone agreed. She even had her own priest-confessor. Her patronage and good works for the churches in Puivert and villages further afield were well known. She was a gentlewoman, the chatelaine of a large and rich estate, and she was expecting her first child within weeks. In the light of all these considerations, Madame Boussay found it hard to imagine that such a person would be involved in the kidnapping of a child or the imprisonment of Bernard Joubert. Her brother-in-law was a moderate man, a bookseller and – despite the regrettable range of the works he sold – a faithful Catholic.

'Lizier,' she said, 'I intend to go to the château myself and pay my respects to Lady Bruyère in person. I'm certain this is all a misunderstanding and can quickly be resolved.'

Lizier frowned, caught between deference and common sense.

'Forgive me, Madama, but is that wise? Cécile Cordier was—'

'Madame Noubel is a fine woman,' she said sharply. 'No doubt she believes her fears justified. But Alis is my niece. And if, as you suggest, my nephew Aimeric has now taken it upon himself to go to the castle, then I should be with them.'

'But –'

'Make the arrangements, please.'

Reluctantly, Lizier hurried into the village. Within a quarter of an hour, the groom had been roused from his bed and a horse was bridled. As the sun came up over the distant hillside and lit the valley, the church bell rang for six o'clock. The carriage was already rattling its way up the switchback track towards the castle gates.

'Only through fire can we be redeemed and purified,' Blanche said, forcing Alis forward with the point of a knife. 'We are all sinners. Fallen, corrupted by the Devil's work. But we can be saved. The Burning Chambers, though the Huguenots denounce them, are a beautiful gift. It is the only way to save those who have turned their face from God, from salvation, from the endless damnation of their heresy.'

Alis didn't speak and kept her head bowed, though her eyes were darting to left and right. The cord was loose around her neck, and she thought that if she could take Blanche by surprise, she might be able to snatch the end of the tether from her hands and run into the woods.

But if she did manage to escape and it was true that Minou was waiting for her, what would happen then?

'Only with fire can sin be defeated,' Blanche was muttering, as if talking to herself. 'Evil will be vanquished. God's kingdom on earth will be made pure again. We will drive them out, the heretics and the blasphemers and those who disobey His laws.'

Alis thought Blanche had lost her wits. Her mood seemed to swing from ecstatic in the one moment to anguish in the next. She kept looking up to the sky, conducting a conversation with the clouds, just like poor Charles Sanchez in Carcassonne.

They left the shadow of the castle and stepped out into the morning. The sun was starting to paint the valley golden.

'You said Minou would be here,' Alis said.

'They are bringing her,' Blanche said, pushing her forward. 'She will be so pleased to see you. You can be together in the life everlasting.'

Vidal woke to find the bed empty and Blanche gone.

Quickly, he sat up, setting his head spinning. A wave of nausea rocked him, like water at the bottom of a scuttled boat. When the chamber stopped spinning, he picked up the goblet beside the bed and sniffed the dregs of the liquid. He felt heavy, weighted down, as if his limbs did not belong to him.

Had he been drugged?

Vidal swung his legs over the side of the bed. Again, the movement sent his head spinning. It felt like iron, not blood in his veins, and like an old and wounded animal, he could barely move.

Slowly, he stood up. His robes and crucifix were scattered on the floor, where she had pulled them from him in the heat of their lovemaking. He was relieved to see her black dress hanging on the back of the door. Perhaps Blanche had only gone to wash. Then he realised her white underskirt, and the ornate rosary that she always carried, were both missing. When he bent down to pick up his crucifix, he saw her shoes were no longer there.

Had she gone to the dungeon without him? He prayed she had not. Her behaviour had been becoming increasingly alarming. Ungoverned. She was afflicted with some deep melancholy in the one instant, then an ecstasy of equal passion in the next. Was it the baby that so affected Blanche's wits? Would she return to herself after the birth, or was she changed forever?

No, the affair must end. He would take steps to distance himself from her and from Puivert. He had already intended to go north into the Tarn, before returning to Toulouse. This confirmed that was the right decision.

Once dressed, Vidal made his way down the winding stone stairs of the keep, looking into each chamber in search of her.

'Lady Bruyère? Blanche? Are you here?'

She was not in the musicians' gallery, nor the chapel.

He descended another flight and stepped out into the courtyard as the bells of the village church chimed the half-hour. What time was it? From the light, between six and seven o'clock in the morning? The grass glistered with dew, but sun was painting the tops of the towers golden.

Vidal went into the logis. Servants bowed and moved out of his way. Taking the stairs two at a time, his muscles fighting him every step of the way, he burst into the chamber where the child had been held.

An empty chair, the ties cut in half and lying on the floor.

He felt a kind of panic mounting in his chest as he doubled back, trying to run. He staggered from the upper to the lower courtyard, heading for the Tour Bossue, when Bonal came rushing to meet him.

'Monsignor, I had not thought to see you so early.'

'What is the hour?'

'The clock has struck the half after six.'

Vidal paused, a wave of nausea felling him.

'Have you seen the Lady Blanche?'

'I thought she was with . . .' he began, then remembered himself. 'I thought the lady to be in her chamber, Monsignor.'

'She was, but is no longer. The girl is gone too.'

Bonal's eyes narrowed. 'No one has come through the gatehouse.'

Vidal waved his arms. 'Where is she? We must find her.'

'I know not, Monsignor. I can report, however, the grave news that Paul Cordier slipped from the path in the dark and fell. He is not expected to recover.'

Vidal nodded, then another surge of sickness hit him, and he swayed. Bonal stepped forward and caught him only just in time.

'Is there something wrong, Monsignor? Are you unwell?'

'I . . . she . . .' He steadied himself. 'Fetch the captain. I would have access to the dungeons.'

'I don't think I should leave you –'

'Go!' Vidal shouted, his voice echoing through the silence of the courtyard.

Bonal bowed, then the sound of raised voices at the gatehouse made them both turn.

'No. Madame,' a guard was insisting. 'If you please. You cannot come in without permission. My lady does not allow –'

Vidal frowned, trying to focus on the short and stout figure striding into the courtyard. A familiar figure, but in unfamiliar surroundings. There was the same look of consternation on Bonal's face.

'Forgive me, Monsignor, but is that not the wife of Monsieur Boussay?'

Salvadora Boussay did not like to arrive unannounced.

In Toulouse, there was a correct way to do things and she took great pains not to make mistakes. The wives of the other secretaries at the Hôtel de Ville were quick to judge and it made her husband angry when she embarrassed him. But these were strange circumstances. Madame Boussay put her qualms to one side and, ignoring the continuing protests of the guard at her back, walked towards the keep.

It was only then she realised the courtyard wasn't empty. There were two men, standing close together. She frowned, then she realised one wore the red robes of a priest, and she was reassured.

Her relief lasted only an instant. If his robes made him look like any other, his hair gave him away. Jet black with a white streak. Momentarily, she weakened. Was her flight known? Had her husband sent Monsignor Valentin to bring her back?

But how would he know she was here? He couldn't possibly.

The experiences of the past week travelling with her nephew had given her a new strength. She raised her chin. She would brazen it out.

'Monsignor Valentin,' she said graciously. 'What a great surprise to see you here, a very joyous surprise, yes indeed. Are you here to visit Lady Bruyère also?'

To her astonishment, she saw panic flare in the priest's eyes, though it was quickly masked.

'You are well met, Madame Boussay. As you say, a surprise.'

He glanced over her shoulder. 'And your noble husband? Monsieur Boussay is accompanying you?'

'He is not,' she said calmly. 'He is always thinking of my welfare, so thought Puivert would be safer while the situation in Toulouse resolved itself. And you, Monsignor Valentin? Are you avoiding the troubles?'

'Not at all. The chatelaine is only recently widowed,' he said. 'With a child due at any time, there is need for spiritual guidance.'

Madame Boussay inclined her head. 'Of course. How good of you to come so far to fulfil your duties. It is no wonder my husband speaks so highly of you.'

For a moment, they held one another's gaze. Both smiled insincerely. The stalemate was broken by his manservant, who had withdrawn during the conversation, reappearing at his master's shoulder and whispering in his ear.

Vidal's eyes widened. 'What did you say?'

'It appears that the woods are on fire,' Bonal repeated, not caring to drop his voice. 'And the nurse says she saw Lady Blanche and the child walking that way before dawn.'

CHAPTER SEVENTY-ONE

⚜

With the soldiers flanking her on either side, Minou walked on through the trees. She could hear the crackle and hiss of green branches burning. The pungent smoke came slinking eerily through the woods like a black mist.

Minou reached the glade, and stopped.

For a moment, her eyes couldn't make sense of what she was seeing. It was like a painting, an arranged tableau, the light and the colours and the style all speaking to an artist's hand. The early sun filtered through the canopy of fresh spring leaves, a whole spectrum of yellows and greens and silvers. On the far side of the clearing, a line of beech and alder looked like sentinels marking the boundary. Behind them, the rougher brown trunks of the evergreens stood in the deeper forest.

She raised her bound hands to shield her face from the heat of the flames.

In the centre of the glade, the fire was burning. Built on the foundation of a rotting fallen tree, its roots twisted like an old man's hand, it glowed red in its hollow centre and charred black on the outside. On top of it had been piled branches and hewn planks of old timber, the flames licking and darting between the gaps.

Then Minou heard singing.

'*Veni Creator Spiritus,*

Mentes tuorum visita . . .'

The same few words over and again, the battle hymn said

to have been sung by the Crusader armies as they massacred the Cathars of Béziers and La Cité.

'Come, Holy Spirit,

And in our souls take up Thy rest.'

Despite the fierce heat, Minou shivered. She glanced at the soldiers beside her, then saw a wooden stake had been hammered into the ground. And though it made no sense that such a thing could be happening – on a May morning in Puivert – she understood that a pyre had been built.

A hundred paces beyond the glade to the north, two men and a boy crouched in the undergrowth.

'Why would anyone be wanting to build a fire here, of all places?' Bérenger muttered. 'If the wind changes, the whole woods could go up. It's so dry.'

'What can you see?' Aimeric hissed.

'Nothing much. The smoke's too thick.'

'Someone's singing.'

'I can hear it too,' Piet said; the thin sound carried on the breeze above the cracking of the fire.

The air cleared for a brief moment of clarity.

'Hold, I can see someone,' he said. 'A priest, I think. In white robes. Some kind of special service for Pentecost? What say you, Bérenger? Could it be some older ritual observed up here in the mountains?'

'We don't have anything like it in Carcassonne, that's a fact.'

Piet turned back. 'In fact, no. It's not a priest. It's a woman.'

'Madame Noubel?' Bérenger said quickly.

'I'm sorry, my friend, no. Younger. Black hair.'

Bérenger drew breath. 'Could it be Blanche de Bruyère? I

only had that one glimpse of her in La Cité, but her hair's as black as a crow's wing.'

'And she has someone with her. A child.' Piet beckoned Aimeric to join him, putting his hands on the boy's shoulders. 'Is that Alis?'

Piet felt him tense when he saw the rope around the girl's neck.

'Yes, that's her. My little sister.'

Aimeric's hand went to his dagger.

'No,' Piet said quickly, pulling him back. 'We will save Alis, but we've got to be careful. If we act too soon, we'll put her in greater danger. We don't even know how many we're up against.'

'There are at least four soldiers,' Bérenger said. 'Two are stoking the fire and there are another two, possibly three, to the south. There might be more.'

'Firearms?'

'Can't see. They're carrying fuel for the fire, and swords, certainly.'

Piet slipped forward between the trees to get a better look, then stopped dead in his tracks. He saw two soldiers with Minou standing between them. Her hands were tied in front of her. As he watched, he saw them drag her to a wooden stake. Anger roared through him, but he forced himself to take deep breaths. Heeding his own advice to Aimeric. To act rashly, precipitately, could see them all killed.

'Come forward,' he whispered. 'Quiet as you can.'

Bérenger and Aimeric crept alongside him.

'She has Minou too,' Piet said. 'So now you've got to hold twice as firm. Don't lose your head now. Your sisters need you. Do you hear?'

Aimeric was pale, but he looked determined. 'Yes.'

'We'll get as close as we can without being seen,' Piet said. 'So far as we know, there are no more than four or five soldiers. There are three of us. Not good odds, but not too bad either.'

'But Minou and Alis are both tied up, and so near the fire.'

'And the Lady Blanche might be armed too,' Bérenger said.

'Even if she is not, there is a madness in her as dangerous as any sword,' Piet observed quietly.

Desperate, yet powerless to intervene, they watched Blanche walk to where Minou was now tethered, pulling Alis behind her like a dog on a leash. When Alis saw her sister, she cried out and tried to reach out her hands to her. Blanche dragged on the rope and jerked her away.

'Leave her!' Minou shouted. 'Do not hurt her.'

'I will kill her,' Aimeric hissed to Piet. 'I swear to God, I will –'

'What matters is saving Minou and Alis,' Piet said roughly. 'Don't let anger cloud your judgement.'

'It will be well,' Bérenger said solidly, though the doubt shone clear in his voice. 'Right is on our side.'

'Let Alis go,' Minou said. 'It's me you want.'

'You are not in a position to bargain, Mademoiselle Joubert. You have been too slow. Kept me waiting too long.'

Minou's heart was thundering with fury, but she was determined not to let it show. And though she kept her gaze firmly set on Blanche, alarmed by her over-bright eyes and unnaturally pale complexion, she could not but be astonished by the change in her little sister.

For so many days, Minou had been tortured with images of Alis ill and hungry, paler and thinner with each day passing. The opposite appeared to be true. In the seven weeks she'd been held hostage, Alis had grown taller and stronger. Her cheeks were pink from the mountain air and her curls a black halo around her face. For an instant, the relief of seeing her so transformed gave Minou courage.

'Where is the Will?' Blanche said. 'You must give it to me.'

'It is not in my possession.'

'I don't believe you.'

'It is the truth,' Minou said in as steady a voice as she could manage. 'It is also true that I want none of this. Puivert, the château, the inheritance you are fighting so hard to keep, you can have it all. I will sign over any rights to you in the presence of the notary, the priest, whomsoever you want. I give you my word I will do this, if you only let us go.'

'Too late,' Blanche murmured. 'A time to live, and a time to die.'

'I do not understand you,' Minou said.

'All would have been well if he had stopped talking. My dearly beloved, much mourned late husband, as he lay stinking and rotting and dying in his bed, railing against the world and the Devil waiting to take him. Talking and talking, sinner that he was. I couldn't stop him. Setting the rumours going. Stealing my inheritance from me.' She put her hands on her swollen belly and squeezed, as if trying to expel the baby ahead of its time. 'I forbade the servants to listen, but they would not stop their ears. I had them flogged, but they would not stop talking. I told them his mind was wandering, he was confused. It was this thing inside me – *this* was the child he meant – but the rumours wouldn't be stopped. Too many words, too many.'

'You killed him,' Minou said in a level voice.

'A time to keep, and a time to cast away. A time to kill. Yes, that is it,' Blanche said, as if it was nothing to take a life.

Minou cast a quick look at Alis, wanting to give her courage.

'God spoke to me and I obeyed,' Blanche was saying. 'As must we all. We are nothing, we are sinners. And then he was buried deep in the ground, his mouth full of earth, and he was no longer speaking. But there was the old woman, you see. Riddled with the sin of pride, she was. Like a cancer. Spreading sinful lies through the village about a Will and a child that she had delivered. Not dead. A time to keep, and a time to cast away. The voices told me.'

'Anne Gabignaud,' Minou said. 'She wrote to warn me.'

Blanche carried on as if Minou had not spoken.

'A time to get, and a time to lose?' Blanche pulled Alis to her, who cried out as the rope cut into her neck. 'Is it time for you to be lost?' she whispered. 'For you to lose?'

Instinctively, Minou leant forward but her bonds kept her tied to the post. She was powerless to help. Then, with a jolt, she realised the wind was moving round, sending the smoke billowing towards the beech trees on the far side of the glade. Spots of black ash started to settle on Blanche's white gown.

'The wind's turning,' Minou cried. 'Step back from the fire.'

'It is only through fire we are redeemed,' Blanche cried.

Minou struggled harder, managing to loosen the ropes a little.

'She took a long time to die,' Blanche said. 'She had more fight in her than her years should allow.'

'Are you talking of Madame Gabignaud?' Minou asked again, thinking that if the soldiers heard her admit to murdering the old midwife, then they would surely refuse to serve such a mistress.

Blanche brought her wild gaze to settle upon Minou again, stepping in closer.

'More fight than my husband. He was like a mewling baby in the end.'

'Who had more fight in her?' Minou tried for the third time.

'The midwife, don't you understand anything? She could not keep her mouth shut either. Told me one of my predecessors, your sainted mother, was a heretic. Did you know that? A Huguenot. She saved a Protestant baby! She deserved to die for that alone.'

Without warning, Blanche's hand suddenly shot out and grabbed Minou round the throat.

Minou struggled frantically, but Blanche pressed tighter, crushing her windpipe. She could no longer breathe.

'I will not let the child of a Huguenot whore steal my inheritance from me. A time to live, and a time to die. It is the only way. This is the word of God. It is God's will. It is His will.'

Minou caught Alis's eye as Blanche's grip suddenly loosened. 'My favourite sister,' she whispered to give her courage.

'Your only sister,' the little girl mouthed back.

Then everything seemed to happen at once. Minou kicked out at Blanche's knees. At the same time, Alis put both hands on the rope and yanked it hard, pulling the end free from Blanche's hand. She started to run.

'Stop her!' Blanche screamed.

The soldiers sprang forward, but Alis was already hurtling for the cover of the woods, trying to get the noose up and over her head as she went.

'Now!' Piet yelled.

Piet, Aimeric and Bérenger broke cover and ran roaring into the glade. Piet took on the soldiers stoking the fire. Aimeric ran to help Alis. Bérenger tried to reach Minou.

The wind spiralled and spun in the glade, as the northerly wind swung round, and a strong south-westerly began to blow along the river valley. Smoke was gusting and billowing, swirling in all directions at once.

Then, a spark jumped from the pyre onto the oil-soaked noose carried by one of the soldiers chasing Alis. The rope burst into flames in his arms. He screamed as the fire caught at his beard and hair, trying in vain to beat it out with his hands. Minou could smell the scorch of his skin as he stumbled and fell.

Another spark jumped and caught a pile of dry leaves at the foot of the beech trees at the corner of the glade. A ribbon of golden flame went shooting up the trunk.

'Get Alis away!' Minou shouted to Aimeric.

Aimeric swept her up in his green cloak, pulling her into the deeper woods.

Minou's relief was short-lived. Through the black smoke, she saw Bérenger intercepted by another soldier. She looked for Piet, but at that moment her breath was knocked from her as Blanche hurled herself again at Minou's throat.

'Piet!' she heard Bérenger shouting. 'Look to Minou!'

Minou was struggling to get her head free, trying to ignore the taste of blood in her mouth. Despite her condition, Blanche seemed possessed of the strength of several men.

Piet ran through the glade and hurled himself at Blanche, knocking her back and away from Minou. A soldier charged with his sword drawn, crashing his blade against Piet's poniard. Piet buried his dagger in the man's belly. Blood bubbled, then exploded from his mouth, staining the green ground red. He dropped to his knees and fell forward. Another soldier attacked, but Piet kept going, sword against sword, tirelessly driving his assailant back towards the pyre.

Still the wind was blowing, fanning the flames. The roaring of the fire grew.

Suddenly, Minou realised Blanche now had a knife in her hand.

'Only through fire can we be born again,' she whispered. 'You must die, but you will thank me. I am saving your soul, Minou.'

Minou recoiled, not knowing what she could do against a blade. She was trapped. She kicked out with her foot, trying to keep Blanche at bay. Another belch of smoke was taken up by the wind, wrapping them both in its suffocating embrace and catching in their throats. Blanche began to cough. Then, into the chaos, came another voice.

'Blanche. My Lady.'

In her shock, she dropped the knife. Minou saw the dismay on Piet's face and twisted round to see Vidal walking into the glade with two soldiers, his manservant and two others between them.

'No,' she whispered in defeat.

Vidal was holding Alis by the collar of her gown. Bonal had angled his blade across her brother's throat. Aimeric's left eye was swollen shut and there was a gash of red on his cheek.

'I'm sorry, Minou,' Aimeric said. 'We ran into them. There was—'

'Be quiet,' Bonal threatened.

'You will put down your weapons,' Vidal said. 'Throw them where I can see them.'

Piet's fist momentarily tightened on the hilt of his blade, but then he did what Vidal said. Bérenger followed, his blade landing on top of Piet's sword. Bonal removed Aimeric's dagger from his belt and tossed it onto the pile.

Vidal nodded and the soldiers tied Piet's and Bérenger's hands behind their backs and forced them to their knees.

'That's better,' he said.

Minou saw a change come over Blanche. Her demons seemed to leave her and she became gracious and elegant. As if receiving guests to a banquet or a masque.

'Valentin, you are most welcome. Forgive me but, as you can see, we were obliged to begin without you. I trust you slept well, my love?'

Piet's eyes narrowed. Bérenger looked disgusted and Minou, remembering the rumours her father and Madame Noubel had shared with her, looked at Blanche's belly and another piece of the puzzle fell into place.

Vidal's child – not her husband's child. Not an heir to the estates of Puivert at all.

'You talk too much, Lady,' Vidal said sharply.

'Will you join me?' she said. 'I have gathered them all for you.' She waved her hand wildly. 'Can you see? Here they are.'

Vidal nodded curtly and the soldiers moved to stand behind Blanche. They didn't touch her, but there was no doubt their purpose was to restrain her, not obey her.

'No?' she said in her strange, flat voice. 'This does not please you? The fire does not please you?'

Vidal walked over to Piet. A soldier pressed his dagger down on his neck, keeping Piet on his knees.

'I will not waste any more time on you, Reydon. You've led me a dance, preyed on my former goodwill. Because of you, many people have lost their lives. This is on your conscience.'

Piet's face tightened in anger. 'Damn you to hell.'

'Do you not remember your scripture, Reydon? Sins of omission and sins of commission, the law of intended and unintended consequences. Because of your obduracy, Crompton and the poor fool you paid to copy the Shroud – they suffered much because of you. McCone too, though he was the architect of his own misfortune. Selling secrets to both sides, so foolish.'

Vidal hesitated, as if waiting for Piet to speak, then stepped back, rubbing the smoke from his eyes.

'You want the Shroud, Vidal. Is that it?'

'You have one chance to tell me the truth. If you do not, I shall kill the girl first, then the boy, and then Mademoiselle Joubert. If you are honest, I will spare them the sword.'

'He's lying,' Aimeric shouted. 'He intends to kill us all.'

'Tell him, Piet,' Minou said, trying to edge away from the fire. Another spark had leapt from the fire onto some dry bracken. A smoulder of tiny flames was starting to burn along its fingers, creeping now across a fallen branch.

'Where is the Shroud now? I know you gave it to your – what is she to you? Your Catholic mistress?'

'You pretend to love God, Valentin,' Blanche said suddenly. 'You pretend all this is for His glory, but you have turned away from the Lord. You seek your own advantage only.'

Vidal ignored her. 'Where is it, Reydon?'

Piet said nothing. Vidal stared, then turned and walked instead to Alis and reached out his hand.

'No!' Aimeric shouted. 'It's here. In the lining of my cloak.'

'At last.' Vidal clicked his fingers. 'Bonal.'

Bonal untied the cloak roughly from Aimeric's neck and handed it to his master. Vidal ripped the stitching, reached inside and pulled out the leather document container.

For a moment, he hesitated, as if he might allow himself the time to look upon the Shroud. But then he reconsidered.

'I shall not defile so sacred an object by unveiling it in such impious company,' he said.

Blanche let out a scream. 'You have in your hands a sign of God's mercy to man, in the gift of His son who died for us, yet you care nothing for it. You are a sinner, Valentin.'

She leapt forward, but the guards held her firm.

'Take the Lady Blanche back to her chambers,' Vidal said, his voice cold. 'She is much afflicted and deserves our pity.'

'What about us?' Minou said. 'You said you would let us go.'

Vidal gave a thin smile. 'Ah, but I did not. What I said was that I would spare you the sword. Reydon is a heretic. You too, now, I warrant. It's like poison. Heresy gets into the blood. The others are contaminated by association with you both. Bonal, bind them. Let the fire do its work.'

CHAPTER SEVENTY-TWO

⚜

Vidal stood back from the pyre, a kerchief over his mouth and nose, watching Bonal secure the prisoners. His red robes snapped in the wind.

Blanche stood beside him in the custody of the soldiers. Her face was marked with smuts from the fire, her white and silver garments ruined with ash. Her hair had come loose from her cowl and hung down her back. She had an expression of serenity on her face, though her eyes were blank like those of a plaster saint in a church. Only the clenching and unclenching of her fists betrayed her turmoil.

Piet, Bérenger and Aimeric had each been bound to trees at the edge of the woods to the north of the clearing, directly in the path the fire would take as the south-westerly wind continued to fan the flames. They were too far apart to help one another.

Minou was still tethered to the stake closer to the source of the fire. Alis was now tethered to the same stake; they were back to back in a complicated twisting of rope. There was no hope of untying themselves. For the time being they were safe but, if the wind swung round again, it would be only a matter of minutes before the flames engulfed them, too.

* * *

'I shall return to the château, Bonal,' Vidal said. 'Finish with the girl and the child, dispose of the bodies, then prepare the horses. I shall await you at the keep.'

'We are leaving Puivert?'

Vidal looked down at the leather container and the cloak draped across his arm. 'Indeed. I have what I came for.'

'And to return to Toulouse, Monsignor?'

Vidal smiled. 'No, we will ride to the Tarn. To Saint-Antonin-Noble-Val, to be exact.'

Bonal met his eye. 'Very good, Monsignor.'

Vidal took a final look around, as if checking all was to his satisfaction, then, leaving Bonal, he set off with the soldiers escorting Blanche between them. Though she was chatelaine and these were her lands, there was no doubt who was now in command.

'God will damn you for this, Vidal,' Piet shouted after him.

Minou saw Vidal pause, then continue along the path without looking back.

The swirling wind was sending the noxious smoke billowing through the glade, turning the air a mottled black. It was impossible to see now.

Piet called out again. 'Minou?'

'I'm here,' she called over the crackling of the pyre.

'It does my heart good to hear you,' he said, but she heard the despair in his voice. He could not reach her, nor could she reach him.

She saw Bonal moving around on the periphery of her vision, dragging the bodies of the dead soldiers towards the fire. She heard a hiss, and a crackle as their hair began to burn, then the sickly, sweet smell of burning flesh began to permeate the air.

Quickly, she began to talk to Alis.

'What stories we will have to tell,' she said, desperate to distract her sister from the horror unfolding around them.

'I missed you,' Alis said, so sweet and simple a statement it brought tears to Minou's eyes.

'I missed you too,' she said. 'We both did. Even Aimeric.'

'I knew you would come, whatever Blanche said, but I also didn't want you to.'

'I understand.'

'She told me we were going to Toulouse, which is why I went with her even though Madame Noubel had told me to stay in the house. It is my fault.'

'It is not your fault,' Minou said fiercely. 'Anyway, it doesn't matter now.'

'Are you sure I will not be in trouble?'

'Quite sure.'

'All right. When I realised Blanche had lied, I waited for you to come. But weeks went by, so I decided to run away. Then the baby tried to be born and Blanche nearly died. She has been ill ever since. I tried to run away again, but they caught me and brought me back. The priest kept asking me questions.'

'Did he hurt you?' Minou said, knowing she had to ask, but dreading the answer.

Alis hesitated, then Minou thought she shook her head.

'I can't see you, Alis, you must say it out loud.'

'Not really. He pinched my cheeks, hard, but I didn't cry.'

Minou breathed a sigh of relief.

'I have a lovely surprise for you,' she said. 'Papa is here in the château. Madame Noubel is with him. And as soon as we are away from here, we will go and find him. What do you say to that?'

'Will they come to find us?' Alis said in a small voice. 'How will they know we are here?'

'They will,' Minou said firmly, though she had no hope of

it. 'Or someone else. The smoke must be visible from miles around. Someone in Puivert will see.'

Minou fell silent as Bonal reappeared to make a final check on their bindings.

'There,' he said, jerking at the rope to test it was secure.

'This is wrong,' Minou said, making a last attempt to reason with him. 'You can't want our souls on your conscience. Please, at least let my sister go. She's only a child.'

Bonal leant over and whispered in her ear. 'I won't have anything on my conscience. I shall confess my sins and the slate will be wiped clean, whereas you – you Huguenot whore – will go to your Maker unshriven. With all your sins upon you.'

He spat on the ground beside her, then straightened up and walked away towards the path. A gust of wind lifted another cloud of smoke into the glade, obscuring her vision.

Then Minou heard Bonal cry out. Within the haze, she saw he was swaying on his feet, then he seemed to collapse sideways onto his knees. Another pocket of clear air and Minou saw Bonal was lying on the ground, with a knife sticking out of his throat.

'What's happening now?' Alis whispered.

'I don't know,' Minou replied. 'Keep quiet.'

'Is it Papa coming?'

'I don't know,' Minou whispered again, struggling to see.

She could hear footsteps coming closer and closer on the dry and trodden leaves, then a figure lumbered into view.

'Aunt!' she cried.

Madame Boussay was perspiring and breathing heavily. Panting. To Minou's astonishment, she leant over Bonal, pulled out the knife and wiped the blade clean on the grass.

Minou didn't know whether to laugh or cry. Her aunt

seemed to be utterly unafraid, not at all perturbed by the fact that she had just killed a man.

'Aunt, dear Aunt,' Minou said. 'Can you cut me loose?'

'I'll do my best, dear,' Madame Boussay said.

'I didn't know you could . . . use a knife.'

'Oh, I cannot. I am so clumsy, my husband always . . .' She faltered. 'It is a trick your brother taught me. Useful, so it's turned out. He said your Huguenot suitor taught it to him.' Then, before Minou could answer, she turned. 'And you must be little Alis, is that right?'

Bewildered, Alis could only nod.

'I am Madame Boussay. I am your aunt, from Toulouse,' she said, cutting at the rope to free Minou, then doing the same for Alis. 'That's better. Now, where's that nephew of mine? Aimeric?'

At first there was no answer. Minou turned cold. The fire could not yet have reached them, but what about the smoke?

'Aimeric?' Madame Boussay called again. 'Answer, please.'

This time, her brother's voice came calling back across the glade.

'We're here, Aunt. Though if you might hurry . . .'

Minou darted round the outskirts of the glade, sheltering from the fire as best she could.

She cut Piet free and, for the lightest of moments, they let their lips touch. Then, together, they cut Bérenger and Aimeric loose, before rejoining Madame Boussay and Alis, and retrieving their weapons.

Exhausted, still in shock, the little group forced themselves to walk back up the slopes towards the castle compound.

'Bérenger,' Piet said, when they reached the edge of the dense undergrowth. 'Go to the village and raise the alarm. If the wind doesn't abate, the woodlands all the way down to Chalabre are at risk.'

'We have to find a way into the Tour Bossue,' Minou said in a low voice. 'My father and Madame Noubel are being held there.'

'Do you think they are still there, Niece?'

'I don't know. Father says no one knows who he is, but that might change now since Vidal has the Shroud. As for Blanche, well –'

'Her wits have gone, Aunt,' Alis explained. 'The baby tried to come early and it made her mad.'

'Our only hope is that since she, too, has what she wanted, she will be calmer.'

'What was it that the Lady Blanche wanted, Niece?'

'A Will,' Minou replied. 'It was hidden inside the bible my mother sent to you, Aunt. I took it from your hiding place in the Eglise Saint-Taur. Forgive me, I meant to tell you. I thought it might be destroyed when the fighting started.'

'Are you saying there is a Will hidden within my bible?'

Minou frowned. 'When you first received it from my mother, did you not examine it, Aunt?'

'Well, no. I did open the bible, but when I saw it was in French – and knew how displeased my husband would be – I immediately closed it and put it back inside the bag. Then, as you know, I hid it. Is it a Will made by Florence?'

'I –' Minou began, then decided this could wait. 'It's a long story, Aunt. Sufficient to say that Blanche believed it would deprive her of her inheritance. I sewed it into the hem of my cloak to keep safe, together with something precious Piet had asked me to keep safe for him. That's why, when we were stopped at the toll house on the covered bridge, I gave my cloak to Aimeric.'

'Which he never let out of his sight. He is an obedient boy, after his own manner.'

'For all that,' Minou sighed, 'Vidal now has it and there's nothing to be done about it.'

Madame Boussay cleared her throat. 'Well, as a matter of fact, he does not. I hope you will not take offence at this, Minou, but the stitching on your cloak was really very poor. I took it upon myself to repair it, when you were asleep, Aimeric. I used to be good with a needle when I was young, though Monsieur Boussay did not want his wife . . .' She stopped. 'Well, no matter. The point is, I found the container and the bible. I didn't think it was my place to look inside the leather holder, so I put that back. But I did recognise my own bible, and it was such a pleasure to see it again that I own I kept it.'

Minou and Aimeric exchanged glances. 'Are you saying you have the Will, Aunt?' she said.

Madame Boussay fussed at her hair. 'Well, I don't know about the Will, but the bible? Certainly I do. Here.' She reached into her ugly velvet purse, tied at her waist. 'It was the only gift I had from my dear sister. I couldn't bear the thought of being parted from it again.'

Minou opened the bible and found the Will, just as she had left it in the pages of the book. Aimeric bent over and kissed Madame Boussay.

'Aunt, you are a wonder.'

'She has a fever, Monsignor,' the nurse said.

'I am aware of that.'

Vidal peered down at Blanche lying motionless beneath the sheets, her hands still on the white linen, her face calm and her eyes closed, like a marble effigy on a tomb. Yet, though she did not move at all, he was certain she was not asleep.

Vidal looked around the bedchamber that had been a place of satisfaction and refuge for him. Now he saw only signs of his folly. To have placed his reputation in the hands of such a woman . . .

'Stay with her,' he commanded. 'Do not leave her untended even for an instant. When the child is born, this affliction will pass.'

'Very good, Monsignor.'

Vidal made the sign of the cross above Blanche's forehead and murmured a benediction, then walked to the table in the corner of the chamber where he had placed the Shroud.

'Avert your eyes,' he ordered.

The soldiers and the nurse all turned away.

At last, in the heat and smoke of the burning wood, God had deigned to answer him after so long a silence. His path was suddenly clear. He was impatient to turn his back on Puivert, on Blanche and her bastard child, and never return.

Vidal realised he had set his sights too low. The Bishopric of Toulouse was a rank to aspire to, but why should he not aim higher? Blanche's patronage, far from helping him to rise, had held him back.

Vidal picked up the leather container. Was it true the Duke of Guise was in Saint-Antonin-Noble-Val, a town Vidal knew well from the early years of his ministry? Indeed, it was in that small town in the Tarn he had first set eyes upon Blanche, an innocent girl mourning the death of her father. Her simple grief had moved him.

Vidal pushed the memory from his mind.

He would go directly to Saint-Antonin-Noble-Val and offer his service to the Duke of Guise and his son. Although Guise's health was rumoured to be in decline, his was still the strongest voice speaking against Condé and the Huguenot threat and, unlike many of his allies, the duke was a man of genuine devotion. What preferment might His Grace be prepared to offer to one in possession of the true Shroud? Vidal removed the lid, put his hand inside and drew out the fragment of cloth. He felt the texture of the delicate weave beneath his fingers, found the tear in the corner of the material that proclaimed it to be the true relic, and waited. He waited to experience the glory of God made manifest in the world. The grace that passes all understanding.

But in this dull chamber, with the averted eyes of the soldiers and the nurse, the afflicted breathing of Blanche in the bed behind him, it did not come.

Vidal slipped the Shroud back into its case and secured the lid. He would wait for a more propitious, a more private, moment.

'Where's Bonal?' he said roughly. 'He should be here.'

The soldiers stood to attention. 'Monsignor?'

'Go and see.'

The nurse turned around, her hands clasped in front of her. 'You are leaving, Monsignor?'

'My responsibilities require my presence elsewhere,' he said. 'I will return when I can to see how the Lady Blanche fares. A mind disturbed is no less beloved of God.'

Holding their kerchiefs close to their mouths, they stood as close to the castle compound as they could without risking being seen from the watchtowers.

Piet put his arm around Minou's waist.

'What matters now is to find your father, Minou, and Madame Noubel, and get them to safety. Vidal might still be in the château, or he might not, but there will be soldiers and servants.'

'They must have seen the smoke. Smelt it.'

'The priest is leaving,' Alis said. 'He told his manservant to saddle the horses and meet him at the keep.'

'Did he say he was returning to Toulouse?' Piet asked quickly.

'In fact, no,' Minou replied. 'As they left the glade, I heard him tell Bonal they were going to a place called Saint-Antonin-Noble-Val.'

Piet frowned. 'That is where Vidal's first parish was.'

'Does he have family or lands there?'

'No, but . . .' He stopped. 'There was a rumour that the Duke of Guise and his oldest son, Henri, are in the Tarn.'

'Do you think that's true?' Aimeric asked.

'I don't know, it might be. It doesn't matter. Our only concern is to rescue your father and Madame Noubel, and then to get away from Puivert,' Piet repeated.

Aimeric nodded.

'While Minou and I attempt to get into the Tour Bossue, can you go to the river, Aimeric, and fetch our horses?'

'I'll go now.'

'Take good care,' Minou said quickly, as her brother nodded and turned away.

'If you will forgive me for presuming to issue orders, Madame Boussay, could you and Alis wait in the woods? Once we are all together, we can decide what to do for the best.'

She inclined her head. 'We will be fine here, Monsieur Reydon.'

'We can't go down to the village,' Minou said. 'If the soldiers are looking for us, it is the first place they will search. We should head back to Chalabre.'

'But if they think we're dead,' Alis said, 'why will they be looking for us?'

'That might be true at the moment, *petite*, but when Bonal does not return, Vidal will send someone to look for him and discover us gone.'

'Then you will have to be quick,' Madame Boussay said firmly. 'Alis, we will seat ourselves here and you can tell me about life in La Cité. I regret I have never had the opportunity to visit.'

'Come, *mon coeur*,' Minou said to Piet. 'The sooner we start this, the sooner we will return.'

Her aunt's eyebrows shot up at the endearment.

'Is Piet your husband now?' Alis asked innocently.

'Not yet,' Minou laughed, hugging her. 'But when the time is right, yes. We hope to be married.'

Valentin. An undistinguished choice at his ordination. The name of an Italian martyr, not French, and a February feast day. In England, where heresy pollutes every part of life, he is a patron saint of lovers.

The voices in my head are sleeping now, but there is too much talking in the chamber. The soldiers and the drunken nurse, her breath stinking of ale, bowing and scraping.

'A time to be born, to be . . .'

The pressure of a hand upon my forehead.

'She has a fever, Monsignor.'

'I am aware of that.'

Valentin speaks and they obey him. How should that be? Are these not my lands? Without me, he is nothing. He has no jurisdiction here. No authority. He is not beloved of God. The Lord does not speak to him.

But he loved me once, didn't he?

The creature in my womb is trying to kill me. I can feel it, writhing in my belly. A succubus sucking the life from me.

'I will return when I can to see how the Lady Blanche fares. A mind disturbed is no less beloved of God.'

He thinks I cannot hear him. His specious and lying tongue. It is his own ambition taking him away, not his service to God.

Footsteps across the chamber. He is leaving. The

soldiers are leaving. A moment, then the stinking, foul breath of the nurse gone too.

A fiend, set to torment me.

The voices are whispering now. Quick, now. Go, now.

Beneath the bedsheet, the blood is flowing. I understand now it is God moving inside me. The Lord's blood was shed for us and for many for the remission of sins.

'A time to break down, and a time to build up, a time to . . .'

No, that was not right.

I am standing. Walking across the chamber. I have no need of cloaks of gold or satin for God is by my side. And I have what I need. The soldiers had not dared to search me and Valentin can no longer bear to touch me. I have still my rosary beads and my knife.

Down the winding stairs of the keep into the burning chambers of the woods where Minou Joubert is waiting.

CHAPTER SEVENTY-THREE

⚜

Puivert Village

'Bring as many men as you can muster,' Bérenger said. 'We need horses, traps and carts. Bring pails for dirt. We can suffocate the fires, put them out one by one.'

'I will.' Lizier nodded. 'They're saying terrible things are happening. Paul Cordier found with his neck broken, many dead within the woods. Two of the guard, terrified, deserted at first light and fled here, saying the mistress has lost her wits.' He peered up and down the street. 'When Guilhem comes, he'll tell us what's what.'

Despite the urgency, Bérenger stopped. 'My friend, I have ill news.'

The old man's eyes clouded. 'My nephew? My Guilhem is one of those who is dead?'

Bérenger put his hand on Lizier's shoulder. 'He died defending others. He was a valiant young man, courageous.'

'He was that.'

'You should be proud of him, Achille. Because of him, other lives will be saved.'

A single tear rolled down Lizier's withered cheek. 'It's not right when the old outlive the young. They have all gone before me.'

'I know.'

For a moment, the two old men stood there remembering those they had lost. Old warhorses both, they had fought in the Italian campaigns and seen many of their number fall. Then Lizier wiped his eyes, leaving a black smear across his face, and squared his shoulders.

'I will gather everyone I can, women and children too. The Bruyère family has done enough damage to Puivert. I know better than most. Time for it to end.'

CHÂTEAU DE PUIVERT

Minou and Piet had made their way unseen through the small stone gate in the walls, through the kitchen garden and into the lower courtyard.

They heard footsteps in the logis, so ducked out of sight and waited, but no one came out and the door remained closed. Every now and again, a grey ribbon of smoke appeared in the sky above the castle, then was carried away on the wind.

Minou thought it was strangely quiet for mid-morning and wondered if news of the fire had already spread to the household. But it suited their purposes. They kept moving, alert to every sound, keeping to the shadows.

Another noise stopped them, this time seeming to come from the keep. Quickly, they hid beneath the high steps, waiting until again the sound had receded, then pressed on to the small stone arch that linked the *basse cour* to the lower courtyard.

'My father said the main courtyard is like a market square. Artisans and stalls selling bread and cloth all along the walls. With luck, we might be able to conceal ourselves behind an awning and tables.'

'He is well informed.'

'He said he can hear the sounds of the traders, but it is mostly from what his student, Guilhem, has told him.'

Piet stopped. 'Guilhem is dead, my love. I found him slain in the woods last evening.'

'Oh.' Minou fell silent for a moment. 'I grieve for Jeannette. She talked so sweetly about the life they would have together. She was so proud of how he had learnt to read and write in French.' She shook her head. 'And my poor, poor father. He had become fond of him.'

'I can be the bearer of the ill news.'

'No, I'll do it.' Minou took his hand. 'I'll tell him when the time is right.'

They walked a few steps further in silence. 'Even if we get past the guards, have you considered how we are going to get into the dungeon itself? The cell will be locked and the door is designed to withstand any assault.'

Piet put his hand into his doublet and pulled out a ring of keys.

'I took these from Guilhem's body last night,' he said quietly. 'This might be the final – the greatest – service he does for your father. Saving his life.'

* * *

Blanche looked up into the blue canopy of the sky and wondered why the sun was so high.

Was it morning?

Morning glory. God's recreation of the day. Was it summer now?

She was standing in the shadow of the battlements. The air was filled with the scent of ash and burning. The Christian martyrs of old, broken on the wheel or the cross or burnt on the pyre. Refusing to recant their faith. Their souls rising to heaven in columns of fire.

But she was still bound to the earth. Her work was not yet done. She had to return to the woods where Minou Joubert was waiting to be saved. The child was with her too. The girl who had saved her life, so the apothecary said. She looked down and saw her shift was heavy with blood.

She walked past the Tour Vert, through the kitchen garden to the small gate in the wall. Valentin had opened it and must have left it unlocked. That was wrong. Her own servants knew better. Her enemies would come inside and kill them all.

Why did they do his bidding now? Was she not Chatelaine of Puivert? Her hands went to her rosary and the clicking of the ivory beads soothed her. So too did the cold blade of the knife. She twisted it until she felt the relief of blood on her palm.

Minou looked at the gatehouse. It was like a block from a child's building set, squat and rectangular.

'Why are there no soldiers on duty?' she whispered.

'Perhaps there isn't a watch kept on the inside of the castle during daylight hours,' Piet said.

'There's no one on duty outside the Tour Bossue either,' she said.

Piet looked around. 'Most of the traders' stalls are boarded up.'

'They have fled because of the fire?'

Piet frowned. 'I don't know.'

Blanche stepped out through the gate. A black column of smoke spiralled up from the heart of the woods. The burning and cracking of the fire. Ash, like black snow, danced lightly above the tree line. She could smell charred flesh, like the spit at a winter's banquet, sweet in the air.

Then she saw them. Facing away from her, a woman and a girl. They seemed to be looking down the valley towards Chalabre.

Minou Joubert and Alis? Could it be? No, they were in the woods. She had given orders for them to be taken there. They had been tied close by the pyre, she remembered.

Blanche moved forward. Her bare feet were silent on the grass. She watched as the girl lifted her hand and waved her arm in a wide arc, attracting the attention of someone else. Blanche listened, then heard the clump and fall of horses' hooves coming up the track.

Why did they have their backs to the beautiful fire? Did they not understand it would take them closer to God?

She could hear their voices now. Always, voices. But not speaking to her. Not meant for her. Closer. Almost there. The whispering should stop. She would stop it. No more talking. Blanche shifted the hilt of the dagger in her hand. She was within striking distance. Then a bird, startled, flew up out of the undergrowth, and the child suddenly turned.

For a moment, their eyes locked.

Then the girl screamed. Blanche attacked just as the figure turned, putting herself in front of the child as the knife came down.

Metal sliding through flesh. Striking bone, something hard.

Blanche smiled. Her work was done. Now might she be granted peace? No more whispering. She had done what God commanded. Now she could rest.

She pulled the knife back to deliver a second blow, but the woman was falling to the ground already. A tangle of flesh and blood and velvet. Such fine clothes. Had Minou Joubert been dressed in such fine clothes? The hood sliding back from the face.

It was not Minou Joubert.

'Aunt!' the child was screaming.

Blanche staggered back from the body. How could this happen? Then, on the periphery of her vision, a young man, leading two horses, appeared on the brow of the hill. He saw them, dropped the reins and started to run towards them.

The child was sobbing, shrill and endless.

'Aunt, wake up . . .'

Blanche put her hands over her ears. Feeling the drip of blood trickling down her forearm from the knife and the inside of her thighs.

Not Minou Joubert.

She took a further step back. Another sound behind her. Out of her domain, through the unlocked gate, now others were coming. A thin old man, stumbling as if the world was too bright, and an old, weathered woman. A man with red hair, like the heretic Queen of England.

And her, the one she was supposed to have killed. God willed it.

Blanche looked down at the body on the ground. Not Minou Joubert. She saw the child attempt to stem the bleeding with her tiny hands. A flash of memory. White fingers, the stone floor of the chapel, pain cleaving her own body in two.

Her head was filled with shouting. Echoing. Chastising. How had she got it so wrong? The voices told her to kill the child, but she had misunderstood. She thought they meant the child of the Huguenot whore, but that was wrong. She understood now.

Blanche looked down at her belly and felt the creature writhing inside. Her enemies were all around. She was beset on all sides like God's people of old. They were coming from the château through the open gate and from her villages in the valley and the ghost armies from the blackened woods walked with them.

These were the last days, the final days, when darkness covers the earth. The end of time.

Blanche glanced up at the keep and, for a fleeting moment, the smallest of moments between one heartbeat and the next, she thought she saw a face at the casement looking down.

'Valentin . . .' she murmured, then remembered he had left her.

Blanche pressed her hands against her skin, to find the place. There was a moment of stillness. Then she smiled and turned the knife on herself.

'A time to keep silence.'

She thrust the knife again, lower down this time, into her womb. Straight away, the voices in her head stopped. They were pleased with her, yes. Quiet. Peaceful now. The air shimmered and glistered, then settled.

No more words.

'Minou,' Alis cried. 'She won't wake up.'

Minou cradled her aunt's head in her lap.

'Aunt.' Aimeric was crouched beside Madame Boussay on the ground, pressing his kerchief against the wound. 'Don't sleep. Look at me. Try to open your eyes.'

'Ah, Nephew. Always so loud.'

'Please, Aunt,' he sobbed.

'I really am very cold, Aimeric,' she said, 'though it is such a pleasant day.' She turned her head. 'Are you here too, Minou?'

'I'm here, Aunt.'

'Niece, I think we should go inside. I had a thought someone had lit a fire to keep us warm. In fact, I am sure of it. No, I am muddling things again. It will be warm inside by the fire.'

Minou was struggling to blink away her tears.

'We'll take you inside. Don't worry. Look, here's Piet come to help. And Bernard too.'

'Bernard?' Madame Boussay's eyes fluttered open as she tried to hold out her hand.

'Stay awake, Aunt,' Aimeric whispered. 'Don't leave me.'

'Nephew, you talk too much.' Her voice was fading. 'Bernard, how very nice to make your acquaintance after all this time. I have had the great joy of Minou and Aimeric's company these past months, but of course you know that.'

'I know it. Thank you for your great kindness.'

'Well, that was my pleasure, and I think I know my duty to my own flesh and blood, whatever Monsieur Boussay . . .' Her voice faded lower. 'Is Florence with you? Is she here? I would see her.' She peered, then frowned. 'Sister?'

Madame Noubel knelt beside her. 'Florence is not here, Salvadora, but I am. I'm Cécile. We met yesterday in the village.'

'So we did. You were Florence's matron of honour, I remember. I did so want to be a bridesmaid, but dear Papa wouldn't let me come.'

'Put her onto this cloak,' Minou said. 'Use it as a stretcher. We'll take her into the castle.' She took a deep breath. 'Both of them.'

'Not her!' Aimeric shouted.

'We can't leave her here for the crows and the wolves, it's not right.'

'No,' Alis said, running into Bernard's arms. 'Not her.'

'We must take them both,' Minou repeated.

'What about the soldiers?' Aimeric said. 'We'll be seen.'

'The soldiers have gone,' Bernard said quietly. 'Some deserted as the fire began to take hold. Others absconded when her confessor fled. They had been under his authority.'

'Quick,' Minou said. 'She will die if we don't get help.'

Blanche felt herself being picked up. The voices were sleeping now. No more movement inside her. No more voices.

She breathed a long sigh, a last sigh.

Then, a blessed and beautiful silence.

CHAPTER SEVENTY-FOUR

⚜

CHÂTEAU DE PUIVERT
Friday, 29th May

One week later, Minou stood on the open ground outside the northern walls of the castle, watching as Blanche's coffin was lowered into the ground.

'*In nomine Patris, et Filii, et Spiritus Sancti.*'

The clod hit the lid of the coffin with a soft thud. Brown earth slipped through the palsied fingers of the Catholic priest summoned from Quillan to perform the burial. Then another hand, stretching out across the open grave, then another. Soil and stone pattering on the wood, like rain. No tears were shed, though every face was solemn and many bore the scars of the events of that day.

For seven days, Puivert had been burying its dead. The tolling of the angelus bell for those much loved, such as Guilhem Lizier, as well as those like Paul Cordier who, though disliked, still belonged to the village. The soldiers killed in the woods had been buried here, too. As had the priest's manservant, Bonal, and a few – still loyal to Blanche de Bruyère – who had fallen in the battle when Bérenger's civilian army stormed up from the village.

And now this, the final burial. A closing of the account.

'Amen.'

It was a small party at the graveside. Minou and Piet, Bernard with Alis standing close beside him, Madame Noubel and Bérenger, with old Achille Lizier at his side. A little further back, Aimeric stood behind a litter, in which an invalid was sitting. Set in the shadow of the castle walls, the chair had been carried down from the logis and brought out into the countryside for the sombre occasion. Aimeric fussed as much as any mother hen, rearranging his aunt's blanket over her knees, offering sweet biscuits and wine.

'Aimeric, really. Is it too much that you might stand still for a moment?' she said fondly. 'You are making me tired.'

For two days, Madame Boussay's life had hung in the balance. The wound was deep. Blanche's knife had been deflected by Florence's bible, so had missed the vital organs, but she had developed a fever. The physician summoned from Chalabre had kept the sickness at bay. Minou, Madame Noubel and Aimeric had not left her side. On the third day, her fever broke and she slept. Madame Boussay was still very weak and could not walk unaided, but the danger had passed. When Minou had told her of her husband's death in Toulouse, a glassy tear had slipped from her eyes, and then she had thanked God and smiled.

The fact that a Protestant bible had saved their aunt's life greatly amused Aimeric. He had taken to teasing her about it and Minou, seeing the pleasure the gentle mischief gave their aunt, did not scold him. For her part, Madame Boussay held resolutely to the belief that it was her older sister Florence, watching over her, who had kept her safe.

'Are you sure you are quite comfortable?' Aimeric asked again. 'Shall I ask Alis to fetch your fan, or—'

'You are too noisy, Nephew,' Madame Boussay said affectionately. 'Altogether too noisy.'

The priest looked to Minou, who nodded. He made the sign of the cross, then stood back to allow two villagers to begin the work of refilling the grave.

'Are you sure you wish to do this straight away?' Piet said, as they walked back towards the castle gate.

She smiled at him. 'I am, *mon coeur*. Will you gather everyone together in the upper courtyard?'

Piet nodded, and went to make things ready.

Already time was starting to heal the horrors of that longest day.

As Achille Lizier and the village women and children battled to save the woods, finally extinguishing the fire at dusk, Bérenger and his comrades had taken the gatehouse. The instant the soldiers heard news that the Chatelaine of Puivert was dead and Monsignor Valentin had fled, most had laid down their arms. Those who continued to resist were swiftly overcome and imprisoned, or given safe passage to leave.

For the next days and nights, Minou had barely slept. When she closed her eyes, her dreams were filled with blood and terror. Images of Aimeric beaten and bleeding, of Piet trapped as the fire got closer and closer, of Alis with marks of a noose around her neck and of Salvadora fallen to the ground, the green grass around her body turning red. Of Blanche with her belly cut open, smiling as her life – and that of her unborn child – ebbed away.

To keep the darkness at bay, Minou had talked to Piet. Working everything out in her mind. Everything she had heard from her father and her aunt, from Blanche too. Everything she had learnt for herself. Talking, so that her dark memories would not overwhelm her.

It would get better in time. Her father promised her so.

Last evening at dusk, Minou had climbed to the top of the keep and looked out across the beautiful landscape. The colours of summer, greens and pinks and the yellow of the fields, the silver of the river Blau flowing in the valley, and the copper sunset over the hills. She thought of her mother and father, and the woman with the mismatched eyes who had died giving her life.

She thought of the quietness of true love. Not the heat and passion of the old tales, burning bright and quickly gone. But silence and the companionship of years. Of the man who would be her husband.

Minou stood a while longer, watching the sun sink down to earth in the west. Saw the silver moon come up in the east above the blackened remains of the woods. And her thoughts returned to Piet and what, here, they might together build in Puivert.

Minou waited until everyone was gathered in the courtyard, then climbed up onto the steps to the keep to address the crowd.

A sea of faces looked up at her. Her family knew what she was going to say, but the household servants and villagers were watchful, some even fearful. There was also a small knot of younger men who had served the Bruyère family, and had been persuaded to return, by being given reassurances that they would not be punished for deserting their posts.

Alis was grinning. Madame Noubel and Bérenger stood close together, close enough to make Minou wonder. Her aunt, though sitting with her eyes shut and clearly weary, was grumbling at Aimeric for not standing up straight. To her pleasure, Minou saw Piet and her father were standing side by side. Already, they had found much in common and her father had given his unreserved blessing to their marriage. At this moment, her father looked proud, Piet nervous.

Minou took the Will from her pocket, though there was no need of it. The terms were already common knowledge in the village, thanks to Achille Lizier. But it was oddly comforting to have it, knowing that Marguerite and Florence had both held it in their hands. For Minou, it had become a talisman.

'Friends,' she began, 'we do not need to talk about the terrible things that happened here. We are each marked by them. We each bore witness to them. What we experienced – fear and loss, anger and pity – all these emotions will live in us for a long time to come. We grieve, but we will recover. We will overcome.'

Minou broke off, the words rehearsed in her head suddenly catching in her throat. Who was she to say such things? Who was she to want such things?

Then she caught Piet's eye and saw that he was smiling. Slowly, he raised his hand and pressed it to his heart. She felt the ghosts of all those they had lost standing beside her, as real for a moment as the faces looking up at her.

'Now we must look to the future,' she said, her voice steady once more. 'I did not seek this. I did not wish to become mistress of Puivert and these lands, but the burden has fallen to me. And I accept it.'

A murmur went around the crowd. Minou saw Bérenger scowl and attempt to quieten people. His determination to protect her always touched her.

'We –' she said, holding out her hand and inviting Piet to step forward – 'we wish for Puivert to be a place of sanctuary for any who are in need. Catholic or Huguenot, Jew or Moor, any driven from their home by war or faith. What happened in Toulouse must never be allowed to happen again.'

Piet nodded and she took another deep breath.

'So, I say this. Any of you who now wish to leave, may do so. There will be no judgement. Those of you who wish to stay and serve, you are most welcome.'

For a moment, there was silence. Then one of the younger soldiers stepped forward, and bent his head.

'You have my sword, my Lady.'

Then another. 'And mine.'

Aimeric's voice was the loudest of all. 'And mine, Sister.'

Alis started to clap, then her father and Madame Noubel joined in, until the courtyard was filled with the sounds of applause and cheering. Madame Boussay waved her fan. Even Bérenger was smiling now.

'Well spoken, my Lady of the Mists,' Piet whispered in her ear as she stepped down onto the grass. 'Chatelaine of Puivert.'

EPILOGUE

⚜

Château de Puivert
Saturday, 3rd May 1572

It is seven o'clock in the evening. The woman now known as Marguerite de Puivert is standing at the top of the keep, looking down over the valley towards Chalabre.

Her seven-year-old daughter Marta – named for Piet's mother – stands impatiently beside her, waiting for their visitors to arrive.

'*Reste tranquille, petite*,' Minou says.

'I am being still.'

'They will be here soon.'

Far below, Minou can see Piet, with their two-year-old son Jean-Jacques on his shoulders, supervising the preparations in the main courtyard below. They look tiny from this distance, but she treasures every crease and smile on her husband's face, each dimple on her son's cheeks, and knows how they will look.

It has been another beautiful day in the mountains. Skies of endless blue, a gentle wind blowing through the woods, setting the silver undersides of the leaves shimmering. Whispering. There is no evidence now of the blackened alder and beech, or the firs and the thin oaks that once stood there, though Minou thinks the forest still holds close the memory of what happened ten years ago, in the bark of its oldest trees and the earth and the bracken now regrown.

The old superstitions of the mountains have led to a small shrine springing up in the glade to remember those who died that day in May in the year fifteen hundred and sixty-two. Minou does not encourage it, but women bring posies and scraps of ribbon, verses in the old language to keep the spirits at bay. To keep the dead sleeping safely in the cold earth. It is only Minou who, on the anniversary of her death, lays flowers on the grave of Blanche de Bruyère.

It is important, she thinks, not to forget.

Minou looks at the journal in her hand. She writes down everything, a way of remembering the truth of things. A treasure chest where she stores letters received – from her aunt, from Madame Noubel – now Madame Bérenger – from Aimeric as he travels with his regiment through France. The last Will and Testament written by her birth mother, Marguerite, and Florence's old map of the Bastide drawn in chalk.

The château de Puivert is a thriving place now and, for the most part, a happy and secure one. Many women and men have found sanctuary within the walls during a decade of war and armed peace. The old Duke of Guise is long dead – murdered by an assassin in the pay of Coligny at the siege of Orléans in the year fifteen sixty-three – but his eldest son, Henri, leads the Catholic armies in his stead. At his right hand, stands a rising star of the Catholic Church, Cardinal Valentin. His power – and his wealth – are said to be greater than any other of the young duke's advisors. It is also said that, within a jewelled reliquary held in the family chapel of the Guise family in Lorraine, is kept a priceless and holy relic. A fragment of the Shroud of Antioch.

When, from time to time, Vidal's name is mentioned, Minou notices how a shadow still falls across her husband's face.

The Prince of Condé, hero of the Huguenot resistance, is also some three years buried. It is Admiral Coligny who now commands the Huguenot forces. Minou is proud Aimeric is one of his most trusted lieutenants, but she still sees no reason for the fighting to continue. For ten years, nothing has really changed. The arguments have grown stale. Faith and the consequences of faith have bankrupted both the country and men's souls.

But now, there are hopes of an end to the conflict. It is women who have brokered this latest peace, bringing the third period of war to an end. The Protestant Queen of Navarre has agreed to the marriage of her son, Henri, to the daughter of the Dowager Queen, Catherine de Medici, sister to the King. It will be the finest wedding of a generation. All the Huguenot nobility, Minou and Piet included, have been invited to join in the celebrations in Paris this coming August, a few days before the feast day of St Bartholomew.

Piet and Aimeric will go. Possibly Alis too. Minou has not decided whether to accompany them, and she thinks the children too young. She likes her life in the mountains and, in truth, there are only three cities close to her heart: her beloved Carcassonne, Toulouse – where Madame Boussay holds a salon of her own in the house in rue du Taur – and Amsterdam.

'Is that them?' Marta asks, squinting into the setting sun.

She is an inquisitive, sharp-witted child, always asking questions. She is the favourite of her Aunt Alis, who comes to visit from Carcassonne with Grandpapa Bernard to spend the summers in Puivert.

'No. They will arrive in a carriage,' Minou says. 'Look again.'

She moves nearer to Marta, in case she strays too close to the edge. Her headstrong daughter has inherited Aimeric's love for heights and is fearless. But for now, she stands perfectly still with both hands shading her eyes.

Minou and Piet had married in the chapel of the castle on the eve of her twentieth birthday. Madame Boussay stood as matron of honour, though they made their vows before a Huguenot pastor. Minou wore a simple silver ring on her marriage finger, though she still keeps the band of twine that first bound them together on the banks of the river Blau, safe with her other treasures inside her journal.

A few years later, Aimeric and Jeannette of Chalabre made the same vows before the same pastor. While she mourned her first love, Aimeric waited, and then fell in love with her. He proposed on his eighteenth birthday. On that occasion, Alis served as bridesmaid and, at the wedding banquet, told outrageous stories of her brother's many childhood exploits and misbehaviours.

Minou often sits in the chapel when she wishes for solitude. It is a place of peace and contemplation, away from the business of running the estate or looking after the refugees who find their way to Puivert still in winter, spring, summer and autumn. It is a Protestant chapel now, not Catholic, but the same light shines through the southern window at dusk, sending patterns of diamond light dancing on the walls and flagstones. Minou thinks it is in such things – the light and the stone, the woods and the sky – that God is truly to be found.

'There!' Marta cries, pointing to a puff of dust drummed up from the road by horses' hooves. 'A carriage coming up the Chalabre road.'

'I think you may be right, *petite*,' Minou says mildly, but her daughter is already shouting over the parapet to her father and brother. 'It's them! They're here!'

Piet turns, see them and raises a hand in reply.

'Don't run on the stairs,' Minou shouts, but Marta has already gone.

Minou lingers a while longer, listening to the sounds of the wheels getting closer. The rattle on the drawbridge and the guards opening the gates. The cries of welcome and laughter in the lower courtyard. This is the first time the whole family will have been together in a long time. Aimeric and his Jeannette, Alis and Bernard, even Madame Boussay is making the journey from Toulouse, in the company of Bérenger and Cécile who have detoured from Carcassonne to accompany Salvadora on the journey south.

But for these final moments, Minou stays high in her eyrie in the sky. She looks down on her beloved Piet, walking hand in hand with Marta and carrying Jean-Jacques on his other arm. She can see her little son is pretending to be a soldier, his wooden sword striking at the air.

Minou sits down on the parapet, opens her journal on a new page and begins to write.

'*Château de Puivert. Saturday, the third day of May, in the year of Grace of Our Lord fifteen hundred and seventy-two.*'

In the west, the sun sinks below the hills. The sky turns from blue to pink to white, promising that tomorrow will be another perfect day.

Note on Language

The langue d'Oc, from which the region of Languedoc takes its name, was the medieval language of the Midi from Provence to Aquitaine in the Middle Ages and beyond. It is closely related to Provençal, Catalan and Basque. The langue d'oïl – the forerunner of modern-day French – was spoken in north and central France.

In the past twenty-five years, there has been something of a linguistic revolution in the Midi. Occitan is now seen on all major signs, there is still a bilingual French/Occitan school in the heart of the medieval city of Carcassonne and Occitan is promoted and advertised on television. However, in the sixteenth and seventeenth centuries, Occitan was considered both provincial and a sign of a lack of education. To distinguish between the incomers and the local inhabitants, I have used both Occitan and French. Certain words, therefore, appear in both forms – for example mademoiselle/madomaisèla and monsieur/sénher.

This independence of language – along with independence of spirit that can, in part, be traced back to the invasion of the south by the Catholic north 1209–44 – is one reason certain historians offer for the fact that Huguenot communities were more prevalent in the south, and why they held out against repression for so much longer. As with the *soi-disant* Cathar Heresy, for many Huguenots – those who followed the Reformed Religion – there was a simple desire to strip back religion and return to the words of the Bible, as opposed to the interpretation of the Bible by bishops and priests, and to reject Latin as the language of worship. Otherwise, Cathar belief and Protestant doctrine have little in common in terms of doctrine and theology. On the other hand, it is fair to suggest that the freedom of spirit and thought that led to Catharism taking so strong a hold in Languedoc in the eleventh, twelfth and thirteenth centuries, before being all but wiped out in the fourteenth century, was reflected in Huguenot communities during the fifteenth and sixteenth centuries.

The translations of the Bible into French by Jacques Lefèvre d'Étaples in 1530 in Antwerp and Pierre Olivétan's revised version in 1535 were important landmarks, as were the translations by the poet Marot of the Psalms into French in the 1530s and 1540s.

Extracts of poetry and sayings are taken from *Proverbes et Dictons de la Langue d'Oc*, collected by Abbé Pierre Trinquier, and from *33 Chants Populaires du Languedoc.*

Acknowledgments

All novelists know how family, friends and neighbours make all the difference between daily life keeping going in the middle of researching and writing a book, and collapsing altogether. I'm incredibly lucky to have people around me who've given emotional, enthusiastic, practical and professional support, in particular:

my brilliant publisher at Mantle (and oldest publishing friend) Maria Rejt, and the entire Macmillan London gang, especially Anthony Forbes Watson, Josie Humber, Kate Green, Sarah Arratoon, Lara Borlenghi, Jeremy Trevathan, Sara Lloyd, Kate Tolley, James Annal, Stuart Dwyer, Brid Enright, Charlotte Williams, Jonathan Atkins, Stacey Hamilton, Leanne Williams, Anna Bond and Wilf Dickie, Praveen Naidoo and Katie Crawford in Australia, Terry Morris, Gillian Spain and Veronica Napier in South Africa, and Lori Richardson, Graham Fidler and Dan Wagstaff in Canada; my fabulous agent, the one and only Mark Lucas, and all at LAW, ILA and Inkwell Management, especially Alice Saunders, Niamh O'Grady; Nicki Kennedy, Sam Edenborough, Jenny Robson, Katherine West, Simon Smith, Alice Natali and George Lucas; my wonderful foreign publishers, in particular Maaike le Noble and Frederika van Traa at Meulenhoff-Boekerij; all those at the Franschhoek Book Festival in South Africa and the wonderful Huguenot Museum, where the glimmers of the story first took root;

to friends in Chichester, Carcassonne, Toulouse and Amsterdam who've supported, made tea and brought good cheer (and sometimes wine!) from the outside world during the long writing of this novel, in particular: Jon Evans, Clare Parsons, Tony Langham, Jill Green, Anthony Horowitz, Saira Keevil, Peter Clayton, Rachel Holmes, Lydia Conway, Paul Arnott, Caro Newling, Stefan van Raay, Linda and Roger Heald, friends at CFT, the Women's Prize and the NT, Mark Piggott KBE, Patron of the Arts, Dale Rooks, Harriet Hastings, Syl Saller, Marzena Baran, Pierre Sanchez and Chantal Bilautou.

Huge thanks to my family, in-laws, cousins, nieces and nephews including my mother-in-law Rosie Turner, cousin Phillipa (Fifi!) Towlson and sister-in-law Kerry Mulbregt, brother-in-law Mark Huxley, my lovely sister Caroline Grainge, especially my brother-in-law Benjamin Graham for his superb photographs, nephew Rick Matthews and my wonderful sister Beth Huxley, for her endless and generous support of all kinds (not limited to dog-walking and balloon-buying!); to our parents, Richard and Barbara Mosse, much loved and much missed.

Finally, as always, I could do none of this without my beloved husband Greg Mosse, my first love and first reader, and our brilliant, amazing (grown-up!) children Martha Mosse and Felix Mosse. Were it not for you three, there'd be little point to any of it. I'm so proud of you all.

KATE MOSSE
Toulouse, Carcassonne & Chichester
December 2017